Cover & Interior Format
© KILLION
THE GROUP INC

THE GIRL
WITH THE
IRON WING

BROKEN VEIL
BOOK I

MARIE ANDREAS

DEDICATION

To everyone who keeps dreams alive—
both their own and others.

Acknowledgements

Writing is a wonderful journey that takes a lot of support from folks around you. Thank you to everyone who has helped me, bought my books, let me cry on their shoulder, or helped in any way.

Extra thanks to editor extraordinaire- Jessa Slade for her magic skills of helping me make sense. Thank you to Laura and Liesel Schilling, Sharon Rivest, and Lisa Andreas for trying to catch all the word shenanigans. And to Ilana Schoonover for working to keep me out of too much trouble. Any errors or mistakes that survived are completely mine.

And thank you to Aleta Rafton for a lovely cover and the Killion Group for the formatting.

OTHER BOOKS BY MARIE ANDREAS

CHAPTER ONE

———◆———

THE DESOLATION AND MAYHEM BEFORE her could only mean one thing—the house brownies had well and truly abandoned her. Or at least the ones working in the kitchen. There was no way the housekeeping service would send more, not at the rate she'd been running through them.

Damn it. I told them I was sorry. Aisling studied the refrigerator again, but as with the last five tries there was nothing even remotely edible in it. In fact, the few remaining clumps of food had become even less recognizable as food and more like an evolving new life form; one possibly able to kill her in her sleep. She slammed the door shut with a shudder.

Maybe throwing her shoes at the brownies during her last bender had been a mistake. Then again, the end of that sentence could be applied to any of her questionable actions after one of her benders. Which was one reason her police partner, Maeve, had been hounding her to lay off the drink. Elves, like Aisling, were immune to human alcohol, but nectar brewed the old-fashioned way could definitely knock most fey for a loop.

With a sigh, she grabbed the stylus dangling next to a tablet stuck on the side of the refrigerator. "Chased away brownies-still have no food." She scribbled into the left column. The list on that side was much longer and the writing was beginning to crawl up the side, but she refused to go to another screen. It had been two weeks since she finally swore off nectar, and she told herself she'd stay off of it if the PRO list outran the CON list.

So far the CON list had one item: Family.

Since there was a lot she wanted to forget about her family in general, and her mother in particular, she felt that really should be a much larger word. Especially after today, when what was supposed to be a short family business meeting ended up swallowing her entire day off. Unfortunately, she was honest enough with herself to realize that, no matter how large she scribbled it, it was still only one word. She ignored the eye twitch that came from simply thinking of her mother.

A sharp chirp from her phone brought her out of her forlorn search for food. *Thank the gods.*

"Aisling here. What's happened?" She tried not to sound excited; a call on this phone meant there was a dead body of unexplainable origin somewhere. But the fact was, her job was currently the only thing going right in her life and it was a distraction from the myriad of things that were going wrong.

"We've got a body down by the old pier in New Town. Do you need me to send someone to bring you here?" The voice on the other end always managed to give Aisling a chill—and not the good kind. Surratt was her boss, as well as being disgustingly attractive, rich, charming, and annoying.

He made the back of her neck so itchy she usually wore scarves when around him, just so she'd have a reason to reach back and rub her neck.

And he never risked his high-end wardrobe by going to an active crime scene—or rather, he had never done so in the past. That he was at the scene wasn't a good sign.

Aisling took a deep breath to keep the stress out of her voice. "No, I can get there. Um, thanks. What's going on?" As she spoke, she walked over to find her boots. One was good and had stayed right near her front door where she'd kicked it off an hour ago; the other had vanished.

"An *interesting* body was found. I'm bringing in the entire squad."

That bit of unusual behavior made Aisling pull back and check to make sure the number she was speaking to was, in fact, her boss. It was already after four and the daytime crew would be heading home soon. Not that crime kept to a time clock, but, when possible, Surratt tried not to overwork his detectives. That was, pretty much, his one redeeming quality.

"Ah!" Aisling said as she finally found the missing boot wedged under her sofa.

Surratt took it as a reaction to his words. "I can't explain over an open line, just get here immediately. The address is in your phone." He cut the call.

Aisling looked at the phone, then slid it into her back pocket. It must be big if Surratt wasn't going to try and fit in something obnoxious.

She gathered her gun, looped her badge around her neck, checked the address, and laid out a small bowl of milk in case she hadn't totally alienated the brownies who cleaned her house. If she could win them back, the ones in the kitchen might follow. Her hand was on the doorknob when she caught a glance of herself in the entryway mirror. The long white-blond ponytail showed far too much of her ears and the jewelry on one of them.

"Crap! That would have been just what I needed." She dumped her stuff on the bench near the door then marched back into the bathroom. The delicately ornate chain of rubies that trailed from the top of her sharply pointed left ear to the bottom would have caused her no end of grief had she gone out wearing it to a crime scene. That she hadn't taken it off the moment she was no longer in her mother's presence indicated how annoyed she'd been with the woman.

She took the time to take the chain and posts off carefully, locking them back in their ornate opal charged spell box and securing it under a spell shield. The opals were magic imbued and would keep the massive amounts of spells layered on it running indefinitely. These boxes blocked anything from sensing whatever they protected.

Then she rearranged her white-blond hair so her pointed ears were less noticeable. There was no doubt she was an elven full-blood; her features would never let her deny that. But she didn't want anyone she worked with to know the entire truth of it. High-ranking elves wore their hair high, delicately pulled back from their ears to display the elaborate clan jewelry they wore. Lower ranking ones usually wore it like she did, loose or in a low ponytail.

Her family was a high-ranking pain in the ass; she wasn't going to let who they were destroy the small slice of life she'd created for herself away from them.

Satisfied that she'd managed to look as good as she was going to on little food and plenty of annoyance, she returned to gather her belongings from the entry and went outside to find a Quick car.

The small electric cars were single-day rentals. They were slower than magically powered vehicles, but she liked supporting the burgeoning electric market. There had to be cheaper ways to have the luxuries of life than magic. Besides, since the fey folk still hadn't decided if the vehicles were trendy enough to bother with, they were usually available, even in her neighborhood.

"Ah, Aisling, good evening, fair one!" The old human next door smiled and waved as he sat on his stoop. The term was one from a long-ago time, one even older than Mr. Graves. But he still followed the ancient ways. Truth was, she would probably smack any other human who called her "fair one", or any other names used to honor her people after they'd saved the humans from the Black Death. But Mr. Graves had a sincerity behind his words that brightened her heart.

"Good afternoon, Master Graves. May the sun shine on you and yours." The elven blessing was far older than even her mother, and she would never use it for anyone but him.

His smile increased a few watts and he nodded like a pleased schoolboy.

Making him smile like that made her happier, so she wasn't paying attention when she walked a block down the street, got into her chosen Quick car, and a knife appeared at her throat.

"Start the car slow, see? I want your coins, that's all."

This day was spiraling into the crapper faster than she could blink. Even if she hadn't smelled the lactic on the hot breath curling onto her neck, Aisling would have known there was a junkie in the seat behind her by the way the knife shook.

Lactic was strictly a human drug, having no effect on any of the fey races, but an extremely detrimental effect on humans.

"You don't want to do this," Aisling said in the calmest voice she could muster. "I don't have enough coin to make it worth it. Really." She slowly raised her left arm to show him her police badge tattoo wrapped along the underside of her wrist but had only gotten half way up when he freaked.

"Give me the coins! Now!" The blade pressed into her skin and drew blood.

Moving faster than any human could hope to see, Aisling swung her head back into his. A sickening crunch told her she'd broken his nose. He was lucky she hadn't shot him.

An instant later the glass behind them shattered.

"What in the hell?" Aisling scrambled out of the front

seat and dragged the addict out from the back seat. He was dead. A tiny red dot on the back in his bald head showed her where the bullet went in.

Only a professional would have a bullet that small. And that brutal. She dropped the body and swore as whatever exotic mixture that had been added to the bullet started to eat away her attacker's face.

Moments later his entire body was little more than a pile of goo on the asphalt. But still no sign of the shooter, nor any other shots fired. She had stayed low to the ground in case the shooter was still active; but it had been too perfect of a kill shot in her opinion—someone was aiming for the junkie. Rustling from the small park across the street indicated whoever shot the junkie had fled. She scanned the car and what was left of the body with her phone; at least there'd be something to show, even if it didn't even slightly resemble a person at this point. Magic or herbs could have been used to destroy the body, but she'd never heard of something this strong before. She cautiously stood, scanning the street in case she'd been wrong about the shooter running off. Her sharp elven eyesight showed nothing beyond a quiet leafy street. The Quick car had been parked away from any of the townhomes, so not even the shattering of glass drew attention. Not a single door opened or curious neighbor popped their head out.

Damn it. First an all-day family feud, aka meeting, then no food, a mysterious case with her boss lurking around, and some vigilante kills a guy trying to rob her. She must have pissed off a lot more than her house brownies on her last bender—the gods themselves were gunning for her.

Inventing a few new swear words, she grabbed her phone and slid it open. "Danaan?" Her boss yelled before she could even get a word in. "Why aren't you here?" Surratt's voice was about as pissed off as she'd ever heard it. Whatever this case was, he was freaked. And being freaked made him pissed. Actually, everything that didn't fit in his perfect worldview made him pissed.

"I was attacked by a lactic junkie in a Quick car. Then someone shot the junkie and took off." She studied the thinning goo. There wouldn't be much soon. Whatever combo of spells and herbs the gunman had used, it was a vicious pairing. "Okay, there *was* a body. I need to call it in, get some uniforms out here—"

"No. You need to get here *now*. I'll take care of your new crime scene and I'm sending a car for you. Stay put." He hung up before she could even draw a breath to respond.

"Seriously?" Aisling raised her face to the sky in supplication. "Whatever I did to piss you off, I'm sorry. I'll never drink again, ever. Promise."

"Promise who what? You nipping the nectar again, girlie?" The rumbling voice behind her made her think maybe her prayer had been heard. Garran was older than anyone she knew, wouldn't tell anyone exactly what he was, and pretty much did whatever he wanted on the police force. Surratt was captain only because Garran refused the job every year and was currently amused by Surratt's reign. At least Surratt sent someone useful. Even if she knew damn well he broke a half dozen magic speed laws getting here as fast as he did. She'd say it was Garran being himself, but something had Surratt twitching about this case.

"No, not that. I was promising never to drink again if my life would stop going sideways." Leaving an active crime scene, one that she was directly related to, was unheard of. For a moment she thought of making Garran wait at least until the uniforms showed up. Then she noticed the flashing comm light on her phone. Surratt, most likely making sure she got in Garran's car. She turned off her phone but slid open the passenger side door of Garran's two-seater and buckled herself in. One thing Garran liked was speed. The cost for the magic that fueled this X-IH Chariot for one day would cover twice her normal annual salary.

"What was that on the ground?"

"Long story. I'm sure you'll read my report anyway." She watched the rapidly vanishing fluid that had once been a human drug addict. "I hope the uniforms get here soon though, hard to explain an attack with no body." She didn't know how helpful the images she got on her phone were going to be.

Garran grunted in agreement. "You did that?"

"No, I——" Aisling's words cut off in a grunt as Garran gunned the Chariot into gear. "Damn it, warn me!" She shook her head as her friend smirked and played weave and bob with the slower traffic. "Some junkie attacked me in the Quick car then someone else shot him with a trancer point bullet. A spelled one. I've never seen anything like it, but it started dissolving the body immediately. Surratt wouldn't let me tell him why I needed to stay back there."

Garran let out a low whistle and rubbed the back of his head. He always managed to keep his head shaved enough to have an odd baby fuzz on it. His pointed ears were longer and more tapered than most elves and rumors were that he was actually older than the elven races. "Damn, that's not good if someone's out renegading with a trancer. Surratt needs to up his game."

Aisling held back what she thought of that happening. Garran probably liked Surratt even less than she did, but the fact was, words had a way of traveling where you didn't want them to go. Even words said to friends.

As usual, Garran sensed her mood and changed the topic. "Where's that partner of yours? Ain't seen her around the station this week."

Aisling laughed and shook her head. Why and how an ancient giant gnome of a fey would have a fondness for an attitudinal human ex-British secret agent she had no idea. But Garran took a liking to Maeve. Sometimes Aisling thought he liked Maeve more than herself.

"Maeve is on vacation. Some people like to do that you know. She'll be back in a bit." Aisling hoped her partner would be back anyway. Maeve hadn't been herself for the last month or so but wouldn't confide in Aisling as to why. Her decision to go home to Mother England for a few weeks shocked no one as much as Aisling.

"My lady, this is your stop." Garran pushed a button and her door opened.

"You're not in on this?" While Garran wasn't technically part of Surratt's crew, she figured he'd been called in for whatever this was.

"Not if I can help it." He tried to flash his usual mischievous grin, but it faltered. "I have to look into some things that might tie into this. It's not good, so watch yourself."

Aisling watched his eyes, but whatever he was keeping locked behind them was staying there. "Fine. Snacks at Tappers?" She almost automatically said drinks, but nectar was the preferred beverage at the elven pub.

Garran nodded slowly. "Maybe. Call me when you're done here."

Aisling was barely free of the car when the door snapped shut and he was gone.

"Detective Danaan, good of you to join us." Surratt nodded to her from the edge of a demolition site. "This way, if you please."

Aisling followed and only then noticed where they were. It hadn't been clear from Garran's car, but she knew this place. What she'd taken as a dump was actually the remains of a small group of buildings. A clump of mismatched apartments that had been the center of an artist commune. One of the few places that was fully integrated by all the fey races and the humans.

Was.

It was little more than a mound of dust and rubble now.

Whatever had happened to it had pulverized the bricks, mortar, and wood.

A sick feeling kicked its way through her gut. What in the seven levels of the abyanon could have done this?

"Anytime, Detective, I know we wouldn't want to rush you. But we do need your intel on this." Surratt's voice didn't even hold the rancor the words would imply. She'd thought the building destruction was what she was there to see, but it appeared he was taking her to a ravine behind the mountain of former buildings.

Her entire squad was there, some taking readings and samples of the rubble, most standing around peering at something laying right out of the water of the culvert. Something bulky and covered with a tarp.

Aisling found herself reluctant to go further. "What is it?"

"Come and see for yourself." Surratt actually sounded remorseful as he continued past the rest of their squad.

None of her squad mates would meet her eyes as she moved past them. There was no way in any known hell that could be good.

She understood why when Surrat pulled back the tarp as she moved closer.

Before her lay a young fairy, one of the winged fey that rarely lived within city limits due to their love of trees and plants. She appeared to be a bit shorter than Aisling, with long skinny legs and light lavender wings. Rather, wing. Half her body was fine, completely normal; as if she'd simply taken a nap by the side of the ravine. The other half...

Aisling turned away quickly as her stomach made a pointed comment that it was a good thing she hadn't been able to find any food at home.

Blowing her breath out through her mouth to slow her breathing, she turned back to the form.

The rest of the body was horribly mutilated, and the

destruction had come from within the girl. The bumps and explosions that covered her body spoke of something moving violently through her with the intention of destroying as much internal tissue as possible. Worst of all, her wing, the mate to the perfect one, was heavy and dull. It looked like…iron?

Aisling's investigative side overwhelmed her horror and she reached out to touch it. What could make tissue and cartilage resemble—

A hand snatched hers back before she touched the wing.

"I wouldn't. I doubt even you are immune to pure iron." Surratt released her hand and stepped back once he was sure she wasn't going to keep moving forward.

"That can't be iron. How did it get inside her?"

Freddie, a gnome tech, moved out of the crowd with a grim nod. "Aye, lass. It's pure iron. We've sent for a human squad to help out since your…partner…is not here."

Aisling knew Freddie was most likely going to say 'your human', implying Maeve was her property. A holdover from a darker time that some of the old fey still slipped into.

"But how? And why would I have any knowledge of this?" Surratt had said *her intel*, as if she knew of this case, or the dead fairy.

"Ye dinna look close enough." Freddie bobbed and pointed to the sand next to the body.

Aisling had to twist her head, but there, in fine script that could only have been written by magic, lay a series of words: *Lady Aisling, this is for thee.*

CHAPTER TWO

———————

SHE TOOK A DEEP BREATH to keep the bile down, and then spun to the semi-circle of police around her. "That's sick, guys. Jokes are one thing, but who in the hell tampered with my crime scene?"

Goldkowsky raised his hands and stepped back. "Come on, Aisling. You can't think any of us would do something that macabre?"

"It's not your crime scene." Surratt's voice told her all she needed to know. There was no joke; the killer had left that message for her. And—waitaminute…

"Not my crime scene? I'm the lead detective for this area, this is my turf—"

"And you are directly involved and not in a way that can help solve this case. You can't solve it and can't be involved. We'll have someone question you about your knowledge of the victim."

Aisling backed up and ran her hands over her hair. How could this be happening? "You're benching me? That may not even be me; Aisling is not the rarest of names, you know. Maybe it was her name. And why in the hell would you bring me here if you didn't want me to work on it?"

Surratt took a deep breath through his nose, managing to angle his face so he stared down at her as he did it. Not easy when in her high boots she was probably a good three inches taller than him.

"We had a mage out here earlier to scan the crime scene. The sentence was magically etched into the ground, we couldn't move it even if we wanted to. And the emotional intent behind that name was you, there was no doubt in the mage's mind. That can't be faked. But beyond it being aimed at you, the mage couldn't retrieve any other information. I wanted to see your reaction." He nodded to the coroner techs to come take images of the body. Usually victims of suspicious deaths were humans or half–breeds. Pure blooded elves and the other fey lines were damn hard to kill. She glanced around at the milling cops and techs and took another deep breath. Hard to kill was by no means the same as impossible to kill.

Aisling was one of the elves gifted with healing, something her partner called into use far too often. Aisling's abilities weren't extremely strong, but they were enough to keep Maeve from having to see a hospital healer on many occasions. An advanced healer could bring back any fey from the dead. Except in a case of iron poisoning. Any fey who touched the body would get violently ill, if not die themselves. Iron was a rare commodity in the modern world for that reason.

"How did they do it?" She wasn't asking anyone specifically, just completely at a loss to be at a crime scene yet not be on the investigating end. Not to mention Surratt would probably put her on some sort of leave as soon as he got back to his desk empire. They'd never gotten along well, but her track record kept her valuable. Now he had an excuse to get her out—at least for a while.

"We don't know. The human team from lower east end is coming to take her to the morgue. They have a full human coroner team. Our folks will have to make do with images and computer scans." Goldkowsky seemed to be the only tech or detective who wasn't consciously avoiding her now. "They think she tried to heal herself and made it worse. That's where all of the lumps came from." He shrugged and worked his way back into the waiting mass of detectives and uniforms.

Aisling stepped back from the scene to clear her head. She also reached for her phone to call Maeve, and then stopped. Maeve hadn't returned anyone's calls since she'd left. But she'd warned them she might be too busy with family business to respond. Still, it would be so much easier to face this with her partner at her side.

"Why the long face? The other kids won't let you play?" The voice was one of those low, easy-to-like-in-an-instant voices. Probably one of the reasons that Aisling had never warmed up to Reece. Whenever someone expected people to like them, even if it was by their voice, it made her look for reasons not to. Her own family were perfect examples of why trusting appearances was often a fatal mistake.

"What are you doing here? This is our jurisdiction, not the feds."

Reece was a member of one of the alphabet agencies—CIA, FBI, KGB, FHP—but which one he actually belonged to seemed to change with each encounter.

But his high-ranking security clearance didn't.

"Our?" His smile was perfect and held no warmth or friendship in it. "From where I stand it looks like you've been removed from the case. Which actually works well for me, as I have some questions for you."

Aisling shook her head and gave him her own smile. One advantage of being from a high-ranking family of elven blue bloods, nasty smiles were taught to the children at a shockingly young age.

She raised her voice, but didn't turn away from Reece. "Surratt, we have a spy." Surratt was an ass, but he was more annoyed by Reece than she was. This murder didn't meet any federal criteria—not yet anyway. Reece had no right to be here.

Her grin grew as the sound of feet coming up off the gravel came up behind her.

"Ah, good timing, Agent Larkin, I got what I needed. She's all yours to interrogate." He turned to Aisling with a growl. "Consider yourself on administrative leave until I figure out what to do with you." With a tip of his head toward Reece, Surratt turned back toward his crime scene. But he'd only gotten two steps when he spun back. "Oh, and we'll be talking about the Quick car incident. The call came in and the uniforms didn't find anything. No car, no body, and no broken glass." The glare that accompanied his words could have shattered windows if any of the buildings around them had still been standing.

Surratt was a pompous ass, but he'd never been downright nasty. His attitude had been so out of character she hadn't even had the urge to scratch the back of her neck once. If Aisling had been raised in a normal household, or anything even remotely close to one, this would be where she'd break down and cry. This day had gone from crappy to catastrophic in no time. It also showed no indication of doing anything but a continuing downward spiral in the near future. How in the hell could the car have vanished? What was happening to her life? But Garran had seen the car and what was left of the body. Of course, who knew where Garran went after dropping her off. But she'd get him to clear things up. Eventually. Hopefully.

Right after she dealt with Reece. He was good-looking; there was no denying that. Probably about six-two; she and he were close in height when she wore boots, and she was five-ten. Average for a human male, a bit short for one of the elven lines. He was a human-fey breed, and the breeds took after their human side more so than the fey, even in appearance. Rich, dark brown hair curled in a casual way around his collar. Standard, symmetrical, non-descript features. Attractive, but not a single aspect that could be picked out as being the reason. Until you got to his eyes. Intense gray eyes that could pull you in and take you hostage on a moment's notice. Extremely *not* non-descript eyes.

Aisling made it a point to avoid full eye contact with him whenever possible. She found that staring at the space between his brows gave the impression of looking him in the eye but saved her from any foolishness. Some races of fey could spell with their eyes. No human breed should be able to. She wasn't going to take a chance that he was some sort of new mutant in breed abilities. He wore his standard outfit of a frumpy duster—odd in LA—and a loose dress shirt and pants.

Fey lines were difficult to breed true when mixed with any other blood. In fact, having children at all wasn't easy and had almost led to the decline of the fey races entirely. Humanity was far more populous three thousand years ago than it was today. They out bred the long-lived fey and soon would have pushed the fey underground.

Until the plague.

Aisling shook her head. What in the hell was she thinking about? Damn it. She must have met Reece's eyes. "I don't know why you and Surratt are now buddies and I don't care. I'm going home and putting my feet up. You heard the man, it's not my case, and I'm on leave."

She started to push past him, ignoring for a moment that she'd gotten a ride out there and had a missing and possibly destroyed Quick car on her record. She wouldn't be borrowing one of those anytime soon.

"Actually, what I heard was your boss removing any reasons why I couldn't question someone who has a connection to an extremely odd murder which might be attached to a huge federal mess." Reece tilted his head and gave one of those cold federal agent smiles. "I could order you to talk to me. If you want to refuse, I could bring in the Agency to force you to follow through or face jail time."

Aisling folded her arms and glared. Pissing him off wasn't worth this much of a headache. One more poke though. "Which agency?"

Reece's new smile was possibly even more false than his previous one. "FBI. This time. Want to see the badge?"

Fey Bureau of Investigations, the big hitter. Usually he flashed badges for smaller, less influential agencies. That he was using FBI didn't bode well.

"No. Thank you." She looked at him expectantly. "Well? What did you want to ask me? I don't know the flyer girl, nor do I have any idea who did that to her." Her stomach took that moment to remind her she hadn't eaten in a long time.

Reece ignored her words but nodded. "Not here. I don't want to be influenced by the local investigation. Besides, I'm hungry, and I know a diner nearby. I'll drive."

She started to shake her head; clearly, he'd heard her stomach and was trying to use her hunger to get her to open up around him. Like that would work. Her stomach growled even louder. Aisling sighed, betrayed by her own body.

"Lead on. You can feed me, but I'm telling you I don't know anything. And I have expensive taste in food." They started walking. "And I eat like a pig."

"Fine by me, then I won't embarrass you."

They were walking away from the direction she'd come in and had to walk much closer to the shattered buildings than before. The damage was even more impressive up close. "Do you know what happened to the buildings? How come there's no one investigating that?" Five buildings at least were destroyed, yet all of the focus was on the small dead fey with iron in her wing.

They approached Reece's car and he clicked the driver's side open. "They really didn't tell you anything, did they?" Reece got in, then unlocked her door from the driver's seat. He did it with such a deliberateness, Aisling figured he normally opened doors for women and was intentionally making an exception this time. She quickly slid in.

"Tell me what? I was there all of five minutes. There wasn't much time to tell me anything."

He tore out of the crime scene and moved quickly through the heavier traffic in this part of town. He was heading further into the older part of the city.

"She did it. That flyer destroyed the buildings before she died. Whatever they did to her, they messed her up good. The calls came in about an hour ago. She went feral fey and exploded the stones themselves from inside. Then she crashed where you saw her. Luckily, they had time to get everyone out before the buildings turned to dust. There were injuries, but no fatalities."

Aisling braced herself as he turned a sharp corner. Extremely few fey could destroy brick, stone, and wood that quickly. Certainly, none of the flyers. "Feral fey?"

"Yup. What we've been calling it at the home office. This isn't the first, although it's the first time we found the feral fey in question. If she's the same as the other cases, or rather what our scientists are hypothesizing about the other cases, something altered this girl's DNA. Something changed what she was and then killed her. Before she died, any latent powers she had exploded. For a brief time, judging by the damage she inflicted on those buildings, she was the most powerful fey in the state. The other ferals we've heard of all vanished or self-destructed, so like I said, it's all theory at this point." He glanced over to her. "It's also the first time we've had a clue."

"Me."

Reece smiled as he brought the car to a halt in front of a questionable dining establishment. "Yep, lucky you."

Aisling wanted to make him take her home; she didn't know anything about the flyer, the destruction, nor the feral fey—a term she'd never heard of before. Then the smell of French fries flooded out of the greasy-looking diner and pounced on her.

Damn it. If she was honest, this current entrapment could be blamed on her missing house brownies, and thusly on her nectar binging. This officially put the score soundly in the giving up the flower juice for good.

"I want lots of food." Aisling pushed past him and entered the diner. The waitress ignored her until Reece wandered in behind her.

"Reece! Usual table?" The petite waitress appeared human at first, then Aisling realized she was a changeling, up close the millions of tiny lines marked her as heading into her second century. When Reece smiled and nodded, the older woman scurried off.

The diner looked far better on the inside than it did on the outside. Warm colors practically shouted comfort food and instead of hard cracked banquet seating, lush, over-stuffed sofas and chairs provided an invitation to sit and relax.

Aisling frowned, and then narrowed her eyes at Reece. "So, you come here often, I take it?"

The waitress motioned them over to where she was clearing a table. If anything, the sofa seats appeared even more comfortable there, and the seat had an actual view of the small creek that ran behind the place. It was the same water that eventually went to the ravine, but at this end it was flanked by thin willows and tall grasses.

"Enough." Reece motioned for her to slide in to one of the seats, but she noticed he carefully took the one facing the door for himself. "I never have time to cook and love to eat. I can recommend everything on the menu."

Although her stomach was about to crawl its way out of her throat and start stalking its own meal, Aisling tried not to appear too excited. This was a different side of Reece—

almost warm and fuzzy.

And less trustworthy than his usually snarky self. Good-looking smartasses were dangerous; good-looking *nicer* smartasses were deadly.

Plus, there was one point she was in full agreement with her family on: That no fed could be trusted. Ever. Regardless of their species. That she wasn't completely sure which agency he was really with made him that much more questionable.

She might not believe she knew anything about the current case—but he thought she did. Watching her words around him would be a good idea, especially until she figured out what his game was.

She leaned back and feigned relaxing; actually her relaxing was only fake for the first two minutes, after that it was like the sofa had enveloped her in a warm hug.

The waitress came back with a smile. "I know what the big guy will have, but what about you, sweets?"

She was classic diner in manner and looks, and would have been a cheesy stereotype if she wasn't so charming. Aisling flashed her a smile, then flipped open the menu.

"I think I'll have some chicken fried steak. And fries. And some fried chicken. The mixed veggies sound good." She glanced at the waitress's tattered name tag. "What kind of soup do you have today, Stella?"

A quick grin told her she'd won the older woman over. "Well, we have honeysuckle stew, clover leaf and barley ragman's combo, and clam chowder."

Aisling pondered as her stomach did the cha-cha. "Which would you suggest, Stella? I'm Aisling by the way, since my co-worker hasn't seen fit to introduce us."

Reece rolled his eyes, but kept his mouth shut. Smart man.

"Ah, you're one of his co-workers! Exciting work he does, right? Well, you do too, don't you, doll? I thought

you looked different from the other women he brings in."
She turned to Reece with a shrug. "No offense, Reece, but
your taste in companions is seriously lacking. Good to see
it's improved with your new partner." She slid in next to
Aisling on the sofa and leaned forward, her voice dropped
to a releasing of state secrets level. "I'd say stay away from
the chowder—the clams ain't fresh—not even sure they're
clams. The ragman's is a good choice today though."

Aisling was glad for the warning about the chowder;
she'd been about to get it since seafood was one of the
food groups she'd missed in her ordering. Ragman's stew
was wonderful if made right. A hodgepodge of bits and
pieces, it always tasted different, but with proper spicing it
was always good.

"Ragman's it is." She handed back the menu. "I'll order
dessert after my meal though."

Stella picked up the menu—she hadn't bothered to give
Reece one—and vanished back into the kitchen.

"You're not my co-worker."

"In a way I am. We're both law enforcement. And I'm
sure if you ever told me whatever agency you truly worked
for, I'd be the first one to come visit your office." As soon
as Stella had left, Reece focused his eyes on the door. She
knew better than to turn around. Besides, she could read
his expressions well enough. If something dangerous came
in, she'd know. "You expecting company?"

"Always. Part of my job." He let his gaze drop for a
moment and met her eyes. Then flashed back to the door.
"I'm not sure, but something feels…wrong."

Aisling laughed and relaxed a bit. "You've been hanging around *us* too much. You're a human breed, Reece.
You don't have second sight." Some humans believed they
could sense important events before they happened, but so
far none had ever been proven reliable.

"There is instinct, you know." Reece pulled his gaze

from the door with a shake of his head then folded his hands in front of him on the table. "Now, what do you know about Mott Flowers?"

Aisling pulled back. That was a name from the past, and possibly one of the most random things Reece could have asked, aside from what color underwear are you wearing.

Mott was an old school mate, not a friend, but someone she'd had classes with in primary school. And someone she probably hadn't thought of since way before Reece's great grandparents would have been born.

"I know he was awful at math and not too good at language either. Oh, and he liked to play keep-away with the wee one's acorns." She narrowed her eyes at him. "What has this got to do with anything? I went to primary school with the guy."

Reece nodded as if she'd handed him the key to unlocking the universe. "And yet you recalled him immediately when I said his name."

She leaned forward. "I'm an elf, and we have freaking good memories."

Stella appeared then to place two huge bowls of soup on their table. From the look of his, Reece's "usual" was ragman's stew also.

Stella stood there beaming. Aisling wanted to know what in the hell Reece was doing asking about some childhood acquaintance, but not in front of the waitress.

So she dove into her stew. The first mouthful was quickly followed by the second.

"Ah, there we go." Stella nodded then went back to her other tables. It appeared that making sure that Reece's friend and co-worker was happy was high on her priorities. Reece must spend *a lot* of time here.

"Again, why are you asking about him? Do you want me to rattle off all of my primary school classmates?"

"Have you seen him in the last month?" He'd tried to

make it casual, but there was a tension in his voice as he said 'seen'.

"No, I haven't seen him for over two hundred years. Is that what you wanted to know? My age? There are easier ways to ask." She knew some elves, especially those who dealt with humans fairly often, felt odd about their ages. She didn't. It wasn't her fault her people were damn near immortal. And his weren't.

"Are you sure?" His stew was shoved to the side and he grabbed her hand. "Think hard now, and carefully. Have you seen him?"

His intensity startled her and she met his eyes. Not a good idea. She'd have to check with Garran to make certain that no breeds could spell cast, but damn, those gray eyes held her.

Of course she hadn't seen him. Hell, she hadn't thought of him at all since probably the day after primary graduation. He'd moved away and she never saw him again.

"No, I haven't seen him. Not since..." Her voice dropped as an image snuck into her mind. Mott. Not as a child. Not something she'd noticed at the time, just off to the side. Too vague to notice when or where the image came from. But for some reason, she knew it was him. Even though they'd never been close, and it had been over two hundred years, it was him. *Why hadn't she noticed it at the time?*

"There's something, isn't there? You've seen him." Reece dropped her hand, but he still watched her intently.

"It's not like I was lying. I honestly didn't know I saw him at the time. Hell, I don't know where or when it happened." She narrowed her eyes, breaking the intense contact between them. "The bigger question is, how did *you* know I did?"

"Ah, well, he had a note on it." Reece shrugged then went back to his stew.

"He left a note for you? Then why ask me? What game

are you playing, Reece? Is this about that flyer, or not?"

"He didn't intend to leave the note, it was in things we found a few weeks ago. Reece held up both hands in a defensive stance. "Easy there, it's all tied together, trust me." His voice dropped. "I'm just not sure how."

"What?" She couldn't recall him ever admitting that he didn't know something.

"Mott Flowers went underground about fifteen months ago. You wouldn't know this, but he became a big name in the scientific community once he grew up. Something to do with working on some of the tech end of magic, he was behind some big inventions that no one would have heard of. Anyway, he vanished right after the first feral fey attack. The computer scientists ran an analysis and his disappearance showed a forty-five percent chance of being connected."

"You think he went feral fey? Is that what is connecting him to the girl flyer?" Aisling chose to ignore the stats.

"No. I do think he's watching you and might have been the one who shot at you this morning. We aren't sure how he's connected and the official think tank he worked for has sealed all of his studies." He paused as Stella swooped in with full plates for both of them. With a nod she vanished just as quickly. "As for where you saw him at, it was two months ago on a murder case in gnome town. There would have been no reason for you to notice him at the time."

Aisling had already sliced up her chicken fried steak and had one tantalizing forkful almost to her mouth when he said that. "You said he went underground fifteen months ago, yet I saw him two months ago? And you really think he shot at me? Waitaminute, how did you know about what happened in the Quick car?"

"We've found recent traces of him and his prior hideout. He's moving around. And he left quickly and abandoned many things, including some notes and photos of you." Reece shook his head. "As for the Quick car, the agency knows about a lot of things—who do you think took that car of yours before the cops got there? But I don't think he was trying to kill you—I think he was trying to protect you."

This time the bit of food traveling toward her mouth went back to the plate. A missing ex-classmate was stalking her? One with an uber high scientific clearance? Shit. "He had a trancer gun—a modified one by the way the body dissolved."

Reece's smirk vanished. "I know. One he's modified based on his own experiments. That goo trick I heard about isn't normal."

"So you weren't actually there. Just lurking outside my building after I was almost mugged and shot?"

"No, *I* wasn't. One of my associates was and two more came to help clean up." He sighed. "My associate went to watch you after we heard about the message next to the flyer. Yes, we heard about it before Surratt and his people took over. Seeing Mott was a bonus, but everything happened too fast, Mott got away."

Aisling wasn't sure which intrusion to focus on first. Super-secret feds watching her, then stealing evidence, or an old classmate shooting at her. "And what kind of photos of me did he have?" Not sure she wanted to know, the answer might increase her current weirded out level, but knowing was better. She hoped.

"Not *that* kind," he said. "We think he was investigating something, we're just not certain what or who. You're in them, and your partner is in some as well. But they are all off center, as if he was taking photos of something near you. Something that we can't see."

Aisling had managed to sneak in two quick bites while he talked, but between Mott and the dead flyer, she was losing her appetite. "And he's leaving these photos around for you to find? Don't you think that's a bit odd?"

Reece nodded. "We found them in a bolt hole he'd had to abandon quickly, and they were partially burned."

"Okay then, Mott is a dead-end right now, even though he's running around with a trancer gun. But how in the hell does he, and whatever he was working on, tie into the girl?" Her voice dropped. "What was her name?" It might not be her case, but, somehow, she was involved. She needed to know who the poor girl had been.

"Julilynn Marcos. Artist, free spirt, moved here with her boyfriend into an apartment way above their means."

Aisling filed the name away; she wouldn't forget her, regardless of why her name was left next to Julilynn's body. No one deserved to die like that. She also knew what Reece was getting at about living above their means. In the cop world, that term usually meant drug runners.

The color in his face vanished suddenly and he grabbed her hand. "Out now." His gaze was locked on the door.

Aisling turned toward the door. "I'm not leaving—"

"Now, damn it." Reece had come to her side and with an unexpected strength pulled her free of the seat.

She expected a horde of raving bikers, but there was nothing. Then the nothing turned to rattling and the door flung off its hinges. A massive shape emitting heavy dark smoke flooded into the front of the diner.

There was only one creature who moved like that—a smoke beast. A rare breed of base fey, they had snuck through the Veil when the mass exodus occurred as the fey fled through the Veil thousands of years ago. They weren't made of smoke, but released it for defense and hunting. They were supposedly seven feet tall, covered in a dark gray mass of fur, and had claws as long as a human's hand. Aisling had never seen one and didn't know anyone personally who had. Explosive magical smoke and a strength like three trolls left few survivors. But they usually stayed in their solitary caves deep in the woods. She had no idea why one was here, but she had to save who she could.

"Get everyone out the back." Reece let go of her arm and ran toward the whirling smoke. Aisling knew she could handle whatever he could, and probably better since her elven body was tougher than his. But he was almost to the front door and she was surrounded by confused patrons and diner staff.

She held up her gun and let the cuff of her shirt fall free from her badge tattoo on her inner wrist. "LA police, everyone out the back door, now!"

People were scrambling, but many were crawling under their tables, or worse, trying to run for the front door. Aisling raised her voice and fired a magic charge from her gun at the ceiling. It wouldn't damage things like a bullet would but it caused enough sparks to grab their panicked attention.

"Now that I have your attention, LA police—go out the back—now!"

Stella held open the kitchen door and between them they herded the patrons out into the back alley.

Stella grabbed her hand as they ran out when there was no one left inside. "Officer? I thought you seemed more like a cop than a fed." She gave a smile. "But what was that we were running from? And where's Reece?"

"I don't know, he must not have—"

An explosion swallowed her words and knocked both her and Stella off their feet. A fireball blew out the back of the diner.

CHAPTER THREE

———◆———

THE EXPLOSION SLAMMED HER TO the ground and clouded her senses. For a few terrifying moments she couldn't hear, see, or sense anything. Unlike some elves, Aisling wasn't a strong sensitive, but whatever abilities she had got blasted by the fireball.

Her vision came back and the milling mass of human and fey diner patrons around her came into view. Stella roused when Aisling checked on her.

The world was still mostly silent, and while she could see that people were talking, it was clear that no one else could hear anything either.

The billows of smoke coming out of the diner told her there was no way anyone could have lived through that blast. A wave of sorrow hit her. Reece wasn't a friend, but no one should die that way.

Her hearing must have started coming back because the telltale sirens of both fire department and police echoed as if they were bouncing off tin in her head. The building wasn't burning, at least not from what she could see as the smoke drifted off. What in the hell could make that kind of explosion with no fire remaining? Smoke beasts could kill, but they usually didn't explode. At least no studies ever mentioned it.

She turned to Stella, then to the others still wandering around and lifted her voice to a level she hoped the other woman could hear. "We need to get everyone pulled away from the diner. Not too far, we may need to talk to them."

Well, Surratt might. There was no way he was going to put her back into active status anytime soon with this event added on.

Stella frowned and nodded. She didn't say anything but started organizing the patrons and other staff with a mix of yelling and hand gestures.

Which left Aisling watching the diner. Damn it, Reece was a pain in the ass, a professional class PITA as Maeve would call him. He was extremely good looking, but after realizing what a jerk he could be, she didn't acknowledge the attraction anymore. Their interactions were usually a contest of one-upmanship with a side of annoyance thrown in for good measure.

So why did his loss slam into her gut like a rock?

Granted, he had information that she needed, but it felt like more than that.

"You look like you lost your best friend. We can get you more food somewhere else." The voice behind her almost made her jump out of her skin. Reece had somehow not only survived, but also snuck up behind her. Considering her ears were still ringing, the sneaking part wasn't so hard to believe.

The surviving part was.

"How in the hell did you get through that?" She poked him in the chest and swung her other hand toward the diner. His long duster was now an odd gray color, and there was dust and ash in his hair, but he was intact and alive.

He shrugged and started dusting some of the larger flakes of ash off of himself. "I ran out the front when I realized that I couldn't stop the explosion. The building is surprisingly intact for going through the motions of blowing up."

Aisling rubbed her forehead. Here she'd been thinking he'd gone up in a blaze of glory, and the bastard was simply watching the disaster from the other side of the diner.

"You were still in there as I ran out the door. You were running toward that smoke beast when it exploded."

Reece's laugh didn't endear him to her. "It wasn't a smoke beast; it was a smoke *bomb*. With a full level one explosion attached, in fact. Once I realized that, I ran out the front door and waited for the inevitable. Thanks for making sure everyone else got out."

Smoke beasts weren't common, but like all other forms of fey, knowing what they were was part of her cop training. She seriously doubted that some high-level spook didn't have that training as well. The bastard was lying to her. Again.

"Is it a game with you?" That hadn't been what she'd intended to say, but it was where her mind was. "Do you lie to me because it's fun? Or is it some psychological allergic reaction to the truth? Something from your deep dark childhood that makes you unable to be honest with people?"

He took a step back and frowned. "I know what I was facing. It was a simple—"

"No." She cut him off as she followed his steps and poked his chest again. "No more lies, damn it. There is something big going on, and I know what was in there."

The look in Reece's eyes scared her. In the time they'd known each other she'd never once seen confusion, not real confusion at any rate. He feigned it enough when he didn't want to give her a straight answer. But this was different. It was real. And tinged with a bit of fear.

He shook his head as if there had been a bug flying around it, but the confusion stayed. "I am not lying. I swear it was an incendiary smoke bomb that should have destroyed the diner, but malfunctioned. Someone was trying to take out the diner, but there wasn't anything alive there." He studied her face, and then dropped his voice. "Was there?"

"Crap." Aisling ran her hand through her hair. She knew what had been in that diner, and she also knew that even if he'd never seen one before, there was no way that Reece would have confused a smoke beast with a bomb. Unless something magical didn't want him to see the smoke beast. "Does your mysterious agency have a Seer on their staff?"

Seers were standard in most law enforcement agencies, mostly to help with the law enforcement officers them-selves. They were there to help officers cope with their daily lives, but also to track things they may have seen but had no recall of. High-powered magic users could mask what actually happened at a crime scene. Seers were a way to combat that.

"Yes." He looked ready to argue, then ran his hand over his eyes. "I'd normally accuse you of trying to pull one over on me, but you've got that deadly serious look in your eyes. Okay, one that is more deadly serious than usual."

"What would my detective be trying to pull over on you, Agent Larkin?" Surratt wasn't emanating the open hostility he had back at the ravine, but he didn't appear happy to see either one of them at his newest crime scene.

"I thought I had seen a bomb inside the diner." Reece's face was thoughtful and he nodded toward her. "Aisling saw something different."

She still wasn't completely sure that Reece wasn't pull-ing her along on some elaborate trick, but she'd have to act as if he wasn't—at least for now. "It was a smoke beast. It wasn't clear, as the smoke hid most of it, but the thing vibrated the doors off of the diner before it attacked." She folded her arms and rocked back on her boot heels. "I know what I saw."

Surratt nodded and his shoulders dropped as some of the tension left them. "I believe you. Not that I doubt you, Agent Larkin, but I trust my detective and what she sees more than I trust my own eyes, let alone yours. If something didn't want you to see a smoke beast, you wouldn't see it." He held up a hand quickly. "And no, not only because you're not pure blooded fey. There is something going on that is far bigger than any of the agencies investigating it. Go visit your Seer, see what they say."

Aisling's eyes grew round. Earlier, Surratt was nasty and overly dismissive, something out of character for him, now he was going out of his way to support her, also extremely out of character. Maybe they needed to use a Seer as well, to find out if this was the true Surratt. He was usually a distracted slime ball who stayed in his office and shoved paper around. She had no idea who this person in front of her was.

Reece seemed surprised by Surratt as well, but like her, he kept his opinion to himself. He nodded. "Yeah, that's already been suggested."

"I have good detectives, none better than Danaan."

If she thought she was surprised before, by now her shock meter was running at full tilt.

"What, you think I keep you around for your pretty face?" Surratt gave a crooked grin. "Trust me, you're where you are because you're good."

Aisling watched as more detectives arrived from the ravine crime scene. Most of the techs were still back there, but the detectives were here taking eyewitness statements.

"If I'm so good, then why am I on leave?" Granted, the use of her name next to the victim was probably a good indication that she was intimately connected with the case even if she wasn't sure what that connection was. But still, she should be on that case, especially if it was as big and potentially nasty as it was shaping up to be.

Surratt glanced around them carefully. Then leaned forward and kept his voice low. "I had to do that, I can't go into things now, but we believe there may be a problem in the department. That's why I asked Larkin to come get you.

I needed them to see you and your reaction, and then get you out of there. Someone is trying to connect you to that victim, and I want to know why. Of course, I didn't know this was going to be the next crime scene." He raised his voice for Reece to hear the last line and shot him a glare.

Reece shoved his hands in his duster's pockets and actually looked a bit embarrassed. Or flustered. Whatever mojo the smoke beast had used on him had shaken him.

"I didn't expect this place to be attacked." Reece turned away from Surratt and thoughtfully gazed at Aisling. "Although maybe I should have."

She had been watching the interviews down the way. Most of the patrons were cooperating, but Goldkowsky seemed to have his hands full with one little old lady. She whipped back at his tone. "What's that supposed to mean?" Aisling was about done with Reece. He might have information she could use, like why Mott Flowers was stalking her after a few centuries, but she was sure she could find that information from another source. "Sir, permission to rejoin the department on this and help out Goldkowsky. He seems to be having problems."

Surratt rolled his eyes and turned back to where the short detective and the even shorter little old lady gnome were locked in a rapidly escalating yelling match.

"Not now, Danaan. I need you here and focused on the issues." He shook his head. "Actually, focused on *the issue*. Larkin's right in that there is something big going on, but we're not sure who in which agencies is aware of it. I need you and him to work on bringing these bastards down. First, find out who murdered our winged victim, then who went after a bunch of diner patrons. You can come back to the station tomorrow for a temporary re-assignment, after you two have finished figuring out what each of you know. But you two will still need to be together on this." With a nod at both of them, he stalked toward Goldkowsky and the battling granny.

"Ah, excellent. Now, where were we?" Reece might still be disturbed about the smoke beast issue, but the chance to annoy her brought him out of it.

"I was going to tell you how to spot a smoke beast?" Aisling asked sweetly. She hadn't been in the mood to talk with him to begin with; that was more true after having a diner almost blown up out from under her. And instead of helping her figure out what was going on, he'd added more issues with Mott. The fire department came out of the diner and nodded to Stella. Whatever that smoke beast had done, there must not have been that much damage or they wouldn't be letting the staff back in.

After a moment, Stella came back out and motioned for Aisling and Reece to come in.

"I was spelled. And until the Seer says otherwise, I'm saying it was a bomb." Reece looked down the alley as the old lady gnome switched her energy from Goldkowsky to Surratt.

Aisling finally coughed to get his attention and pointed to Stella waving from the door. "Look, my boss wants us to talk, and I want to know what you know about Mott Flowers and Julilynn Marcos. We need to make sure Stella and her people will be okay, but is there some place we can talk that's not a crime scene?"

Reece nodded and they stepped inside the diner. Smoke stained the walls; one or two places near the front were solid black where the creature had tried to burst into flame but hadn't been able to. It had failed, then vanished. Or failed and was taken out by someone else.

Smoke beasts were primitive fey, and they stuck to themselves deep in the San Angeles Mountains. There was only one way that one would be roaming around in the center of one of the largest cities in the world; someone was controlling it. To get such a creature under control would take a seriously powerful magic user. Which made her wonder why someone of that level would spend all of that power on trying to blow up a diner. She'd have to get a look at the file with all of the diner patrons in it tomorrow. That thing was after someone. The way her luck had been today, it was looking for her.

"Nothing but cosmetic damage they say," Stella said and broke Aisling out of her thoughts. "Should be up and running in a day or two." The way she wiped her hands on her apron, Aisling had a feeling there would be a lot of magical gifts being used. Most fey were magic users of some level and from the almost visible magic crackling around the tiny woman, Stella was one of the powerful ones.

Reece leaned forward and gave Stella a hug. "If you need anything, give me a yell."

Stella looked back from her contemplation of the smoky diner and smiled. "I will be fine. I expect to see both of you back here soon." With a nod, she marched off to attack the mess.

Aisling went out the front of the diner.

Reece fell in next to her. "Where are we going?"

There were still a damn lot of issues adding on to the already crappy day she'd had. But her stomach reminded her that she only had a few bites beyond the soup. "Someplace else with food. You pick."

"I could take you back to your car if you want to pick it up."

"Yeah, I don't have one at the moment." She nodded and dodged two techs with equipment leaving the diner. "There was an accident, and that's why I was trying to use the Quick car."

She glared at Reece to emphasize the unspoken words of, "and no, you shouldn't ask me about it." That was the fourth car to self-destruct in two years. At this point the motor pool wasn't allowing her to sign out anything with more than two wheels.

"Ah, yes, you had one a few weeks ago as well. And then we had to pick up that Quick car you got attacked in. Sorry if that compounded things, but we needed it for our case on Mott." He didn't look sorry in the least. He probably would have ordered her car to be picked up simply to cause her grief.

She got to the passenger side of his car and slid in once he unlocked it. "I still don't get why he shot the mugger. The guy was a human junkie with a knife—he didn't stand a chance."

Reece gave her an odd look as he started the car. "You probably didn't see whatever he had with him, but there was iron dust where that junkie sat in the back seat. Our techs reported it when we pulled in the car but our scientists are still analyzing it. Whatever it was from turned to goo along with the junkie when Mott shot him. But he was carrying iron of some sort. Mott possibly saved your life."

CHAPTER FOUR

J ULILYNN'S MANGLED BODY FLASHED IN her mind
and she rubbed the small nick on her neck where his
blade had touched her. Had the iron residue from whatever he was carrying been on that blade, she would have
been dying a horrific death right now. "I'll have to send
him a thank you card." Being flip about it allowed her to
shove that terror aside for now.

"You *and* us, too. Although if we'd found that junkie
intact, we'd have a better idea who we are dealing with."
He paused at an access road that led to the freeway. "Which
way—you want to go home, or try for more food?"

As disturbing as this recent revelation was, she was still
starving. And more importantly, she still hadn't finished
questioning him about Julilynn. "Food, but no restaurants.
How about Centaur Burgers?" She looked around his car.
"Or are you a no eating in the car kind of guy?"

He laughed and turned the car away from the freeway.
"With the amount of time I spend on stakeouts, I'd starve
to death if I didn't eat in my car. Centaur Burgers it is."

It was late enough that the line wasn't as horrifically long
for the drive-through as it could be. It helped that it was a
Thursday night. Friday or Saturday and they'd be there for
an hour or more. Aisling didn't frequent the burger place
often, but stress made her want meat, and lots of it. This
day had started with nine hours of harassment from her
family and ended with a smoke beast and a death by iron
poisoning. She needed burgers.

Reece ordered a classic burger, some fries, and a coffee combo. He sat back out of the way to let Aisling lean forward and order. "Four mega burgers, one small fry, and an iced tea."

She smiled at Reece when he raised an eyebrow. "I'm still hungry, and leftovers would be good."

"Don't you have food at home?"

"I was ripped off by brownies." Now *that* she hadn't meant to say to him. She blamed the insanely intense smells of burger nirvana coming from the drive-through corridor on loosening her tongue.

"You were robbed by a pack of brownies? I didn't know they had a gang. Did they clean up your place after they robbed it?"

"Funny. They didn't break into my house, they were hired house brownies." There had to be something she could tell him that didn't involve her overactive love of nectar and the resulting outcome to the house brownies. "They went on strike." She shrugged.

Luckily the car before them left the window and Reece had to pull forward. "Someday I'd like to hear what you did to make them go on strike." He paid for the food, handed it over to her, and found a place under a light to park.

Reece studied people, and then used whatever would make them uncomfortable to get them to do what he wanted them to do. Good thing the sneaky bastard never became a cop; she'd have to kill him if they worked together for more than a week solid.

Reece stepped out of the car and took off his duster, then got back in.

"You took off your jacket."

"Yeah, I often do that when I'm staying inside places." The look he gave her clearly said that he thought she'd been hit in the head by flying debris recently.

"No, don't be a smartass. You didn't at the diner."

"Yeah, I did, why wouldn't I..." The scowl that crawled across his face told him he was re-thinking who got hit in the head. "I'll be damned. You're right."

Aisling paused in unwrapping her first burger when he looked like he wasn't going to expand on it. "And? Why didn't you? You don't know why, do you?"

He shrugged and tried a glare, but he wasn't feeling it. "I'm sure I had a reason."

She kept staring until he finally shook her off. "I don't know. I'd say it was intuition about the *bomb*, but I didn't notice that I didn't take it off at the time. I'm sure it's nothing. Unlike someone who is going to starve because she's alienated the hired house brownies. Now, that's a story to hear."

Aisling wanted to push about the duster, it could be nothing, but it had been her experience in her thirty years on the force that little things had a tendency to turn into big things. Whether they were a good or bad thing remained to be sorted later.

"They left. Probably on a vacation, some mix up with the agency who hires them. How about instead you tell me what you know about Julilynn Marcos and why you think she's related to Mott and me."

Reece ate a few fries, then pulled up his phone and set up a series of projected images. "I was able to pull these photos of her off social media." He handed her his phone.

The girl looked much better alive. Tiny and delicate, she was of the pixie lineage of flyers. Her short blond hair was tipped with a rainbow of colors and in each photo she was with a tall faun. He looked as smitten with her as she was of him.

"Look in the corner of the third and fifth photos, lower left," Reece said.

Aisling scowled at the projection until she was able to

enlarge and focus the small image. Mott Flowers. Swearing, she did the same to the fifth one—different day, different shirt, but there was her old school chum with a camera aimed at Julilynn and her faun boyfriend.

"He was stalking her too? Damn. Was he a creep?"

"We think that he found out something in his think tank, or his day job at the tech company, that scared the hell out of him. He ran, but he also was clearly trying to resolve something, or things."

"And the connection between her and I? You have something or you wouldn't have been so agreeable to help Surratt out." She knew the two men didn't get along and she didn't think Reece helped Surratt out without his own massive list of reasons.

Reece took back the phone and set up another image. "We found this."

It was older than the others; the first set were from a month ago, this one was dated almost four months back. A crime scene photo, but definitely not an official one.

In the center were she and Maeve, plus a few other members of the force. It was taken at a downtown bank heist that had revealed a pair of murders. Standard circle of onlookers trying to get as close as they could to the police tape without getting a magical zap. Julilynn was right in front, a huge human man was too close not to be with her, and next to him was a grim-faced Mott. He was pointing right at Aisling.

Aisling kept the photo up and looked for anything else that would explain what was going on. She couldn't think of anything about that case that was weird or different. That this wasn't the case Reece had originally mentioned about her seeing Mott at also gave her food for thought. He hadn't wanted her to know. Something had changed in the last hour.

"Can you send me this one? I might be able to figure

out what caused them to be so interested." She added the last part when Reece looked ready to shake her off.

"Fine, don't show it around if you'd mind." He took his phone back, hit send, and then put it away.

"Eat up, fed-boy, you still need to get me home and I need to be back in the precinct tomorrow a.m. to find out what's really going on."

Reece shrugged and increased his eating.

A half hour later, Aisling unlocked the door to her house to the sound of Reece peeling out. As if acting like a fifteen-year-old would impress her.

His car tricks didn't, but the sizeable doggie bag he'd sent her home with did. She'd mindlessly eaten all four of her burgers while trying to figure out the connections in the cases. Reece had driven them back through the drive-through and ordered her three more burgers and a salad to take home.

She let out a low whistle when she flicked on the lights. Whether the kitchen brownies had forgiven her or not was still to be seen, but the house brownies had. Her house was spotless. They'd taken the bribe of whole milk and fresh bread she'd left for them. Good thing too, an annoyed kitchen brownie would usually sulk; but a seriously annoyed house brownie could destroy your house.

The cold box door opened without any foodstuffs trying to grab her; in fact the most vicious looking of the remains was gone.

Which hopefully meant it had been kicked out by a kitchen brownie and not gotten out on its own. She put away the leftover fast food and grabbed some more milk for the brownies. Yes, it was spoiling them to serve it twice in a night, but she didn't care. There were enough things out to get her, she needed something to be on her side.

And if it took copious amounts of whole milk, she'd go find a damn cow.

What she should do, after the long dramatic day she'd had, would be to take a hot bath and crawl into bed. She was intending to do that very thing when instead she found herself going over to her computer.

Mott Flowers had popped up out of nowhere, stalked her and her partner, and possibly been involved with a horrifying fey death. She needed to find out what she could about her long-forgotten classmate.

CHAPTER FIVE

———◆———

THE ALARM CRACKED OPEN AISLING'S skull at some unholy hour. Squinting across to the clock told her it only felt ungodly—it was actually seven a.m. She managed to shut off the clock without destroying it and stumbled out to her kitchen. The coffee maker was popping away cheerfully, but that was more machine technology than returning kitchen brownies. With an optimistic smile, she flung open the cold box door.

Nothing. Not only was there nothing for breakfast, the fast food from the previous night was missing.

The hired kitchen brownies were still here, but they weren't helping her, and they'd started taking hostages.

"I said I was sorry." Rustling through her cabinets uncovered some honey in a dust covered bottle. "I don't know what else I can do. I've promised to stop drinking." As she offered appeasements to the hidden sprites, she poured out all of the honey into a small bowl. Hopefully a direct apology combined with enough sweet stuff to keep them on a sugar high for a week would bring them back to normal.

Or cause an ant invasion.

Bribes placed, and lamenting her lack of breakfast burgers, Aisling got ready for work and went out the door. Then realized she didn't have a car, and most likely the Quick car folks wouldn't let her have anything.

Standing on her stoop, she was about to start calling everyone in her phone until she found one of her friends who could come get her, when a green cab pulled to a stop in front of her house. Considering cabbies rarely came this far out searching for fares, it had to be someone lost. But it never hurt to check.

"Can I help you?" Hopefully his missing fare was on the other side of the police precinct from her. As if her luck would have been that good. But her luck had to turn around eventually, right? Her stomach grumbled its opinion on that.

"Yeah, you Detective Danaan? I've been sent to get you."

A tingle of fear crept down her spine, but there was no way this guy looked anything like Mott, about a foot too tall and the wrong species for one thing; the driver was fey but wasn't elven. Besides, hopefully anyone with the reported amount of brains Mott had wouldn't be that stupid.

She sized up the driver, winged fey, it looked like wings were tucked in a holding vest under his jacket. Light lavender skin. Yeah, there was no way this was Mott.

And more importantly, she knew she could take this guy in a fight and had her hand on her gun in the pocket of her vest. Just because he wasn't Mott, didn't mean he was who he said he was.

"My boss Johnson send you?" she asked as she locked her house behind her.

"Not sure who Johnson is, but the guy who sent me said his name was Surratt and he was your boss. How many bosses you got?"

Aisling felt her shoulders drop a bit although she hadn't been aware of hunching them up. Paranoia was a common side effect for a cop, but this was pushing it. Forcing a smile, she slid into the cab.

"Nope, Surratt's my boss. Johnson likes to play games sometimes."

The cabby looked at her sideways from the mirror as she buckled herself into the back seat. He didn't say anything the entire trip.

When Aisling paid him, tipping him graciously for the imagined slight she might have given by mentally accusing him of being a killer, he grunted, pocketed the money, and sped off.

"Geesh, Danaan, ya go through another car? Now you're taking cabs into work?" The tall, bulky detective lingering outside the station should be inside at his desk by now. Probably hanging out here to smoke. Trott was about the only cop she knew who smoked, but since Surratt forbade him from smoking inside, he had to take a lot of breaks.

"I lost my car a week ago, just took you this long to notice." She hadn't, but she liked the way his face scrunched in on itself when he was confused. Trott was muscle, pure muscle and not much else.

Surratt kept him on the force because he was family… or so it was rumored.

He took a long drag of his cig as he tried to recall the last time he'd seen her car. Aisling moved past him. He'd figure it out eventually.

"Good of you to join us, Detective." Surratt was back to his slightly acerbic self. Whatever flash of decent behavior he'd had yesterday was gone. Although he did send a cab for her. Interesting. Maybe he was changing. Or maybe he found a new way to mess with her.

"We've been ready to start the briefing on a case for five minutes. Did you let that cabbie take the long way?"

Aisling dropped her purse off at her desk and swung wide to grab some coffee. She hadn't thought about it, too busy making sure the cabbie wasn't working for someone trying to kill her. But yeah, now that she thought about it, he had gone a few miles out of the way. Great detective skills on her end. No wonder she hadn't noticed Mott Flowers following her.

"Um, no. Just running late. Is there a new lead?"

Surratt shook his head. Obviously, he'd seen her face when she'd realized she been taken for a ride, while being taken for a ride. "If you'll join the rest of the boys and girls, we can all learn about it together."

She smiled to the assembled officers and detectives, at least the few who weren't watching something at the front of the room, then took her seat.

Her much needed coffee almost took a header when she realized what the others were watching.

It was a series of close-up photos of Julilynn Marcos. Having been there in person didn't prepare her for the shock of what had happened to the girl.

The close-up photos of her left wing and entire left side of her torso were truly horrific. With these views, it was clear that there was no flesh left in the wing, and there were huge gaps in the remaining flesh on that side of her body. The rest was pure iron.

Aisling felt the chill that she was sure was running through all of the fey minds right now. Iron kills. Their precinct was about half human and half fey, they had a larger portion of humans than most, but considering that Los Angeles probably had the largest single group of humans in the world, it wasn't surprising. Judging from the looks around her even the humans were freaked out by a body turned to The Deadly Metal as it was called. Since the fey had saved the human race from extinction in the 1300s, the remains of humanity had taken great care to keep iron out of everything. The Black Death had taken away humanity's ability to bear children, worldwide, reducing their numbers more than the plague itself did. The fey managed to destroy the plague after twenty hard years, then within the next fifteen were able to create magics that allowed some human conception. The fey still out-bred the humans, something that would have been unheard of when the humans hit their population peak in 1290.

"How did they do that to her?" Aisling knew a briefing wasn't the time to be muttering out of turn, but the shock of what had been done caused an irrational response.

Surratt took the front of the room and ignored her blurted comment. "People, I can't tell you how crucial it is that we find this killer. The data we know is that our victim, Julilynn Marcos, was fine and healthy when her boyfriend last saw her at 0900 yesterday. He'd left their apartment to go look for work. At 1700 yesterday, witnesses say the victim flew out of her top floor apartment in a rush, then headed for the east side. No one knows where she was until calls started coming in about a rampaging flyer in the art district at 1940; by the time black and whites got there the buildings had been turned to dust. Witnesses pointed officers to the ravine to look for the attacker and they found Julilynn as shown in these pictures."

As he spoke, Surratt clicked through the various photos, ending on a map of the time-line for Julilynn's last day. Aisling was grateful he didn't leave the image of her mutilated body up.

"Her family doesn't live in California, so we're trying to track them down. She and her boyfriend were part of one of the artist flocks that roam the country but had been in LA for six months and seemed to be settling. Her boyfriend has gone into a state of shock and can't tell us anyone who would want to do this to her—and no, we're not taking him off the possible suspect list."

He stood there staring at the timeline for a few moments. "That list is damn short, people. We've got a killer who managed to use the feys' greatest enemy against one in a way unimaginable. The medical examiner still doesn't know how it was done."

The entire room was silent as the words sank in. This case shouldn't be a shock to most of them, Surratt had damn near called out the entire precinct when the body had been found.

Aisling knew she'd been called because of the whole finding her name next to the body issue. But why did he call everyone out? Yesterday he'd mentioned he thought that someone in the precinct wasn't what they seemed—was it connected to this case? How could he know that if the timeline he gave was right? He was deliberately implying this was the first case of its kind whereas both Reece and he had directly stated that wasn't true yesterday. They simply hadn't found any bodies before.

"Could this be a new weapon? The gangs have been amping up their designs," Claughten said. He was originally from narcotics and pretty much directed everything back to drug smuggling or the drug-based gang warfare.

"It could be, we've no idea, and we won't until we catch the bastards behind this. That's why I'm pulling in all the departments on this. We don't know if it's an isolated incident or the start of a larger attack."

Aisling waited a few minutes as the usual series of random and useless questions bounced around the room. This always happened, as if the stupid comments and ideas needed to be eliminated before the real brainstorming could begin. Not to mention half of the precinct was probably dealing with their own iron terrors. Most fey were extremely long-lived, yet not immortal like the early humans had believed; but they were hard to kill and slow to reproduce. But some things could still kill them, and nothing was more painful than death by iron poisoning. It was as if every single atom and molecule in the body burst into its own tiny ball of flame, ripping its way out of this world and into the next one.

Or so she'd read. No fey who had gone through it survived.

Surratt brushed off the worst of the questions and shrugged for the better ones, his assistant taking notes of them all. Including the dumb ones. But Aisling waited for him to bring up the fed involvement. Then was surprised a few moments later when he called out assignments to track the case and still hadn't mentioned the other potential cases.

Interesting. He'd had Reece get her away from the others at the scene, so they had to have known a fed was involved. He'd made a point of mentioning that Reece was questioning her loud enough for most everyone to hear. And the ones who didn't hear about it earlier would do so when this meeting broke up and the gossip began.

What game was Surratt playing? For that matter, what game was Reece playing and why was she being pulled into it?

Her thoughts had drifted so far away from the room that she almost didn't hear her assignment. Or rather she didn't hear it correctly.

"Excuse me?"

Surratt had already gone to the next name, but he paused. "Did we wake you up, Danaan? Very well, as I said, Danaan working with narcotics on the new smuggling case."

The shock on her face was echoed by the faces closest to her. She was a homicide detective, and one of the best. But here in the time of a nasty and interesting case she was being moved to narcotics? What the hell? If he wanted to keep her benched, then why bring her in at all today?

She opened her mouth to argue but Surratt shot her a look that said it wouldn't be a good idea. While she usually didn't take his opinions into consideration, this seemed like one she should.

He faced her glare for a few moments as if to make sure she was letting it drop. Then she realized that he was waiting for something else. "Aye, sir." Calling Surratt sir was also something she didn't do often, but again, it seemed like she needed to this time.

Surratt nodded and then finished his list. The group left without their usual level of talking, only a few mutters were heard over the shuffling of feet and scraping of chairs. And most of them seemed to be directed at her. Great, now the entire precinct would be sure she was on Surratt's shit list. Since he was working so hard to convince them of that, she hoped he had a damn good reason.

Aisling waited for some cue that he wanted her to stand by, but when he seemed to be intent on a discussion with his assistant she left.

"Wow—who did you piss off?" Goldkowsky shook his blond head at her as he leaned against her desk. His desk was a good ten feet away in the opposite direction. He'd detoured.

"What do you want, Goldie?" Normally she and he had a nice bantering relationship; they were friends of a sort, the type that were found on the force between non-partners. But she wasn't up to battling wits right now.

"Easy there." He held up his left hand as a warding gesture then opened the right one to hold out a huge chunk of imported dark chocolate wrapped in fancy foil. "My wife got this as a gift, but she's decided she's unhealthy again, so she suggested I bring it to work. I thought you could use it."

Aisling refrained from ripping the chocolate out of his hands. That she could use it was the understatement of the eon. Goldkowsky was a solid man and a good cop. His people came from human farmers in the Midwest somewhere but were originally from Norway. That solid and slightly bland persona was a nice change to some of the drama queens in Aisling's life. His wife was a regular character on one of the soaps and often had her husband bring in the offers of tribute from her fans that she refused.

"Thanks," She muttered as she shoved a piece into her mouth. Damn, that was good. She'd never gotten to know his wife but that might have to change if she could get this directly. A second piece quickly followed the first and she felt the tension flee her shoulders.

"Seriously, are you okay?" His light blue eyes went from joking to concerned. Something she rarely saw. "I'm not sure why Surratt's out for you—"

"It's nothing. I pissed him off again. I knew eventually he'd retaliate. Besides, it's the whole 'my name was with the victim' issue. He wants to keep me clear of it as much as he can so he doesn't look bad." She cut him off. She wasn't sure what Surratt was doing but she had a gut feeling she needed to go along with it. If Maeve were here, she would have told her the truth—that she had no idea what in the hell was going on—but everyone else was going to be under watch until she got a handle on this situation. Or at least a glimpse of an idea of a handle on it.

Even though she came from a family of professional liars, she wasn't as good as she should be. Goldkowsky's face showed he wanted to ask more questions but wasn't going to.

"If you need to talk…" He nodded his head toward his desk.

Aisling smiled. "Thanks." One advantage of working around cops, they were naturally curious, but they also knew when to back off. She was sure he was asking what the rest of the department was thinking, and while they were all holding back now, they wouldn't stay that way for long.

She needed to talk to Surratt.

With a longing look at the chocolate—there was too much for her to eat all of it at once, even in her current stressed condition—she shoved the remainder into her secret stash in her desk. The lack of real food could mess her up if all she ate was a pound of chocolate. A sugar crash wouldn't be the best way to start her time with the narco squad. They might haul her in for being drugged.

But Surratt hadn't come by her desk, which considering that his office was directly behind her desk should have been impossible.

Not trying to appear like she was looking, Aisling wandered by his office. Nope, lights off, and door shut. With a sigh she walked over to the war room. He shouldn't still be there, but who knew.

Nope.

Damn it, he was trying to make folks think there was a wedge between them, and she was willing to play along, but she still wanted to know why. She needed to figure out what he was actually doing. And after his moving her to narco for the meantime, folks would figure she'd be pissed and avoiding him. It wouldn't look right to have her hunting him all over the place.

Besides, she needed to go check in with the narco squad and find out about this new case.

Narcotics had the entire third floor to themselves and she was going up the first flight of stairs when her phone rang. Blocked number. Great. It could be any number of people, some of whom she avoided like the plague, others she couldn't afford to not answer.

At the landing she gave in and answered. "Danaan."

"Oh lovely, you answered," The voice on the other end was cultured and dry. A perfect example of elven breeding at its best. "I did try to leave a message for you at your home, but I believe I missed you. I wanted to make sure you were all right with the arrangements the family mentioned." Crap on a cracker. Her mother topped the plague carriers' list. This number didn't come up on caller ID, so it must be a new one for her. With all that had happened since she'd left the impromptu—

or so they claimed—meeting she had managed to shove their plans and manipulations to the side.

"I'm at work, Mother. What do you want? I told you I needed time." She thought about hanging up, but she knew her mother would call back. Or worse, send someone here to fetch her.

Lady Tirtha Lasheda Otheralia did not come off the hill for anyone, including her own daughter.

"Testy, darling, one should never be testy. It shows bad breeding." The last four words were automatic and Aisling doubted if her mother heard them anymore. They came out of her mouth in almost every conversation they had. Must be a result of Aisling's ongoing testy nature.

"What. Do. You. Need. I'm at work, Mother." She spoke slowly and kept her voice low in hopes that she could manage to keep from yelling.

"Have you had a chance to think about our idea, dear?"

Aisling was grateful she was the only one in the stairway as had anyone seen her glaring and scowling at her phone as she held it at arm's length they probably would have reported her to someone.

"As I'm sure you noticed on the news feed, things have been a bit hectic around here." She hadn't seen anything on the news but she'd only half listened to it as she'd showered this morning. But there was no way they would try to sweep what happened under the carpet.

"You're dealing with a building collapse? Isn't that beneath you? Really, none of us understand your fascination with that…*job*." That was her mother, always able to make job sound the vilest of four-letter words even though it was only three. And in her mind, it probably was. Her mother wouldn't admit to her full age, but historians had estimated her to have been around since before the Black Death. Aisling secretly believed her mother had probably been the carrier.

She swore to herself. Damn it. If Surratt and the brass were keeping Julilynn's death out of headlines, he should have said something at the briefing. Then she thought of the chunk of time that she'd been lost in thought during his brief. Shit, she had to pay better attention.

"The building was a major collapse, a deliberate one; they are pulling some of us in on it." She sounded like she was lying, and worst of all she knew her mother knew it.

"Right. So glad you're a *detective*." She heard her mother speaking to someone else, someone she mostly covered up the phone for. "I'm sorry, dear, we'll have to continue this later. Something has come up. Do think about what we talked about."

With that dismissal, she clicked off on the call.

Aisling stared at the dead phone and shook her head. She wasn't sure how much of a reprieve she'd gained, but she'd take whatever she could get. She quickly tagged that new phone number to at least pop up with a warning; later she'd see if she could block it. Their plan was to have her leave the force and become more involved in the family business. Nothing new there. What was new, was the more aggressive campaigning her mother was doing to get her to agree. In short, join a stodgy company worth billions that Aisling couldn't say for certain what the hell they did. Besides make money. She'd take dealing with criminals over her family any time.

CHAPTER SIX

WITH A SIGH, SHE FINISHED the climb to the narcotics floor. She had nothing against the men and women working here, but it wasn't homicide. Even if she went along with the vague premise that Surratt knew what he was doing, she didn't like being taken off her squad. Especially with a case like this one hanging in the works.

"Danaan, they're in the briefing room." One of the women nodded at her and pointed down the corridor. Aisling couldn't think of her name; she'd probably only talked to her once, but she'd have to work on finding out all their names.

She went into the smaller version of the main war room downstairs. Although with all the maps and photos this one looked far more like its namesake than Surratt's usually barren version.

"Hello, Detective Danaan, don't think we've been formally introduced before. I'm Dixon, I'm a special consultant for the narcotics department." The tall human male held out his hand. His coloring was darker, like someone with a West Indies heritage. And his eyes were so dark as to be almost black. But those differences and the facial hair didn't change the fact that it was Reece in disguise before her. Maybe others couldn't tell, but she knew. Probably from spending too much quality time with him yesterday.

By all of the gods—what the hell was going on? Surratt keeping her off the case, but then assigning her to a department where Reece was doing something undercover? At no time during their chats yesterday did he mention being up here. Obviously, he thought some of the answers concerning Mott Flowers and Julilynn Marcos were to be found in the narcotics department.

"I've been helping out the department for about a year now, but never had a chance to meet you." He shook her hand and flashed her a completely non-Reece smile. Damn it, he wanted her to play along too. But a year? The sneaky bastard had been in her place of work for a year and she didn't know? There were going to be so many people that needed to explain things to her they were going to wait in line to have their asses kicked.

"I'm so glad to meet you. I'd heard there was a former druggie come back to the straight and narrow helping out the folks here." Aisling gave a harder shake than Reece expected and pulled him forward and dropped her voice to a hiss. "I swear to god, I'm going to hurt both you and Surratt. Badly."

Reece said nothing but his forced smile became a bit more grimace-like.

"Now that you two have met, we can get on with our brief." The supervisor for narcotics was standing at the front of the room. Captain Losien was a tall mixed fey breed, a mix of human and elf. She was smart, sharp, and her dark skin hid almost a century of age. Aisling didn't know much about her personally, but she was well respected in the station. "I think everyone else knows Detective Danaan, she's on loan from homicide for a while."

The looks sent her way weren't mean—they were all on the same side after all—but oftentimes departments had to compete for resources and since each department felt they were the most important, animosities could occur.

"And yes, I think she'll come in helpful. The current case is why I pulled in Dixon too." She tapped a clear screen in the front of the room and a map of the city opened. A few more taps and a corner of Poor Town came into focus. An area known to detectives of each division far too well.

"There is something coming in, something coming from Alaska via Seattle. We can't get ears or eyes on it, but a rumor showed up two days ago. The source that got the information to us was found murdered in a ravine yesterday."

Aisling held back her gasp of surprise. The victim from yesterday had been an informant? If so, wouldn't Surratt have known? She shot a sideways glare to Reece—he sure as hell would have known. But he kept looking forward.

"He was found miles from the ocean with fifteen more holes than he started life with." *He* not she. Aisling wasn't sure if that bit of information was better. Two victims that close in location and timing could be connected.

She felt eyes on her and turned. Reece, or Dixon as he was calling himself, was now watching her closely. She spared him another scowl, and then went back to listening to the captain.

"We need to get information. Right now, we don't know what the shipment is, but we know the Cymru and Scottish clans have unified on this. I don't need to tell any of you what could happen if the three biggest drug gangs in Los Angeles start working together."

Aisling rubbed the side of her face. There was no way this was good. And a cold feeling in her gut told her it was connected to Julilynn Marcos. And possibly Mott Flowers. Somehow. Even though Surratt hadn't mentioned any known drug or gang connections for the poor girl. Drug runners kept their affiliations hidden if they wanted to stay alive.

"Sorry to interrupt, but Special Agent Larkin is on the phone for Detective Danaan and he says it's important." The kid who stuck his head in turned bright red before he finished his words. A newbie in the department, he was afraid the interruption would be blamed on him.

She would tell him that it was Reece's fault, that it was always Reece's fault, if the jackass hadn't been sitting right next to her. Which begged the question of who exactly was on the phone?

"I am sorry, Captain, but I'd better take it. Agent Larkin is impatient and not too bright. He might be trying to figure out how to open his garage." Ignoring the glare Reece gave her, she left the room and picked up the department line. Never mind that had he actually been calling her he would have used her cell.

"Hello?"

"Hello, Aisling, yes, it's me. I preset this recording and triggered it. It's scrambled so the station can't record it. I know you want to find out what's going on, but we can't tell you. Not now anyway. We need you to stay as out of the loop as possible on this. Smile and nod to me in the room if you understand and agree."

This was the most asinine thing he'd done yet. Pre-programmed a call to her while he was right next to her to tell her to stay quiet. But she nodded and flashed a grimace. That was as close to a smile as that bastard was getting for a while.

"Great."

Aisling glared at the phone. How cocky was he that he knew she'd agree?

"Now listen to me, not only is there something going on, like I'm sure the captain has told us, but there is a connection higher up as well. Maybe in your department, and for sure in narcotics. That's all for now." The call cut off.

Aisling handed the phone back to the newbie and stalked back into the war room. "Sorry for that. I was right, Agent Larkin couldn't find his ass and his head was stuck."

The resulting laughter made her feel a bit better. Evidently, she wasn't the only one annoyed by the fed's antics.

Wait until they found out he'd been spying on them for a year. Never trust a fed, but don't piss off a narcotics detective—they had nasty ways of payback.

"That was charming," he whispered as he leaned close as she sat.

Aisling continued smiling at her newfound best buddies. The narcos really didn't like him judging by the nods of approval she was getting. "As charming as what you've been doing for the last year." She kept her voice to a whisper.

"Okay, if you kids have finished your fun, I have the assignments. Dixon, I want you to take Danaan around to some of your haunts. Danaan, leave your badge and gun here. Where you're going it's your life if they know you're a cop."

"Aye, sir." She didn't bother to mention the whole badge on the wrist bit. She'd only done two undercover ops before, but each time the wrist tat had been magically glamoured. Regular undercover agents never got them in the first place.

"Aisling? If you come with me, we'll take care of making you a bit less presentable." The tall red-haired human woman came into the room from the hall, winked at Reece then smiled at her. Thank the stars; Aisling had totally forgotten that Heike was back in LA. She and Heike had been fast friends for Heike's first few years in LA. Heike had started in homicide, then transferred to narcotics. They lost touch after that even though they were in the same building. About ten years ago she'd left the country, moved to Sweden or Norway—one of the northern countries, Aisling couldn't remember which.

They'd completely lost contact then.

"Heike, I'm so glad you're here." She hugged her tall friend and followed her out in the hall. "I didn't see you in the briefing."

Heike tossed a wince over her shoulder, then led them down a short hall. "I'm not on this case. Captain has me cleaning up some old cases first. But it's great to see you." She held open the door for her. "Did you ever marry that guy? Ric, I think his name was?"

The name caught Aisling by surprise. Ric had been over way before Heike had left. They weren't close friends by then anymore, but Aisling figured that everyone in the precinct at the time knew about her doomed love affair.

Heike caught the look on Aisling's face as she stepped around her and sat behind a small table filled with an odd selection of paint, makeup, tiny lasers, and needles. "Damn, I stepped in it, didn't I? Should have noticed the lack of ring."

Aisling slid into the chair across from the various implements of torture and shook her head. The glamour was a spell, but it was always administered via machine. Supposedly made it much harder to detect. "It's okay, took me by surprise, that's all. Ric took off two days before the wedding. No note, no nothing. Cleared out his condo and vanished." Aisling thought about the terror she'd felt when he first disappeared. Until one of his brothers told her he was fine. He'd left the country and was in love with someone else.

Heike stopped looking through the labeled containers and met her eye. "Oh, sweetie, I am so sorry! It doesn't matter how long ago it was, that must have been awful. But look on the bright side, maybe he's dead now."

From anyone else that comment would come across as callus, but Aisling knew what she meant.

She flashed her a grin. "Thanks. To be honest, I haven't cared in years." She leaned forward. "Doesn't mean I wouldn't accidentally run him over if he wandered in front of my car though."

Truth was, when he left her, she was devastated. It

had been a whirlwind romance, from first blind date to engaged in record time—for her family anyway—of less than six months. Her second cousin had set them up, and the entire family approved of Ric. Even her mother. Aisling had never been able to prove it, but there were times when she thought her mother had somehow been involved with setting them up. She seemed to know way too much about Ric and his heritage than she would have been able to casually find out.

He had totally not been the kind of guy she normally went for; he was nice, charming, and funny. Her trend was more toward the bad boys. But Ric won her over almost immediately on their first date. His leaving like he did left her a walking zombie for a few months.

She shook off the old feelings and smiled. "Now, what about you? How have you been?" She wasn't going to ask about her husband specifically, nor if there were any kids. Heike was pure human, getting a permit to have a child would have been extremely difficult, if not impossible.

Heike kept the laser she held in her right hand and fished about in the bag behind her with her left. "Oh, you really are out of the loop! Mark and I have three children. Must be the cold air, but the doctors finally approved us for one, and three eggs became active. They let us keep all of them and we had them each two years apart." She finally finished fishing through her purse and flipped out a vid picture holder.

Ten minutes later, Aisling was wondering if her friend had been taken over by aliens. Heike had been a fun-loving girl, always wanted to have kids though. Now having them had turned her into uber mom. Aisling wanted to ask how in the heck two low-ranking humans got permission to have three kids, but there would be no tactful way to do it.

"Okay, enough about family life. If I could, I'd go on all

day. Anyway, hold out your left wrist." Heike had put the pictures down, but Aisling noticed she kept glancing to them. No doubt they hadn't gone through all of them.

Aisling quickly shoved her wrist in Heike's hand before more precious family shots could be shown. Heike gave a smile and went to work with her laser.

After another five minutes, during which Aisling couldn't see her arm, Heike released it.

"There you go, no one would know it was there."

Aisling tilted her arm back and forth and had to admit, she couldn't see anything. That was some excellent spell work; although Heike didn't create the magic, she wielded it well. There was some slight redness from the laser, but it was a tiny handheld unit. Wouldn't go deep enough to remove her badge tattoo; just enough to let the makeup change the coloring.

Reece stuck his head in, still disguised as Dixon. "You ladies done? We need to get on the road, I have a lot of turf to show our guest."

Heike shrugged. "I'm done, it's hidden."

As soon as Aisling joined him, Reece turned down a smaller hallway which led to a side entrance for the stairwell. "I have certain areas I hit at regular times. Sometimes folks reach out to me with info, but only if I'm there when they expect it."

That was hopeful. Aisling detected a slight emphasis on the word 'info'.

"There's a chance some high-ranking Scotties are coming into town, a few of the higher lieutenants. Most likely connected to whatever Losien mentioned." Reece's eyes lit up and anyone who knew Reece would have easily seen through the dark coloring and disguise right then.

Not the Mott Flowers case after all. "Reece—Dixon," Aisling shook her head at her probie level mistake of saying the wrong name. She'd caught it, but still, anyone could have been in this stairwell. "How do we know this? Shouldn't Interpol or something like that be involved?"

Reece leaned into her far too close to be respecting any personal space. "They are." He all but whispered and the look in his contact-disguised eyes was serious.

The damn bastard was Interpol, too? It was bad enough that he flashed badges—legit ones—from a dozen US agencies. But he was international as well? Her headache went up a notch.

"Hey, don't forget to log your miles this time, Dixon. Maggie's not going to help you out if you come back with a blank sheet again." The unidentified narcotics officer was a stair grating above them, but he'd just stepped out so she knew he couldn't have heard them.

"No worries, Smith. I'll have my ride-along do it. Homicide is good at note taking, right?"

Aisling heard a laugh, then it was cut off as the narco officer went back into the office.

"Funny, *Dixon*. I think as the only actual cop between the two of us, I should drive."

Reece had started down the stairs again and his laugh echoed all the way up. "Right. Not going to let you drive my car, and there are rumors all over that they won't let you get another car out of the motor pool."

Reece ignored her grumbling behind him as he smiled and nodded at some beat cops who called out to him as Dixon. Of course he knew their names as well. People Aisling had seen for years, but couldn't seem to keep their names straight, and he not only knew them all, he seemed to know their families.

"How was Johnny's game last week, Macks?" He shouted out to a tall, stern, elven beat cop.

The man flashed a smile that Aisling knew she had never seen and gave thumbs up. "He won. Thanks for asking, Dixon."

Aisling smiled and nodded to folks who watched her, but half the time the smiles weren't returned, and a cautious look graced the ones who did. Surratt's list of crap he had to answer for was getting longer by the moment. He'd made them question her status by his exclusion of her.

She let out a sigh of relief as they finally pushed through the double glass doors and into the perpetual LA sunshine.

"Now about the car?"

Reece led her down the street to a beat-up green/gray/rust colored Arctic Cruiser. Aisling hadn't seen one of those in years and thought they were all extinct. A far cry from the state-of-the-art showroom model Reece normally drove. Dixon was a man of little means.

Reece smiled as if he was a ten-year-old showing off his elven warriors' action figure collection. "Isn't it a beaut?"

With a sigh, Aisling touched the side of the vehicle and grimaced as a layer of rust practically came off in her hand. "How does it still run?"

He reached forward and held open the door. Okay, so Reece didn't hold doors for her, but this Dixon character did? A little odd considering they were the same person and he knew she knew that. She'd never heard of a method actor in a federal, or international, bureau. Aisling peered inside the car first, judging from the exterior who knew what had crawled in there to die.

The inside was actually in decent shape, simple dark leather, new from the feel and shine, new dashboard, all the dials looked authentically old in style but bright and clean. Most likely taken off other cars of a similar make but in better shape.

Oh, gods. Aisling knew what this meant; she'd made the mistake of dating one of this type of men in college. "You're *rebuilding* it."

"Yep, isn't it grand?" Reece all but petted the dash as he slid in behind the wheel. "I've been working on it since

Dixon started helping out the force. Now *these* were classic cars."

Aisling used the old-fashioned lap belt as Reece gunned the engine to life. "Between you and Surratt, my life has become far too annoying as of late. I can't take any more annoyances." He hadn't pulled out into traffic yet, so she grabbed his face and turned it toward her so he couldn't miss her expression. "You telling me about repairing, fixing, or finding cars, this one, others, future ones, *any cars,* will be considered annoying."

Reece scowled a bit, then pulled free of her hand. "I hadn't said anything."

"No, but you were going to." Aisling folded her arms and slouched in her seat. Gods, the three weeks with that guy in college had been hell. He'd been hot, and she was sure if she tried she might remember his name. But all he talked about was rebuilding old cars. It was like a religious cult.

"No…okay, yeah I was. You would have loved it, but it's your call. No car talk." Reece shrugged and let himself get cut off by another car as he entered the roadway. Unlike his driving of the night before, Dixon drove like an old lady.

"Do you need me to get out and push? I thought you had a timeline?"

Reece adjusted his extra-long rearview mirror and slowly picked up speed. A few more hours and he might be within spitting distance of the lower end of the speed limit. "Now, just because some of us don't drive like bats out of hell and wreck everything they drive is no reason to mock." Which would have carried more weight if she hadn't been riding with him last night.

Aisling leaned forward and tapped on the sad bouncing speedometer. A car whizzed by and managed to flip them off out of all four windows. Tricky, since she only saw two people in it.

"You're not sure how fast you're going are you? And those cars weren't all my fault. Mostly. But that's not the issue. You're now going to be the cause of accidents because everyone is having to zoom around you."

When he didn't respond but continued to slowly move his way into the freeway lane, she added. "You didn't drive like this last night."

He turned and flashed the type of smile you'd give to a slightly idiotic child who made a silly mistake. "Reece drives like that, Dixon doesn't. Dixon knows that his car is still working some bugs out and if he goes too fast it could cause a break down. Or an explosion. Not sure which."

"You are both men, you moron! Who is going to notice if Dixon drives the same way as a screwed-up federal agent that no one likes?" Aisling braced herself as a car trying to pass them before they got on the freeway nearly slammed into her side of the car. "You're going to get us killed, whoever you are. And cars don't explode unless they crash into something."

Reece gave the car a bit more gas and cleared the freeway entrance. Thank god he stayed in the slow lane.

"Rule one of undercover work, always act as if you are being watched every second of every day. Bathrooms, restaurants, in bed. In cars. Everything. It's for your own safely more so than the fact anyone is watching. Because the moment you drop your guard, you'll be dead." He didn't turn to her, but smiled. "Be grateful you're with Dixon today, because Reece wouldn't have told you that."

Aisling pounded her head back against the soft seat. She had to admit, grudgingly, that the interior of this car was nice. And not so grudgingly admit that she may have seriously underestimated Reece's eccentric behavioral tendencies.

"Fine. Does Dixon intend to talk about himself in the third person a lot? Because that could be a dead giveaway."

"Hey, I know who I am, I've been using third person since you seem to have issues with it. And for the record, people do too like Reece. And cars can explode if someone has been messing around with their fuel intake valve with some slightly illegal upgrades that haven't completely worked yet, but are still attached to the car."

Aisling shuddered, but continued to tell herself he was speaking hypothetically.

It was an odd time of day to be on the road, not rush hour, too late in the morning, but that weird time when the freeways were full of the odd mix of dawdlers and speeders. Luckily, they seemed to be able to sense their own kind and the speeders gave Reece a wide birth. Or Dixon. No, damn it, she wasn't going to play along with his fantasy world.

"Right, the narcotics department loves you."

Reece shrugged and stuck close behind another dawdler. "Yeah, well, Reece had some problems with them a few years ago. He had to expose a well-loved team member as a smuggler. Even though they knew the person was bad, they still blamed Reece."

"Homicide isn't fond of you either. Surratt pretty much wishes you were dead. I've heard him say your name as he runs his coffee beans through the grinder. Kinda grisly." She held up her hand. "And before you answer, remember, I have been a cop there longer than Reece has been an annoyance. I know you didn't expose anyone in our squad."

Reece slowed—how that was possible Aisling wasn't sure, there were bicycles that could move faster than this—as he approached the off-ramp.

"I don't know, why do you guys hate me?"

Aisling grabbed the dash as a bit of Reece poked through the Dixon façade and he gunned the car to clear an orange light at the base of the off-ramp. Whether it was because he wanted to make the light, or she had annoyed him, Aisling wasn't sure.

"You're a fed, or at least sometimes you say you're a fed. Now you're implying you're Interpol," she paused but he gave her an innocent smile and shrugged, "anyway, feds and local LEOs usually don't get along. You guys have a tendency to stick your noses into all of our cases."

"Only the good ones."

"Only the ones you shouldn't be poking around in. We have one of the best police forces in the world. We don't need you tossing around your assorted badges and tromping over everything."

Aisling was going to add to the list of why he annoyed her, working from the assumption the rest of the squad felt the same, when she noticed Dixon started to slide lower in his seat. He also dropped his right hand from the wheel, and leaned more into her side of the car than was needed.

"What are you doing, *Dixon*?" Aisling hadn't intended to whisper, but his actions seemed so questionable it came out that way.

The neighborhood had gone from freeway to the middle of the ghetto in minutes. Unlike most blighted areas, this one had never been a nice place to live. The houses were tiny and poorly built, with minuscule yards that never would have had much in the way of plants. Clearly no elves had ever lived here. Even those who had forsworn their family ways, such as herself, were automatically drawn to nature. Areas like this hurt her soul.

Although she'd be damned if she'd ever admit that to Reece, or Dixon for that matter. Great, now she was thinking of him as two people as well.

"Name isn't Dixon, its Leifen. Lose the jacket and drop the ponytail." His voice was now a full tone lower and the words were clipped. His faint accent sounded like an odd combination of a human from Sweden combined with one from one of the Middle Eastern deserts. He reached over and grabbed a small box next to him. He held it up to his face, clicked, and his coloring changed to almost paler than hers. She'd thought his eye change had been contacts, but his eyes were now a swampy green color.

"You have a glam box? How? Never mind, I don't want to know. Just tell me how many people you think you are?" The box he was now sliding away was a seriously high-end product. It would be coded only to him, and it could change his appearance to one of a few preset disguises with a touch.

"Yes, it's a glam box, and I have as many disguises as I need in it." He watched the streets carefully.

"You need to warn me about these changes, unless you want me to give you away." But as she grumbled at him she started changing what she could. She pulled the jeweled hair band free of her hair, sliding it around her wrist as an obnoxious bracelet. Then she tossed her jacket in the back—luckily it wasn't one of her favorites, who knew what had gone on in that back seat—and un-did the top two buttons of her shirt.

"Missed my original exit, so plan changed. I need Leifen right now, not Dixon." He looked her over with a lecherous, and very non-Reece or Dixon, smile. "Good, now you'll work better as Leifen's woman."

Aisling shook her head but managed to keep from hitting him. Wait, she as Aisling might not hit another law enforcement officer, but whoever was riding along with a thug like Leifen would probably hit. A lot.

"Bastard, I told you not to come this way." She smacked his right arm with a sharp blow.

The wince he gave wasn't acting and made her feel a bit better. She didn't like being caught off guard. She doubted he missed his exit; he'd been driving slow enough to catch every single one. He had planned on changing into this next character and not warning her.

She struck him again, in the shoulder this time. "I told you, you're lost." She roughed her voice a bit and gave it a shrill edge. He wasn't the only one who could role-play.

Reece/Dixon/Leifen glared at her but stayed silent. Well, that was an improvement over the other two. She could hit Leifen and he was quieter. She might like this one the best.

"I need…" His voice drifted off as he started looking down alleys as they cruised by. That was another thing; there were ugly, junk filled alleys every five houses or so, too close together and made the area feel more squished than it already was.

"Perfect." He finally spotted whatever he was searching for, but to Aisling's eyes, the alley they drove in was exactly like the other six they'd passed. He turned into it and she knew why he'd chosen this one. The end narrowed through illegal room additions and became impassable within one hundred yards. No one would be coming from that direction, and the locals would have long ago learned they couldn't use it as a thoroughfare.

"Now come here." He grabbed Aisling's right arm and pulled her toward him. He un-did her seat belt so fast she hadn't seen him move. He didn't kiss her but started nuzzling her neck. "We're being watched, and there's no one in this neighborhood that I want doing that." His voice was soft and sounded far more like Reece than Leifen or Dixon.

Aisling played along, cooing at him, and moving around to make it appear that far more was going on than actually was. With an artful flip, she straddled him. It allowed her a view back out of the alleyway.

Their tail was good; she had to give him that. It took a few moments of far closer contact with Reece than she'd ever thought she'd be exposed to before she noticed who was following them. A thin shape, all in black, with solid black glasses on. A top hat and gloves completed the ensemble. He was all in black, but Aisling had a feeling that wasn't what made his skin so glaringly white.

Someone who looked like that would stand out anywhere, especially a run-down neighborhood like this one. And he would have, had he not been sliding between worlds, as it was called.

A tricky move, one that could only be done by highly trained and insanely powerful full fey, and a move as dangerous and illegal as hell. Her heart stilled as her mind caught up with the terror of what she knew was behind them.

The majority of the fey races had come from a different plane a millennium ago. They'd lived on earth as little more than myths and rumors to the humans for almost as long before they had to come out from the shadows to save humanity from the Black Death. But the veil between worlds prevented some of the nastier underworld things from coming to Earth. Crossing it was not to be taken lightly, and sliding between the worlds was dangerous for many reasons. There was only one category of being that Aisling knew who could pull it off, even though there had been no sightings in a few hundred years.

They were being spied on by one of the Old Ones.

CHAPTER SEVEN

"REECE, WHO ARE YOU REALLY, and more importantly, who have you pissed off? Big names only." Aisling forced herself to stay calm as she nuzzled his ear, but having an Old One take an interest in you was akin to having someone slide a nuclear bomb under your seat. There was no doubt what would happen when it went off. And no survivors.

"I told you, hot cheeks, it's Leifen." He kept his voice low. He knew someone was following them. But there was no way a human, even a half breed, should be able to sense an Old One.

She glanced behind them again and a chill clenched her gut. She'd never seen any of the Old Ones, but there were a variety of them. Creatures who couldn't cross to this side of the veil—or supposedly couldn't. Some were far more dangerous than others. At her second glance, she knew what was back there. Taking a deep breath and forcing herself to look away from the Old One, Aisling rocked back a bit to see Reece's face. His eyes weren't as distracting with the different eye color, which was good because staying alive for the next few minutes depended on being able to stare him in the eye. Vallenians were nothing more than myths told to scare young fey. Deadly monsters reaching out from the other side of the veil to suck away souls.

And one was right at the end of the alley.

"Listen to me carefully. There's something following us. Watching us right now. It is not a man. Unless you want to be so far removed from existence that your grandparents will never have been born, you need to do exactly as I say. *Reece*, you need to blank out your thoughts about anything beyond this car and right now." She hoped that the importance of him focusing on her right now came through.

A small bead of sweat appeared on his upper lip. "You're terrified."

Aisling nodded slowly. A damper grew around his mind. Not that she would have been able to read his thoughts before, but there was definitely a psychic interference going on that wasn't there before. "Can you see the one following us?"

Reece answered by turning them both and pushing her into the seat. "No, I can tell we're being followed, and it's not good. I can't see anyone though."

Aisling let out a short sigh of relief. Bad enough that a vallenian was somehow involved; it would have been ten times worse if Reece had the ability to see beyond the veil. His ability to *sense* the watcher, something she'd have to deal with later, was disturbing enough.

"He is still there. We're being watched by an Old One." The vallenian were more of a fey secret. Humans never went through the veil, and fey hadn't for centuries. The cold-blooded killers of the other realm needed to stay hidden. Old One was a vague term used for any of the Underhill creatures who never crossed over to this side. Until now. It was far safer for Reece if he had no idea what was actually following them.

Aisling rolled Reece back over, leaving her on top this time and bruising them both in the process. It wasn't easy for two tall people to deal with the front seat of a car, but she was actually glad now that he had this old beater, at least it had the old style bench seats. Reece winced as she hit a tender spot but kept quiet. The concern in his eyes said he was still picking up on her terror.

Which was another issue she was going to have to deal with—maybe he was that good at reading people. But the other option was that he'd inherited some active fey genes. Something unheard of, that while wouldn't be an immediate death sentence, would definitely be grounds for him spending a few years under study. Then probably followed by a quick, silent death.

Fey/human breeds never carried forward the fey talents. The High King and Queen were obsessed with making sure that never happened. Supposedly, there was a fear such a thing would trigger another Black Death.

Once she was sure he was going to be able to keep his reaction to being inadvertently kneed to a wince, she raised herself up as if in the throes of passion and looked to the street behind them.

The tall, black-garbed being was still there, his focus caught by something down the street, and then he faded away.

"It's gone now, isn't it?" Reece tried pushing her aside so he could sit up but there wasn't enough room with the way they were sprawled on the seat. She got the gearshift in her tailbone and pushed back.

"Stop it. Let me move, then you can get up." She folded herself to the side, extremely grateful for those damn yoga classes Maeve kept making her take. Once they were both seated normally, Reece turned and squinted into the empty street behind them for a few moments. She poked him.

"How did you know it was gone? For that matter, how in the hell did you know it was there?"

Reece kept squinting toward the street, then finally turned back to her and shook his head.

"I'm not sure. Coldness in the back of my head. Coldness and pressure. I knew they were gone when the feeling left."

Crap. Aisling tried to remind herself that she didn't care

about Reece. That even if the High King's people found him, it was probably nothing. Reece had been around fey his entire adult life and no one had noticed anything.

And a tiny little voice, which sounded suspiciously like the British accent of her vacationing partner, kept reminding her she couldn't live with herself if she didn't try and warn him. Humans had lived beside the fey for so long, many forgot they weren't equals. If the High King and Queen felt he was a threat, having developed fey powers as a half breed, they would lock him up without question.

"Reece, Leifen, whatever you want to call yourself, you need to pay attention to me. Right now." She grabbed his chin and forced his eyes to meet hers. "Nothing happened." She felt resistance but he didn't say anything. There was no way she could count on his ability to keep *this* secret. Vallenians hunted people through their thoughts—they could find him from his memory of sensing them. "Nothing happened. You saw a gangbanger who you thought recognized you, so we hid. But he left and *nothing else happened.*" She weighted the words with as much magic as she could afford without giving something away. Spelling someone against his or her will or knowledge was a High Council crime. But so was hiding a potential breed with powers. Damn it, she couldn't let Reece be taken or killed on her watch.

Reece took a deep breath, finally letting it out with a shuddering sigh.

His eyes stayed on hers and for a few tense moments she was afraid the spell wouldn't hold. This situation was going from bad to hellish. If this didn't work, and he recalled everything, including her attempt to spell him…

But then his eyes slid closed and his head dropped to his chest.

Aisling pulled him forward a bit so he was draped over his steering wheel, then scooted back to her end of the seat.

A second later he came to with a snort and a shake of his head.

"What happened?" He blinked his eyes and twisted his neck to get out the kinks.

Aisling leaned forward, not having to fake her concern. "Are you okay? We tore into this alley for no good reason, then you smacked your head on the steering wheel."

He blinked a bit more, this was a mixed blessing, spelling someone often left them confused of the immediate situation, which was good and helped the spell take hold. However, she needed him functioning in order to get out of here. The ability to cross the veil between planes was limited, but she didn't want to take a chance the vallenian would come back. And getting Reece away from here would help solidify the spell she'd placed.

"Do you remember anything? Like why you tore down a dumpy alley like a possessed man?" She chased the concern out with a healthy dose of her usual snark. Then she rolled down the window. "A nasty, smelly, blocked alley I might add? Or is this part of your plan? If we're stinky no one will suspect us?" She quickly rolled the window back up; she had lowered it to have something else to complain about, but the fact was the place stunk like a fifteen-day-old corpse.

"My plans work, and no, this wasn't part of it." Reece shook off the remaining stupor her spell had left and started the car. Snarkiness and sarcasm had so many uses. "Why is this thing out of gear?" He glared at her, but she shrugged.

"Never mind. We need to get out of here fast. That gang-banger may have spotted me after all; if he tells people Dell was here, I'm toast." At her questioning glance he added, "Yes, another one of my personas. Dell died a few months ago—long story."

Aisling buckled herself in an instant before he gunned the

car into reverse. A good spell would wind itself so well into the victim's conscious that they added parts of reality to it without knowing. The mental plant that she'd supplied, of a gangster spotting him, had caused Reece's subconscious to construct a scenario that fit it. And exposed yet another persona. She sighed. At least this one was dead.

Chapter Eight

"How long was I out?" Reece slowed his wild dash once he got free of the alley and went back to his low level of seating and in general appearing as if he was cruising.

Aisling thought fast when she realized he'd seen his watch and realized he'd been "out" for more than what she'd implied.

"Only a few minutes. To be honest, at first I thought you were faking it. But you were out." Okay, so much for thinking on her feet, she couldn't come up with a plausible lie, so it was better to let him think he passed out.

He rubbed his head, then turned to her and narrowed his eyes. "Then why don't I have a bump?"

"Everyone knows your head is made of rock. Maybe that fey ancestor of yours was part rock troll."

He opened his mouth to argue, then started swearing instead and whipped the car into another alley.

Great, was her spell making him run into repeats?

"My phone, my *real* phone, is buzzing—they'd only call me for something big."

He pulled as far over as he could. On the side of the dirty road was a car-shaped outline cleared of dust told her that a car usually sat here. For all she knew it was this one.

He pulled out a phone that was hiding in a pocket sewn into his jacket; she hadn't noticed it when she'd been on top of him.

"Reece." His eyes went wide as the person on the other

end spoke, and although she couldn't hear the other end of the conversation, Reece wasn't happy.

"Understood." He clicked off and hid the phone again. "That big thing that Losien referred to? It's massive. And not coming from Seattle. We have a Welsh man and a Scot, both landing about half a mile from here in an illegal and hidden landing pad. Want to guess who?" He let out a huge breath and shook his shoulders, one of the few times she'd seen him stressed.

"I have no idea."

"The captains of the Scots and the Cymru Celtic gangs are on their way here. They are coming in for a secret meeting with some other gang. One so damn secret Interpol just found out about it. We can't stop it, but you and I are going to find out what the hell it's for."

This couldn't be good. The Celtic drug gangs hated each other almost more than they did the rest of the world.

"And we can't chance driving into the location—we're walking," he said, then glanced at her boots. "You are going to have a great time in those. And no, I'm not carrying you." The attempt at banter wasn't strong; he still looked upset.

Aisling ignored him and got out of the car. Her favorite high black boots probably weren't a primo choice for undercover out in the 'hood. But no one told her this morning she'd be playing gangster moll.

"Come on." Reece was sounding more like himself and a lot less like Leifen. That alone told her how rattled he was. It was possibly more than finding out about the meet. That spell of hers might be causing some problems.

"Leifen, don't order me around, k? You ain't the boss of me." She poked him in the back with her finger. "Dontcha forget that." She put a heavy East Coast slang into her voice. West Coast mobs would know each other, but a bitch girlfriend from the east would be unknown and hopefully unnoticeable. She hoped that no one saw them at all on this trip, but she agreed with Reece's earlier comment that if you always carry the act around, you won't forget to put it on.

Reece immediately dropped his left shoulder and appeared a good two inches shorter than he actually was. He also developed a slight limp. Not so much as to be an affectation, but enough of a hitch it may be real. She had to admit he was good.

"Hey, I'm the boss of the world, bitch." He turned and grabbed her close, his half smile telling anyone who did happen to be watching that the bantering was for play. "Thanks," he whispered, then kissed her light on the lips, but enough to look real from a distance, and started down the alley.

Aisling shrugged and followed. She wasn't quite sure how her character would respond to that, so she'd ignore it. For now. Like Surratt, Reece was amassing a long list of things he needed to explain and/or answer for. Aisling would make sure both debts were paid in full soon.

Reece was ambling faster than she would have thought someone with that odd walk could, and she jogged a few steps to catch up. "Where we going?" She kept her voice low, but still kept the accent.

"I know a place we can watch the landing pad without being seen." He glanced at his watch. "Damn it, we're almost out of time. That plane is landing in five minutes." He slapped her ass then started jogging through another smaller alley.

Aisling kept her grumbles to herself as she took off after him, but he would pay for that ass slap. If he asked her, which she noticed he wasn't, jogging in this part of the city was an uncommon event and was going to make them stand out. People were either walking or running for a life—to take someone's or save their own. But Reece didn't full out run, and he kept his body oddly stiff.

Mimicking his movements did bring her pace up a bit, but still gave the feeling of not really running.

"Stay low," he said as he dropped into a crouch and slowed down. They were coming out between two buildings and a mountain of wooden crate refuse over their left side. It was easily fifteen feet high and appeared ready to fall over at any minute.

"This way." He grabbed her arm and pulled her into the crates. Or rather, almost into the crates. A thin passageway, invisible unless you were at the right angle, led them into the pile of wood. The inside was narrow and dusty but surprisingly stable. Even though the exterior looked like the crates had been dumped here recently, this crawl space had been here for a few years if not longer.

"Why did we come in—?"

She froze and dropped her words as the unmistakable sound of a gun being cocked, and far too close to her for comfort, was heard.

"What you doing here, Leifen?" The voice was low and slimy, the type of voice to be expected hiding in a passageway of refuse.

"Bilth, my friend…" Reece put on a grin that would have made hardened prisoners check for a shiv in their backs and held out his hand.

The unseen man holding a gun to Aisling's temple didn't reach to take the hand. Nor did he drop the gun.

"Leifen, what the hell game you pulling?" Aisling piled on her East Coast bitch accent but kept her head cop still. "I told you, I ain't doing your friends."

The gun pulled away. Aisling shook out her shoulders and turned to the man. Or rather, the elf; a full-blooded elf stood before her. One with clan jewelry and everything. He shouldn't know this part of town existed, let alone be hiding in a pile of junk. Nor should he be friends with someone like Leifen.

"Although, for someone this pretty, I might change my mind." She leaned forward like a cat would to sniff new prey. She wasn't too surprised when Bilth's hand reached out and slapped her. The trick was making it appear that she hadn't been expecting it.

Many high-level elves disdained their lower caste cousins almost more than humans. The higher quality ones hid it. She'd caught a quick glance of amber on his ear when he struck her.

Glothin caste, lowest of the official clans. Had he realized her clan he would have most likely gone for a ritual suicide rather than face a tribunal for striking her. Well, a law-abiding Glothin would have. She doubted that had ever been something Bilth had been called.

"You could have said no." She rubbed the side of her face and moved behind Reece.

Bilth kept his dead-eyed stare on her for a few more seconds, then turned to Reece. Aisling wished she could let this bastard know who and what she was.

"I won't ask again. Why are you here, Leifen?" Bilth was a clan elf, which should provide him some stature in the world. But Aisling recognized the type. He hadn't been happy being lower middle class, so went to the lawless side.

"Same reason as you; was sent to watch." Reece had kept himself composed during her entire interaction with Bilth, and Aisling admitted she was impressed. Reece was still a pain in the ass, but there was a good chance he could teach her a lot about undercover work.

Bilth holstered his gun, then motioned for them to continue through the passageway. It got narrower as they went in, but a long bar of light told her where they could see out.

Reece shrugged and led the way, waiting until they'd stopped at the small area hidden there. The thin band of light she'd seen from the entrance was carefully crafted by strategically placed pieces of wood that would allow whoever was inside it to see out without anyone outside seeing in. Aisling pushed past Reece and peered out. Goddess, there *was* an airstrip out here. Okay, not a legal one, nor a large one. But there was a strip of land patched together that was barely long enough for one of the small hopper planes to land.

If who they thought was coming in was actually arriving, they weren't coming directly from the United Kingdom. The size of plane that would be able to land on that strip would have a short radius, less than three hundred miles most likely. She'd have a better idea when she saw it.

"Why did you bring your bitch? This isn't a place for… candy." Bilth had positioned himself with a clear view of both of them, and his own back against the wall of the small enclosure. Aisling hoped Reece, or rather Leifen, was on decent terms with this guy.

"She's more than a piece of ass, we're partners. I needed someone to watch my back after Dell got it." He didn't seem too concerned about Bilth's watching them, nor his questions.

Aisling swallowed her surprise, but only barely. She knew Reece was good at being multiple people. Hell, Reece might just be a persona. But how in the hell had he been his own partner?

"Heh." Bilth actually took his first real look at her. "Not a bad set up." He held out his hand. "I'm Bilth. Leifen can fill you in later. Sorry I pulled a gun on you."

Aisling was so surprised by his change she actually held out her hand. She was more surprised when he gave it a quick shake. Handshakes and apologies? What kind of criminals was Reece hanging out with?

"Take it they ain't here yet, since you still are." Reece ignored the handshake and stood closer to the window.

Aisling joined him.

"Naw," Bilth said. "You know them Celtic gangs, can't be on time for their own wakes. But I'm surprised you're here."

Now Reece looked nervous, or rather, as Aisling corrected herself, Leifen looked nervous, which was a totally different thing.

"Yeah, I screwed up. Gave the boss some shady information about some flyer bitch. I need to get things fixed." He went back to staring through the crack but Aisling felt all of his attention focused on the elf next to her.

"Ya mean Franko's runner? What was there to tell on that?" Bilth's laugh was as ugly as he was attractive. "She meddled; she died. But I ain't going to get in your way. I got my job to do for my boss, you got yours. This is neutral territory."

Reece gave a twitch in agreement that turned into a nod. "Agreed. You hear what happened to her?"

Aisling wanted to tell Reece to shut up; there was no reason for Leifen to be asking about Julilynn Marcos—especially if he supposedly already knew. But she kept her eyes out the thin peep hole and prayed he was as good as she hoped.

"The bitch talked. Talky bitches die, especially addict ones. End of story."

Aisling said a few mantras that Reece let that go.

For once the gods seemed to have been listening.

"Gotcha. That's what we thought." Reece turned back to watching the tiny landing strip.

Bilth pounded him on the back. "Checking to make sure you guys weren't missing anything, right?" His laugh crept down Aisling's spine. "I'd do the same if it was your guys who whacked her."

Aisling filed that information aside. Even though he was all but admitting that his cartel was responsible for Julilynn's death, she couldn't help but think that it wasn't the truth. There was the slightest bit of question to his voice. As if he was waiting to see if Reece was going to claim the kill.

But Reece gave that odd twitch and nod, which said nothing. Aisling turned slightly so she could see Bilth and his briefly narrowed eyes told her what she suspected. His cartel didn't kill the girl.

Her speculation as to who did kill her and with what was pushed aside as a small chopper came into view.

Two thin forms freed themselves from where they'd waited invisibly against a pile of wood. They were both human, so Aisling was sure they'd done their trick with skill, not a spell. Not that humans couldn't buy spells, but it seemed that in the last fifty years or so, humans were losing their ability to successfully use spells. Any spells. The only one not affected seemed to be the childbearing spell. But human rights' activists were in arms that that would be next and that somehow the fey races were behind it.

She felt Reece tense as he stood next to her. Bilth had moved to the long viewing area as well and his reaction was far less controlled.

"Aw, screw the pooch." He ran his hand through his thick hair but never took his eyes off the scene before them. "Why did it have to be the Klowsky twins? "

The chopper made a smooth and silent landing, attesting to the skill of the pilot. The two humans approached as soon as the blades stopped whirling. Two, possibly three people moved inside.

"They friends?" Since Reece wasn't reacting to the name of the humans, she hoped it was safe to feign ignorance. She'd heard of the Klowsky twins, brothers who dabbled in anything they could to move up the ranks in the seedy drug underworld. But as they hadn't killed anyone, that the cops knew of, they hadn't directly crossed her path before.

"Naw, they just make regular donations to my poker fund. Damn, gonna miss that income." He stepped back from the wall of wood and shook his head, his right hand pulling a small device out of his pocket. "Too bad."

Aisling was about to ask him why he kept saying that when the landing strip exploded and took the front of the wood pile with it.

CHAPTER NINE

A ISLING WASN'T SURE HOW LONG she'd been out, but judging from the dust still drifting in the air, it hadn't been long. That and the lack of sirens. Then it hit her, in this part of town there was a good chance any police presence would be seriously delayed. As in they'd wait until they were sure who ever set the explosives was gone. They'd want to make sure that if anyone was going to retaliate, they had done so and moved on. When she'd first joined the force she'd started in areas like this and, as bad as it sounded, she couldn't blame the cops.

She felt around and aside from a copious amount of small wood pieces and shavings dumped on her, she didn't seem to be injured. Reece was a still form next to her and Bilth was nowhere to be seen.

Not too surprising since she'd recognized the device in his hand as a detonator a fraction of an instant before the world exploded. Reece may have come here to spy on the mobsters, but Bilth clearly had different orders.

After she dug her way out from under the wood pieces and dusted herself off, Aisling crawled over to Reece. The roof had seriously lowered, but not collapsed, during the explosion and they needed to get out of here before it became their tomb.

"Leifen." She shook his shoulder. There was some blood near his temple, but no other injuries that she could see. "Damn it, *Leifen*, wake up."

Reece twitched and his eyes fluttered, then closed.

Damn him all to hell. She should leave him here and hope the roof didn't collapse while she went to get help.

Except that her luck hadn't been good enough to rely on for anything anymore.

A few more shakes of his shoulder and she got little more than another twitch. That blow to the head must be worse than she thought. She went out a bit to see what she could of the demolished landing pad and wished she hadn't. Blood and body parts mingled with the mechanical remains of the small chopper. Surprisingly, little beyond the pad, and the former occupants, was damaged.

Aside from this damn wooden blind anyway.

"Wake up." She spoke as loud as she dared and gave another tug on Reece's arm. There was a chance he'd sustained more damage than the head, and moving an injured human was always iffy. But the wood above her seemed to be resting completely on one single post. And while she wasn't a wood expert, it didn't appear solid. Chancing to try to heal him here wasn't an option either when the entire thing could collapse at any time.

"Damn it." With a few favorite swear words softly blistering the air, she grabbed under Reece's shoulders and started pulling.

The passageway out seemed to have taken less of a hit than the front of the blind and a light up ahead told her the way was clear enough that Bilth had made good his escape.

Holding onto Reece was difficult. While she was stronger than a human of similar build, he was heavier than he looked and his shoulders were hard to keep a hold of. Plus, she found the way had narrowed and she kept smacking her knuckles into the wooden pieces along the sides.

Finally, she got them out of the entrance. Now she faced another problem. She couldn't drag him all the way back to his car; it had to be a good half mile, and she'd be far too noticeable. She was looking around for a place to hide him when he smiled and opened his eyes.

"I knew you'd save me." He rolled to his side and rose gingerly, but with enough ease to reinforce the dark thought flinging around Aisling's brain.

"You were awake?" She held up the backs of her bloody hands to him. "This, you caused this. And I think I wrenched my back pulling your sorry ass...and you were awake!" She was going to kill him.

"Easy there, I needed to make sure you had my back, right?" He took her arm and started briskly walking away from the landing area. "No harm done."

"Except to me. And hopefully you got some good bruises." Aisling tried to pull her arm free, but he had a solid grip on it. She could pull free if she forced it, but if he was holding on this tight, he may have a good reason. She needed both of them to stay alive long enough for her to kill him.

He kept them moving quickly, but put his mouth close to her ear. "We are being watched, and there are at least two snipers with their sights aimed squarely at our heads. Right now, I'd say they are determining if we're people they should kill. That they haven't yet means they aren't sure. But, if we don't get out of range, and quickly, there's a good chance that we are going to die."

Aisling increased her speed. She hadn't seen anything, but she wasn't out in the field as often as he was. Reece was an ass, but he did have skills. "Then why were you playing dead? Seems like a stupid time to prove a point."

"I made a mistake, okay? Now isn't the time for blame. I misjudged who was behind this. I spotted one of them when I was getting up from the ground. Top of the brown building across from the landing pad." He turned to face her. "It was one of the Lazing."

Aisling seriously thought about breaking into a run. The Lazing were an almost mythological gang, one from the

Far East who almost never came to the West. They had minions to do that. Lead by an eastern fey of mysterious origins, they kept to themselves.

Until now.

"Do they know who you are?" She figured that it would be unlikely that they would have a clue, nor an interest once she left, of who she was. But Reece seemed to be known far and wide. If there was a chance that the snipers guarding the explosion scene knew who he was, they were seriously screwed.

Reece increased his speed, all but dragging her along until she got her feet under her.

"Leifen," she emphasized the name but she wanted to yell Reece. "Do they know you? *Any* of you?" She'd hissed the last part, lowering her voice to barely a whisper.

"Yes." He shook his head. "Not now, not here. But yes."

It had only taken them five minutes to get from the car to the landing pad when they came in, but the route he led them on going back took three times as long. And managed to cross every gang territory in the area that Aisling knew. He was hoping to not only confuse anyone following them, but also hoping they'd think twice before they crossed into another gang's turf.

His beat-up cruiser finally came into sight. Aisling started to move toward it, but Reece pulled her back as they got to the car. "Not yet, baby." He had been slowing his pace for the last few minutes, but now he stopped completely and pulled her into his arms. She was sure the kiss he gave her appeared passionate to anyone watching, if there was anyone watching. But he was all business as he spun her around so her back was up against his car.

Her back and his wristwatch. He held her tighter and she realized it was him pressing something on the watch. A minute later he relaxed and released her. Obviously the watch, like its owner, was far more than it seemed.

"It's clean." He raised his voice, "Now that we've kissed and made up, let's head for home. I've got some ass to bag." He slapped her ass—again—and casually clicked the alarm off of his car.

They were secure in the car and heading back toward the freeway before she finally gathered her thoughts to ask questions.

"So in no order, what were you checking for with the watch, who is Bilth, and which one of your personas knows the Lazing? I have a hell of a lot more but they'll wait. Our drive to the station won't be that long."

Reece kept watching for cross traffic as he continued toward the freeway. He was one block away from the freeway when he spun the car down the last side street. And he still didn't say anything.

"Crap, you think we're being followed." She didn't ask a question, it was a fact. She'd been watching the traffic behind them but she hadn't seen anything. Damn it.

"I know we are. I just can't see them." He turned onto a few more streets rapidly, and then whipped the car around to swing backwards into a driveway, and into an open garage. He shut the engine off immediately and slid low in the car.

Aisling followed suit. She wasn't used to feeling like a novice, but riding with Reece was making her feel like she had just joined the force. Crap, what if the Old One had come back? She couldn't block Reece's memories like that a second time.

Minutes ticked by slowly, Reece's watch loudly counting each one in the silence of the car. Aisling was about to tell him they were clear when a small Quick car drifted by. The electric cars were near silent, and this one had been modified with a reflect skin. A special spell laminate that reflected almost all light. It was only used on the air force's stealth fighters.

And one little Quick car. Luckily it wasn't near as effective on the ground as it was in the atmosphere. They could make out the shape of the car at least.

Unfortunately, because of the reflective skin, they couldn't see inside, but she instinctively knew whoever it was had been hunting for them. The car moved almost like a living thing, as if it was using senses a living predator would have to sniff them out.

Reece's breath stopped and Aisling held hers as well. There was no way that a car could have become sentient; most likely the feeling she had was because of the person or persons inside of it. But whichever it was, she knew she didn't want anyone in that car to know they were there.

It had drifted two houses past their location when it sped up and left the area.

Aisling waited a few moments, daring to breathe, but little else. Then Reece nodded and slid back up.

"What...no, you know what? I don't want to talk about any of this until we are the hell out of here." Aisling put her seat belt back on and motioned to the street before them. "We probably want to get out of this garage before the owners come back, ya think?" Just what she needed on top of this insane morning would be some gun-toting homeowner shooting at them for trespassing.

Reece turned the key. "Agreed on both counts."

The way back to the station was silent, but Aisling had way too many things going on in her head to notice it. She liked homicide; each case was a mystery, but for the most part a mystery she was damn good at. Like doing a crossword that was one level below her skill. Intriguing, but not too challenging.

This shit with Julilynn Marcos, Mott Flowers, Reece, the explosions, being followed by an Old One, and the murder of two major players in the drug world was challenging. Very challenging. If she admitted it to herself, she had started to like her comfort zone. This man next to her was ripping her right out of it.

"Okay, what was that?" Reece's voice startled her after the silence of the drive. He was pulling up to the same curb he'd been at that morning. He quickly glammed himself back into Dixon. Aisling almost chastised him for not parking in the police lot, then her brain caught up and reminded her that her fellow cops all thought he was Dixon, a criminal informant, not Reece, some sort of spook.

Keeping who he was straight was going to be a pain in the ass—especially since he was fooling her own police force. Her head started pounding. "What was what? I didn't say anything, and after all the shit you need to answer for, I get to be the one asking that question."

He'd turned off the car, but neither of them moved to get out.

"I…felt something. Are you sure you didn't say anything?" His brows were pulled low and he looked sincerely confused.

Aisling gave him her best "I have no idea what you're talking about" glare and tightly shook her head. But inside she fought a moment of panic. She hadn't said anything, but she'd been thinking it. And he'd sensed her emotions.

Shit. Shit. Shit.

That spell she'd cast on him had somehow linked them temporarily. He hadn't sensed her before, or if he had he hadn't noticed because she was talking and reacting in conjunction with what she was feeling. But this time she'd just been thinking.

Some elves used magic a lot; she'd never been one of those—at least not since an incident in college left her with a healthy fear of it. From what it appeared, her attempt at spelling Reece hadn't gone completely as planned.

"Nope, I didn't say anything. I do have a hell of a lot to

ask you, some of which should wait until we get to narcotics, but some of it needs to be answered later by Reece. I
don't think you want narcotics to know who Dixon really
is. Or Leifen for that matter. They may or may not like
Reece now; they are going to hate him if they find out he's
been spying on them for a year."

"Agreed, but I swear I thought you said something."
Reece opened his door. "But we need to make sure we
watch what we tell narcotics, you can feed Surratt what he
needs to know later."

"Surratt knows you're Dixon?" This was getting out of
hand.

Reece smiled and shoved his hands in his pockets. "He
has a good idea. He doesn't ask, I don't tell him. But Dixon
gives him info that he probably wouldn't have access to
otherwise."

Aisling followed him down the sidewalk toward the station. "But he hates you, even more than I do."

"You hate me, Aisling?" Reece's gaze was far too con-
templative for her tastes. She didn't want him thinking
about how she felt about him. Another level of crap hit
her. If she didn't hate him—which if she was honest with
herself, she didn't—he was going to feel that emotion too.

"Ya know, hate has different levels, and I am so not
talking about them with you." She looked him up and
down. "And glam magic aside, you're a lot more Leifen
than you should be right now."

Reece froze and adjusted his posture. Taking a deep
breath, he shook himself and Dixon was back in place.
"Thanks."

Without waiting for her he strode up the precinct steps.

CHAPTER TEN

THE REPORT TO CAPTAIN LOSIEN was short and edited. They'd gone on Dixon's rounds and been caught up in an explosion that might have been a fight between gangs. What Reece withheld was more interesting than what he told her. He didn't mention the Scot and Cymru mob bosses, Bilth, or that the Lazing had been involved. Whatever agency Reece truly worked for, they kept a lot of their data to themselves. Normally, Aisling would be worried about not passing on the information, but there were weird and dangerous things going on, and until she figured them out, she'd follow Reece and Surratt's direction. Both felt there was a leak of some sort in the station.

Captain Losien took the information in dryly. But Aisling was certain if she'd known the reality of it the captain wouldn't be so calm.

"Good work. Aisling, since you're the officer, I leave writing it up to you. Dixon, make sure she gets all the points straight, but you can't write it." From the emphasis of her words it was clear Reece liked to dabble in some exercises of creative writing on reports from time to time.

Aisling had been assigned a small nearly empty desk, the ones used by short timers or, as in her case, temporary transfers. There was no reason to make someone comfortable if they weren't going to stay was the mindset. Still, sitting at such a blank desk made her homesick for her regular one downstairs.

"Okay, so what else goes in besides what you told Captain Losien?" She opened the computer, one handed down from a few retrofits and about ten years older than any other computer in the station. It took a few minutes to figure out how to use the old operating system, but she got a file open and started typing.

"Nope, you got the time wrong," Reece had pulled his chair over so he could see the screen, then he reached over a hand to the keyboard to change a few sentences.

Aisling slapped his hand. "You heard the captain. I write, you talk." She dropped her voice, although after the initial interest at their return no one seemed to be paying attention to them. "What do you mean the time is wrong? That's when we got there."

"We wasted some time getting lost, remember?" He reached over and made her type in time good twenty minutes after when they actually got to the area. Great, he was covering up the gaps in their story by changing the timeline on an official report.

Even though she knew she shouldn't mess with it—the spell she cast was unstable—she couldn't help herself. Aisling sent a concentrated thought of pure irritation at him.

He pulled back as if struck and glared around the room then back at her. His eyes narrowed slightly and she knew she couldn't play that again. She needed to find her brother Caradoc; hopefully he could fix the spell before it blew up in her face.

"Oh, yes, I'd forgotten." She pulled her mental annoyance back but let it drip out with her words. Hopefully Reece would think he was losing his mind. A little sanity questioning might be good for him.

She adjusted the time and Reece refrained from trying to control her typing, at least physically. He made little grunts and nods to get her to change the real facts to what he felt the department needed to know. It was already so censored from reality; she wasn't sure what else to put.

Aisling wasn't a huge rule follower, but she'd never outright lied on an official report. She understood his reasons, and whatever agency's spook he ultimately was, he definitely out ranked a homicide detective. But she didn't like it.

The rest of the day was spent going over reports of drug smuggling from the British Isles. So now Aisling and Reece got to plow through masses of old data. Reece got a call a few hours in, claimed his ailing mother needed him, and took off. Since he was in a unique position as a special consultant, he could leave when he wanted. Unlike Aisling who had two more hours of drudgery.

Aisling had shut down her prehistoric computer and was heading for the elevator when Surratt called. She seriously thought about letting the call go to voice mail.

For a few seconds anyway.

"Aisling here, what?" She let her annoyance come out in her voice. Surratt was directly responsible for her current situation and the hellish day she'd gone through. But he was still her boss and not answering the call would make things worse.

"Good, you're still in the building. I need you to come to my office." He clicked off without waiting for her answer.

"Fine. I'll be right there. Thank you for asking me to drop by," she said to the dead phone line. Damn it. She wanted to find a cab, get home, eat, and take a long bath.

She was halfway to the homicide floor when she realized another irritating fact—he'd known she was still in the building. Damn it. He was tracking her. He couldn't seriously think she was involved with the death of Julilynn Marcos, could he? First off, no one, but no one, called her Lady Aisling, not even her family. And even after seeing numerous pictures of the girl before her horrible transformation, she didn't recognize her. Yes, she'd been at one of Aisling's prior crime scenes, but so were lots of people. She didn't have any interaction with her. To be fair, sociopaths didn't need to have logic on their side and may have picked Julilynn as a random target. Then added the tag to her. For some unknown reason.

Except that Bilth knew about Julilynn, and the implication was that she was killed by a drug cartel. Since Aisling had never been involved with the narcos, nor for the most part the cartels, it wouldn't make sense for one of them to have targeted her.

The homicide floor was staffed thinner than usual at this time of the day. Yes, it was the end of the workday for some people, but cops didn't follow regular hours. Especially homicide cops with a twisted case on their hands.

Most likely a huge chunk of the task force was out chasing for clues in the destroyed building and the ravine. Exactly where she should have spent the day.

Nods from the few folks staffing the desks seemed amiable enough, so things must have been said about her current exclusion that made her less of a pariah.

"Danaan, in here." Surratt stuck his head out of one of the smaller interrogation rooms. Aisling couldn't help her sigh of relief at the fact he was coming out of the viewing side, not the suspect side. But if he didn't think she was a suspect, or involved with a suspect, then why in the hell was he tracking her phone?

Surratt sat at the far end of the table and nodded for her to shut the door and sit. The lights were on in the interrogation room, but no one was in there.

"Okay, so tell me what you and Larkin were doing in poor town and in the Fluns gang's turf?"

After the cloak and dagger ways of Reece, Surratt's bluntness was startling. And it answered the question about Surratt knowing who Dixon really was.

She wasn't completely sure to what level she was supposed to tell Surratt. Reece had been vague enough, and Surratt clearly knew who he was. But she didn't think she should be telling him everything.

As if he was reading her mind and not just picking up on her emotions, Reece's number flashed on her phone. "Speak of the devil, let me grab this. He probably forgot where he put his car."

At Surratt's terse nod, she answered the call. She knew she couldn't leave the room, but hopefully Reece wouldn't make things difficult.

"Aisling here, what?"

"We shouldn't mention our friends from the east yet." The tone was very Reece, but short and terse.

"Gotcha."

"You're with Surratt now?"

"Yup."

"Okay, I think we need to talk about the stuff in my head, but right now you can tell him everything except about the Lazing. I'll pick you up in the a.m."

He clicked off before she could respond. "Bastard." She shut her phone off this time and put it back in her pocket.

"Trouble in paradise?" Surratt's grin grew. "Don't tell me you two still don't get along?" The smile on his face said he knew that was the case, and he was pleased by it. Considering that he was keeping plenty of secrets for Reece, and probably didn't dislike him near as much as he pretended, she was surprised he was happy about them not getting along.

"He's a bastard and you know it. I don't know who I pissed off enough to leave me saddled with him, in a persona the narcotics team doesn't know about by the way, but I'd like to find a way to settle my debt." Better to play along with Surratt's perceptions. Sadly, she had found that while Reece still annoyed the crap out of her, she didn't hate him. But Surratt didn't need to know that.

"Agreed on that front." Surratt's laugh confirmed the wisdom of her move. "But it's handy having him around, whatever agency he's actually with. Which brings me to today's adventures. I know he wouldn't have told narcotics any more than they needed to know. But what happened?"

He had a pad of paper with lines already scribbled across it, but from what she could see they were written in some sort of code.

She gave as much detail as she could, still leaving in their "getting lost" detail and blaming Reece for it completely. She excluded the Quick car, the Lazing, and the Old One.

"He crashed into an alley? Was he drunk?"

Aisling kept the alley story at what Reece knew just in case he brought it up. Besides, if he didn't it might be fun for Surratt to have something to needle him about.

"I honestly don't know. He said he thought we were being followed, freaked out, and misjudged a closed alley." She shrugged and feigned ignorance, but something in Surratt's eyes told her she'd mis-stepped.

"He freaked out?" He watched her reaction carefully.

Damn. "Well, okay, maybe that was my interpretation. He and I were arguing because he took the wrong damn exit and got us lost. He may have been reacting more to that than whoever he thought was following us."

She swallowed the thought of what would happen if anyone knew what had been following them or that Reece had sensed one of the vallenians.

"I could see that." Surratt relaxed and asked a few basic questions, mostly about Bilth, although he seemed to know about him already.

"You're certain that the people on that chopper were the Cymru and Scots mobsters?"

Aisling shrugged. "Reece said they were, and it was one of his agencies that told us about the landing. That jackass

Bilth seemed to think so as well."

She was hoping that mentioning the cartel thug by name again might lead Surratt to let some information slip. He'd raised a single eyebrow when she first mentioned Bilth, but hadn't seemed too surprised. Considering Bilth knew Reece as Leifen, and possibly as the late Dell, it could mean that Surratt knew more of Reece's aliases than she did.

And if so, he wasn't going to let her in on it. Nor give her any more information than what she already had.

She decided to switch gears. The mystery behind whatever drug the cartels were trying to bring in was interesting, but to be honest, even with all the layers on this one, she wasn't that interested in the cartel members killing each other. Her idea would be to take all the mobsters, gangsters, and cartels and dump them somewhere that they could kill each other in peace.

While her thoughts were probably shared by many of her fellow officers, they weren't something she would ever say out loud.

"Any word back on Julilynn Marcos?" She carefully avoided looking at him, trying to appear less interested than she was.

"Good try, Danaan. But while I technically shouldn't tell you anything, since we're still not sure of your connection to the girl or the case, I will tell you that we don't know anything. Right now, the medical examiner is pulling his few remaining hairs out and will most likely list it simply as accidental extreme iron poisoning."

"What? How in the hell could any member of the fey races get that much iron in their system accidentally? It would kill them before they got anywhere near that amount in their blood stream. Once she touched it her organs would have started shutting down."

Surratt shrugged and raised his hands. "We know, but the medical examiner hasn't been able to figure out what happened. There was extensive damage to all of her internal organs almost at once, and the more she fought the effects the worse it got. But they can't find the source. It's iron poisoning, but nothing like they've ever seen before." He got to his feet. "Thank you for updating me on the gangster situation. Have a good night."

He was out the door before she'd pushed her chair back. What was it with that man and cutting her off when he no longer needed something from her? She leaned back in the chair and rubbed her eyes. In a way, all of this mayhem was helpful; it was keeping her mind off of her mother. Popping open her phone, she confirmed that there were no missed calls. Even though she hadn't called back, Aisling knew that woman hadn't let this issue drop. Lady Tirtha Lasheda Otheralia didn't let anything drop. Ever.

Putting away her phone, and ignoring the sudden skin crawling feeling she'd gotten about being watched, she left the precinct.

Cabs didn't like hanging around a police station unless they were desperate. They often ended up with fares that recently got out of jail and had no money to pay. And a desperate cabbie was not a good cabbie. So Aisling walked a few blocks away from the station. There was a small shopping area and park that might be more conducive to picking up a cab. She could call for one, but she felt like a walk right now.

Everyone raved about LA's weather, but for her the best weather was at twilight. When any heat of the day had vanished, and the sky was starting to turn. A slight breeze made it even better.

The street wasn't busy, uncommon for this time of day, but not enough to worry her. LA traffic was capricious.

The small group of males huddled around something at the small park next to the shopping center was worrying though. She walked closer when she noticed the group was made up of a bunch of local punks, her worry and her speed increased. None of them wore gang colors, but that didn't mean they couldn't be dangerous.

"Hey, LA police, what's going on?" She swore when she started to raise her wrist only to remember she hadn't seen Heike back in the station and the glamour was still on it. Fortunately, Surratt had been making them carry backup badges lately. She'd picked hers up when she'd reclaimed her gun before leaving the station. A serious criminal would never take the word of a badge kept in a wallet, but it should be enough for punks.

"Yeah, right." The leader, a scarred low caste elf with half of his right ear missing, stepped forward. "You ain't got a tat, you ain't a cop." He looked her up and down and she realized that she hadn't fixed her clothing from her little run as Reece's bitch. His gaze quickly changed from annoyance to something far worse.

She pulled out her gun, but kept it pointed up. What she didn't need was to be under report for a shooting. "Well, then I stole a cop's gun. And unless you guys want to see how well I did at the shooting range last week, I'd suggest you bugger off."

There were five of them, two humans, two elves, and a troll. Trolls weren't common in LA or any of the warmer parts of the world. They hated heat and it made them slow and sluggish. She swore as the troll turned its tiny head toward her. His eyes were red. Great, one way troll kind could handle the heat was to dope up—like this one did.

"Grab her, Tiny. We found us something more fun than rolling a stiff." The leader hadn't pulled out a gun, and none of the others had either. Thugs pulled guns when threatened if they had them. Her pulling out hers would have led to more had they been armed. Which meant unless her life was seriously in danger, she couldn't justify a shooting. They weren't armed.

She could try to get back to the station and find some uniforms to follow her back, but now that they were moving around she could see a body had been at the center of their circle. A body that might not be dead yet, but could be, or at least relocated, by the time she came back with help.

Only one thing for it then, prove to them she was an alpha bitch. While she couldn't shoot them, she also couldn't risk that in a fight one of them might get her gun. So she opened the clip and threw the bullets as far as she could. Not the brightest thing, she'd have to find them all later, but it showed them that grabbing her gun would be useless.

"Boys, we got us a suicidal piece of ass here. Don't worry sweetie, we won't be gentle."

"Seriously? You use that line a lot? What, you're hoping your victims will double over laughing so you can grab them?" She was slowly walking backwards so to follow her they'd have to move away from the body. She was pretty sure it twitched a bit which hopefully meant whoever they were they were still alive.

As she moved, she judged the other punks. None of them were big, nor moved like fighters. The only two real threats were the troll and the leader. Luckily for her, and bad for them, since they appeared to be counting on the troll as their muscle, she'd spent a few rebellious decades in the frozen north. Around lots of trolls far bigger and nastier than this one.

The troll took the lead and lumbered forward. Even doped, he was still slower than he should be. And short. At seven feet tall he was taller than her, but the trolls in the Alaskan mining town of Farthing would have laughed him right out of the pub.

The troll lunged, and she darted out of his way, then came down hard on the back of his neck with both hands.

The move jarred her—her hand-to-hand combat instructor Torrance would be disappointed at how bad her troll fighting had gotten—but it still dropped him to his knees.

The move left her slightly off-balance and the leader took the opportunity to grab her from behind. Arms tight as steel bands began to squeeze the breath out of her. Or most of it. She still had enough to smash her head back at the same time she stomped on the top of his foot. His grip lessened as he pulled back in pain and she dropped low and swung a groin shot in. The elven thug curled up in a fetal position and whimpered.

The troll was groggy but too drugged to stay down. She gave a few solid kicks to the side of his thick skull and watched as his eyes rolled back.

Aisling turned to the rest and held out her arms, ignoring the twinge across her ribs where the leader had grabbed her. "Who's next, boys? Not only will I kick your ass, I wasn't kidding about being a cop. A homicide detective even." She leaned forward a bit and gave them an evil glare. "I know where to hide the bodies."

The remaining three gave their fallen comrades a whole two seconds thought, then turned and ran.

With a glance to make sure both of the punks were staying down, she hit her phone and called in some uniforms. The cars were pulling up before she got to the body the punks had been beating up.

The man appeared to be breathing but was in bad shape. She gently turned him over and started swearing. She knew him. But she hadn't seen him since primary school, except in some very recent photos.

It was Mott Flowers.

CHAPTER ELEVEN

———◆———

HIS FACE WAS A MISHMASH of cuts and scrapes that were already starting to bruise. Either these guys had been working him over for a long time or, most likely, he'd been beaten somewhere else then dumped here.

It would be more like the kids she chased off to pick at remains than actually take down new prey. They only went after her because they were pumped up from their beating up someone who was already badly injured. Plus, they figured four big teenagers and a troll against a single woman were good odds.

Mott hadn't aged well, even with the bruising taken into account. He must be close to her in age, based on them being in school together, but while Aisling still appeared to be in her twenties had she been human, Mott looked closer to his mid-fifties.

Things could happen to an elf to age them unnaturally. They had to be drastic though, and from Mott's appearance, he'd lost close to half his life span to whatever aged him.

"Ma'am? Did you report this in?"

The uniformed human beside her caught her lost in thought.

She turned and held up her metal badge; when he automatically glanced to her left wrist, she shook her head. "I'm Homicide Detective Aisling Danaan. I'm on an undercover case and had the tat glammed." She held up her photo ID as well. The uniformed cop was young and was visibly concerned as he went from her badge, to the ID, to her, and the body.

"I'm in Surratt's department. Do you want me to call him to confirm?" She knew she wasn't being nice to the young cop, but she was tired and annoyed. She needed to get Mott to a hospital, and needed the cops to do it without knowing who he was. She'd call Reece and let him know what happened. "I'll tell you what happened, then you can have police escort the victim to the hospital. His name is Rick Moore. Agent Reece Larkin of the FBI was looking for him. Call him and tell him which hospital he gets sent to and tell him I told him to go there." This way he'd get to the hospital faster, she didn't even want to say Mott's name on the phone until she was safe in her house. Reece wouldn't know the alias, but she knew he'd recognize the face when he saw Mott. It was the best she could do. If she tried to stay with him, or put too much attention on Mott, it could make it harder for the feds to get him somewhere safe.

The uniformed officer watched two other policemen load up the two thugs while an emergency crew was putting Mott on a stretcher. When he finally glanced her way, his expression was more than a little concerned.

Aisling beat him to the punch. "Officer Manling is it?" At his terse nod, she continued. "I have been on a case for most of the better part of the last twenty-four hours. I am tired. I want to go home. Call Surratt if you want, but I need to get this done." Fatigue was kicking the crap out of any polite inclinations she had.

A newer SUV pulled up, and Garran hopped out. Aisling hadn't seen him since he'd picked her up yesterday morning, but was glad to see him now. Especially when it was clear the uniformed kid in front of her recognized him before he held up his left wrist.

"Garran, I'm damn glad to see you. I caught these punks

beating on this man over here. I need to leave my report with this officer and go home. But he seems to doubt who I am."

Garran back slapped one of the other officers and nodded to Officer Manling. "Tats not good enough anymore, son?"

Aisling sighed and held up her arm. "I've been undercover and they glamoured it."

"Ah, good call then, Manling. But I can vouch for this one." With a nod, he walked over to where the ER techs were loading Mott into the ambulance. A brief frown crossed his face before he turned back to them.

Finally, Manling took her story of events, then nodded and went to examine the scene.

Garran came up to her as she started to walk out of the park. "Need a ride?"

"Weren't you going into the station?"

He shook his head and shoved his hands in his pockets. "Nope, I live about a block away and when I heard the call that you had stopped a mugging, I thought I'd come see."

Aisling followed him to his car. Much better than a taxi. "But wait, they mentioned I was the one who found the body? Then why in the hell was Manling giving me such a hard time?"

"Because he's new. You're pretty. He freaked out." He laughed. "Take your pick. Anything new on the case from yesterday?"

Garran was in the homicide department, but he usually dealt with cases no one else knew much about—not even Aisling. He kept weird hours and was often not seen for days. But Surratt trusted him more than he did his own mother.

"Nothing except for Surratt kicking me out." She briefly filled him in on Julilynn Marcos—he already knew—the message left behind—knew that too—and her evening with Reece. He sort of knew about that.

His new car was a welcome change from Reece's beat-up monster they'd been in today. And different from the one he'd picked her up in yesterday morning. Still, the seats were soft and broken in enough that she wanted to curl up in them and sleep. She needed some rest.

"You want a new car every day? Or are you trying to break my record and destroy the last one?" She hadn't destroyed her previous cars herself. One had been stolen about five months ago outside of a double murder; one had a giant boulder roll on it at a case out in the valley about three months ago; and the third was totaled when a wrong way high-as-an-angel driver slammed into it outside her favorite restaurant. That none of them were her fault didn't seem to make a difference to her friends, the cops' car pool, or her insurance.

Garran slowly moved his car into traffic. "Naw, you're doing so well at that." He grinned to take any sting out. "The other one was the wife's. She needed something bigger for a few days so we switched. Now what's this about you being blown up today? I assume Larkin was involved?"

Aisling had to admit, the way Garran turned Reece's last name into a swear word was endearing. "We weren't blown up; yes, Reece was involved; and why do you ask questions when you already know the answers?"

Garran's smile fell and he seemed to take too long to gaze at the trees across the street before he answered.

"I'm not sure. Rather, I'm not sure what's going on in the department." He held up a hand. "No, I don't know anything. I have a feeling, you know? It's something my people have."

Aisling bit her tongue to keep from asking him *who* his people were. Garran was fey, but it wasn't clear what type. But one of the reasons he handled the odd cases that he did was because of what he was.

"Good girl," Garran said. "No, I'm not telepathic, but you have an expressive face when you're exhausted. There is no doubt that something is going on. I'm not sure who's involved, so watch your back. I'll be gone the next week or so, taking the wife up to visit her folks in Canada. Stay out of trouble."

He'd managed to time things so that he pulled up to her house just as the final words left his mouth.

Aisling's laugh turned into a yawn. "Will do, you as well. I hear in-laws can be tricky."

With a nod, Garran drove slowly down the street. He nodded to Mr. Graves, who bowed slowly before going back into his house.

The sight brought a smile to Aisling, but also another bit of food for thought. She might have to ask Mr. Graves if *he* knew what Garran was.

Her thoughts were slammed out of her head as a shoe whizzed by her face the moment she opened her front door. The second projectile, a slipper luckily, managed to catch the side of her head.

She ducked by the time the toaster came cruising at her on its way to doom and destruction on the sidewalk below the short flight of stairs to her stoop. There was already a pile of her belongings scattered about the ground.

Her gun was in her hands an instant before she remembered she hadn't reloaded the bullets. Damn it, this exhaustion was going to get her killed.

But what kind of serious intruder would hurl her own things at her? She ducked as a large portion of her wardrobe came sailing overhead.

"Whoever you are, come out with your hands up and empty. I'm with the LA police and I will use force if I have to."

The only answer she got was a series of pans from her kitchen flying out the door.

Damn it. She crouched low and nudged the door open further. Hopefully she could at least get a glimpse of who was trying to rob her by throwing everything out of her home.

At first nothing, then she spotted a fast-moving tiny red cap. And another. They were hard to see due to their speed, but it looked like the house brownies she'd hired had brought in friends and were trying to destroy her home.

"Damn it! Stop! I have a contract with you—"

Her desk chair flying through the air cut her off as well as made her flee down the stairs to the sidewalk below.

An instant later, her apartment exploded and the force sent Aisling flying.

CHAPTER TWELVE

A ISLING DIDN'T REALIZE THAT SHE'D been knocked out by the explosion until a concerned med tech appeared in her field of vision. Well, partially in her field. Her right eye didn't seem to be working.

"Can you see me? Nod if you can see and hear me." The med tech was stereotypical: young, good looking, built, and probably saved little old ladies on his way home from work daily. But he also seemed to know what was going on, which was one up on her.

Aisling thought about speaking, but it seemed too much effort. She settled for nodding.

Bad idea. Her eye wasn't the only thing not working right. Her balance must have been blown up in the explosion. That little bit of movement made her fight to keep from throwing up.

"Easy there, you've taken a pretty serious hit. Or rather hits. Looks like you got out of there just in time." He reached up with a cloth and dabbed at the side of her head. Aisling didn't need to see it to know there was blood on it. The dampness was starting to creep down her face.

"How bad?" She wasn't sure if she was asking about herself or the apartment—at this point both were in question.

The scowl across his face might have marred a lesser man, but on the med tech it only made him appear more gallant.

"You're going to be okay. A night in observation is all I ask, as I said you took a hard blow. Your place? Not so much." He turned to glance over his shoulder and Aisling steeled herself enough to peek. Flames were dying, but there wasn't much left.

"Others?" Talking wasn't much fun, but she needed to know.

The med tech shrugged. "It was the weirdest thing. Your immediate neighbors all got chased out by a band of brownies about a half hour before the explosion. And it didn't spread to their homes."

She dropped her head back to the ground. Maybe the brownies had been trying to save her? All this time she thought she'd alienated them, and instead they'd gone through and saved everyone in the apartment building?

"Oh, and the brownies left you this," He handed her a tiny envelope. "I guess they knew the explosion was coming."

Aisling's right arm was stiff, but she could hold the envelope with that hand. Nope, she was right. She had alienated them. Or the little bastards were more mercenary than she thought. It was a bill for saving her life and those of all of the tenants of the adjacent apartments.

Things seemed better when she wasn't thinking about them, so she leaned back and let the med tech do his job. They had a slight altercation when he insisted on an ambulance. She was winning the fight when a familiar face appeared within her limited range of vision.

Reece flashed his badge at the med tech. "Agent Larkin, FBI. I'll see that this officer gets in an ambulance, and we appreciate that you saved her life." He paused and glared expectantly at the med tech. "You can go, thank you, we've got this."

Aisling watched the exchange. Leave it to Reece to butt in about this too. The man was becoming a menace. No, he had always been a menace. She'd never had to be around him this much before. The case better end soon. For his sake.

Reece stood with his arms folded while he waited until the tech left. The handsome young tech opened his mouth to argue, but instead gave Aisling a short nod and went back to the crowd near the apartment building.

"You didn't have to be so bitchy; he did help me, you know."

Reece turned to her with a sigh. "I know. And it wasn't him personally, but we have a situation and at this point I need you to only be around people you know." The scowl on his face had relaxed a bit once the med tech left. But not enough to suit Aisling.

Her left arm was in better shape than her right—she'd landed on her right side when she was blown clear—but it worked well enough for her to lift up her hand and rub her eyes. She wasn't happy but climbed onto the gurney under Reece's prodding scowl.

"What else?" Her home being blown up wasn't going to be the worst thing of the day?

Reece shook his head. "Not here." He motioned to a tall, slim man wearing the uniform of an ambulance driver. But he had the gait and moves of an assassin. "I didn't lie to the tech. We do need to get you checked, but not somewhere public. Jones here will take us."

Aisling grabbed his arm as he moved to go past her. "I thought you said I need to only be around people I know?" She kept her voice low, but knew the ambulance driver heard her anyway. Those types of killers heard everything, or they didn't live long.

"Jones, meet Danaan. Danaan, meet Jones. There, now you know each other. I should have been clearer. We need to keep you around people *I* know." He freed his arm and stalked to a second ambulance and climbed inside. Jones gave a quirky half smile, then set the spell that would cause Aisling's gurney to follow him to the ambulance as well.

Aisling watched as Reece waited for her and her gurney to join him inside. That scowl on his face was going to leave a permanent mark by the way it was etching itself in.

She'd seen almost all of Reece's emotions, and now those of Dixon and Leifen. But this one was new. Anger she'd seen before, but this was a whole new level, thrown in with something else. Fear? That was something she'd never seen—Reece scared. Rattled a bit, but he always covered it up with some trick of smart ass-ness so it never stayed long.

From his face as she was lifted into the ambulance, this was staying awhile.

"I'm the one who lost her home, why the hell are you so cranky?" With most people, Aisling might try to see if they'd shake out of their moods on their own. But Reece wasn't most people, and for the first time in her life, at least since she'd turned old enough to walk, she felt her survival might actually depend on someone else. Him. It was going to take a while to process that thought.

Reece's scowl dug in a few more inches, but he stayed silent until Agent Jones had locked the back of the ambulance door and started the engine.

"You weren't the only one under attack." His scowl softened to concern and sorrow. "Your partner's place in London was blown up almost a half hour before yours was. I was coming to tell you when I heard your place went up too."

Aisling tried to fling herself off the gurney, but Jones had secured her in too well. "What? Is she okay? What about her family? I need to talk to her."

"Easy there, tiger." A bit of his usual sarcastic self crept back to the surface. "We don't know yet, but it appears she may not have been there when it went off. But it was her place, not her folks'. Her family moved to Bath a decade ago and they haven't seen her in years." The way he dropped the last line, he knew what she was going to say next.

"But she was going home to stay with her family...no one was sick, were they?" A coldness hit her gut. Maeve had been planning on a vacation, but then left earlier than planned due to a family emergency. Yet, she'd not been in contact with them. "So why did she go to London?"

Reece sighed and ran both his hands across his face. That was a new look too—he appeared as exhausted as she felt. "We're not sure. To be honest, we thought she was going on a vacation, so no one was concerned. But this goes deeper than we thought."

Aisling waited for him to finish; when he didn't do anything but stare out the back of the ambulance window, she coughed. "What goes deeper? What the hell is going on? We need to find Maeve."

"*We're not sure.* And when I say *we*, I mean the real agency I work for. And no, I can't tell you who they are yet. But the fact that none of my superiors know what is going on makes me want to go find a bunker out in Montana somewhere and hide for a few years."

The residual pounding in her head from the explosion grew worse. What in the hell was going on? That all of these events were enough to freak out a super spook like Reece? This was the first time he'd admitted that there was an agency behind all the IDs he flashed around, he must be rattled.

She needed a chance to sit and get things sorted. When she had a tough case, she often resorted to an old-style murder board. A huge old drawing board she'd saved during the last station upgrade and remodel. Drawing all of the pieces of a tricky case on it and having it in her living room had resolved many a difficult case.

The fact that her beloved murder board was probably a pile of kindling now caused the pain in her head to increase.

"I know this is a spook central ambulance, and not a real one, but I think I do need something for my head. Can we at least swing by a pharmacy before we go wherever it is we're going?"

Reece shook himself free of whatever thoughts he was pulling through the mud and grinned. "Actually, we are going to a hospital, but not one most people have ever seen. Speaking of which…" He leaned forward quickly. Aisling didn't see the needle until it was in her arm. "Sorry about this, but we can't have you seeing everything yet."

Aisling reached over to pull out the needle, but her eyelids were already starting to close.

"You bastard," she got out right before everything went black.

CHAPTER THIRTEEN

———◆———

THE SMELL HIT HER FIRST. That antiseptic, burning scent that could only be found in a large hospital. The smell that usually made her stomach clench the moment she stepped inside one and made questioning injured witnesses pure torture.

The urge to throw up didn't come as much of a surprise.

"Be at peace." A soft female voice came from somewhere next to her and she found her bed raising up slightly and the smell drifting away. To be replaced by the light smell of jasmine.

Aisling opened her eyes, blinking back tears at the brightness of the room for a moment. Then the room darkened a bit.

She wasn't surprised to see the ethereal being seated next to her. Flalin were a rare type of fey, but they were highly sought after in the health care profession. Considering that this one's silvery hair drifted to the ground and back up in elaborate knots at least a dozen times, she was one of the ancient ones. Healing powers flowed from them and they were once the caregivers to kings. But as technology began to weave its way into daily life, more of them had died and no new ones had been born.

"I guess that makes sense," Aisling said as her stomach settled.

"What does, child?" The voice was softer than a summer breeze but soothed her soul.

"That the super spooks would have a flalin on call."

Aisling softened her words with a smile and a slight touch on the woman's arm. Flalin were gentle, and touch was important to them.

A laugh that sounded more like silver bells in the wind than the sound coming from a voice lifted Aisling's heart. Things couldn't be as bad as Reece said, not when there were beings like this woman around. Aisling caught herself and shook her head.

Falling under a flalin spell, even one supposedly on the same side as her, was a rookie mistake.

"Sorry, I'm feeling better now. Is Reece around? I'd like to get back on the case."

"Right now, you are the case." Reece's voice as he came into the room brought reality slamming back into Aisling's head.

He'd taken off his duster, but the clothes were still the ones that he wore as Dixon the day before. His skin, hair, and eye color had returned to Reece though.

"What day is it?" There were so many other questions flooding her brain but that was the only one that made it to the surface.

Reece laughed and pulled forward one of the ubiquitous hospital guest chairs. That a super spook hospital had the same little quirks in furniture was reassuring. The worry lines that still creased his face, however, were not.

"It's Tuesday. Also known as the late afternoon after the night your home blew up."

Aisling sat up a bit more in bed, the pillow and bed following her movements exactly. She flashed a quick smile to the flalin; the healers were highly intuitive and telekinetic. "Well, at least I got some sleep. We'll talk later about how you kidnapped me and knocked me out. But right now I want to know what you meant."

He moved his chair a bit closer, then leaned back and rested his feet on the metal frame of her bed. He looked like total crap. She might have rested, but he'd been up the entire time.

"The same highly specialized components used to blow up your townhome were also used on Maeve's place." He paused and leaned forward. "And it was the exact same exotic mixture that was used to blow up a certain pair of mobsters yesterday."

Aisling wasn't too shocked to learn that the evidence pointed toward the same persons blowing up both her and Maeve's places—or at least the same organization. It was doubtful the same person hit both LA and London within a few hours. But the mobster killing connection surprised her.

"The Lazing have taken an interest in you and your partner. An unhealthy one. Any idea why?"

A soft hand gently caressed her forehead. "You are upsetting my patient, Agent Larkin." The flalin voice was still a thing of beauty, but there was a hint of the steel that a few thousand years of life left behind.

"I know, but we'd like to keep her alive, and knowing whatever in the hell is going on might help us do that." Reece wasn't disturbed about being chastised by the healer. But he did look ready to fall asleep.

Aisling shook her head. "I have no idea why they would know I exist, let alone want to blow me up."

Reece unsuccessfully fought a yawn. "Think hard, there has to be some connection. The Lazing don't leave Yokohama, but now we have multiple attacks." Another yawn interrupted him. He shook his head. "There is no way there's not a connection. We have to…" This time Aisling echoed his yawn, which launched him into a new one.

"I'm going to sit over here. But we need to discuss…" Reece moved over to the small, hard guest cot also found in most hospitals. His conversation dropped off as he fell face first onto the cot and was sound asleep.

"Could you teach me that? To put him to sleep like that?" Aisling asked the healer sitting next to her. The woman's smile gave no doubt as to why Reece had suddenly been unable to stay awake. "Please? That was awesome." She found that she couldn't stop her own yawns. "Oh, come on, that's not fair, that's…"

Aisling's dreams were dark and chilling, but none of them made the trip back to consciousness with her when she awoke, just the feeling of them. She wasn't sure if she should be happy or upset about that. She had a feeling they weren't things she wanted to remember; her heart was pounding and she was covered in sweat when she woke up.

"Good of you to rejoin us." The voice was up to its normal snarky level; clearly the spell induced sleep had helped clear Reece's head. A bit too much if the tone was any indication.

"Can't an injured and currently homeless woman get some rest?" Aisling opened her eyes and gave Reece her family-patented once-over glare. Although her annoyance with him did chase away the last shakes her dreams had left in their wake.

"Ah, but good news, we've found you a place to stay. They were able to rescue a large number of your possessions that were on the street and we're moving them to a vacant apartment on the east side owned by the department."

Aisling shot him another glare then shook her head. She knew the type of place he was talking about, a crappy little safe house. Most likely a studio with a flophouse rejected bed.

"Nope, I'm going to stay at Maeve's." She raised a hand when he opened his mouth. "I am staying there. She said I could if I needed some time away from my house." No need to explain why Maeve had thought she might need a change of place—he didn't need to know that Maeve feared the house brownies would kick her out at some point.

Reece stood in the doorway, but his annoyance came forward in waves. "We need to keep you under—"

Aisling sat up completely and swung her feet out to the side of the bed. She thanked the gods that her legs didn't shake when she stood. "You are whatever in the hell it is you are, but I am a cop. Pure and simple, a cop. And a damned good one. Good cops are often threatened—it means we're doing our jobs." She turned away from him and grabbed some fresh clothes. Someone had been to her locker at the station and grabbed her spares for her. Obviously Surratt knew what happened. "I can't work on this case if I'm under guard and hidden. And I *will* be working on this case." She let a bit of her elven high-blood heritage reinforce her words. Her family was very old and very powerful, and possibly not as honest as they seemed. Centuries of that energy surrounded Reece. She didn't like to use that power; it would be difficult, at the least, if anyone figured out who her family was. But she was still mentally and emotionally wrung out and she needed him to back off on this.

Reece gave a little shake of his head and slightly narrowed his eyes. A huge uncontrolled reaction from someone like him. And one that added to her own theory about him. He claimed to be a half-fey, a human with a fey parent but no fey traits. Yet his reaction was one of a fey to her power.

She mentally added that to her notes. Worrying about his real heritage was possibly extremely low on the hierarchy of weirdness surrounding her right now, but the fact that they were now partners in this mess meant what he was could impact her and that moved it up on the need-to-know list. There might have been a damn good reason that vallenian was following them—a reason that had nothing to do with her.

"I know you think that you need to protect me, but isn't it more important to solve this damn case?" She stepped behind a screen and changed.

When she came out Reece was studying her carefully. Then he shook it off. "What case? Technically you aren't on the case."

She knew he meant the Julilynn Marcos case, but she also knew that he realized there was a much bigger case going on. One she was right in the middle of even if the police department wouldn't, or couldn't, admit it. That sent up another red flag for her to check into. She understood, mostly, why Surratt kept her off the flyer case. But he had to have known there was something bigger going on. He dumped her with Reece for a reason beyond simply throwing off any moles that might be in the force. If he couldn't admit there was something bigger going on, perhaps he was counting on her and Reece to resolve it.

A new twinge hit her head, joining the echo of both her nightmare and the explosion from the night before. Politics. She knew what would make Surratt suddenly go into stealth mode, especially when it meant he was going to have to work with someone like Reece. Only politics.

She sighed; give her good old serial killers over politicians anytime.

"What?"

"Nothing. There is a case and you and I both know it. What the brass and higher ups think is going on, I have no idea. And if I recall anything from last night, your higher ups don't know either." She brushed past him on her way out of the door. "You coming or what? We need to get my surviving possessions moved over to Maeve's, I need some non-hospital breakfast foods, and then we need to find some answers."

CHAPTER FOURTEEN

———◆———

ONE THING ABOUT REECE, ONCE he changed directions, he changed directions quickly. As much as Aisling felt breakfast should take precedence, he felt getting her possessions over to her new homestead should.

A moving van waited for them outside the hospital, not too shockingly it was driven by the same, "no, I'm not an assassin, just a driver—really" Agent Jones from the night before. That it was right outside the hospital exit was a bit exasperating though. Like right outside at the end of a short tunnel that meant she couldn't get a single clue as to where the hospital was.

"Well played," she muttered under her breath as she crawled into the passenger seat.

"Pardon?" As before, Agent Jones oozed polite concern. It did nothing to offset the knowledge that he could probably find eighteen different ways to kill her with nothing more than a washcloth.

Aisling smiled back. "Nothing. I assume my things are in the back?"

"All packed and ready. Agent Larkin will meet us there." He handed her an eye mask. "Unless you'd like to be knocked out again?"

Aisling debated fighting, but it was a useless and one-sided debate. She was good, and if she wanted to tap into her full abilities gifted to her by her family, she might be able to win a fight against Agent Jones. But it would still be a crap shoot and it would leave her in a far worse state if she lost.

"Fine." She settled the mask over her eyes. "Lead me home, Jones."

After about twenty minutes, more than a few of which she could tell they were going in circles, Jones finally pulled over. "You can take the mask off."

Aisling blinked in the bright morning sun. Maeve's ground floor condo seemed to be nicer than normal. Or it could be the head trauma talking.

"How much of my things survived? Maeve's a pack rat, so there may not be much room in there…" She let her sentence hang there as a crease darted between his brows. "What?"

"Your friend's place was empty. Didn't you know?"

Aisling bolted out of the car. There was no way Maeve could have cleared everything out—not in the time between her fake emergency and her flight. Although since the emergency was a fake, maybe she'd been planning it for a while.

Her hands shook as she undid the lock. No, she couldn't have had time. Aisling had been at Maeve's for drinks two nights before she left. Maeve was a major world traveler, and she never left a country without buying enough crap to support a family of five there for a year.

She couldn't have cleared everything out that quickly.

The lock stuck a bit, but finally she got the door open. Had Maeve had a landlord instead of being the owner, they would have been ecstatic—the place was not only empty, it was cleaned within an inch of its existence.

Aisling didn't say anything as she stalked throughout the rooms of the small condo. This needed to be treated like a crime scene—someone or something moved Maeve's belongings out of here. Two reasons to do that: one, there was something in her belongings that someone was after; two, someone wanted it to appear as if Maeve moved away of her own accord and wasn't coming back. Most likely the answer was a bit from each side and perpetrated by the same person or persons.

The rooms were professionally cleaned; on a hunch she brought out a mini black light scan wand that she kept in her pockets to scan for blood at crime scenes. She knew for a fact that there should be some drops leading to the downstairs bathroom. The party that led to them was etched in her mind.

But the scan revealed nothing.

"Damn it."

"I take it you didn't know she'd moved her entire household out?" Reece said from behind her. She hadn't heard him pull up his car or come inside.

Aisling widened her search, but nothing appeared. "She didn't move it; someone took it and cleaned the hell out of this place. There have been bloodstains here for the last two years. Couldn't see them anymore, but I know they were there. Look." She held the scanner out a bit so that he could see the confirmed nothingness.

"Maybe she was selling the place?"

"You may not have any friends in your job, I wouldn't doubt it." She put away the scanner and motioned to Agent Jones as to where she wanted her boxes. "But Maeve and I were friends. Best friends. Call each other if there is a body to hide friends. She wouldn't have done this."

Reece looked ready to argue, and then shrugged. "You're right that she's still the owner and no sales have been filed. But if that's the case, then this is a crime scene."

Jones had been about to put a pile of boxes on the floor, but then silently turned and took them back out.

She'd been counting on Maeve's familiar place and things to give her some comfort. Comfort she wasn't going to admit to the likes of Reece that she needed.

Instead she picked up one of the boxes Jones had brought

in earlier and started for the door. "Agreed. We need to get a team in here immediately."

What in the hell had Maeve gotten into? They'd been friends and partners for over ten years. While Aisling knew there were some things in Maeve's past that no one would ever know, she knew a hell of a lot about Maeve's life, and most importantly, she knew Maeve—there was no way that Maeve would take off like that. Not without leaving word.

Word.

Aisling dropped the box she was holding, ignoring the clatter it made. If Maeve knew she was in danger and was lying about why she left to everyone, even her best friend, she would have left word.

Now the question was where. It would have to have been something not in her possessions. Granted, Maeve might not have known that her things would all be lifted, but she wasn't stupid. If whatever was going on was bad enough for her to leave and lie, she would have figured it would only get worse.

"What are you doing? You can't stay here." Reece stood in front of her. "Crime scene, remember?"

"Shh, I'm thinking." Aisling closed her eyes and tried to tap into anything of Maeve in the room. The cleaners had been damn good; they'd done a psychic wipe of the rooms as well as a physical one. That spoke of big money. Fey who were strong enough to do a full psychic wipe were mostly hired by cops and agencies—anyone doing it freelance was walking a dangerous line and would charge accordingly for it.

There was not a single bit of Maeve's presence left in the living room, nor in the bedrooms, bathrooms, or dining room. But the smallest of sparks flickered from the kitchen.

However, Reece hovering right behind her was messing things up. The more she sent forth her senses, the more

Reece mentally intruded.

"Get out." She pointed toward the door, still concentrating on the spark in the next room. She didn't want to go into the kitchen until he was gone.

"There's nothing here, you can't—"

Aisling mentally tethered herself to the spark, then turned and begin pushing Reece. "I might have something, but I can't do anything unless this room is clear."

Reece let her push him out but didn't help. "Then what about Jones?"

Aisling glanced over her shoulder where the still black clad form of Jones stood. That she hadn't felt him when Reece was all but drowning her was spooky. And something else to be filed away for later thinking. Either Jones was that scary or she was having a specific reaction to Reece.

"Him too. I need both of you out. It may take a little while, so no one comes in until I come out." Her connection with the spark was fading. "Now. I need you both out now."

Jones didn't move, but his eyes were on Reece.

Reece watched her carefully, as if he was trying to read her mind by studying her face. Finally he shrugged. "Fine. Jones, we wait outside for her ladyship." He gave a half bow then turned and left, Jones followed with a nod.

Aisling let out a breath. He was being a smartass; he didn't know who she was. Shoving that fear aside, she turned and stalked toward the faint ember of psychic energy in the kitchen. It was weak, as if someone had deliberately kept emotions free of whatever it was when it was being placed. Since living beings left emotional fingerprints on almost everything they encountered, the extreme lack of such an energy indicated deliberate planning.

The kitchen was bare just like the rest of the house and Aisling moved into it quickly. Too quickly, the spark winked out of her mind. She carefully took a few steps back out, concentrating on the energy and slowing her heart rate.

There. A flicker across her inner eye caught her attention. It was coming from a high cabinet, the type built above the refrigerator that usually went unused since there was no way to easily get to it.

She needed to climb on the adjacent counter—it was doubtful that anything in there would be up front.

The cabinet appeared empty at first; she finally braced herself to be able to crawl into it as far as she could. The spark came from the back corner, but there was nothing there.

Unless…

She started tapping the back panel of the cabinet, the one that should have solid wall behind it. Sure enough, the lower corner gave a little. A few more well placed taps and a partition slid out. The revealed spot was mostly just dust and wood bits, but some digging revealed a small, rolled document. No more than six inches wide, it was pale and brown on the edges. The faded black ribbon tied around it appeared to be older than Aisling. Moreover, it was covered in Maeve's psychic presence. Now that she'd found it she let her senses relax to normal instead of keeping them hyper aware. A damn good thing because the moment she touched it a feeling of pure evil slammed into her mind.

CHAPTER FIFTEEN

———◆———

THE LEVEL OF HATRED THAT stabbed toward her mind knocked her off her perch on the counter. Only excellent balance and decades of training kept her from landing on her head. As it was, her left shoulder was going to have a nasty bruise by the end of the day.

After she rolled to her feet, Aisling sent a protect spell around the document that modified the hate and anger into a dull throb. This needed to be examined by the precinct magic users. Aisling was a decent one, but since she needed keep some of her skills under wraps, she probably shouldn't be digging into it herself. Not to mention there was way more to this scroll than paper, ink, and ribbon and having the resources of the entire force would be a benefit.

So then why was she rolling the scroll between her fingers and seriously thinking about unrolling it?

Damn it, she didn't know what Maeve had gotten herself into, and partners covered each other's asses, right? What if there was something on here that could ruin Maeve's career? A good best friend and partner would make sure everything was okay before she turned over evidence.

The reason for the negative mental blast she'd felt became obvious as she undid the first roll. The scroll wasn't ancient at all but made to appear that way—and a small spell token was glued inside the seal. The token would successfully keep any nosy humans away from the scroll without them knowing why. And most low-level magic users would see it as an ancient scroll and avoid it as well.

Unrolling it further brought a short burst of swear words on her part. Maeve had been in communication with the Irish mob. A note rolled inside the scroll was dated five years ago, a good five years after Maeve had supposedly cut all ties with her murky past back in England. Most of it was in code, and not one that Aisling recognized at first glance. The scroll outside the letter was completely illegible. It was elvish, but such an archaic form she couldn't even pick out a single word. Or there was a spell on it scrambling the words.

There was no way Reece would stay outside for long, and there was also no way she could let him, or the police, get a hold of this. At least not until she was able to decipher it and make sure it didn't incriminate her partner in some way. Another vote for dragging in her brother Caradoc; he could break any code.

Once the scroll was re-rolled, and securely hidden on her person, she did some deep breathing exercises and a few calming stretches. She had to appear calm and undisturbed. At least not more disturbed than she was when she came in here. Reece and Jones might only be human, but they were both so well trained they might as well have magic.

After a few mantras tossed in for good measure, and a check to make sure her heartbeat and breathing were normal, she went to go find the men.

"So? What did you find?" Reece was leaning against a tree right outside of the front door, managing to appear nondescript and sexy at the same time. Damn it. She was hanging around him too much if she was thinking he was sexy in that awful shapeless duster.

Chasing that thought away with a large nailed club, she shrugged and did her best to appear annoyed. Not hard considering her reaction to him. When this case was over, she was going to have to stay far away from him. Getting involved with a super spook like him would be worse than getting involved with another cop, and she'd sworn that would never happen.

"Nothing. I thought I sensed something in the dining area, but there wasn't anything." She glanced around the empty street. "Where's Jones? More importantly, where is the truck with all my things?"

Reece used his shoulder to push himself away from the tree. "Your belongings had to go somewhere. Jones went to go take it there, and I called Surratt about a new crime scene on his turf."

Luckily for Aisling, Reece's tone was condescending enough to get any inappropriate thoughts of him out of her head. That he didn't say anything as he turned and walked toward his car—assuming she would follow—helped also.

"What, the case of a missing cop too much for your alphabet agency?"

Reece had reached his car and finally turned. He didn't appear shocked that she remained near the tree, but he did nod to the passenger side of the car. "Not sure how else you're going to get anywhere unless you ride with me. As for the other, yeah, no offense, but a missing cop and her things are a bit below us." When she still didn't move, he rolled his eyes. "You wanted breakfast earlier, right? How about we go get something to eat, then you and Dixon can go report in."

What she wanted to do was find someone to help her with the scroll. Although the Irish mob was primarily human, and Maeve definitely was, the code appeared vaguely elven.

With a sigh, she tamped down her rising anxiety and let herself drift toward the car. "I thought they pulled us off the case after yesterday?"

Reece's smile made her want to turn and walk the other

direction. "Nope, we get to go back to the scene of the crime and see what was left behind. At least what's left after the big kids went through it. You're a benched homicide cop, and I'm a consultant; we don't rank high." He slid behind the wheel, not waiting until she was in before starting the car. "But first, food. I can hear your stomach all the way over here."

Breakfast was uneventful except that Reece ate enough food for three starving trolls—or one very hungry elf. On the whole, humans required much less food than most all of the fey races due to having far slower metabolisms. Reece seemed determined to break that rule every chance he got. And he was in good shape. The perpetual duster hid most of his physique but the muscles were noticeable when it was off—and when she'd been dragging him away from the explosion. That he might be something other than what he claimed got another tick in the yes column. She just wasn't sure what.

A quick change of appearance via the glam box, clothes, car, and demeanor later and Aisling found herself walking into the narcotics debriefing with Dixon.

"Hooking up with the consultants now, eh, Danaan?" Volpe said as they passed through the bullpen.

Aisling forced a grimace and shook her head. "Not in this lifetime. Just making him useful and getting a ride into work." She ignored the grunt of protest coming from Reece. *Dixon,* she reminded herself. No, even when he was Dixon or Leifen, there was still something uniquely Reece about him. That an entire police force couldn't tell was more than a little disturbing, but at least in her head she would keep with the one name.

The morning brief was smaller than last time, but when she asked about it all she got was the same grunt as before and a shrug. Reece was feeling peevish and, therefore, so was Dixon.

The updates were short, and Captain Losien ended with the biggest. "Thanks to Danaan and Dixon we have a good idea that it was the Scots mob behind the drug deaths, but it does appear that their top post and that of the Cymru mob were killed yesterday. They probably won't be active over here again for a while. Our department is still holding onto this case due to the drug connection, but I have to tell you all the feds want it badly—they know something about who killed those two and aren't going to share. If they push too hard they'll get the case in their laps and we'll be out. So let's make sure we solve this before that happens, shall we?" She dispersed the group but gestured toward Aisling and Reece to stay.

"We got the autopsy on our chopper victims." She raised her hand to ward off the question Aisling was about to launch. "Yes, they examined the pieces. Both of them had fairly high concentrations of the same drug they found in the flyer. It's officially being referred to as Iron Death and doesn't react like any known controlled substance."

Aisling shook her head. "Why…no, how…no, *why* would humans have an iron-based drug in them? Unless there's some high you folks get from it that no one knows about?"

Reece dug his hands in his pockets, a very Reece, and not very Dixon, move. He caught it a moment later and pulled them out. "Humans don't get anything from it, nothing positive anyway. How much are we talking about?"

Captain Losien turned to her computer screen. "Way more than what is healthy for a human."

Aisling studied the screen. Chem had never been one of her strong points, but those numbers were so bad even she recognized it. There was no way even a human could have that much Iron Death in their system and still be alive.

"Could anyone tell if they were alive when they blew up?" She'd seen them move in the chopper, or so she thought. It wouldn't be that hard to rig the helicopter to fly in on its own with a few well-placed spells. The Lazing had thought they were alive or they wouldn't have had snipers watching for them.

"We thought about that, too. Our early examination indicates the explosion killed them. They were alive until then."

"Which brings us to how were they surviving with such high concentrates of the Iron Death drug in their blood?"

"And why?" Reece reacted as if Losien had just slapped him and rubbed the side of his head, but Aisling couldn't tell what was actually going on.

"Why what?" Captain Losien didn't raise her head as she spoke, which was good in that she didn't see Reece's face.

He quickly recovered, so the shock wasn't showing on his face anymore, but he still looked off balance. Unfortunately, whatever had happened would have to wait until they were out of the station to discuss.

Aisling caught what he meant though. "Dixon doesn't think they were accidentally transporting that much Iron Death."

Captain Losien glanced from one to the other, then back to the screen. "You got that from this?"

Reece still appeared confused and worried. "No. But it makes sense. No one, fey or human, can carry that much Iron Death in their system and live. But I'd wager if the techs dig a little deeper, they might find there's a way the human blood stream is being shielded from the Iron Death at a molecular level." Reece started to shove his hands into his pockets again but caught himself and dropped into Dixon's slump.

Aisling tried to catch his eye; he was disturbed by something more than the drug for him to almost slip up twice. And in a building full of cops no less. Nothing seemed off to her, beyond the horror of this entire case.

"That's how they're getting this crap into the US?" Aisling whispered it but both heard her.

Reece stayed silent but a brief nod indicated that was his thought as well.

"How are you making that connection?" Losien turned to them with narrowed eyes and crossed arms.

Aisling liked Losien but she was one of the more suspicious people she knew. The fact that Aisling made a leap she hadn't yet gave her the idea that Aisling had information she hadn't shared. Even if she wouldn't say it out loud.

"Why else would they do this? Two top tier members, of two of the world's largest and most powerful mobs, carrying enough Iron Death in their systems to bring down dozens of people? And yet, they weren't affected?" Aisling said. "Julilynn Marcos was killed by a huge overdose of the same controlled iron product, and yet we haven't seen this drug coming in through any of the normal paths."

"So you think that it makes more sense that they are using themselves as mules? Their top two leaders?" Captain Losien closed her computer screen and shook her head. "I have a problem with your logic. But I'll pass the idea on to the eggheads downstairs to keep an eye out for it."

She all but pushed Reece and Aisling out the door. "Until then, you drag what information you can out of any contacts you can find—we need to know who blew up those mob bosses before the feds steal my case."

The door slammed shut before either Aisling or Reece could comment.

"What did you freak out about?" Aisling kept her voice low, but Reece responded with a tight shake of his head, followed by a frown. That, she understood. He wanted to wait until they got out of the precinct before they said anything.

She didn't know if the feeling that there were way too many eyes on her was real or a side effect of suddenly wondering if she was in enemy territory. But she couldn't get out of the building fast enough.

Reece kept silent until they were in Dixon's car. "Damn it. I never thought she was the mole until today. There were no indications she was anything other than what she appeared." He stared out over the steering wheel but Aisling couldn't see that anything was out there.

"Wait, you think Captain Losien is behind the Iron Death case? Where in the hell did that come from?"

He didn't answer at first, nor turn toward her, but the tightening of his jaw gave him away. "If she isn't, someone above her is. My agency had some tox screens pulled, they were able to grab some evidence before the cops got in. That screen she had of the tox results was doctored. The lines on the right were off. She wanted us to see it, maybe to make the conclusion we did. But I'm not sure if she's with the Scots or the Lazing."

He still hadn't turned toward her, but Aisling grabbed his face to force him to look at her. "Isn't that a bit of a jump? A mole? The Lazing?"

"I don't know, okay? Something is horrifically wrong, and I don't know. Rather, I didn't know."

He acted like he was slipping into shock. Aisling shook him hard. "What the hell is wrong with you?"

"I don't know what's going on. I don't know who is on what side and what the final game plan is. She's probably been the mole we were hunting for and I never picked up on it until today." He took a deep breath, "This doesn't happen to me. Ever."

Aisling let out her breath and relaxed her shoulders. "Is that all? I appreciate your super spook status, but no one ever knows everything in all of their cases. That's why we have to investigate things. Some never get solved, but we're nowhere near that with this one. What's bugging you?"

"I've been around her for over a year. And I never once

picked up on her duplicity. It hit me like a bullet when I saw the tox screen." Reece's gray eyes grew wide. "I always see the connections, always see where it's coming from even as I'm working the case. I didn't see this one." The last was muttered under his breath with finality and mourning that one would expect from someone who'd just been told they'd lost a limb.

CHAPTER SIXTEEN

A ISLING WAS AFRAID SHE WAS going to have to slap him. Not that she'd mind under normal conditions, but he looked horrible. They were still outside the police station and people were starting to watch them. *Cops* were watching them.

She shook his shoulder. "We need to move. If you're going to have a breakdown, crisis, whatever is going on, we need to get away from here." She shook him again when he didn't respond. "I will haul you out of that seat and drive your damn car."

He blinked and turned to her. "Sorry, this is an extremely disturbing feeling. I agree we need to get somewhere safe and sort it out. But we need to be seen out and about first." He started the car and moved into the road.

"And where is this place we are going to?" She was glad they were moving but he still seemed out of it.

"First, we'll go to the crime scene. At least be seen there for a bit. Then I want to see the area you found Mott Flowers in. We got him over to our hospital but he's still unconscious."

There was nothing new at the crime scene, just markers left from the narco and homicide squads, a pair of techs climbing over the collapsed wall, and some uniforms standing guard along the crime scene tape.

After a few hours of being seen and finding nothing, they went through some of Dixon's known areas. Aisling had no idea what he was searching for, and Reece wouldn't say. But whatever it was, he didn't find it.

Finally, he gave up and they headed toward the park. Reece parked down a side street a ways from it and they went down a walking trail to get to the place she'd found Mott. Given the closeness to the police station, a wise precaution.

Unlike the first scene, there was no police tape, no investigation. A mugging stopped by a cop, nothing more. Only a couple people knew there was more.

"We interviewed the two you caught after the cops locked them up, and the guys who were rolling him claimed to have found him dumped back there. Not sure why they brought him up this way where I found him." Aisling walked back toward a clump of bushes. It seemed Mott was on the run from many people, and yet the people who found him dumped him instead of killing him? There had to be a reason.

A piece of torn fabric similar to the shirt that Mott had been wearing was stuck on a branch.

Reece glanced from it to the ground. "He wasn't unconscious when they brought him here. This is where he tried to run." He pointed to another more scuffed-up area. "And they subdued him. Why didn't they kill him?"

"My thoughts too. Don't suppose since we're working together you can tell me why your agency, or one of them, is hunting for him? Beyond the vague information you already gave me?"

Reece got to his feet and dusted his hands off. "Nope. But if whoever grabbed Mott knew we wanted him, we'd never find his body." He glanced around as if noticing the time. It was already after five p.m.

"Now let's go where we can get some food and try and figure out what in the hell is going on in this city."

Aisling followed him toward his car.

"And where would that be?"

He turned back to her. "Your new place." His grin was more like his old insufferable self.

"How is going to a cop safe house going to be a good place for us to avoid cops?"

"Not a cop safe house, one of *ours*." His smiled faded and he kept walking. "One that is now going to be sold after this case is over since you'll know where it is. The fact that my superiors practically threw it at me for you, knowing they'd be dumping it after, is almost as disturbing as me being clueless."

He changed his hair, skin, and eyes back to his own with his glam box, and put his duster back on. Then got them on the road.

They headed toward the seedy side of the city, almost directly toward Old Town, but then he went on the freeway. Within ten minutes they were in an area that her mother might almost approve of.

"You've got a safe house in Gossamer Hill?" Aisling's eyes went wide as they rode through the rolling hills and elegant townhomes in the middle of the city. They closed in on a security gate. Had they been in Reece's normal car, it might have fit in; but she knew there was no way that Dixon's clunker wasn't going to cause notice here.

Reece lowered his window as they rolled up to the gate. He held up a badge, but put it away before Aisling could see it. It was good enough for the small, horned, fey guard, however.

The gates pulled back magically and Reece drove up the winding hill to the left.

"Okay, how in the hell is this subtle?" She glanced around at the splendor. More hills, more trees, flowers, even the buildings appeared plant-like.

"It's not," he said. "But sometimes hiding doesn't work, so hiding in plain sight does." He got an odd expression as he parked the car. "My superiors thought you'd feel at home here. I told them your clan, but someone must like your family." He shrugged. Most humans were vague at best in understanding the various elven clans and their statures. He seemed to understand them.

Aisling claimed a lower mid-level clan as her family in public. Yet, somehow, she had a feeling Reece's mysterious bosses knew who she really was. She'd be more upset, except that they clearly hadn't told Reece. Considering the group was so secret she was certain her mother didn't even know about them, her own secret was probably safe.

"I don't see how your car isn't being thrown out of here though."

Reece sheepishly flipped open a small panel on the dashboard. The control panel inside was not an original part of this car. Nor from any vehicle outside of a few secret agencies.

"A comp-skin?" Like the one they'd seen on that mysterious Quick car, this disguised the car itself. "What do people think they're seeing?" That explained far more than him flashing a badge of some sort as to why the guard let a piece of rusted crap inside the gates.

"An H-22 speedster." He smiled as they approached one of the two-story standalone homes. He hit another button and the garage door, which hadn't been visible up until that moment, appeared and opened. Reece drove in, and it shut silently behind them.

"Why does your agency have this kind of place as a safe house?"

Reece got out of the car and the lights in the garage trailed up a short stairway toward a door. "Sometimes we have high-end guests." He shrugged. "Until we brought your boxes over, I'd never seen it. Hopefully you'll be fine here without rented house brownies." His crooked smile told her he knew all about her problems with them even if she hadn't told him most of the details herself. "Brownies refuse to work up here, but we have enough tech to get around that."

He opened the door in timing with his words.

Aisling had grown up in extreme wealth, but she was impressed. The place wasn't huge, but this door opened to a state-of-the-art kitchen that was so elaborate it almost made her want to start learning to cook. And every piece of equipment appeared untouched. A small alcove built into the corner grabbed her attention.

"A food synthesizer?" Her father had been trying to get on a list for one for months. But her mother kept fighting him. She was older than he was and believed in the old ways. For some things.

"Yup. There are only a few in the world right now." He was far too smug as they went through the entire house. The living room was well enough furnished that it would make a showroom seem shabby. Two bedrooms upstairs were spacious and well appointed. Jones had obviously made it here hours ago, and the sad boxes of what was left of her townhome were rattier by comparison.

Once the tour was over, Reece sat her at the dining table, called up food and wine, and served dinner.

"Now you need to start talking, and fast." Aisling waved her fork around the room. "This isn't a normal safe house, and it sure isn't one an agency who had it would dump by letting me stay here and exposing it. Tell me what's going on." She took a long sip of the wine. Like most elves, her metabolism was too quick to be affected by wine or other human alcohol, but she did love the taste.

"There's only so much I can say," he said then raised his hand. "Seriously. I can't tell you who is behind this, and I'm not high enough in the organization to know the why for everything they do. This case, the one that includes Jul-ilynn Marcos, the drug cartels, Mott Flowers, Maeve, and you, is massive, that's all I know." The concern that flashed across his face was brief but telling. He wasn't lying and he was uncomfortable with whatever was going on.

That made her happy in a perverse way. At least she wasn't the only one freaked out about what had been happening.

"There is something big and nasty behind this, we're sucked in, and I'm trapped in a showroom." She glanced down and realized her food was almost gone, and so was the wine. "I still don't have answers."

Reece smiled and walked over to the synthesizer and got another plate for each of them. "If I had anything I could tell you, I might."

"Is there any word on Maeve?" She'd been deliberately trying to not think about her partner. Short of flying to England and trying to hunt her down herself, there wasn't much she could do.

The confident, lying Reece popped back into place. "We've had leads, but she's gone to ground. There's no evidence that she was in the house when it blew up though."

"I know you're blowing smoke. Your crack team of agents don't have a single lead, do they?" Aisling pushed back from the table.

Good on Maeve for hiding from everyone, but it didn't make Aisling feel any better about her missing friend. "You're as rattled as I am. You froze back at the station. You sat there in your car almost having a meltdown. Stop feeding me the same bullshit. Like it or not, we're trapped in this thing together."

Reece looked ready to argue, then shrugged. "Fine. No one can find her—or her body. They've reviewed enough footage to believe she hadn't been in her home in a week, but since even MI6 can't find her, no one knows for sure. Happy?"

"Thank you," Aisling said. "You *can* tell the truth sometimes." And the few times she'd caught him actually doing that were now making it easier for her to tell when he was lying—she didn't need to tell him that part. "Are we going to talk about the station now? Losien? Your freak out?" Without waiting for a response, she picked up her wine glass and moved to the living room. It would be a shame to not enjoy the luxury here.

Reece stayed at the table for a few moments, then wandered over. Unlike her, he didn't relax back into the soft furniture.

"I've always been able to see the game plan in a case. I might not see all of the players, not at first anyway. But I see where it's going. I screwed up on this one. I've been in that station undercover for a year, and I never picked up anything questionable from Losien. Nothing." He shook his head. "How did I miss her?"

Had this happened a few days ago, Aisling would have taken joy at his obvious impending breakdown. He'd always been one of the cockiest bastards she'd known—next to Surratt. Having grown up in a family of high-powered elves that said a lot. But seeing him like this was upsetting and not only because she had a feeling she needed him to get her out of whatever was going on.

"She could have shut us down because it was a long leap of an assumption." Aisling didn't believe it and from the look on his face Reece didn't either. She'd felt something was off this last time they'd spoken with Losien, a tension that hadn't been there before. But she wouldn't have thought much of it had Reece not noticed the changed tox results and had his freak out.

"I should have noticed." Reece dropped his head in his hands.

"What type of breed are you anyway?" Aisling asked. His reaction was far more of a muted fey sensitive than a talented human. Fey sensitives could lose their abilities through illness or injury—they usually didn't take it well.

"What?" That brought his head up and the look he gave her said he was leaving pity party-ville. "Not that it matters, but our family has water fey in our line. Ocean fey of some sort too, according to my grandmother."

Nymphs and Naiads. They were definitely sensitives. His reaction to being shut down on a skill that was more and more appearing to be beyond human intuition was making the hair on the back of her neck stand up. Human breeds had no gifts. That was how it was.

So what the hell was going on? Aisling was more sensitive than she let on, part of her cover of not being a member of the ruling families was to not disclose that. But even if she tried, she might not get to whatever was going on in Reece. If magical gifts were crossing the human-fey divide that could change everything. And not for the better. Fey were long lived and while some were mercurial, most of them mellowed after centuries of life. Humans were too young and violent to have such gifts.

She had wanted to pull in her brother Caradoc before, but now she really needed him.

She'd drifted off into her own thoughts, but now Reece was narrowing his eyes at her.

"You think that has bearing?"

"No, of course not. But there have been some studies done on the influence of fey blood in breeds." Aisling scrambled; she wasn't an academic sort, and Reece knew that. "My brother has been doing some research on the topic. I think he'd like to talk to you, might be able to shed some light."

"I didn't know you had a brother." A scowl joined the narrowed eyes. "Your family information didn't mention siblings."

"He's much older. And what the hell are you doing going into my private files?" She knew he hadn't seen her real files, but maybe pushing back at him would get him back to something resembling normal.

"I have my reasons," he said. "But if your mysterious brother can help me figure out what's messing up my psyche—sure. If the connection is within the station, we can't risk tipping our hand."

Aisling nodded and pulled out her phone. She had a message sent to Caradoc before Reece could reconsider.

"I didn't mean bring him here."

"It's being burned by your agency, right? We need to figure this out sooner rather than later and my brother can be hard to pin down." She shook her head and lowered the phone. "Most likely he won't respond for a bit. He goes off on his own a lot."

He leaned back with a sigh. "Fine."

She needed to keep digging at what he knew. "Do you think Surratt is working with Losien?" It would help explain so much within her life if he was one of the bad guys.

His smirk burst her delusions. "He's done a good job, hasn't he? But no. He's actually working with the agency and has been for the past eighty years."

"What? He's human. I would swear he is full human, not even any breed." Now it was Aisling's turn to lean back. "Damn it. High family shifter fey. It's illegal as hell for them to hide as human, you know that." The shifters were a specialized fey line—and fortunately a small one. They rarely had successful births. If she hadn't been blocking who she really was the entire time she was around Surratt, she would have sensed him at some point over the past twenty years. But her block worked both ways and numbed her own sensitivity.

"The agency works with its own rules." The smug bastard was back. He might only be a smaller cog in the massive beast, but he was part of it and that was enough for him.

Before she could respond, or chase him off and get some

sleep, Reece's shirt pocket started buzzing.

His phone was one of the newer high-end ones that started as a small tab, then expanded on command. "Reece." The heavy line that had appeared between his brows when he glanced at the caller ID didn't bode well. Now that the idea of a good night's sleep had crawled into her head, Aisling wanted to follow through.

"Understood. We'll be there." He closed his phone and silently put it back in his pocket. The line between his brows dug itself deeper.

Aisling gave him a few seconds. "Well? We'll be where? What's happened?"

"Another iron overdose. Male fey this time, but also a flyer."

CHAPTER SEVENTEEN

AISLING SWORE. "DAMN IT. THAT wasn't the cops on the phone, was it? Where this time?"

"Down in the lake district. Yeah, that was my superior, my *real* superior," he said with enough emphasis on 'real' that Aisling knew he hated telling the truth. "He's annexing you, unofficially, for this case. Surratt knows." He sighed, got to his feet, and walked to where he'd left his duster. "Your tat is still hidden, right?"

Aisling hadn't gotten off the sofa yet but she raised her arm and pulled back her sleeve. "Nothing to see here." She rubbed it self-consciously. She'd been on the force over twenty years and probably only gone undercover twice. But being without her badge tattoo being visible made her feel under-dressed. She'd be glad when they took the glamour off and she could get back to life as normal.

She stood and Reece shook his head. "You might want to change. All black at a crime scene might make people think police detective. We want them thinking fed consultant if they notice you."

She stared him down, then surrendered, and went upstairs to the larger bedroom. His tread was quiet, but Reece was right behind her. "I don't need you to pick out my clothes." That was where she drew the line.

"I think guidance would be a good idea. The flyer crashed in the club zone—you need to look like you belong there." He held up his hands and motioned to the luxurious rooms. "And not here."

"Jeans, flats, and a t-shirt and jacket. Providing they survived the explosion. Is that okay with you?"

He nodded. "That'll do. You have a gun?"

She pulled back from the room she was about to enter. "My service pistol. But I can't take it if I'm not supposed to look like a cop."

He held out a small snub gun. It was legal—barely. "Keep it in the small of your back."

Aisling wasn't going to argue about the levels of deception going on right now. She took the small gun, then slammed the bedroom door in his face.

She had changed and was just tucking the gun in her waistband when her phone rang. Caradoc, her brother.

"Took you long enough."

"How is my favorite baby sister?"

"I am your only baby sister," Aisling had automatically gone for her boots, but grabbed her running shoes instead. She'd bought them ten years ago and they were still pristine.

"Looks like you've been having an interesting time lately, even Mother is picking up your distress."

Damn it. That was not what she needed. "Can you assure her I'm fine? Slip her one of your cocktails maybe? I need to talk to you. The coordinates are in your phone—but I'll be gone for a bit. It's a spook house, but make sure they don't see you when you come in." Caradoc was almost as underground in terms of denying the family connection as she was. But she didn't want the wrong people knowing who he was.

"The second death flyer?"

Aisling was reaching for the bedroom door when he said that. She froze. Her brother was a tech hound and a strong magic user. But how in the hell had he known about the flyer?

"What did you say?"

His laugh was low. "You heard me. I think I need to see it as well. I'll meet you and your fed boy toy at the event."

"He's not my boy toy, and no one says that anymore." She shook her head; he was distracting her. "How in the hell did you know?"

"I have my ways. Your handsome friend is becoming impatient. Tell him a few more minutes will save him in the long run. See you in a bit." He clicked off before she could respond.

It took a second for her to realize he had said 'death' flyer, not dead flyer. That was another thing to grill him on—once they got away from Reece. If he knew about the deaths, and knew where they were, she certainly didn't have the ability to stop him from appearing at the crime scene. She flung open the door and almost had Reece knocking on her face.

"Sorry, but we need to go. Who was on the phone?" He didn't wait but turned and jogged down the stairs.

She took her brother's words to heart—if he said to slow down, she would slow them down. She dropped to re-tie her shoes. "Hold on a second, the laces are loose. It was my brother, checking in. He might be able to help you." She hadn't mentioned Reece's issues, but she knew if anyone could help it would be Caradoc. Satisfied that she'd delayed a bit, she got to her feet and passed him in the living room. "Are you coming?"

The drive to the district wasn't long and both of them stayed wrapped in their own thoughts. Aisling was trying to figure out what Caradoc's angle was. Her brother was a semi-socialite and tech business magnate. If he knew about the flyers, he was connected to them in some way. She had no idea what was going on in Reece's head.

They were turning into the housing area for the district, a rundown slum surrounded by dance clubs that had once been the height of living for the middle class fey, when sirens came from behind. A fire truck and ambu-lance passed them as Reece pulled over.

In the next block, two cars were engulfed in flames and police motioned them past. Two other cars were in the accident, but weren't engulfed yet. The entire street was glowing orange and red.

Reece shook his head as a cop sent them through the small space allowing cars to leave the area. "Good thing you're fussy about your shoelaces. That just happened and we would have been in it."

A chill went through Aisling. Not so much at her brother knowing about this ahead of time, while he wasn't near the level of sensitive that their oldest brother Harlie was, he had some flashes from time to time. She was more upset that she couldn't figure out how the accident had hap-pened. This wasn't a wide street and was heavily travelled enough that building up speed for that bad of a collision should have been impossible. As they made their way past, she noticed that the cars resembled toys where a child had picked them up and smashed them together in a fit of rage.

"Did you see something?" Reece was focusing on get-ting through the space that opened up so wasn't looking at the wreckage itself.

"Not sure."

Unlike the first flyer incident, most of the buildings were standing. But as they pulled closer it was clear that some-thing had slammed into a number of them, just not at the same level of destruction as Julilynn Marcos. The scene was blocked off and two cops that Aisling didn't know stood watch with their hands on their weapons. This wasn't her precinct's district, so she hadn't been expecting her own officers, but she knew a number of cops from the nearby districts.

Reece stopped the car and dropped the window. He held up his badge before the cop could ask.

The cop nodded and peered inside the car. "Agent Larkin, we can let you in. And this is?"

Before Aisling could respond, Reece jumped in. "My CI. She has intel on the problems. There have been connected events."

The cop was old school and narrowed his eyes as he peered around Reece to Aisling. Finally he nodded and hit his communication badge. "Two coming in. Special Agent Larkin and…"

"Clarabeth Jones." Reece again jumped in before her.

"Clarabeth Jones, his CI. They have access." The cop's eyebrow shot up at Reece's name for her.

A tingling and disturbing feeling slid up her spine as they passed the blockade. They couldn't go fast, so she had time to study everything around them for the source, but nothing specific appeared to be causing her reaction.

The team involved had already gotten some spotlights on the scene, magically driven giant lights. While the damage to the surrounding buildings wasn't as widespread as in Julilynn's case, it was still catastrophic. The building they pulled in front of was half missing and would have to be torn down.

The disturbing feeling that had hit her when they drove up was getting worse. She wasn't a true sensitive—there were fey who could pick up a situation at five miles out—but all elves had some sensitivity to psychic instabilities. And right now Aisling's was going off the charts. It took far more will than it should have to push open the car door.

"Are you okay?" Reece was standing next to her door.

Aisling had taken so long to get out of the car that Reece had time to get out on his side and come around to hers. She got out and rubbed her arms. "I'm fine." She couldn't explain what she was feeling to herself, she certainly wasn't going to try and explain it to someone like him.

"Are you actually cold?" He almost looked ready to hand her his duster.

"No. I'm fine. Shall we see what happened?" She stalked past him. The feeling of ill ease got worse the closer she got to the focus of the lights. And cops. And judging by the clothing—more feds. A quick glance told her Caradoc wasn't here—or at least he didn't want anyone to see he was here.

The cops didn't block their way, and after a glance at Reece, neither did the feds. They stepped back to let her and Reece through.

Aside from the increased creepy feeling, the scene was a lot like the one of Julilynn Marcos. A golden-green male fairy was curled up before them. At first it looked like he'd not suffered the same mutations that Julilynn had, and then the wing came into view. It wasn't attached to him anymore and seemed more like a twisted art installation rather than a body part. On his final crash, the weight of it must have sheered it from his body. Aisling hoped that he'd died before that happened.

"Agent Larkin, thank you for coming so quickly." The man before them wasn't human, but beyond that it wasn't clear what he was. A true mixed fey was rare, most fey-breeds took after one parent. But he looked like not only was he true-mixed, both of his parents had been as well.

"How long ago was this called in?"

Aisling tuned the standard questions out; she was still listening if anything pertinent came out, but there was always that layer of telling each other what they knew on a case. Even though Reece's contact most likely filled him in when he first called him. Cops and feds always did an exchange of information, more as a courtesy ritual of introduction to a case. Over years on the force, Aisling had developed the ability to use that time to analyze the scene on her own—without appearing to disregard the other cop. It was easier to do when she wasn't the one being spoken to.

CIs were used differently by different agencies. Right now, the rest of the law enforcement around her were trying to figure out if she'd been mob or drugs before she came clean and became Reece's CI, and one high enough to have a special license for a gun.

Another chill hit her, and this wasn't subtle. No slow cooling of the soul, this was as if death itself had body slammed her. Had she not been focusing on her surroundings and the flyer, it would have knocked her to her knees.

And it came from right in front of her. The body wasn't doing it, but the crowd directly across from her had parted. She doubted that they even knew why. A dark shape, vague and disturbing, flowed into the space—a vallenian.

She dropped her gaze and focused back on the body. Her own body wasn't playing nice and it took her precious seconds to get her heart rate back to normal. Two sightings of the beings in as many days couldn't be coincidence. This was something she actually needed to notify her mother about considering her stature on the High Council. Providing she and everyone in the immediate vicinity survived the next few minutes.

CHAPTER EIGHTEEN

THE VALLENIAN BENT LOW AS if sniffing the ground. Even though Aisling was focusing on the body before her, she was also keeping a perception of the creature open. It was a way of watching but not watching favored by the higher elven caste levels. As with all of her growing up, she'd had no choice about learning it—but for once in her life, she was grateful for it.

She ignored the building pressure in her head but tried to recall the feeling—she knew both her mother and her brother would be asking detailed questions about this encounter. Even her mother, with all her advanced years, had never admitted to seeing a vallenian. Of course, anyone who viewed one was supposedly on their way to death, so there was that.

The creature sniffed the body, then gazed around the oblivious crowd and vanished. The removal of the pressure in her head sent Aisling stumbling forward a step. She caught herself before actually falling into the crime scene.

Reece grabbed her arm. "Are you okay?" His voice was low and actual concern flashed across his face.

"Yes, just a bit unbalanced." She nodded toward the body in front of them. "That is unsettling, to say the least. Especially for full fey." Shoving the horror of another vallenian sighting aside, she focused on the body. Aside from the wing being torn off as he crashed to the ground, the dead flyer had far less damage to his body than Julilynn Marcos had. She glanced at the buildings still standing around them. He'd also caused less damage before he died.

Considering that Julilynn was about half the size of the man, she should have collapsed first if they both had an equal dose of the drug. And if the strength was similar. In days, whatever had caused these deaths had grown significantly more deadly, as this male fairy died much quicker than Julilynn, based on the time between him going feral and when he died. It appeared that the Scottish and Cymru mobsters had died smuggling something in their bodies, but hadn't been impacted by it. Had these two also been smuggling drugs and somehow whatever kept them safe dissolved?

Aisling shuddered both at what kind of drug could do that and at any fey who would be that desperate to risk becoming a drug mule for something that horrific. Unless they brought the killer iron drug in unawares. "The coroner should test for more traditional drugs as well as whatever killed him." She kept her voice low, more to herself, but Reece's grunt indicated he'd heard her. With a nod, he stepped toward two dark suited men nearer the body and started asking questions.

"Gruesome, isn't it."

Aisling startled at the voice behind her but didn't jump. She hadn't heard her brother creep up. Nor did she have a clue as to how he got into an extremely guarded crime scene. He was unlike their mother in almost everything, but an unnatural ability to move into places unnoticed but in plain sight was one thing they shared.

"How are you in here? This is a crime scene after all." Aisling didn't turn but shook her head. "Never mind, I don't want to know. Do you know anything about this?"

"Not at all. In fact, no one on the council does, and it's worrying them."

The somber tone in his voice caused her to turn to him. Nothing caused the council to worry. At least not since the

Black Death curtailed the humans' evolutionary lead in reproduction. Over two thousand years of non-worrying.

"Does *she* know I'm investigating?" Her mother hadn't acted as if she did, but she didn't acknowledge what Aisling did unless it impacted the family.

"No. I'd keep it that way. Right now, she's only on the fringe regarding information about this. The High Council's scientists are stepping in as much as they can without appearing to do so." His tone of voice echoed what she felt. The elven High Council wasn't a secret, but they appeared to be more figurehead than anything. In reality, they were far more powerful than anyone, even other elves outside of the ruling families, knew.

Aisling couldn't help but smile at her brother. Tall, dark blond hair, and sharp blue eyes left him noticeable wherever he went. Yet he often had a disheveled air about him, as if he was a university professor who'd been tricked into coming out of his lair. The times he wasn't a rumpled academic, he was glammed up and on magazine sites. The two sides of Caradoc were refreshing, not like the rest of their family.

"How are you here by the way?" She turned back to the body. The coroners were taking measurements at the direction of the feds. Reece went to ask more questions.

"They all think they see someone they expect, but not who I am." He shrugged. "A twist on a standard glamour spell that I've been experimenting with." His smile dropped. "But there is more than that body and the one from before. Something else is chilling your soul."

She couldn't bring herself to say the word—not even to him. At first, she thought it was simply a healthy dose of fear, then she realized that she physically couldn't. No matter how hard she tried, the word vallenian would not come out. Was that how they managed to not be seen? They were actually seen but no one could talk of them?

"This is bad. Something that can make my little sister silent." The words were light, but heavy at the same time. He couldn't tell what she'd seen but he knew it was bad. "I've seen what I need to, and I know where you're staying. I'll find you in a bit." With a whisper he vanished.

She knew he'd actually been standing there, but he was gone. Even for one as powerful and inventive as her brother, that was a new trick. She'd have to ask him how he did it later. The attempt to say that she'd seen a vallenian had caused a massive headache. The council and other high-powered elves had speculated that although some Old Ones made brief trips to this world, the vallenians hadn't; they couldn't. Obviously, both assumptions were wrong.

Reece came back from his brief conference with two other mysterious fed types. Both were dressed more appropriately in Aisling's opinion. Black suits, white shirts, black ties. Reece didn't fit in with them and they were supposedly his kind. "They are going to run a full tox screen—and see what differences there are between this one and Julilynn. The iron component is making it almost impossible to scan for anything. Including what caused the iron." He started walking back to the car.

Aisling glanced back. The human coroner loaded the body onto a floater gurney and led it to the ambulance. The rest of the cops and feds continued to search for anything that could explain what happened. Normally, she'd be right there with them. A case of this magnitude, even if the general population needed to be kept in the dark, was a career maker. Not to mention terrifying on a personal level. But between what she'd seen and the headache that was still adding new layers, she couldn't wait to get clear of there.

They silently got into Reece's car.

"So aside from the fact that there are now two, this didn't

help resolve the first case at all. Did they have an ID on the victim?" Aisling was expecting him to pull the car out quickly and braced herself.

He did as expected but his response was slow to come. "This confirms it wasn't a one-off aberration, but something much larger." He weaved in and out of traffic, the prior accident had been cleared; most likely by a troll gang.

Aisling waited until he was on the freeway before nudging him. "Are you going to share? Or try to see if you can get us to slam into another car?"

"Damn it, sorry. I'm still not getting a handle on this case and it's eating at me." He shot her a sideways look. "They did ID the flyer and you're not going to like it. He'd only been in LA a few days. Over from the UK. Irish national, but he'd been living in London for the last twelve years—he worked with your partner with MI6 before she left and came here."

Aisling swore under her breath. She knew Maeve. A week ago, she would have told anyone who asked everything about her friend and police partner. In the last few days, that had been blown to hell. Aisling never realized there were so many parts that Maeve kept hidden. And if she'd questioned Maeve's involvement in this case before, there was no question now.

"What's his name?"

"Ryn Trebol. He had been MI6, then went rogue a year before Maeve came here. Was running with some shady types, but I couldn't get much in the way of details yet."

"Damn it, what were you involved with, Maeve?" She'd muttered it under her breath, but Reece's hearing was almost as sharp as some fey.

"You had no idea? Nothing that, thinking back, you might have missed?"

Aisling stared at him, but he kept his eyes on the freeway. There was far too much studied nonchalance in his tone.

"Has she been a major suspect this entire time?" Aisling swore as things started snapping into place. "Is that why I was targeted? By you? Your agency? By Surratt? Was my name planted next to that flyer?" The level of what in the hell was going on was hitting her like a slap in the face.

"No!" He turned to her then quickly faced the road. "Your name in the sand was legit. The people who initially found the flyer and reported it sent in photos with that already there. Our mages confirmed it was spelled there and targeted for you."

Aisling gave him a second while he turned at the exit. "The rest? What the hell is going on, Reece?"

He brought the car to a stop outside the safe house, but didn't open the garage. "I can't tell you." He raised both hands in defense. "I don't know. Seriously. I was told to investigate this and a number of other cases that kept being tied in. You seem to be the center. Or Maeve is and you're adjacent. Either way, none of my agencies are telling me. Take time and think things through. I can get you some time at least."

Aisling stared at him for a few moments; when he didn't budge, she dropped it. "I'm going back to narco tomorrow and doing my job. I'll also find another place to stay as soon as I can. Tell your agency to go to hell." She slammed the car door and marched to the front of the safe house. There was a moment's pause, these houses were coded with fingerprint idents. She had no idea whether they'd logged her in to the front door or not. She let out a sigh when she grabbed the handle and it popped open.

The sigh changed when she entered the front room.

"Aisling, we need to talk. I'm in trouble." Maeve sat on the sofa, leaking blood.

CHAPTER NINETEEN

M AEVE HALITHI WAS PURE HUMAN but almost as
tall and slender as Aisling. Her dark skin and ice blue
eyes spoke of her mixed human heritage. Normally dark
skin. She was almost paler than Aisling right now, and her
attempt to rise to her feet when Aisling came in dropped
her back to the sofa. "Whoever owns this place probably
won't be happy about the blood—sorry about that." Her
normally clipped British accent was slurred, most likely
from blood loss.

Aisling ran forward. There was blood, but not enough to
account for the condition of her friend. "Where are you
hurt?" She tried to gently push her to lay down, then with
more force when Maeve had enough strength to try to
fight back. "Stay down, damn you."

"It's not a new injury, but I re-opened it getting here.
Daft rookie move." Maeve lifted the edge of her shirt and
exposed bloody bandages. No idea what the wound looked
like, but at least it appeared they'd missed her gut. There
were a number of bruises around the bandage as well.

"Can you climb up those stairs?" Aisling shook her head
at herself before Maeve could respond. "Never mind, I'm
going to have to heal you here." She sat on the ground
next to the sofa and started to drop into a trance.

"No, you can't." Maeve swung her hand to push Aisling's
arm aside but didn't have the strength.

"And you're going to stop me how?" That was a common joke between them, but Maeve wasn't smiling.

"You can't. They might have put things in my blood when they hurt me." Maeve winced as a wave of pain hit her. She took a deep breath and a second one until it passed. "I think it's iron. Pure iron."

Aisling scooted back so quickly Maeve most likely didn't see her move. "What? Who? We have to get you to a hospital." The terror that hit her was real. If Maeve were somehow carrying pure iron in her blood, then touching Maeve in a healing trance would have killed Aisling in seconds. Aisling was on her feet immediately, gauging the risk of taking Maeve into an exposed hospital or taking their chances here. Without Aisling being able to touch her... She shook her head and pulled out her phone.

"What are you doing? You can't send me to the hospital. They'll find me, and if they did what I think they did, I'm deadly to any fey there."

"I'm not going to sit here and watch you die. No matter how pissed I think I might be at you for doing stupid shit. Without me," Aisling stopped dialing but didn't put her phone away, "what are the options?"

"You can both stand down and let my people take care of this," Reece's voice came from the kitchen behind her. "We have a secure hospital."

Aisling swore and turned. She had been so focused on Maeve and the iron she hadn't heard him sneak in. Should have known that bastard would come in anyway. "Get out. You're not taking her in. And I thought you were letting me have time." Yes, Maeve needed a healer, but Aisling knew if he got her into his agency, Maeve wasn't coming back out. Being a person of interest to any of the higher agencies was dangerous, if not deadly.

"He was, but that changed because of me," Caradoc said as he stepped out from the garage doorway as well. "Sorry, Aisling. I came to meet you, saw Maeve break in, and then noticed this one sitting in his car arguing with himself."

Aisling held up her hands to motion for them to stay back as both Reece and Caradoc moved into the living room. "She might have iron in her blood. None of us, including Reece, can touch her." Even a breed like Reece could be destroyed by iron; it would just take longer.

Caradoc came a step forward anyway and knelt a few chair lengths away from Maeve. He closed his eyes. "Keep an eye on your friend there—he's thinking of running for it."

Aisling gave Reece a grim smile and took a step closer to him. "I don't care who you work for. If you move toward your gun, the door, or your phone, I will take you down."

Reece slowly raised both of his empty hands and kept them up. "I'll stay here. But my people have this place monitored. If he saw her come in, they would have as well."

"I'm not that sloppy, Larkin." Maeve bit her lip as a spasm of pain slammed into her. "Caradoc has skills that your people dream about." Maeve had met Caradoc once, a year ago. But based on the way she followed him on social media and the tabloids, Aisling was pretty sure Maeve had a crush on him that she wouldn't admit to.

Caradoc didn't move for a full two minutes. Finally, he rolled to his feet and shook himself like a dog after a cold bath. "No iron beyond what is normally in human blood. But they've done some damage and there are traces of a number of other components that shouldn't be there."

The iron in human blood wasn't a danger to fey. There were old wives' tales that before, when the humans outnumbered the fey, their blood was different, more dangerous. Like so much of this world, that changed after the Black Death.

"Is it safe for me to heal her? And what are we going to do with him?" Aisling was ready to step forward but wanted her brother to watch Reece.

Caradoc stepped backwards next to Reece. "Yes, you

can, but don't drain yourself too much. I have a feeling you won't be staying here long." He nodded to Reece who raised his hands higher.

Aisling went to Maeve and resumed her seat on the floor. Trusting that her brother could keep Reece under control with whatever means necessary, she slipped into a healing trance.

The severity of Maeve's wounds was bad. The one at her waist was the largest and most threatening, but many of the smaller ones were poisoned. Not with iron, she trusted her brother on that. Something else, but she couldn't get a good enough feel to determine what.

Normally, Aisling's healings flowed easily. She wasn't strong enough to completely heal this many wounds, but she could usually heal them enough to allow Maeve to recover quickly on her own. This time it felt like both Maeve's body and her own were fighting back at her. She was able to close the major wound when she felt herself fall over onto the carpet.

"Aisling!" Caradoc ran forward and helped her back up. Maeve sat up on the sofa, and Reece spun toward the back door.

The door swung open and Jones, Reece's resident assassin, stepped in holding a monstrous sized gun.

"I'm not sure all of what's going on. This place has too many protections on it for me to get a bug in. But for now, all of you stay where you are." He nodded to Reece.

"Now, there's no reason to think that our agency means you harm, Maeve. And we can help you. Even if you don't have pure iron in your blood, you said you don't want to be found." Reece moved for his phone.

"Not by your lot," Maeve said as she shook her head. "Your people are chasing me too. You forget, I was MI6, I've seen what happens to people an agency is *interested* in."

"And you'll not be calling anyone." Caradoc held out his

closed fist and a small bolt of electricity leapt from it to Reece's phone.

Reece swore and threw the phone across the room. He shook his hand in pain, revealing black scorch marks that now crossed his palm. "What the hell?"

If Caradoc was concerned about Jones holding a gun on him he didn't show it. He held open his hand. A small triangle of metal parts sat there with a few lights flashing then slowly stopping. "New toy. I think the reliance on magic that our society has is unhealthy and potentially dangerous. This can disable any magic-based gizmos." He tipped his head toward Jones. "Including your rifle there. This thing loves blowing up guns of any sort. Might not seem like it, but the firing mechanism of that weapon of yours has a tiny component of magic. You can put it down slowly, or I can see how much of a mark exploding something that big leaves on you." He glanced around. "And the room."

Jones didn't throw his weapon, but he did quickly drop it to the ground. He kept watching Caradoc's face the entire time.

"Thank you," Caradoc said. "Now, Aisling, if you would be so good as to remove the rifle from temptation. Then frisk them for anything else that might cause us problems."

Aisling moved the rifle to the far end of the room and kicked it under the console. After she pulled all of the charges from it.

Searching Jones was an exercise in find-all-the-sneaky-weapons. Twenty small firearms, knives, garrotes, and a few throwing stars later she tipped her head in his direction. "That is a serious collection." She also removed his phone and a small tracking device, used by many fed agencies, and tossed them on the pile.

She started to move to Reece when Caradoc made a tsking sound. "Not your fault, sister of mine, but the one you just searched has two more, extremely illegal, and very magical stiak weapons. He can either remove them himself or I fry them."

Aisling swore. Stiak weapons were on the level of trancer guns—illegal and deadly. And almost untraceable.

Jones held Caradoc's glare for a full five seconds, then swore and reached around to the small of his back and pulled out the two tiny weapons.

"Disable them as well." Aisling had only seen them in vids, but she knew they could be triggered to explode if an unauthorized user touched them.

Jones shared his glare with her then flicked a small button on each. Aisling didn't move forward to take them until Caradoc nodded.

She turned to Reece. "Pat you down, or surrender the weapons the easy way?" Aisling knew that under normal circumstances Reece would fight before he'd surrender his weapons. But he'd seen what her brother could do, and it was clear the electrical burn on the palm of his hand was hurting.

He didn't say anything but removed a collection of weapons almost as impressive as Jones'. "We're not your enemy. None of yours." He focused on Maeve longer than the other two. "Our agency can help you."

"And which one is that again?" Aisling moved all of the confiscated weapons next to Caradoc. She wasn't going to take the time to remove rounds from all the guns. The standing hairs on the back of her neck told her Caradoc was right about not having a lot of time.

Maeve stayed silent, but Aisling noticed she was moving around more. Still staying low, but Aisling would bet she was preparing her own weapons and was more recovered than she was trying to appear.

"I can't tell you, not even now." Reece locked his fingers together over the top of his head. Jones paused, and then did the same.

"Do you have anything that I can use to tie them up?" Aisling didn't recall seeing anything in the house, but she hadn't spent much time here. Caradoc had been full of surprises so far.

But not this time. "Sorry, didn't think to bring that."

"I do." Maeve winced as she got to her feet, but she looked a lot closer to normal now as she got up and walked to a duffle bag tucked behind the sofa. "Wasn't sure why I might need it, but better to have it. It's elven." The grin on her face was matched by Aisling as she tossed her a coil of dark green rope.

Elven rope was impossible to cut. It could eventually be undone, but unless someone was trained in it—and a full-blooded elf—you weren't going to get out of it for a while.

Aisling took the ropes and tied up both men. She tied them to chairs and the chairs were tied to opposite sides of the table. "Now what?"

Maeve hobbled over to the front window, then swore and stepped back out of range. "They might not have seen me or Caradoc, but there is a slow-moving car out there."

Caradoc swore and aimed his disabling gizmo at the light panels. The entire house went dark.

His swearing continued in amount but reduced in volume. "That wasn't me."

CHAPTER TWENTY

"**D**AMN IT, THEN WHO DID it? Reece?" Aisling dropped down to be less of a target if anyone was aiming through the windows, and she and Maeve moved closer to Caradoc.

"It wasn't our people," Reece said. "Unless you called in, Jones?"

Jones grunted in what sounded like a negative.

"We can guess it's not any of the assorted good guys. It's the bad guys and it's me they're after," Maeve said. "I shouldn't have come here. Although even the good guys seem to be looking for me unfavorably." She glared at Reece.

Aisling stayed low, but blocked her friend as she started to move toward the door. There was little light coming from outside and she knew she and her brother had the advantage over the other three in terms of night vision. "You should have kept in contact with me and not lied about going to visit family. Coming to find me now was actually a smart move."

"It was." Caradoc came up behind Maeve and yanked a few hairs. "And now it's time for Maeve to go." He held his hand over the hairs and the softest of glows emitted from them. Then they merged into his skin. "Whoever is hunting you will read me as you for now. This will work for about an hour, but after that however they are tracking you will revert back to the real you again. Once I'm gone, gather everything that's yours and flee. Both of you."

He placed a tracker in Aisling's hand. Another piece of elven tech-magic, it had a direction and location built in. It would lead her to somewhere he considered safe. "I've already removed your boxes from upstairs—they're safe for now. But do a full sweep for anything else of yours here." Magic sweeps meant everything would be cleansed. But they could raise flags if the right type of magic user came across one.

He raced out the garage door, but even had the lights still been on, she doubted the other three would have been able to see him. She went around the living room and kitchen, turning off all the light switches. If whoever dropped the lights put them back up, she didn't want them to see inside the house.

"What about us? If there is someone out there and they know who *we* are?" Reece said.

Aisling shook off the flash of concern she had. "Does anyone really know who either of you are?" Since the lights were still out, she knew she could see their faces, but the reverse wasn't true. "The people chasing Maeve will follow Caradoc and, trust me, my brother could get someone lost in their own house. And I'm sure your people will realize what happened and be here soon enough."

"The car has turned and is quickly leaving the area." Maeve had crept up to the window on her knees and peeked out the window. "Damn it, there was a second one as well, next street over, and a third. They are all high-tailing it out the gates. After your brother I assume. He shouldn't take that risk."

Aisling wanted to make Maeve tell her what in the hell she'd gotten into, but this wasn't the place or time. "He knows what he's doing, don't worry. Do you have anything else here besides the bag?"

At Maeve's headshake, Aisling nodded, then remembered she probably couldn't see that.

"Okay, hold a second." Aisling sent out the magic pulse that would remove everything about her or Maeve from the room. Then she grabbed her jacket and purse and tugged Maeve to the garage. She stopped by Reece and fished the car ignition stick out of his pocket.

"Come on, you can't take the car. It's not paid for."

"Then you'd better make sure that none of your friends follow us for the next hour. I'll leave it somewhere notice-able—in one hour." It wasn't so much a kindness as she figured with Caradoc's spell that was probably the same amount of time they had before Reece's people came after them too. Once they rescued Reece and Jones, that was. She didn't wait for Reece's response but led Maeve out the door. Reece might not have pulled into the garage when he'd dropped her off, but Caradoc must have made him since his car was waiting for her. It still looked like the H-22 speedster that the comp skin projected.

She manually opened the garage, not easy, but possible. This side of the street was dark, so that was to their advan-tage. She couldn't see or sense anyone watching them, so she went back and got in Reece's car. Sliding into the driver's side felt different than being a passenger.

"You do know how to drive this thing, right? I kept up with some of your adventures while I was out of town." Maeve stowed her bag then buckled herself in with what Aisling felt was undue speed.

"I have never crashed because I didn't know how to drive. I'm sure a full investigation will reveal the last two weren't my fault at all." Aisling waved one hand toward Maeve as she backed out. "And they wouldn't have hap-pened at all if you hadn't bailed on me—and tried to get killed."

"I deserve that." She settled in her seat as they approached the gate, but the guard lifted the arm immediately. Aisling noticed Maeve grabbed the dash as she gunned it as soon as they cleared the block.

Aisling almost grabbed the dash as well. Whatever engine Reece had in this thing was insanely powerful. She slowed and got her heartbeat back under control once they were on the freeway. The tracker Caradoc had given to her was flashing the direction she needed to go. Off at the next ramp.

"Where is that thing taking us?"

Aisling got off the freeway then followed it to a long side street that ran parallel to the freeway. "No idea."

"Aren't we going back the way we came?"

"Yup and now we're getting back on the freeway." If this had come from anyone other than Caradoc, Aisling would have thrown it out the window and they'd take their chances finding a place to hide. The next exit was another freeway, this one heading west. Aisling sighed and took it. The light steadied to solid, an indication that this would be their direction for a while. It was only five miles to the ocean, so it couldn't be for that long.

"I still have no idea where this is going. I didn't know Caradoc had a secret hideout, let alone that it was somewhere near the beach."

"And the weird double back?"

"Most likely a failsafe he built into it. My brother can't leave any magic or technological gizmo alone. He has to make them all better."

She glanced over when Maeve didn't say anything. Her friend was unconscious. She almost pulled off at the next exit, tracker be damned, but then she heard her soft breathing. Maeve was asleep. Not too surprising considering how exhausted she'd felt when Aisling had tried to heal her.

The tracker started pinging to the right and Aisling got over into the right lane. There were only two more exits before the beach, both part of a rich and trendy neighborhood that her mother would love—if she didn't hate the ocean. Caradoc didn't hate the ocean, but he was more of a woodsy person. And he definitely didn't go for high-end anything beyond tech toys and gizmos. The tracker led her to an enclave of homes that made the area they left look like a ghetto. It led her through a number of streets, crossing over its own path at least three times. Finally it led her right into a hedge. Aisling stopped the car—luckily there was no one else out right now—but there was also nowhere to go forward unless she wanted to slam Reece's car into an eight-foot-high hedge.

"Either that thing Caradoc gave you is busted, or you need to go into the hedge." Maeve's voice indicated she'd definitely been asleep, and needed way more.

"I know that." Aisling looked up and down the street. "I'm not sure if two cops ramming a giant plant, in a rich neighborhood, at one in the morning is a great idea."

"You have another one? We need to ditch this car soon."

Aisling drummed her fingers on the steering wheel for a few moments. "Okay, hang on. And I want it noted that if I wreck this car doing this, it does not count."

She didn't wait for Maeve's response but punched the car forward. And went right through the hedge. It was now a solid mass of green in the rearview mirror.

"Damn him, he was always too good at illusions. He should have warned me."

"If he's so good, you should have expected it," Maeve said.

"Go back to sleep. I'll wake you if I need anyone bled on." Aisling smiled at the responding grunt. It was damn good to have her partner back.

The hedge appeared to surround a nice, comfortable, average house. Fancier than most outside of this area, but nothing like the monsters in the actual neighborhood. She stopped the car in the driveway and got out. "Stay here in case we need to run." Maeve was stubborn but she wasn't stupid—most of the time. She'd know she couldn't move fast.

The house was old, which explained why it was smaller than the mansions that surrounded it. The hedge blocked the lights from the street. It shouldn't have; they were taller than it was. But she knew it was part of the spell; light wouldn't be able to pass in either direction.

She climbed the four steps to the door and grinned. While the house was old fashioned, the entry tech was not. A palm panel was embedded to the right. Her name flashed in old elvish as soon as her palm touched it. Also very Caradoc. He combined the old and the new on a daily basis. The main lights came on as soon as she stepped into the room. Like the outside, high-end but old. Knowing her brother, he'd had this house for a few hundred years.

Maeve was barely awake when she finished checking out the place and got back to the car. Aisling grabbed her jacket, purse, and Maeve's bag, then helped her friend to the house. Maeve tried batting her away twice, but there was no force behind it. She probably needed to be in a hospital somewhere, but since that wasn't going to happen, they'd have to see what rest and food could do.

Unlike Reece's safe house, this one was a single story with three bedrooms. Aisling got Maeve into the closest one and rolled her into bed.

"Thank you. And thank you for not giving me shit about this. Well, not much anyway."

"Oh, there will be shit, lots of it. Mountains of it. I want to wait until you are strong enough to attempt to fight back." Aisling dropped the banter. "Seriously, you need to rest. I'm going to go dump Reece's car. The house will lock behind me. Go to sleep."

Normally that would be a rallying cry for Maeve. That she nodded and put her head on the pillow wasn't good.

Aisling quietly shut the door then went for Reece's car. Hopefully getting out of this place was as easy as getting in. She slowly backed out. One moment she was in the driveway, the next back on the street. Caradoc must have some way to watch for traffic or he'd only be able to come and go in the middle of the night.

Aisling left the area, trying to find a place not too far; she was running low on reserves herself. But she needed to leave this car a good distance from the house.

A few miles down the coast was a nasty little part of town. With a ton of tow away zones. She found the perfect spot near a troll strip bar, slid the key stick under the mat, and ran toward Caradoc's house. Reece would find it here, or in a tow yard with a record that it was found here. It wasn't much, but it did make her happy as she ran.

Elves, as a whole, were stronger and faster than humans. They could also outlast them. The ten miles back to the house only took her ten minutes and gave her some time to think. Unfortunately, it wasn't long enough to come up with answers. She missed her old murder board. It helped to see everything spread out in front of her.

The hedge worked for someone on foot the same way it worked for a car. But it was a little more disturbing on foot. In the car it appeared that you went through nothing. The hedge passage on foot was as quick, but Aisling would have sworn she felt plant-life brushing against her as she passed.

She checked on Maeve first. She didn't believe her partner was in any state to make a break for it, but she was the most stubborn being Aisling had ever met. With her family, that was saying a lot.

Maeve was out like a drunken harpy—and she was snoring. The sound was so bad, Aisling would almost believe she was faking—except that she'd heard it before when Maeve was extremely drunk.

She shut the door and decided to claim the bedroom furthest from Maeve as her own. This wasn't his regular home and, while furnished, there were no personal items. She had no idea when Caradoc would be back; the time limit on his spell ended about three minutes ago. But he could suffer with taking the room closest to the snorer— Aisling was desperate for some sleep.

There was no way to know how he did it, but the small collection of boxes, which was all that was left of what she owned in the world, was inside the room she'd claimed. Shaking her head at the skills of her brother, she shut the door, showered, changed, and fell into bed.

Only to be woken what felt like seconds later. But the rays of sun peeking through the far too gauzy curtains stated otherwise. A soft muttering in another room was what had gotten her sleeping attention. She slipped into something more substantial than the t-shirt and shorts she slept in and creaked open the door.

"We know you're awake, and Maeve won't go back to her bed anyway, so you might as well come out." Caradoc sounded too chipper. But the smell of fresh brewed tea and cinnamon bagels brought her out of her room.

Caradoc and Maeve were sitting at the table with a full tea service, bagels, toast, a pile of eggs, and bacon. And a woman, dressed in a suit that was so boring she could only be a federal agent, gagged and tied to the dining room table.

CHAPTER TWENTY-ONE

A ISLING FOLDED HER ARMS AND glared from her brother to partner to the fed and to the food. Then she repeated the order. Caradoc and Maeve continued to chat about the weather, or some other nonsense. The lady fed—only someone part of one of the federal agencies would dress so badly—continued to glare at them, with a bonus one for Aisling over her gag. Her hands were tied together in front of her and then to the table leg.

"What is going on? Who is she and why is she here?" Aisling grabbed a plate and a cup of tea and started building a breakfast. "Talk, I can multi-task." Judging by the inane discussion they had been having, she knew they wouldn't say anything of importance in front of the woman. But someone as sneaky and gifted as her brother could have found somewhere else for her.

"This is Agent Paselin. She's my own special agent with the patent office. I was trying to show her that my life and that of my sister and her visiting friend are all above ground and normal." He waved a buttered scone at Aisling casually. But she noticed the motion his eyes made as he spoke. A game she and he used to play as kids when their mother would go off on one of her tears. He didn't want her to say anything but go along with the current premise—they'd talk later.

"Nice to meet you, Agent Paselin, I'd shake your hand, but well, it would be awkward. Why are you following my brother?" She dug into a bagel.

"She believes I stole some proprietary material from my own business. Things I invented." Caradoc's normally calm demeanor faded, although he kept his tone light. Whatever was going on with this woman, he was taking it extremely seriously, but didn't want her to think he was. Deflection through humor and nonchalance had been his coping mechanism growing up. He was an expert at it now.

Agent Paselin might or might not believe his attitude, but she did not like his words. She was yelling through her gag so much Aisling almost thought she could make out a word or two.

"Does she need that on?" Aisling knew if her brother had been able to block light from escaping his hidey-hole, he would have done the same with sound. No one beyond the hedge would hear her no matter how loudly she yelled.

He shrugged. "Not really. She has just been so exasperating."

Aisling moved forward to ungag the agent, then glanced at Maeve. For a brief second, Maeve wasn't sitting there. A small, blond, elf woman was. Then the appearance disappeared. Caradoc nodded. He'd put glamour spells on both Maeve and her. Handy. Not completely legal, and it relied on the person seeing the spell to be distracted while it took hold—like being bound and gagged—but handy.

Aisling lowered the woman's gag.

"First, can I have some water? Secondly, you did steal them. They were patented items that belonged—"

"To me. My company. My patents." Caradoc was annoyed, but he also got up and got her some water.

Aisling went back to her eating, but not before shooting a questioning glance to Maeve. Maeve had finished eating but shrugged and turned to watch the showdown.

"A company that you sold to the government." Paselin's hands were tied with enough room to allow her to pick up and drain her water glass. She sat it back on the table and tapped it for more.

This time Aisling refilled it. Caradoc was far too focused on the banter between him and the agent.

"I signed over the company, but I expressly did not sign over the inventions. I have told you to have your lawyers read the fine print of sub-section 200.7, category b." He folded his hands on the table, his eyes narrowing as he and the agent glared at each other. She opened her mouth to speak, then fell forward onto the table.

Aisling ran over to check for wounds. Maeve started to get up also, but Caradoc pushed her back into her seat as he joined Aisling.

"She's fine. Just an old-fashioned spike to the water. Mother would be proud that I thought of the old ways. Enough elveswort to knock her out and fog her memories of the last few hours." He gently pushed the agent back upright, untied her from the table, and carried her to the sofa.

Aisling laughed. "Well played. The gag made her thirsty, so she didn't notice the tang of elveswort; it also distracted her from you placing the glamours. What did I look like?"

"Wait, what? If you were going to mess with her memories, why change us?" Maeve did get to her feet this time but dropped back to her seat when Aisling resumed hers.

"I wasn't sure that I was going to muddle her. Besides, elveswort can leave traces of the memories—almost like a remembered dream. Better to avoid her recalling you at all." Caradoc came back to the table. "You were different enough that she wouldn't recognize you if she stumbled into your police station. I needed to make Maeve look totally different."

Maeve narrowed her eyes. "Is that legal?"

"Only slightly. This is a private home and it was a low-level glam. Besides, is what you've been doing completely legal?"

"It needed to be done." She leaned back and folded her arms.

"That wasn't what I asked."

"Don't try debating him on these things; it's not worth the effort," Aisling said. "Let's all agree that some actions might not be on the up and up and move on. Why is she here and what are we going to do with her? Isn't this your safe house?" Kidnapping a fed agent, even from a low-ranking agency like the sub-patent office, and then holding said agent in your secret house didn't seem like good planning. With or without glams and elveswort. Nor did it seem like her brother.

"She doesn't have a clue where we are besides somewhere deep in the forest north of LA. I had to grab her; she was somehow tracking me through the forest when I was trying to leave a trail for the thugs who thought they were trailing Maeve. I needed her to see some normalcy, but also not know who you two were." He ran his fingers through his hair. "More importantly, I needed to find out what she was really after. But she honestly believes she is tracking a patent infringement."

Aisling pushed back from the table and sighed. "What were you afraid she was after?"

"It's complicated. But the point is, if she's working for someone deeper than the patent office, she's unaware of it. I'll take her up to the national forest near where I found her and leave her in a cabin."

Maeve shook her head. "Your entire family is like this?" Maeve and Aisling had been partners on the force for years, but Caradoc was the only family member that Aisling had let Maeve meet. Caradoc was about eighty years older than Aisling, but the rest of their siblings were a few hundred years older than him. There were no kids after Aisling.

"Mostly. But the big question now is what to do about Reece and Jones? Their agency freed them, right? Do

Maeve and I need to flee the country?" Aisling was only half joking. Caradoc easily took care of a patent agency worker—but there were too many agencies behind Reece, not to mention how many Jones came from, for even Caradoc to mess with.

"I can go on my own; I don't want either of you in on this." Maeve talked fierce, but she still wasn't recovered. Her normally dark skin was paler than usual and there were uncommon dark circles under her eyes. Aisling's healing couldn't do as much as it normally would. It was speeding things up, but it would still take time. Not to mention that Aisling hadn't been able to identify the poison that had been in some of the weapons used and that could still be affecting Maeve. She needed a doctor, not to go off on her own.

"Someone has to push your wheelchair until you recover," Aisling said. "Besides, I'm pretty sure I've joined you on the most wanted list." She wasn't too worried about Caradoc; he always managed to slip through unnoticed, even when someone was looking right at him. But there was no way Reece and Jones were going to let what she did go unreported.

Caradoc's grin was worthy of their mother's. "Actually, about that. Your two friends might have accidently been in a house that got weed bombed. Someone came along, before they got untied, skunked them, and seriously messed with their memories. The suspicion is a drug lord found them, most likely the people who were lurking around the nice, rich enclave and who appear on a number of vids taken from private homes." His grin clarified how both actions occurred. "From what I could pick up, Reece remembers dropping you off, and then nothing. Jones thought he was still in the surveillance van when he woke up. You are going to need a good story to go along with that though. They know you and your belongings were gone."

Aisling closed her eyes. She was glad that Maeve hadn't been exposed, and that she wasn't going to have to move to some foreign land with no extradition. But filling in the gaps wasn't going to be easy. And making the story cop-proof was almost impossible.

"You could go to where you left his car, and maybe tie yourself up in the trunk?" Maeve said.

Aisling shook her head. "Won't work. I left it in front of Troll's Passion in a fifteen-minute zone. It's probably in a tow yard by now."

Caradoc got to his feet and started pacing. "Maybe we can tie you and Agent Paselin together? You were kidnapped, along with your things, then you woke up in the forest in a stolen car. You freed yourself and rescued her as well."

"That might work. Convoluted, and there's no motivation for any of it. But we criminals don't always need a reason, right?" Maeve shrugged.

Aisling folded her arms and shook her head. "And it allows Paselin to be indebted to me, so we can become buddies, so my brother can keep tabs on her." The plan didn't have motivation, but it did somewhat resolve things, and worked in Caradoc's favor. "You're becoming more like Mother every day."

"Take that back." He narrowed his eyes.

"Are you saying that having me rescue her is for my own good? We could leave me as a bewildered kidnapping victim—although left with all of my belongings is odd—I don't need to be with her."

"It lends an air of goodness to your image. You were confused, and possibly in danger, but you saved another." His grin dropped. "Yes, knowing what she's up to without resorting to kidnapping her would be good. I can't shake the feeling that while she might not be checking deeper than patents, which are legally mine by the way, someone else might be pulling her strings. There were some odd things going on before I finally sold that business to the government."

"Why did you sell it? Actually, which company was it?" Caradoc was the sibling she was closest too, but she didn't see him much. He also tended to start companies as fast as most people decided what to order for breakfast. He usually hung on to them though.

"A small calculating firm; odds, inventions, percentages, that sort of thing. Only had it for a few years, but it wasn't doing much. When the government gave me an offer, I took it. But the intellectual property of anything that I added to it remained mine." He shook his head. "They know that."

"She seemed pretty sure that wasn't the case." Maeve got up with a wince and hobbled over to the recliner facing the sofa.

Aisling shook her head as she watched her slowly trudge a few feet. They still had no idea who was after Maeve, beyond Reece's agency, but the idea that she thought she could take off on her own was ridiculous. Of course, Maeve had been healed faster from worse injuries over the years. It was easy to take healing for granted. And she was almost as stubborn as Aisling's mother.

"Which is why I was trying to find out if she was working with someone or simply a clueless minion set on a task she didn't know anything about."

Aisling sighed and ran her fingers through her loose hair. "Let me get on what I was wearing last night. We can say that the gangsters broke into the house, grabbed me, Reece and Jones fought back, were defeated, and got skunked. As for taking my boxes, they knew Maeve's belongings were gone, so they tried to tie it to that—make it look like the same folks took them."

Maeve almost bolted out of the recliner. "What?"

"Then you didn't do it." Aisling was glad about that, but not happy her friend's things were missing. "Your place has been cleaned out professionally. Probably right after you left."

"Damn it, I have to go find out what happened."

"You're a wanted possible fugitive. Feds want you, the bad guys want you, and you are still sickly looking. You *need* to stay here. Caradoc can find a car to leave Paselin and me in and get this plan going."

Caradoc shook his head. "Now who sounds like Mother?"

Aisling glared. She wasn't going to dignify that with a response.

CHAPTER TWENTY-TWO

AISLING WENT TO CHANGE. THE pile of her belongings was going to be a problem. Thugs might have kidnapped her and stolen her stuff. But fitting her, Paselin, and a mass of boxes in a car was going to be awkward and stupid. This entire stunt was sketchy at best; they needed to make it more plausible, not less. She pulled last night's clothing back on, got her hair back in the low ponytail, and rejoined the others.

"We need a different plan for my things."

Maeve hadn't moved but nodded. "I was thinking the same thing. If they took it, there was a reason. And one separate from taking you and the agent here. In fact, they were probably looking for something in your belongings, and were taking you and the agent to be killed and not found for a long time."

"She sounds like various members of our family," Caradoc came out from the third bedroom. He'd changed into all black. That might be great for skulking about at night, but it was now nine in the morning…on an obnoxiously sunny day.

Caradoc didn't say anything about his new wardrobe. Instead, he checked Paselin's ropes. "I'd better do what our mistress criminal says. We can have your boxes appear in a warehouse in a day or so. Maybe some blood on them to indicate a fight between the people who took you." He waved his hand as he walked toward the door. "I'll have this sorted in a bit. Let me get us a car to dump. Stay here."

He managed to direct the last comment to both she and Maeve in a single shot, then was out the door.

"Wanna talk about it?"

Aisling pulled back. That was what she was about to ask Maeve. "Talk about what? You're the one who needs to talk. And a hell of a lot, I'd like to add."

"About Reece? I watched you two in the other house, and your reactions as your brother talked about him." Her grin was all old Maeve. "Something's happened. The cop has a crush on the fed." She teased in a singsong voice.

That was possibly the last thing Aisling expected to hear. It took a full second to respond. "What? No. We've just been forced to work together a hell of a lot more than normal." Totally against her will, the feeling of the kiss they'd shared—one that was totally undercover and meant nothing, came to mind. And the fake make-out in the car meant nothing. Right up until the vallenian showed up.

"You're thinking about it way too hard. And you blushed for a split second there. Now you've gone pale; are you okay?"

Aisling shook her head. "I will be. I remembered something I need to talk about with Caradoc—something family." If she *could* talk to him. The fact that she hadn't thought to bring it up in the last few hours was disturbing. Regardless of all the other crap going on, a vallenian on this plane—twice—was the biggest issue. Forgetting it was almost as bad as not being able to mention it.

"And the other? I know you, my friend. It's been a while since you've dated, but our mystery fed? Really? He's hot, I'll give him that, and those eyes of his are killer. But he's buried so deep in the agencies that none of my contacts are sure which ones he belongs to."

Aisling threw her hands in the air and stalked down the hall to her borrowed bedroom. There might be some truth to Maeve's words, but she wasn't going to deal with it now.

She automatically went to get her gun, then realized that if someone kidnapped her, the first thing they'd do was frisk her. "I am not falling for anyone," she yelled back down the hall. "I want to find out what in the hell is going on, and why my life seems to be tied up in it. He's probably the best way to find out." She stalked back out to find Maeve still watching her with an amused smile.

"Seriously? You're going to smirk the entire time? That isn't going to free you from having to tell me why you left and who did that to you. Or why you were around Ryn Trebol before he died." She'd thrown the last bit in to get Maeve off her case about Reece. But her friend's face said she'd hit something.

"You *were* with him? Damn it, up until how long ago?" Both she and Maeve had lost friends on the force before. But Maeve was still weak and news like this wasn't good for anyone.

"Not after he came to LA," Maeve said finally. "I saw him briefly a few days ago in London. He was sure he had a lead on a new drug, one that the Scotties were making. Could give the most amazing high in the world, but deadly as hell if things went wrong." She rubbed a hand over her eyes. "He called me two days ago. Said he was burning that phone and all contacts—that he'd blown the case wide open, but had to fly now." Her eyes were haunted. "Those were his last words to me. How did he die?"

"He went feral. That's what Reece said his people are calling it. We had a female flyer take out about five apartment buildings on the north side a few days ago in the same state, although she did more damage before she finally died. There was pure iron in her veins when she died." She paused, Maeve wasn't fey, but she knew what it meant, and she had too many fey friends not to cringe at Aisling's words. "It looks like the same thing happened to Ryn. I am so sorry."

Maeve studied her face for a few moments, then blinked rapidly and nodded. "For a fey, you have a horrible poker face. He died in massive pain, and I can't go claim his body. Or see him."

"I am so sorry."

Maeve wiped her hand across her eyes. "We weren't close, at least not anymore. He could be a bit of a bastard too. But he was caught up in whatever this is, and he died horribly while trying to stop it."

Aisling waited a few moments. "What is *this*? Obviously connected to drugs, but how in the hell can any fey survive with iron inside them? And what's the connection to everything?"

"We don't know. I am sorry I had to leave with a lie, but my old captain called. There's some dicey shit going on back home, but she died in a car accident before I could get there. A single car, no witnesses type of accident." The look that crossed Maeve's face said she fully knew it had been a hit of some kind. "As for what happened to me, I came back to the States in a cargo plane, against my will. There was supposed to be a hand-off, me for some academic geek they wanted. Deal fell apart, both sides were attacked. I got beaten up by the survivors." She rubbed a bruise that still lingered on her jaw line. "I don't know exactly who did it. Woke up tumbled by the side of the road a while ago and hunted you down."

Aisling studied her for longer than she should have needed to, but there had been a lot of things scrambling her brain lately. "How did you find me? That was one of Reece's super-secret safe houses. Rather, it belonged to one of the agencies he works for." The breaking in part wasn't shocking; even in her prior condition, Maeve could break into anything.

"I'm that good?"

"Don't give me that weak-ass grin, Halithi," Aisling said

then she watched Maeve's face. Guilt was all over it. "Wait, you put a tracker on me? What in the absolute hell?"

Maeve shrugged. "Sorry about that. But the shit was hitting the crapper at blinding speed. I wasn't sure how broad it was going to go, and I wanted to be able to find you." Her grin wasn't at all contrite.

"Damn it. You could have done it the old-fashioned way and told me what was going on," Aisling said, then held up her hand before Maeve could respond. "Never mind, I'm not up for the lecture on how bad super spy sneaky shit can get. Where is it?" Aisling knew it would have been one of the nice and illegal subdermal trackers. Just not where it was.

"Your left shoulder blade. That last night at the bar before I left, you were in a serious nectar haze. Gave you one extra pat on the back before I took off."

The night of her last nectar binge. Aisling couldn't help but think she felt an itch there now. "Get it out."

"Actually, that might come in handy." Caradoc had opened the door and gotten a step inside before he spoke. Neither Aisling nor Maeve had heard a thing.

"I'm not wandering around with a damn tracker in me. Besides, what if someone finds out and hijacks the signal?"

He was far too pleased with himself, so she wasn't going to address the sneaking into the house bit.

"That works well with my plan. Although, it will be the cops or feds, whichever, who hijacks your tracker. In the woods." That grin always looked like he'd just polished off the last of the nectar at a frat party. Too pleased with himself and on the edge of doing something incredibly stupid.

"That's brilliant, actually. I would have removed it. But this way it can help deepen the story." Maeve smiled. "I like it. If scanned, the tracker will lead back to a former Scottie enforcer—who died a few months ago."

Aisling had a feeling she knew how he'd died. When

Maeve joined the force she'd made a big stink about being done with the super spy sneak work—obviously that wasn't true.

"I can muddle where it came from even more. We'll leave the real connection to the enforcer in, but make them work to find it." Caradoc nodded and untied Paselin from the sofa, but she was still unconscious. "I have a car out in the woods. A friend left it set up and hidden for me. I'll take our two victims up, hide them, and then trigger the tracker to send a pulse. Easy enough to do and it would happen if it got seriously damaged. Maeve stays here."

"I can help."

"You can blow everything." Aisling knew it was blood loss and fatigue that was making her friend act this stupid. But they didn't have time for it. "You're wanted by too many people, most of which we've no idea who they are. You have to stay here." She stared at her friend for a few moments, then shook her head and turned to her brother. "Spell the house. She'll try and leave the second we're down the drive."

"What? I didn't say anything."

Aisling narrowed her eyes and folded her arms. "You didn't need to. Am I wrong?"

Maeve scowled for a full second, then dropped it, and fell back into the chair. "No. Damn it. I don't like being helpless."

Caradoc set a spell on the house.

CHAPTER TWENTY-THREE

CARADOC WENT THROUGH CARS AT the same pace he created and picked up new companies, so Aisling wasn't surprised that she didn't recognize the huge land cruiser in front of them. She was surprised when she realized it was magic-free. She wasn't a huge magic user, but she had enough to know when the tingle she should feel wasn't there.

Caradoc put Paselin in the back, double-checking her ties before buckling her in. Then climbed into the driver's seat.

"Do you want to tell me why my big, massively power-ful, magic-using brother is staying away from magic? And has invented a gizmo to short it out?" Aisling's family was split. The kids who took after their mother were some of the most powerful magic users on the planet. Her father's side—not so much. Caradoc hated their mother, but there was no denying he got his magic skills from her.

He shrugged and got on the road. "I can't explain it. Part of it is a feeling I've had lately—we rely too much on magic." He held up a hand. "Ignoring what the Black Death almost did to them, and *did* do to them. I'm not denying that magic can be used for good—had our people not stepped up there would be no more humans. I get that. But I don't think we should use it for everything."

There was a pause at the end of his sentence. "And?"

"And Harlie is freaking out about something."

Harlie, or Harthinatle as he was named at birth, was their

oldest brother. He was also extremely eccentric, lived in a cave in Nepal, and hadn't spoken more than a few words to anyone except Caradoc in over two hundred years.

"When isn't he?"

He shook his head. "This time it's big. He went to one of the human temples and prayed. In a corner, and most likely freaked out the locals because there's no idea of what he was praying to, but he went in *public*."

That wasn't good. Harlie never left his cave. Locals left him food—although they never saw him, they knew he was there. He also magicked supplies to himself on a regular basis. But he never left.

"Does he know what's happening?"

"Not at all—that is also freaking him out. A thousand years of precog suddenly shutting down can disturb a man."

Something kicked in her brain. "Reece is freaked out too. As far as I know he's never been diagnosed as a precog, and he is a fey-breed so he shouldn't be. He says he can always follow the pattern of events and that leads to knowing what will probably occur. But he can't right now, and he is wigged out big time."

Caradoc got onto the 5 north freeway and headed toward the Glovin Forest. "That can't be a coincidence. Okay, it could be with only two, but I have a bad feeling that we'll be seeing more of these issues if we search out registered precogs."

The vallenian popped into her mind. "There's something more, something…damn it!"

Luckily Caradoc was a great driver; otherwise Aisling's scream as her brain exploded into a thousand sparks might have caused them to crash. He did piss off a number of drivers as he immediately pulled to the side of the freeway.

"What happened? Were you shot?"

If Aisling could pull enough brain cells together, she would point out that if someone screamed, assuming there had been a gunshot wasn't the normal response. The more her brain kept trying to shove her away from the images of the vallenians she'd seen, the more she fought back.

"Aisling! Look at me!" Caradoc grabbed her shoulders and turned her to face him.

She couldn't force her eyes open, but she wasn't letting go of the image. Something told her that if she did, she'd never remember what she'd seen. The most stubborn, most conniving person she knew was her mother—she hung on to the thoughts and images of her and faced the pain.

"A vallenian! I've seen one. Twice. Damn it all to hell, it's trying to erase my memories!" The words burned as she got them out and although they felt like they were screaming out her throat, she knew they were barely a whisper.

Caradoc let go of one shoulder, and a cool metal touched her arm when he put his hand back. The coolness flowed through her body, chasing away the screaming pain.

And the block on speaking of the vallenian. She let out a sigh and opened her eyes. Caradoc released her arms, but she'd never seen him that worried.

"I don't know what you did, but thank you. I can think about it now. I've seen one twice, or two separate ones. One was trailing Reece and me. I…I wiped his memory so even if he thought he noticed it, it couldn't find him. The second time was last night where Maeve's friend died. I didn't see anyone react to it on any level—including Reece."

"Vallenians. On this side of the veil." He was pale and his hands shook.

Aisling knew what was going through his mind. Vallenians were tales told to keep young elf children in line—they weren't real. As she got older, she realized they were real but believed the stories told as truth, that they, and other equally unsavory Old Ones, couldn't cross the veil to this plane. They were a dark part of the elves and other fey's past and they were going to stay that way. Until now.

She looked at her arm where the coolness was still tingling. A small, flat piece of metal stuck to her skin. She reached to pull it off, but Caradoc's shaking hand stopped her.

"I wouldn't. That is blocking magic, including the web of death one of the vallenians attached to their memory. Eventually your mind will stop poking at the thought and we can take it off. But leave it for now. It will morph to your skin tone in a few minutes and no one will see it." He let out a huge breath. "We're going to have to tell Harlie."

"We? He won't talk to anyone but you. You tell him." Not to mention, while she appreciated this toy of his that kept her head from exploding; she didn't want to test it with a second try.

"Won't work. The truth can only come from the one who has been in their presence. So unless I see one too, and no offense, I'd rather not, then it will have to be you. In person."

Before Aisling could come up with a suitable response, a groan came from the backseat.

"Damn it, she's starting to come around. Toss that blanket next to you over her head, and don't say anything else inside this car."

Aisling did what he said. Paselin stopped groaning and seemed to go back to sleep. The sleeping herbs were still running their course.

With a nod, Caradoc moved back into traffic and headed for the old forests. Much of California was covered in forests, all of them protected by the elvish powers. But this was one of the most undisturbed ones. Aisling hadn't been up here since she'd been a kid, but Caradoc drove as someone who made regular trips.

He quickly got them into a lesser used area and pulled up alongside a mostly hidden beat-up and burned car. He stopped the car and motioned for her to get out and shut the door. Then he joined her.

"The blanket will muffle her awareness of what is going on around her; I'm going to leave it on for now. Take it off when you notice the cops coming. Or the feds. Still not sure who will find you first." He kissed her on the forehead. "Be safe, sister mine. You're the only sibling I can stand." He wrapped regular rope around her hands—easy enough to get out of if someone had time and training. Then he went to get Paselin.

He put the slightly squirming agent into the backseat, and Aisling climbed in the front. Caradoc gave an apologetic shrug as he put a hood over her head. She heard a click. The area where she guessed that tracker of Maeve's was started humming.

She started counting after she heard his car drive off. The bag and tie were a good touch, but she did need to manage to free herself and Paselin before whoever traced her tracker found them. Her brother had been a little too thorough in his work.

Once she'd managed to get her left hand free and could pull off the hood, she noticed that Paselin was moving around in earnest. Not only had Caradoc been thorough, he'd tied her hands separately. Aisling's right hand was still tied to the car seat.

"Hello? Who's back there?" Aisling hoped that Caradoc's earlier glam had disguised her voice as well.

"I'm a federal agent, you can't keep me here." Paselin was still irritating even through the distortion of the blanket.

"I'm a cop. Detective Danaan. I'm not sure what happened to us, but you're under a muffle blanket." Aisling knew it would distort the words a bit, but Paselin should still be able to understand her. "I am tied, but almost free. We're in a car…somewhere in the trees." Her grunts as she worked on the last tie weren't faked—she was going to have to have a talk with her brother about how to fake tie something. "I'm almost free, then I can get you."

"I was tracking a patent runner. I can assure you my agency will be grateful if you help me."

Aisling glared at the moving lump. "I'm a *cop*; it's what we do—agency or not. Now hold on." The tracker in her shoulder seemed to slow down, then rapidly sped up. She wasn't sure if that was good.

The final strand of rope broke, and Aisling got out of the car. Ideally, she'd free Paselin just as their rescuers arrived, but she didn't want to stall that long. The hairs on the back of her neck were up; there was something wrong here, but she couldn't pin it down. Nor be sure it wasn't a reaction to the hell she went through talking about the Old One.

Paselin blinked owlishly as Aisling got the muffler off her, but there was no sign of recognition in her watery eyes as she studied Aisling. "Excuse me, but you don't look like a police detective. What department?"

Aisling nodded to her jeans and tennis shoes. "I'm in homicide and undercover."

"Where's your badge tattoo?" Her eyes narrowed.

"It's been tat glammed. That's what undercover means." Aisling pulled Paselin out and untied her.

"Maybe you're working with them." She took two steps away once she was free.

Aisling wasn't worried; she knew she could outrun her, but running her to ground wouldn't be conducive to getting on Paselin's good side. "What did you say you did again? And what's your name?" She didn't have a pad screen like she would had she been out at a crime scene, but she let her voice slip into bored cop mode.

"Federal Agent Lindsey Paselin, patent office special bureau. And you are?" The cop tone had reassured her, but she kept glancing to where Aisling's badge tattoo should be.

"Detective Aisling Danaan, precinct 626, homicide, working with narco on loan. Nice to meet you. Now let's see if we can get out of here before whoever grabbed us comes back."

The sound of a car slowly coming through the woods was a welcome sound. The weird back of the neck feeling got worse though. "I'm not sure we want whoever that is to see us." She grabbed Paselin's arm and pulled her deeper into the woods.

"They could be rescuers. I've been missing for hours, I think." She glanced at the light through the trees, then at her watch.

"Or it could be our friends coming to finish us off. Look at that car we were in, it's not going anywhere except as a funeral pyre." She tugged again and this time Paselin came along. Aisling couldn't shake the feeling that this wasn't going as planned. To make matters worse, the hum from the tracker in her shoulder was now gone.

Judging from the stumbling way she made her way through the woods, Paselin rarely left her office. Which again raised the question: why in the hell someone sent her after Caradoc while he'd been in the woods in the first place. But it was something to be dealt with later. Aisling had little precog, but there was something to be said for instinct. And right now, hers was saying they needed to get further away from the clearing and the car. She didn't want to pull Paselin the entire way, but they needed to hustle.

The car they heard came to a stop and two doors slammed. "Hey, we know you're out there. Your friend sent us. Gave us the code for that tracker. We want to help."

A chill went down Aisling's spine. The voice was pitched more friendly, but she'd swear that was Bilth, the gangster who'd left them to die in the rubble. That he didn't know who he was after, just someone from the tracker, might help them.

"What are they saying?" Paselin's voice was low, but Aisling didn't think it was low enough.

She held her finger up and shook her head. The best thing would be to keep moving before someone figured out the direction they'd gone. But Paselin wasn't good in the woods.

Bilth yelled out again. "Hey, someone tied you up, left you in a torch-car, and will be back. We know from the tracker you're one of us; we can help you."

They only thought there was one person out here. From the look on her face Paselin's first thought was that it was her, but the talk of the tracker confused her.

Aisling bent to the woman's ear, her voice little more than a whisper. "They are after me. I know that voice and he's not on our side. Right now, they don't know about you, and we need to keep it that way if you want to live." This had been a ruse to cover Aisling's disappearance and rescue Paselin. It wasn't a ruse any longer.

Paselin opened her mouth but Aisling put her hand over it. "This isn't negotiable. Your job is to protect patents—mine is to protect lives. I win here." She waited until Paselin nodded tightly. "I'm going to run and make enough noise once I get a bit away from here that they will follow me. You're going to crawl into those bushes behind you and not come out until I say so, or you see a badge or uniform. Is that clear?"

Fear was starting to show in her eyes. Paselin was tougher than most paper pushers, but this was wearing her down. She nodded.

Aisling removed her hand and gently pushed Paselin toward the bushes. She waited until the older woman had crawled under the plants. Then she turned and started jogging lightly. Elves could be silent if they wanted. Even so, she wasn't familiar with these woods and being silent at a faster speed would be risky. After three minutes, she picked up speed and stopped worrying about the noise.

"That way!" A different voice, not Bilth, yelled. Aisling was grateful for the distance between them indicated by the voice. She barreled down the path.

Bilth was an elf and, most likely, at least a few people with him were as well. Hopefully, she had enough lead to keep them off her trail. How did they pick up the tracker? Caradoc was supposed to aim it at the cops' network. Her brother might be a lot of things but technically incompetent wasn't one of them. There was always the chance that if there were a mole on the force, they got it, and no rescuing cops were going to show.

Which hopefully meant that there were some good guys coming in to follow it as well. She and Reece were suspecting that part of the precinct was corrupt too, but right now them finding her was the only chance she had.

She heard the sound of running footsteps behind her, still not close, but definitely on her tail. Either Bilth, another elf, or one of the faster fey. But not well versed in the woods or she wouldn't hear them at all.

The trails were thin here and going off of them might be safer, but not faster. She knew enough about the woods to know going off trail when someone wasn't experienced could lead to disaster—even without trained killers running behind.

The sound of distant gunshots came from the direction she'd run away from. The person chasing her slowed, then seemed to turn away from her, but Aisling wasn't taking chances. After five minutes of a few more gunshots, some unintelligible shouting, and no sound of pursuit, she stopped running. She wasn't in as good of shape as she should be and stopping brought her to a shaking stand that quickly had her bending over with her hands on her knees. Sitting sounded best, but that wasn't a great idea after running as hard as she had. She'd have to recover a bit before heading back.

"Interesting. You're not Maeve." The accent was cultured, but not strong enough for any one country. "Turn around slowly, I like to know who I'm killing."

CHAPTER TWENTY-FOUR

"WHY SHOULD I HELP YOU if you're going to kill me no matter what? You do need to offer options, you know. I might be worth far more alive than dead." Aisling slowly rose to an upright position and kept her hands out to the side, but didn't turn. Even if she had a weapon, she wouldn't be able to outshoot someone with a bead on her back.

"Well said," the man continued. "Then a deal; if you are not someone I have a bounty on, or a grudge against, and that dysfunctional tracker has lead me astray in truth—I will let you go. Most people recover fine from memory wipes and I promise to keep yours as painless as possible."

Aisling paused; there was no way she would let him memory wipe her. Who knew what he'd destroy? She was getting ready to do some stupid move that would most likely get her killed, when the sound of a chopper came over the small clearing. A blue light flashed around her.

"Hold your fire, we're federal agents, and that's a fully functioning arc screen set to send any force back at the attacker. Back off and maybe you can get out of here before the cops on the ground find you."

Aisling had never been so happy to hear anyone's voice in her life. Reece might be an aggravating fed, but he was an aggravating fed with great timing. She spared a glance up to see the chopper. It was a small one, but not small enough to safely land in this clearing, and from what she'd seen there was nothing else around here that was even this big. Arc screens were rare and couldn't hold for long. If her attacker felt desperate enough, he might hide in the trees and wait for it to crash—he had to realize the chopper couldn't land.

The welcome sound of motorbikes would have made up her mind if she'd been in his place.

"Tell Maeve that I said hi. She'll know what this is."

Aisling jumped as something hit the back of her calf. She heard the sounds of someone running through brush—he didn't care about trails. Then the blue light dropped from around her as the arc screen shut down.

A rope dropped next to her with Reece peering from the chopper. "Those are cops—good ones, hopefully. They found your friend the patent agent. But you might want to talk to us before the cops."

There hadn't been enough evidence beyond Captain Losien's odd behavior to determine if there was something wrong with the precinct. However, getting more intel from Reece might be a good idea before they walked into the lion's den.

The motorbikes were getting closer, but still probably too far away to see her. They were specially designed for search and rescue in deep woods. Faster than a human hiking, but not as fast as an elf running. She scooped up the small, folded envelope that had been thrown at the back of her leg by the gunman, then reached up and tied the end of the rope sling dangling from the chopper around her. Reece had her pulled up and the chopper out of the area before the bikes came into the clearing.

Aisling wasn't terribly surprised to see that the pilot was the only other person up here or that it was Jones. She took an empty seat and buckled herself in.

Reece shut the door and buckled himself in. "Do you want to tell me what happened to you and why you were running through the woods with a patent agent? And why that thug was going to kill you?" The chopper was loud, but much quieter than the police choppers she was used to. Reece only had to raise his voice a little. He looked peeved, but she was beginning to read his expressions better. He was acting mad at her, but he was more worried.

This is where it could get tricky. She had to make sure her story matched what Reece and Jones remembered. "Well, I don't expect you to pay that much attention, but when thugs in masks break into your supposed safe house, tie us up, and kidnap me, I would hope you'd at least recall something." Pissed was going to be the best way to play this. And it would let her work through some of the fear adrenaline from her almost fatal mystery encounter in the forest.

"We were all in the house?"

Aisling gave her best 'what have you been drinking' look. "You and I were. Who else was supposed to be there? I told you to drop me off, but you insisted on making sure everything was okay. You don't remember following me in? And us getting jumped?"

Reece winced and shook his head. "No. Jones and I woke up in the house, both tied up. You were gone, and I don't remember anything after leaving the crime scene. Your things are gone too."

"What? You let them grab me *and* my belongings? And how can you not remember what happened?"

"We got skunked," Jones said when Reece stayed silent. "I'd guess they grabbed you, then came back for your things. I was in the car watching and tried to stop them. Reece and I were in the house when they let off a skunk bomb. The agency found us a few hours ago."

Aisling didn't have to work hard to appear tired and annoyed. She was both already. "Then how did you find me?"

Reece got his smug grin back. "Someone got a tracker

on you. I don't suppose you know who grabbed you?" At her tight shake of her head he nodded. "Neither do we. But it seems that you and Agent Paselin were going to die mysteriously out in the woods. Your belongings weren't in the car, according to the police radio. But a lot of gasoline was."

Caradoc was pushing authenticity a little too far.

"Who was the guy I saved you from? He had a hood on, so we couldn't get a good look from up here. Took a bunch of photos to see if we can break it down later."

"I have no idea. I thought the cops had found us when we got out of the car. Neither of us recall getting into the car, by the way. Then I realized it was Leifen's friend Bilth and some of his buddies. I hid Paselin and ran. I finally shook them, thanks to someone shooting up their friends back at the car. I was getting ready to head back when whoever our hooded friend was threatened to blow my brains out." She gave Reece an honest smile. "Thank you for saving me, by the way."

"Anytime." He held out his hand palm up.

"What?"

"What did he throw at you? You have no idea who he was, he was going to kill you, but then he gave you a parting gift?" He wiggled his fingers.

Aisling paused then took it out of her pocket with a sigh. Flying across the forest in a super spook chopper was not the place to argue about ownership. It felt like a small piece of thick fabric.

"Thank you." He unwrapped the item carefully, a frown growing as it looked like what she'd felt—heavy fabric in a diamond shape. His swearing started when he flipped it over.

Aisling leaned as far as she could to see but his hand was blocking it. "Well? What is it?"

He opened his fingers. It was a badge of some kind, like a

patch used by biker gangs. "This belonged to Ryn Trebol. It is from the Ankhs."

A new round of swearing started and she wasn't quiet about it. "What in the hell? The Ankhs? Now the Egyptian mob is in on this too?" She plucked it out of his palm before he could close his hand. Yup, the Ankh symbol circled in blood and upside-down. It was hard to tell it was upside-down given its status right now, but when on a jacket, she knew that was how it was displayed. The well-known Egyptian symbol of life had been turned upside-down. There were better symbols of death, but this was also an insult to their people.

Reece snagged it back. "I got some of the pictures from last night. Unsurprisingly, given the way he died, a number of gang patches were missing from Ryn's vest, but only one looked like it wasn't torn off on impact with the ground. This is about the right size. No one is going to be happy about this, nor that someone who tore it off of him had you at gun point in the middle of the woods."

Aisling got pulled in by his eyes. She shook her head and sorted her thoughts out. Reece and whoever he worked for were probably the best chance to get to the bottom of this mess, but she also sure as hell wasn't going to tell him the man with the hood was after Maeve. His agency already wanted her; she wasn't going to give them more reasons. "I don't think that I was who he was searching for. He used the same tracker that you did, but thought it was in someone else."

"I don't suppose you know where you got hit with the tracker? Or who he thought you were? I doubt whoever grabbed you and was going to kill you would have wasted a tracker."

"Not at all. It started buzzing when I woke up, maybe earlier but I didn't notice it," she said then paused. "He didn't say a name, just that I wasn't who he expected. But how did *you* know it was me out there?" Bilth had followed the tracker as well, but he wasn't sure who he was tracking—just that he needed to find them. Most likely his higher ups pointed him toward her and said bring whoever it is in. She had no idea if they were also looking for Maeve, or the prior and very dead owner of the tracker.

Reece sighed. "We weren't sure. This tracker was registered to a mobster who died a few months ago. It vanished after his death. We got bio readings from it that said female, most likely elf. But the thing is so damaged they weren't consistent. Figured we were missing a female elf, and had no other leads, so Jones and I borrowed the chopper and came up here."

Aisling patted her shoulder. "Crap, they could still be tracking me." She hadn't felt anything from it for a while, but she felt like she was on a giant map somewhere and any mobster or thug who wanted to, could find her. This thing needed to come out now.

"You're safe. I had a scan and defuse triggered on that thing once we pulled you up," Jones said from the front. He made it sound casual, but wiping out a tracker, without harming important intel she knew their agency wanted, wasn't simple. Especially from a chopper hovering in the air. Every time she figured they couldn't freak her out more with their sneaky gadgets, they did it again. Now she didn't want this thing out of her. If they could disable it like that, they might trace it to Maeve. Caradoc needed to mess with it first.

"Good. So what—" Her words were swallowed by a proximity alarm.

"Stay in your seats. We have a tail and he's chasing us out over the ocean." Jones sounded calm—for anyone else. Just in the few interactions she'd had with him, she could tell he was worried. She grabbed the armrests as the chopper dove hard to the left.

Reece pulled up a small screen next to his seat and was tapping furiously. "Not surprising, their ident is fully blocked. Much higher level than what we have on this thing."

Aisling stared out the window. She wasn't sure at what point they'd gone out over the ocean, but it had been a while before the other chopper showed up. Land was distressingly far away.

Jones banked the opposite direction and her harness cut painfully into her as he almost went vertical. An explosion of light right past her window explained the drastic move.

"Damn it, I can't outrun them. They're bigger and have more reserves. We're going to run out of gas if I keep heading out over the water, and they won't let me get ahead enough to turn back to land."

"Do your people know where you are?" Maybe if they took a deliberate dive into the water, they could survive long enough to be rescued. She could see the other helicopter now, about twice the size of theirs and blatantly armed. It could have blown them out of the sky at any point. It wanted them far from land.

"Not really," Reece said but didn't appear to be willing to elaborate.

The chopper shuddered and almost rolled over completely as Jones dodged another missile. It looked small but the explosion wasn't.

"We don't have a choice. That last shot also had a spider on it that jumped to us before it exploded. It's on our tank and sucking everything out. We're going in."

CHAPTER TWENTY-FIVE

"WE'LL BLAST OUT THE DOOR directly before we hit. Dive as far to the right as you can. Jones? You coming?" The chopper whined as the blades were shut off and folded into themselves at Jones' command. The dangerous blades wouldn't take them out, just the chopper itself. Diving clear of it would be crucial; this thing would sink fast.

"Ready." Jones came into the body of the chopper as it rolled to the left—probably the last command he'd loaded in.

Reece hit a button and the door blew open and flew across the water. Aisling closed her eyes, dove as far as she could, and hit the water.

Growing up near the ocean should have meant growing up on the beach. Except when your family matriarch was one of the most powerful people in the world and she hated the ocean. Aisling learned to swim quite well in the family's lake-sized pool. As an adult, she enjoyed the beach, but was never a fan of the dark murky water.

The water was freezing as she dove into it. She went deep, hoping to get far away from the sinking chopper, then swam for the surface. The tail of the chopper was sinking beneath the waves as she popped up. At first, she didn't see either Reece or Jones, then both bobbed to the surface. Jones was close to the chopper, but Reece had managed to get a respectable distance away. He started swimming toward her then yelled and pointed up. She couldn't hear exactly what he said but she looked up.

The chopper that had been chasing them was crashing; far too close to where she was.

Jones dove just as she did, but she wasn't going to clear it. The weight of it hitting the water, even only glancing her, was enough to tumble her under. She screamed as a body slammed into her—someone from the chopper. His eyes were open, and he'd been dead before the thing crashed.

She kept swimming but had lost her air when she screamed. She was too far down and there was no way she could get to the surface in time. Someone came up from behind, grabbed under her armpits, and then sped to the surface.

She gasped and choked as she got some air in and coughed some water out.

"You'll be okay. Stay here, I need to get Jones." Reece had lost his duster and was wild around the eyes. But he was also swimming unlike anything she'd ever seen.

There were water fey and he'd said his fey line came from them. But human breeds always trended human—there couldn't be any manifestation of the fey side. Anyone who was more than half fey looked fey, not human.

The second chopper followed theirs to the bottom of the ocean. Reece and Jones swam to her but at a more leisurely speed. Reece was calmer too. She was treading water carefully, but land was even further away than when they crashed.

"Why did it crash? How the hell did you save me, and how are we getting to land?"

Reece shrugged. "I have no idea. Jones? Did you hit the other chopper before we crashed?"

"Not me." Jones was also watching Reece carefully. He probably had the same questions concerning Reece's actions that she did.

"Want to explain saving us? I appreciate it, trust me. But

no human can move that fast in water."

Reece shook his head. "I honestly don't know. But right now, we need to figure out how to get out of here. There were three people on that second chopper, all dead and bleeding; they turned on each other before they crashed. We're going to have sharks soon. If you two are up for it, we should leave this area."

Aisling had extremely good eyesight and she could already see a fin in the distance. Being eaten by a shark was worse than drowning. If possible, she'd like to avoid both possibilities. Jones didn't answer but started swimming toward the thin ribbon of land on the horizon. Aisling followed with Reece bringing up the rear.

They'd gone for about a half hour when Jones pulled up. "I need to rest." He was in excellent shape and a trained killer, but swimming called on different stamina than land events. Unfortunately, treading water wasn't a complete rest from swimming and was still going to wear them down.

Except for Reece. Aisling felt drained, Jones obviously did too. Reece looked like he could keep going until he hit land.

"I know you don't want to talk about it, but I need a distraction from a potential watery death. Just what is your fey side? This isn't some distant water fey." The question was considered rude in general public. But they weren't in public and there was a good chance she and Jones were going to die out here. Reece, whatever he was, could help prolong things, but not get them both to land.

"I'm a good swimmer, okay?" Reece tried but then shook his head when both she and Jones kept staring at him. "Fine. Naiad. My mother was a naiad."

"And your father?" Jones' tone showed he understood how hard this was for Reece. Being fey was fine, being human was fine, but being a fey-human hybrid with fey like abilities was not fine. He might be an assassin, but he cared about his friend.

"He was human, pure human. Trust me, they did a ton of testing when my mother was pregnant with me, and I heard all about it growing up. There were no traces of fey on my father's side."

Aisling turned, but there didn't seem to be fins near them. They were probably still snacking on the bastards who had shot them down. "Has something like this happened before? I'm sorry, but there is no way a human could swim like that."

"Never. I liked swimming, but I could never move like I did today. And it's fading. I'm already slowing."

"Ahoy, people in the water. This is the Coast Guard ship *Agorian*. We're coming to rescue you. Please stay calm and let the selkie divers attach floatation devices to you." The ship wasn't close, but still Aisling was surprised none of them had seen it approach. The speaker's voice had been augmented for long distance and two sleek sea lion-like forms were bounding to them. Selkies looked like sea lions when they changed—until you saw their eyes. Fey eyes of a light sea-green met hers as the first one nudged a floatation ring toward her. Once all three of them were secure, the two selkies started circling them. The ship would be here in minutes, but it was probably a good idea with blood and sharks not that far away.

Talking was difficult when they were in selkie form, so Aisling kept her comments to a nod of thanks. She watched the two to see if they reacted to Reece any differently than she or Jones. Fey could usually sense other fey, especially ones that were similar in type—she hadn't sensed him, but maybe people closer to what he was could.

Nope. They secured him with the float ring just like her and Jones and kept him inside their circle.

She didn't get much time for observation anyway as the boat pulled alongside. It wasn't one of the massive sea vessels but a smaller boat about thirty feet long.

They got them up onboard and wrapped in massive towels. The selkies stayed in the water, circled the ship, and then zipped back toward the crashed choppers.

"They'll do initial data gathering, too many sharks for much more. We have a full investigative crew coming out." The ship's captain was a short, round gnome. The type who looked like she should be serving people in a cozy diner somewhere. The tone of her voice however was extremely no-nonsense.

"I'm Captain Colian. Now, who are you and why were you dumping unmarked choppers in my ocean? Neither one showed any flying clearances on my screen."

"I'm Detective Danaan from the LA police. I'd been kidnapped and these two were rescuing me. We were attacked by the second chopper and I can only believe they were with whoever kidnapped me." She'd have to stick to the kidnapped story, but tying it to the chopper would hopefully keep the questions limited. And while whoever had been in it could have been after Reece or Jones, she had a bad feeling she was the target.

Captain Colian looked her up and down, pointedly returning to her left wrist. "I understand not having your badge and gun, alleged kidnapping aside, the ocean would have taken them. But I didn't see a flash of a badge tat as I handed you your towel." She glanced over to Jones and Reece. "On any of you."

"Mine was glammed for undercover work," Aisling held up her wrist even though she knew the captain couldn't see it. Until it was unglammed back at the station, only a police issued scanner would be able to see it.

"We're both with the FBI," Reece spoke and a dark line of a wrist tattoo that Aisling had never seen flashed on his left wrist. It wasn't the entire tat, but enough to look legit and easily be glammed. "I can vouch for Detective Danaan, we're working with the police on a major drug case."

Captain Colian's eyes narrowed. "I don't doubt you're a fed, but I want to check on her tat. Stay here, all of you." She nodded to two of her people and they moved in closer. "I have a mobile scanner. Let me get it."

Aisling shared a look with Reece. That was more than odd. If she'd been on her own, okay, suspicion might be warranted. Heike had done a good job glamming her tat. But the partial of Reece's was legit, and whether she was a cop or not, FBI would outweigh Coast Guard.

She dropped her eyes to the partial tat on his wrist. Granted, he usually wore long sleeves, but she was certain she'd never seen it before. She nodded to it with her chin, not wanting to attract attention from the other two coasties.

His shrug was less reassuring than it could've been.

The captain came back with a small wand. Three quarters of it was flat and about two inches across, it tapered into a thin handle. "I'd like to see all of your wrists, if you please."

Jones pulled back both sleeves and held up his hands. Nothing was visible until she ran the flat portion over it. A thin silvery badge appeared. FBI. Considering that Aisling figured that Jones was like Reece, in that he probably belonged to many agencies, she wondered how they decided which one got the badge tat.

Reece was next; same silvery shimmer underlying the black outline. Feds rarely showed their tats, most of the agencies liked their wallet badges instead.

Aisling pulled back her towel and still sopping shirtsleeve and held out her wrist. The captain swung the wand over her arm. Nothing. Two more times. Still nothing. And the two coasties around them were now four. A knot built up in Aisling's stomach. How the hell could her tat have vanished?

The captain stepped back a few feet and let her hand drift toward her sidearm. "I'm afraid we'll need to take you in." She turned to Reece and Jones. "Your badge tats say you are feds, but maybe this time you got tricked. There's no way a cop wouldn't have a tat, and no tat could be so well glammed that this wouldn't reveal it. We got a warning that there were some fake cops making the rounds. I have authority on this ship and on the ocean. I'd like you two to stand back. We'll be putting cuffs on our *detective* here. You can all sort things out when we get to shore."

Reece was calculating his best angle. The more she was around him, the more she could read subtle changes in his face. Had anyone asked a week ago, she would have said she'd strangle him before she was around him long enough for that to happen.

Jones was ready to fight.

Aisling rubbed her wrist. She'd say the scanner was broken—she damn well knew she had a tat. But why would the other two show up and not hers? The captain didn't say anything, but her eyes narrowed briefly.

"I am a cop. The tat was hidden for undercover work." She held up one hand and dropped her towel. "I won't fight. But you have to promise you'll turn me in to my precinct captain, Captain Surratt." She held out both wrists for the cuffs.

Reece and Jones still looked ready for a fight. But none of them had working weapons, they were out in the middle of the ocean, and the Captain was right about her jurisdiction—for now. Once they got back, Surratt would fix things. He could also find out what the hell happened to her tat.

Aisling gave a quick shake of her head to the men and they stood down.

The captain tilted her head, her eyes narrowed, as she tried to figure Aisling's angle. There was no doubt in her mind she'd found a crook of some sort. She finally shrugged. "Aye, we need to turn you in somewhere. I can surrender you there."

The cuffs weren't comfortable, even more so on cold, wet wrists, but there wasn't much of a choice. After cuffing her, the coasties escorted her to a lockup that doubled as a closet and shut her inside. Yes, exhausted, soaking, and confused elves were known to be dangerous.

She kicked over an empty bucket and sat. It shouldn't take long to get to the docks. She rubbed the place her tattoo should be. Where it had been. Even though Reece thought she'd been unconscious and kidnapped, she knew she hadn't been either. Which meant the removal happened as she sat there fully awake a few days ago. Heike didn't glam her tat—she removed it fully.

Damn it. She knew something was odd about her friend—and about her last few years. But she would never have thought she'd betray her like this. There should have been no legal way she could have been on any childbearing approval list, yet she got three? Humans were naturally sterile, at least about ninety-eight percent of them. Elven doctors with a lot of time, magic, and money were able to reverse that for a select few each year.

Had Heike sold herself out to some gang to have children? And to who? Aisling shuddered as the ramifications of what could have happened had she been deep undercover and no way to prove she was a cop hit her.

Heike had set her up to be killed.

The sounds of the ship docking pulled her out of her thoughts—but not her fury. And fear. Whatever was happening was massive and impacting everything on both sides of the law.

The door opened and three armed Coast Guard guards stood there in the narrow passageway. They looked nervous. Armed nervous people were not good. They were also blocking the door.

"You're not going to be able to get me out that way if you don't move."

The one in the front, a human, aimed his gun at her. "I am sorry. We don't have a choice." He was pulling the trigger when Aisling ducked and charged to tackle him. Not the best move, but she didn't have a choice.

The gunshot went wide and all three of the guards went down with Aisling twisting on top, batting the gun away with her cuffed hands. Her shoulder stung and the warm dripping feeling told her she'd been hit after all. The pain hadn't reached her brain yet.

The door at the end of the causeway burst open and Reece charged in with a military issued gun that he must have taken from someone on the ship. "You okay? The captain went overboard—possibly with help. Jones and I found drugs all over this damn ship."

"The bottom two I'm sitting on still have their sidearms. I can't get off them." Aisling raised her cuffed hands.

Jones came through the door, also armed with a nice new gun. "Everyone is either gone or dead. They killed some of their own when they realized we'd figured out they were running drugs. We're docked at the far end of the pier, and not in a Coast Guard area." He nodded to Aisling. "You comfortable there?"

"No, I was explaining to Reece that they are still armed, and I can't get off of them."

Reece stepped forward and made sure all three guards knew a gun was trained on their heads. "I was trying to figure out how long it was going to take you to bleed all over them. You can get up now, none of them will even blink. I'm exhausted and pissed and have an itchy trigger finger."

Jones squished past him and helped her off the unmoving pile.

"Thank you, does he often talk like that?" She was careful not to bump Reece as she and Jones moved past him.

"Only when he's *really* tired and pissed." Jones took her arm and helped her down the corridor. "Let's get out on the deck."

Aisling glanced back to see Reece stepping backwards toward the door carefully. "One move, I swear I will shoot you all in the gut."

Jones moved Aisling to the side, and Reece backed his way out. She stood by as the two jammed the lock.

"Since our badges are showing, and we have guns, and yours isn't, and you're in cuffs, we're going to have to pretend you're our prisoner for now." Reece stopped and picked up one of the clean towels and dropped it over her head as they left the ship. "We can't take a chance someone recognizes you until we get the tat issue resolved. So, you'll be our injured and light-sensitive prisoner." He nodded to the dock guards and a beat cop making their way down the dock toward them. "You okay with that? We can get the cuffs off at the station."

Aisling nodded. The towel was so threadbare she could see through it. It wasn't the greatest plan. But there was a chance that someone would know her, and the towel would at least slow that. They needed to get out of there and to the station quickly without attracting too much attention.

"I'll need to see some ID and you need to hand over any firearms." The cop wasn't the most observant; both Reece and Jones had their newly obtained guns stuck in their waistbands. Since neither were wearing coats, they were noticeable.

"I'm FBI Agent Larkin, he's Agent Jones, and she's wanted for questioning. Our chopper was attacked and crashed into the ocean. And that Coast Guard vessel is loaded with illegal drugs."

His last words were swallowed by an explosion as the ship in question blew up.

CHAPTER TWENTY-SIX

T HE FIREBALL THREW THEM TO ground, engulfed the ship, and wiped out half of the dock. Aisling rolled to her feet. Unfortunately, she'd fallen on her left side where she'd been shot and almost collapsed. The blood loss from the gunshot wound, combined with fatigue from her race through the woods and the long swim in the ocean, caused the world to sway. Jones grabbed her as she stumbled and steadied her. When she started to sag once more, he picked her up.

Reece helped the cop and dock guards get to their feet. "We need to get everyone off the dock. Now."

"What about the people on that ship?"

"Look at it. Do you really think anyone survived that?" Reece flashed his wrist with the tat. "Federal case now, call it in and get everyone off the dock. Check all the surrounding ships. I doubt anyone could have missed that, but people can be stupid."

Aisling thought about trying to get out of Jones' arms, but she was thrashed. Elves were fast healers, but not that fast. Jones started walking quickly to keep up with Reece leading the way and barking orders.

The cop and the dock guards did have to roust a few people out of their boats, but soon everyone was away from the dock and the fire department showed up.

Three black and whites arrived with the fire trucks. "How are we going to play this?" There was a hell of a lot going on what with her still in cuffs, shot, no tat, and a

Coast Guard ship and dock blazing behind them.

"I've got it," Reece was back in his cocky form. He had a swagger as he approached the first clump of police. For once, Aisling didn't find him annoying.

"Good to see you, Hjalk, how's your husband and the kids?" The officer Reece spoke to was elven, but shorter than most of his kind.

His grin was huge as he grabbed Reece's extended hand. "All are good. What are you doing out here?" He peered at Jones, Aisling, and their fiery backdrop. "And what the hell happened? The three of you look like partially drowned weasels, and that woman is bleeding."

"Long story. I'll buy you drinks sometime and explain it all." Reece dropped his arm around the shorter man. "But we were in the ocean. Can I use your phone to call this in to my superiors? It is a federal case, but we need local support."

Hjalk laughed. "Don't you always? No worries, we got ya covered." He handed his phone over. Aisling tugged on the towel as he came over with the small med kit all cops carried and silently did a quick bandage of Aisling's wound. It was to keep the blood loss down and the magic-infused bandages would hold things in until she got to a hospital. He was quick and efficient and if he felt odd bandaging a criminal with a towel over her head, he didn't give any sign.

While Reece stepped back to make a few terse calls, Aisling pushed back the towel a bit and watched the cops' reactions. They were curious about her and Jones and keeping an eye out in case any civilians decided to help the fire department. But they genuinely seemed to like and respect Reece. A far cry from the bare tolerance he faced in her precinct.

Reece finished his calls and handed the phone back with a smile. "Thanks, I owe you. My people are on their way. For now, just keep the watchers out. Could you spare someone to take us to precinct 626?"

"Sure. I'd do it myself, but someone has to stay in charge." He called over a fey woman, a tall, sinewy naga. "Run them to 626."

Aisling was feeling worse and winced as Jones carefully put her in the patrol car.

"Sorry about that."

Aisling figured at this point no one would recognize her, so she took off the towel. "Thanks, but it was the ass who shot me who should be sorry. Probably is, with that fire." She thought about the looks on the shooter's face and the other two. Once she wasn't bleeding, she was going to have to track them down. There wasn't malice in their faces; they were going to kill her, of that there was no doubt, but there was more fear than evil. That was another mystery to add to the pile. Once she was in dry clothes, without the cuffs, and had the bullet hole stitched up she'd look into them. Explaining this all to Surratt wasn't going to be fun, but for once being injured didn't annoy her; maybe he'd figure she couldn't fight back and would leave her alone.

Jones climbed into the back seat next to her, with Reece up front. "Are you okay?" Jones whispered.

"I will be." She raised her cuffed hands. "These seriously need to come off." Since the owner of the cuffs had gone into the water, getting the key wasn't an option. If they weren't standard, they'd have to cut them off.

"You sure you want me to take you all to the 626? Blondie back there is pale even for a northern elf." The cop was watching her in the mirror.

"Yeah, need to get some things taken care of. She'll get help, not a worry."

The cop laughed. "Not worried, just didn't want her croaking in my car. No offense, honey." She smiled but it was fake.

Aisling forced a sharp smile, showing her how that type of smile was done. "None taken, *sugar*."

The cop's eyes narrowed a bit; she'd probably figured Aisling for a perp, and the blood and cuffs would make most folks think that. Now she was trying to figure out who Aisling was.

They got to the precinct faster than she'd expected, which was good. She got out of the car on her own, once the cop unlocked it. But Jones still came to her side to help her. He didn't pick her up this time, but let her lean on him as they walked up. The beat cops were curious, blatantly trying to figure out what Aisling had gotten into now. But they stayed back as the three made their way into homicide.

Surratt was waiting, and the worry he was showing was a rare sight on his face. "Bring her to my office." He glared out at the rest of the office. "Don't you people have anything to do? Have you never seen an undercover agent get hurt?" There was enough snarl in his voice that all the cops hurried back to what they were supposed to be doing.

Jones helped her to a chair and Surratt activated the dimming screen over the window into his office. Reece was the last in the room and he shut the door.

"What the hell happened?" Surratt still looked worried, but he was also pissed—and not at the three in front of him.

"Can we get these off?" Aisling raised her hands and winced as the brief wrapping the cop had done on her wound pulled. "And yeah, going to need a doctor."

Surratt had gone behind his desk as they came in, but he was back in a second, he took a good look at her. Then he glared at Reece. "She's injured and you brought her here?"

"I thought we should get the cuffs off before the hospital. And we need to keep her under guard."

That snapped Aisling out of her drifting pain. "Why? I'm

now a flight risk?"

Surratt folded his arms and waited for Reece to explain after tossing a set of master cuff keys to Jones.

"No, but someone is setting you up. Where's Heike?" Reece asked Surratt.

Surratt pulled back at the change in topic. "Funny you should ask. She hasn't come in the last two days. No calls, nothing. The house she was staying in is empty."

"Crap." Aisling winced as Jones finally found the right key and the pressure on her wrists stopped as the cuffs came off. "She removed my tat." She rubbed her wrists.

"How? A good glam will hide them."

"The Coast Guard captain that pulled us out of the water had a police-issue scanner. It didn't show anything." Reece nodded toward Surratt's desk. "Get yours and see for yourself. I don't know if she was after Aisling specifically or only trying to endanger as many undercover cops as possible, but you probably want to pull in any who had work done by her."

Surratt grabbed the scan wand and held it where Aisling's tat should be. Three more passes and there still wasn't a tat. There was a lot of swearing though.

He went back to his desk and tapped the speaker. "Fachie, get me a list of everyone who had Heike work on them with tats or disguises. And if she shows up, lock her up immediately." Fachie was Surratt's assistant. A gnome who was so efficient that he usually had what Surratt needed before he finished talking. He was also the soul of discretion.

There was a pause, something unheard of for him. "Aye, Captain. And a medevac for Aisling?"

Surratt smiled at the speaker. "Good thinking. We can let people think she's far more injured than she is. Get on it." He sat back in his chair as he cut the speaker. "Heike. Damn. She was a good cop."

"I think *was* is the correct term. I don't know what happened, but she's working for the other side, either willfully or under duress." Reece tried to rewrap Aisling's wound.

The door popped open and Fachie smiled at Aisling. "Medevac is here. Will your guests be going along?"

"Yes." Reece and Surratt answered in unison.

"Apparently yes. Should I be on a stretcher or anything? In fact, do I need all this? Any doc can sew me up and at least thirty cops saw me walk in here. They'll know what condition I'm in." She didn't add that there was no way of knowing if any of them were corrupted by whoever Heike had been working for. Besides, she knew she didn't look great, but she felt much better than she had. Getting the cuffs off helped reduce the pressure pulling on her shoulder.

"You've had a relapse; I've already spread the word. The stretcher is on its way." Fachie nodded to Surratt and shut the door.

"Before they get here, is there anything you can tell me about what the hell happened?" Surratt was being far more diplomatic than Aisling would have been—and far more tolerant of Reece.

"It's complicated," Aisling said. She could tell as he started to open his mouth, Reece wasn't going to give much, if anything, to Surratt. "But you might want to pull the records for that Coast Guard ship that is burning, and a black chopper, serial CO-459012. It shot at us, then somehow crashed after we did, with three dead men on board. The fed boys said they didn't do it and I believe them. Oh, the Coast Guard ship was loaded with drugs, and three guards who tried to kill me." She tilted her head at an annoyed Reece. "Anything else I forgot?"

Surratt laughed. "I told you she wouldn't put up with your bullshit, Larkin. Thank you for the intel, Detective. You know they wouldn't have told me any of that." His face stilled. "I'll fill you in later, but there is something big going down in the drug lords' turf wars—something has a lot of the smaller gangs scared. But we're not sure of what."

He didn't get a chance to add anything else as Fachie knocked and opened the door. The med staff came in, nodded to Aisling, then got her on the stretcher and wrapped her up.

Jones and Reece went to go out first but Fachie stopped them. "These won't start any fashion trends, but they're clean, dry, and don't smell like brine. Once you get her there, you can change." He handed a pile of clothing to Reece. "There's a change for Aisling as well."

The trip out to the vehicle was muffled; mostly Aisling couldn't see much after being covered from head to toe. The whirling of another chopper wasn't a happy sound, though; she didn't want to get in another so soon after the last. But she trusted Surratt on this. He was as rattled about Heike as she was, and if he felt they needed to make her seem injured in a big way for the moment, then so be it.

The ride was short and within five minutes the doors opened and she heard Reece tell the approaching hospital staff this was the patient called in by Surratt.

They trundled her down corridors and she tried her best to stay still and exude being injured. Wasn't that hard as she *was* hurt and still feeling the effects of the last few hours.

"Officer." Reece had his polite fed voice on as he greeted whoever Surratt put on door duty.

"Agent." The word was too clipped to give her a clue who it was.

The door was shut behind them and two nurses helped remove her coverings. Neither seemed surprised to see she wasn't as injured as they were pretending.

The first smiled at her as he helped her into the bed. "The doctor will be here to see to that shoulder."

"We've secured this floor," the second nurse said as she

adjusted Aisling's bed. "Officer Goldkowsky out front is the only one in uniform. Detective Danaan's records are sealed as well. Is there anything else you need?"

Reece started to shake his head, then paused. "Wait, maybe some food. She's not nice when she's hungry." The grin he flashed was a knockout and the same one he'd used with the cops at the dock.

Aisling wondered why he was such an ass to everyone in her precinct but charming everywhere else. There had to be a reason. He'd been popping up for the past couple of years and not played well at all. So why?

She was so busy trying to figure out yet another layer of the man that she almost missed his dig. "That was your stomach you heard." She shrugged and shared a nod to Jones. "But I think we could all eat and change clothes."

The agents stepped into the hall so Aisling could change. Fachie was right about the clothes not being exciting. But they were clean, dry, and new.

Jones and Reece came in after a few minutes, both having changed.

"I almost forgot, but please tell me that Ankh badge wasn't in your coat?" Aisling made herself comfortable in the bed; might as well play the part. Either this was a deluxe model, or her body was over-reacting after all the recent abuse; it was surprisingly easy to relax.

Reece pulled the packet it had come in out of his pants pocket; he'd obviously transferred it when he changed clothes. "No, but any DNA from the man who threw it at you is gone. The thing got soaked."

Aisling was about to ask him if he planned on telling Surratt about it when yells and screams came from the corridor. Followed by alarms.

Reece and Jones had armed themselves off the coast guards, but Aisling didn't have a weapon. She started to get up anyway.

Reece pushed her back down. "You can't. You are hurt, you have no gun, and we're not sure what in the hell this is." The sincerity in his dangerous eyes got her. "Stay put." And his words echoed her own to Maeve not that long ago.

"Fine, I'll stay." The yelling was getting worse.

Jones was already out the door and with a concerned nod in her direction, Reece followed. Goldkowsky stayed at his guard post, but looked like he wanted to go down the corridor. The alarms had been shut off, but a red light was still flashing.

"What the hell is going on? Did you see anything?" Aisling asked Goldkowsky. She hadn't lied to Reece. She was staying in the room; she just kept the door open a bit.

"Not sure. There was some action at the far end. This is a secure floor for many things, so it could be another cop, a witness, a dangerous patient." He shrugged. "But then the yelling started. And that's not good." He pointed to the silent still flashing red light.

She couldn't see what was going on down the corridor without risking someone seeing her. But the lights were everywhere. "What's it for?"

"Dangerous exposure. And if it—" A klaxon cut him off and doors started slamming. The light turned purple. "Damn it. We're locked down now. Whatever it is, it's bad. That's a class one contagion."

CHAPTER TWENTY-SEVEN

———◆———

T HE DOOR TO AISLING'S ROOM started making a grinding noise as it tried to shut and lock down. She took a chance and looked at the other end of the hall. There were people running toward her. Rather, one fey was running toward *her*. There was madness in his eyes as he stared directly at her and picked up speed. Reece, Jones, and what she assumed were the undercover cops were all running behind him.

"Why the hell aren't they shooting him…oh goddess." Aisling grabbed Goldkowsky, dragged him into her room, and let the automatic lock engage. "I don't have a lot of strength right now, so help me move anything we can in front of that door." The hospital protocol meant the door was electronically locked—Aisling wanted more defenses beyond that.

Goldkowsky was a solid detective and he didn't ask questions in a panic situation. He waited until everything they could move was piled in front of the door. "What the hell is out there?" The yelling was right at her door now. The pile of furniture rattled as something rammed the door again and again. "And why did no one shoot?"

"Remember the girl flyer, Julilynn Marcos? The one with the iron wing? That fey out there is showing the same symptoms. It was crawling up his neck. They must have realized what was wrong with him and what would happen if they shot a diseased, iron-carrying fey."

Goldkowsky's major had been bioscience before he

switched to law enforcement. He paled as he thought about the repercussions. "If the Iron Death goes airborne because of the shot, the vents could carry it to the rest of the hospital and everyone inside would be exposed." He shook his head, but still automatically reached for his gun when the door rattled again.

No one knew what the Iron Death would do if it got airborne because they still weren't sure what the drug really was. But Aisling had a guess that any non-humans on this floor would have become extremely ill; many would have died. Possibly anyone with fey blood in the entire hospital.

Another rumble, almost like a small explosion, caused the ceiling tiles to shake loose. But the door stayed shut.

First the alarms stopped. Then the flashing purple light switched to red. And there was no more rattling from the door.

"Aisling? Are you okay? Where's Goldkowsky?" Reece's voice was a welcome one.

"He's with me. We're both okay. Can we come out?"

The chorus of no's stopped both she and Goldkowsky from starting to pull back the furniture.

"We have a third Iron Death victim, although this one seems to have been sent here. We've got hazmat suits, and he was contained, but it's too risky to come out yet. He died right at your door. The seals around this room will keep you safe, but stay inside."

Aisling and Goldkowsky looked at each other. She climbed back on her bed. Moving around hadn't done great things for her gunshot wound. Goldkowsky freed a chair from the pile at the door and sat to call his wife and tell her he was probably going to be late getting home tonight.

She thought about asking to borrow it to call her brother, but most likely he'd find her.

An hour later there was a knock at the door. "You two

can come out now," Surratt said.

She unlocked the door, but he was alone. The corridor behind him gave no evidence of what had happened.

"Where'd Reece and Jones go?"

"They got called back by a higher up. We need to get that hole in you closed, and you need some rest. Goldkowsky, you good to finish your shift? Aisling's going to have a miraculous recovery tomorrow, but I still want her under guard tonight."

Goldkowsky nodded. "Sure. I thought things might go long, so I called the wife. I'm good."

"I'm glad everyone is good, but there's a patient for me." A dark-skinned, slender, pixie-fey woman came forward. The men stepped aside with respect although she barely came up to their waists.

"I think it's stopped bleeding," Aisling said.

The tiny woman tilted her head. "And you're a doctor now? How fabulous for you." She turned to Surratt and Goldkowsky. "All cops are the same." Then back to Aisling. "Please lie back and let me examine the wound. And gentlemen, if you can shut the door on your way out, that would be appreciated."

Aisling shook her head at their quick escape. "I take it they have been under your care before?"

"I'm one of our sensitive team—we handle the law enforcement types. Surratt got into so many disasters as a rookie, it's amazing he survived." She carefully pulled aside the field dressing. "Military dressing, and a good job too. They kept you from being worse off than you are."

Aisling winced at a few prods.

"Clean, through and through shot. A derma patch on for a few days and you'll be fine." She paused. "Did you know you had a tracker in that shoulder? And the bullet managed to destroy it?"

Although she knew she couldn't see her own shoulder,

Aisling twisted around anyway. "How did you know it was there if the shot destroyed it?" Maybe the guard who shot her hadn't missed after all. That was too much coincidence.

"My scanner is getting residue, though not much."

A snap of cold hugged her shoulder in the front and the back as the derma patch settled in. That the tracker was no longer a concern was fine; that it might have been a deliberate shot wasn't. The tracker had reacted when the Coast Guard captain brought them on board. She might have locked Aisling up for more than just a missing cop tat.

"Now, you're going to be fine, but you're exhausted and need sleep. Since I don't trust any law enforcement personnel to actually rest when they are told to, you'll be staying here overnight. I'll have food sent up, but don't try sweet talking an early release." She narrowed her dark eyes. "Unless I have to tranq you?"

Aisling raised both hands and settled back into her pillows. "After the last few days, rest and food sound wonderful."

———◆———

She woke the next morning without a clue as to where she was and was halfway out of bed before her brain caught up with what the surroundings meant. She glanced around for what had woken her and realized that it was her arm. In all of the ensuing madness, she'd forgotten about Caradoc's gizmo to block the magic concerning the vallenian. It was buzzing, but still not visible to the eye.

A knock followed by the door opening made her stop poking at it. She hoped the buzzing was a good thing. The nurse that came in appeared a bit confused at her being awake, but smiled anyway.

"I heard rustling and wanted to make sure things were okay. Since you're awake, there's a call that's come in for you—if you feel up to taking it."

Aisling scrambled back into bed but nodded. The nurse brought over a standard wireless phone and sat it on the table next to the bed. "Try not to talk too long though. Dr. Watamni can be fierce if she thinks patients aren't resting enough." With a wink, she went back out and shut the door.

"Aisling here."

"Sister o' mine, you really can muddle things up," Caradoc said with far more morning enthusiasm than should be allowed. "Everything is good at the house, but I think I should come get you."

He sounded fine, but it was hard to tell with him. Her initial reaction was that she needed to get to work. But she knew Surratt; unless he needed her for something specific, he'd force her to take the day off. Never mind that she was technically loaned out to narcotics still. "Let me check with the boss, but probably, yeah. Doc won't let me out without a final checkup." There were a lot of things she wanted to ask, but not on an open line. "Oh, and can you get a new phone for me before you come get me? Mine is at the bottom of the ocean, so they'll need to do a remote data transfer."

"On it," Caradoc said then put his hand over the phone to talk to someone in the room. When he came back on the line his voice sounded annoyed. "Someone is going to get tranquilized real soon if she doesn't watch it."

Aisling laughed. Maeve must be feeling better if she was causing him grief. Of course, there were plenty of times in the past she wanted to tranq her partner as well. "I'll call you once I'm sprung...or do I need to?" She had a feeling Caradoc was wired into the hospital somehow.

"Nah, we're good. I'll see you when you're ready. If the boss says you go there first, I can do that." He clicked off.

A soft rap on the door was followed by the door opening. Dr. Watamni came into the room. "You look much better." She motioned for Aisling to sit up in bed so she could check the area around the bullet wound. "Everything appears fine, however, I'd like to keep you longer. But I won't. I know how stubborn elves are." She went to the door. "Call your boss. I'm releasing you, but not back to duty until tomorrow. If he gives you a bad time, have him talk to me." With a nod, she shut the door.

It was still early, and taking her time leaving wouldn't be a problem for the hospital, but Aisling wanted out. She also wanted to know what in the hell happened yesterday in the corridor. She knew that even though it happened right outside her door, and the fey appeared to have been aiming for her, there would be nothing to find. Hospitals could be tighter than police stations.

A nurse came in and gave her a message. Surratt had called last night and told her to stay home today. She quickly changed, gathered her things, and left. Even though she knew they would have sterilized everything last night, she walked slowly down the corridor looking for clues.

Nothing.

Surprisingly, she was left standing out front for three full minutes before Caradoc showed up.

"Sorry, I had to lock up your friend. She's feeling better and doesn't think she should stay put."

Aisling grabbed the new phone sitting on the car seat then slid into the car. "Not surprising. She still talking about going off on her own?"

Caradoc grinned and headed for the freeway. "Yup. She has a serious lone-wolf dramatic streak. How'd you two survive as partners for so long?"

"We're both too stubborn to quit. Besides, neither of us could probably work with any other cop."

"Like Reece? He's not a cop, but she did tell me her theories. Although that would be a different type of partnership." His grin was pure teasing older brother.

"Seriously? We've got more weird and dangerous shit going on than we can deal with, and you two are worried about my love life?" She shook her head and activated her phone.

And almost threw it when it rang immediately. She took a deep breath to steady herself before answering. "Aisling."

"I came by to see you and they said you escaped." Speak of the devil and he shall call you on your brand-new phone.

She shot Caradoc a glare even though he was keeping his eyes on the road. He still had the damn smirk.

"Hey, *Reece*. The doc said it was a clean through and through. Slapped a derma patch on and, after a night's observation, let me go. She forbade me from working today—what do you need?" She wasn't up to dealing with any feelings she might or might not have about him, but if he was calling there could be news about the case.

"It might be better if you rest a bit. Yesterday was intense even by Jones and my standards. But briefly, and we don't know much, there is evidence that your partner is back in the country. And she was the last person to see Ryn Trebol alive."

CHAPTER TWENTY-EIGHT

A ISLING WAITED A MOMENT TO respond. She *knew* Maeve was in the country, but Maeve had pointedly said she hadn't seen Ryn recently. Spoken to him, yes. Seen, no.

"What makes you think that?" She was out of sorts enough that she didn't want to try a pure lie. Reece might pick it up through the phone.

"They've tracked her entrance into the US, on a passenger plane under an assumed name. There's footage of her with him about an hour before he went feral. I'm sorry, Aisling, it appears she is on the other side. We're tracking her, and we will find her."

Caradoc glanced over, as his hearing was sharp enough to hear Reece. He looked confused. Just like Aisling felt.

"Where do you think she is? I'm not going to try and help her Reece, but she's still my partner." She was pretty certain Maeve was still trapped in Caradoc's house, but she didn't have to fake the anxiety in her voice.

"I know." There was a gentleness in his voice she hadn't heard before. "All we have is that she's in the northern part of the state. She cut through the same woods you were left in, but has been spotted twice farther north. Might be heading to the compound in Eureka." Northern California was densely wooded. About ten years ago a gang had taken over a small town and many refugees from the law had made their escapes there over the years.

Aisling had no idea how they were supposedly seeing

her when she was still in LA, but she could make a guess as to why they thought she went through the Glovin woods. She tilted her head to Caradoc. He shrugged and got off the freeway.

Damn it. They'd almost been on long enough for someone to trace the call. "Sorry, Reece, going to a friend's house for a bit, connection is bad up here. I'll call you tomorrow." She clicked off before he could respond.

"Well, that was abrupt." Caradoc pulled into the housing area and went right through the hedge.

"Why are you doing that in broad daylight?" The use of magic wasn't a problem; there were more fey in the world than humans or breeds, so magic was the norm. But she was thinking a hidden house should stay hidden.

"Don't worry, there's a spell casting mechanism in the hedge. Now why were you so rude with your future boy toy?" He got out and was halfway up the drive before she even opened the door.

"He's not my boy toy, and regardless, he was trying to trace the call and track me." She used to have a trace breaker on her old cell; first order of business would be to get one put on this phone.

Caradoc broke the spell lock he had on the house. "Isn't that a bit extreme? Maybe he just wanted to talk to you? Besides, he could have asked where you were."

"Which he didn't because he was tracking me."

"Who was tracking you and you're out of chocolate." Maeve came out from the kitchen finishing up the remains of a candy bar.

"She hung up on our boy Reece and seems to think he was chatty to try and get a lock on her."

"He probably was. He is an uber fed. He probably sneaks up on his mother when he goes to visit on mum's day." Maeve threw herself onto the sofa, but Aisling noticed she was still stiff. Pretending to be healthier than she was again.

"I would have noticed. My car records those attempts." He took Aisling's phone and walked back outside. He came back a moment later looking pissed. "He tried to trace you. Didn't go through, but two more seconds and he'd be on our doorstep. His tech is better than mine." He handed Aisling her phone and stalked to his bedroom.

Aisling and Maeve followed.

It had been clear when Aisling first came here two days ago that this wasn't Caradoc's normal home. But his bedroom now looked like he was planning on spending some time here. One whole wall had been turned into a technophile's dream with two work desks and a bench. His bed was crammed into the corner.

He flipped open a slim black case and took out the smallest set of pliers and screwdriver Aisling had ever seen. "Phone?" He didn't look up as he rifled through the case with one hand, but his other was held out.

Aisling dropped her phone in his hand. He had the interior open and was fussing with things before she had pulled her hand back.

"That will show him." He closed the phone case back up and gave it to her with a smile.

Aisling turned it over and back. "Looks the same."

"Ah! It does. But you now not only have a trace breaker, you have only the second trace breaker reversal slam in the world. Our sneaky fed tries that stunt again and not only will he not be able to trace you, you can trace him. It will show on your screen. And if you hit this screen it will slam a fifteen-minute disable on his phone." He pointed to a small black icon with a skull on it. Dramatic, but Caradoc liked things like that.

Aisling almost wanted Reece to call back to test it out. "Mother doesn't know you can do this, right? She was the main reason I had a trace breaker on my other phone."

"I avoid her as much as possible, and I am certainly never

giving her knowledge of my tech. She's left the city now, by the way. Off to torture Europe for a bit."

Aisling was grateful she wasn't going to run into the woman, but not being in Los Angeles wouldn't stop her from bothering Aisling. Or making real her threat.

"That is not a good reaction on your face, what did mummy dearest do while I was away?" Maeve said as they all walked back to the living room.

"She's trying to force Aisling to give up the force and join the family business," Caradoc said.

Aisling took over the recliner. "I can speak for myself. But yeah, what he said. Even though he wasn't there. Even though I asked him to be there. You know most of our family are jerks. They all sided with her. You and Dad could have helped."

"I'm sorry about that. I'm not sure where Dad was, but I had an issue with that patent agent and couldn't get away. But I heard about it. What's the problem? You have no intention of giving in to her."

Aisling bounced the back of her head on the headrest. "No. But it's just getting on my nerves. The more she pushes, the worse it gets."

"And every time she calls you out there's a chance someone will realize who you are." Maeve tilted her head in that 'I understand you, but I don't get it' expression. "Because being a member of one of the most powerful families in the world is a bad thing?"

"If anyone realizes that I am her daughter, what family I belong to, my days on the force are over. Even Caradoc keeps his family connections down low." Aisling fought the lump of fear thinking about that caused.

"Then if she wants you to join the family, wouldn't exposing you in public as her daughter be the quickest way to get that done? If you really couldn't be on the force with that connection?" Maeve said.

Caradoc laughed. "Our Aisling is smarter than that. When she first decided to join the force, she made Mother commit to a blood swearing to never disclose who she was in public—in any form—if Aisling made it through and became a cop. The rest of the family couldn't either, which wouldn't be that hard to enforce since Mother controls them. If Aisling failed getting onto the force, she would work with the family. Mother was so certain Aisling wouldn't make it onto the force, she agreed. She's stuck now."

Maeve laughed. "That would have been good to see. I've only seen the official records on your mother, but she is a scary woman."

Aisling smiled at the memory of her mother realizing her daughter was going to be a cop and there was nothing she, or any of the family, could do to stop it. "It was a damn good moment. But she can still force meetings in person and accidentally risk exposing me." Aisling shook her head.

"So what happened with my perfect plan?" Caradoc asked. "Your fed boy has locked all the details of what actually happened, or rather the people he works for have."

"First off, it wasn't a perfect plan, it wasn't even a good plan, and when you pretend to tie someone up, you don't *really* tie them up. But it went wrong so many ways I'd need a wall to chart them all."

Maeve smiled and went into her room. She immediately came back rolling out an old school dry board. "Or a murder board? I had Caradoc get you one after I heard about the explosion."

Most police stations used fey boards, magic-charged electronic devices that could tap into Wi-Fi. Aisling preferred a far more physical way to track big cases. Her board had taken up most of her tiny living room in her old apartment—and been blown up when it exploded.

"Thank you," Aisling said and uncapped the first colored

marker. "This is going to sound self-centered, but I have a bad feeling it's right—at least for now." She drew her focus circle in the middle of the board. In most cases, it was usually the victim. This time she wrote her name. This was a case and while she might or might not be an actual victim, there was too much weird crap going on around her to ignore.

Caradoc and Maeve watched as she added every trail she could think of. The junkie who tried to car-nap her and was killed. Julilynn Marcos with Aisling's name next to her body. Mott Flowers. Caradoc looked ready to ask a question at that, but he shook his head. The smoke monster at the diner. The Lazing. Ryn Trebol. Maeve. The Scottish, Cymru, and Irish gangs. Bilth—twice. The man with the hood in the middle of the forest. Heike. Black helicopter that chased them. Who shot down said black helicopter? Coast Guard. The third iron victim in the hospital. Captain Losien.

She stepped back and searched for gaps. There were no details, just the names. She could now think about the vallenian without her brains leaking out her ears, but she wasn't about to write that one on the board.

"Captain Losien? Heike?" Maeve didn't question her own name being up there, but she hadn't been aware of the department betrayals.

"My question is Mott Flowers," Caradoc said. "How did you know about him? He was the main reason I bought that company the feds bought off me. I let them buy it because he took off a year ago and doesn't appear to be planning to come back. Without him and his inventions, the company is useless."

Aisling rocked back into the sofa and leaned against the arm. She briefly explained all of the items on her board to them, then stepped forward and added "Caradoc's company" next to Mott's name.

Maeve was pissed when she heard what Heike had done to Aisling's tattoo. "I know she's your mate from way back, but I will snap her like a twig if I find her. When is Surratt getting your tat back?"

"No idea. At the time he was trying to keep things subtle. They don't know if it was just me or if Heike had been sent to cause as much havoc as possible."

She was going to add to the board when her phone rang. She was expecting Reece, but Garran's number popped up. He was supposed to be on vacation. Even when he wasn't, he rarely called her. Of course, he usually showed up wherever she was at the time if he needed her. There was a good chance even he couldn't find her right now.

"What's up, Garran? Aren't you off somewhere sunny?"

"Sadly, no. I know you're recovering and off the grid. But you might want to come in. Surratt's at St. Belle's Hospital. They just found him in an alley. He's been shot. It doesn't look good."

CHAPTER TWENTY-NINE

"DAMN IT, DID ANYONE SEE anything?" She went to her bedroom to get her gun.

"Nothing. He was supposed to be in his office, had the window dark. Fachie checked when he left for the day, noticed he was missing, called him, but found his phone was still in the office. Uniforms found him less than a half mile from the station. Docs say he'd been shot at close range where he was found."

She almost put her gun back; she didn't have her badge and not even her tat. Wandering around with a police-issued gun and nothing to back it up was a good way to get shot if things went bad. Trouble was, they could do that even if she didn't have her gun. She tucked it into the small of her back and put on a longer jacket to cover it. "I'm on my way. Have you called Reece?"

"Why would I call the feds because our boss got shot?"

"Can't explain, but there's a bunch of shit going on—Reece should know, if he doesn't already."

Silence on the other end. "I know. I can't talk on the line. I'll meet you at St. Belle's. You call Larkin and tell him to join us. He doesn't have this line, and I want to keep it that way. Garran out." He clicked off.

"What happened?" Maeve got the words out before Caradoc, but both looked to be asking the same thing.

"Surratt has been shot. They found him in an alley and he might not make it. I need to get to St. Belle's…damn it, I need a car." She hadn't been worried about not having a vehicle until now.

"I can take you in. Sorry, not letting you borrow my car though," Caradoc said. "I can see about finding you one after this."

"I've had my issues with Surratt—I think everyone in the department has—but damn it, I wish I could go," Maeve said. At least this time she wasn't trying to insist she come along.

Aisling grabbed her shoulder in solidarity. "I know." She was glad Maeve was staying put. Of course, she knew her partner well enough that she was still going to ask Caradoc to lock the house again once they left.

"Okay, you can drive me, but this will make twice that we've been seen together. We need a cover story." Aisling and Caradoc left the house and he locked Maeve in without a word from Aisling.

Maeve's yell of annoyance as the magic shield locked the house told Aisling she'd been correct.

"I *could* be your brother," Caradoc said. He raised a hand as they both got in his car. "Mother has always said the best lies work when they are simple and close to the truth. No one knows our family background. I'll be myself, renegade business tycoon and rabble-rouser. You've never connected yourself to me before because of my reputation—hence us having different last names."

Aisling rolled her eyes. "You don't have a reputation."

"Ha, a lot you know."

She shook her head and called Reece. She wasn't surprised that it went to voice mail. He probably screened calls out of habit. "This is Aisling. They just found Surratt. He's been shot and might not make it. I'm going to St. Belle's now. You might want to be there." She knew she had the tracker breaker on her phone and she was calling him, not the other way around, but she still kept it short.

St. Belle's was an older hospital, smaller, and with expansive gardens around it. It also catered to humans. Queen Bellaquora was the elf who initially found a way to save the humans when the Black Plague was destroying their population.

Caradoc turned into the parking lot instead of taking her to the front to drop her off. "I'm not going in, but since I'm coming out as your brother, it wouldn't be unusual for me to want to wait for my car-less sister." He gave a soft smile. "I know he's been a pain in your ass, but I am sorry your boss got shot."

Aisling got out and walked around to his side of the car. "Thank you. If I don't need you to wait, I'll call."

She walked to the entrance. "I'm Detective Aisling Danaan, here to see Captain Surratt."

"I'll need to see your badge, he's under guard." The surly nurse looked more like a security guard and he probably was. "I can't let you in without one."

"I don't—"

"She's with me," Garran cut in as he came down the hall. "Is that sufficient?" His face was almost a snarl and was definitely not something any sane person wanted to be on the other end of.

"Yes, Detective Garran. I'm sorry." The nurse looked embarrassed.

"Pay more attention next time." Garran took Aisling's arm and spun her down the hall.

She waited until they were well past fey hearing. "Wasn't that extreme? He was doing his job."

"He was being an ass. I already told him you were coming, gave your name and a full description. He's either incompetent or up to something. I've already ordered his records to be pulled."

Aisling pulled back at that. Garran was a lone wolf; he played things his own way and kept to himself and special projects. Now he sounded as suspicious as Reece. "That bad?"

"I'm sorry you weren't pulled into the loop sooner, or that we couldn't keep you clear of it completely. We couldn't keep Maeve out and she almost got killed." His eyes darkened. "So did you. But now we go forward." He stopped outside of a door with two uniformed cops that she didn't recognize in front of it. "He's not doing well. Doc says maybe a few hours." He nodded to the cops and swung open the door.

Surratt was hooked up to so many machines that Aisling had difficulty telling where he was. She left Garran and walked to Surratt's side. His face was the color of the sheets and bandages stuck out along his chest under the edge of the blanket. She watched him for a few moments. As a cop, death wasn't a stranger. As an elf, it still struck her as wrong. She traced the edge of his hand and silently vowed she'd find out who did this.

"He was supposed to leave town."

Aisling jumped at Reece's voice. She didn't hear him enter the room and was surprised that Garran let him in. She turned to find him also watching Surratt.

"We had intel that Heike's body had been found, and there was evidence that someone was coming after him next. After we cleaned up the attack in the hospital, he promised me he was packing up and going deep. Damn you, Surratt." There was real emotion in his voice and Aisling confirmed what she'd come to realize in the past few days—the animosity between Reece and Surratt was a ruse. They probably weren't friends, but they had been working together on something big for a long enough time for genuine respect to develop.

"He didn't tell me that," Garran said from a few feet behind them. "I wasn't on vacation. I was trying to track some leads. He texted me early in the evening to say you'd been shot and tell me about the third iron fey attack.

Nothing about Heike."

The machines around Surratt started flashing and Aisling and the other two moved out of the way as hospital staff came rushing in. Aisling found herself digging her fingers into Reece's arm as she watched them try to keep the lines on the monitors from going flat.

"We need to keep him here, ease some of the pressure. If we can get him stable, we can put him into a coma and give him a chance to fight back." The woman who spoke was a full healer, one of the elves from the higher clans according to her smock and her clan jewelry. Next to her was another elven healer, a male.

"Where is your third?" Aisling didn't want to disturb them but a Triskele was needed to have a chance at stabilizing him.

"She's out sick and we haven't been able to find a replacement." The woman didn't look up as Aisling approached.

"I'm not licensed, but I might make the third side." She let her healing power show so they could feel it.

"Under-trained, but better than nothing," the woman said. Aisling stood back a bit as the doctors stepped out of the way. She and the two healers joined hands over Surratt's body. It was hard to push past the horrible sound of the machines, but eventually Aisling found her balance. She was there to stabilize the healing; the other two would do the heavy lifting. Even so, a few minutes later she was ready to curl into a ball and weep with exhaustion. Two sets of steady hands guided her back to a chair against the wall.

She felt as if her bones had melted as she wrapped her arms around herself.

"She's far stronger than she appears. But get a blanket on her, she might go into shock," the male healer said from where he and the female one continued the healing on a less intense level. The machines had stopped their warnings and the lines were no longer flat.

Reece tucked a blanket around her and stayed at her side. Garran took a few steps closer to Surratt and the healers.

"Does he have a directive?" The nurse assisting the healers asked quietly.

"He's a cop without a family. But I have authorization to make the directive decision." Garran held out a thin data chip to one of the nurses; she scanned it and nodded to the healer.

Aisling had heard of some cops having so few connections with distant family that they chose a fellow officer to make their final wishes known. She knew she'd pick a dozen different friends on the force before her mother.

"What are the options?" Garran was calm and solid, just like he always was. A slight inflection in his voice and a stiffness to his stance told Aisling how upset he was.

"The bullet is out but he lost a lot of blood before he was found. We can try to keep fighting, forcing him back each time, or we can put him in a coma." The healer paused. "We have no idea when, or if, he will come out of it."

She didn't say it, but it was clear they'd dealt with police before. The words left unspoken were heavy and serious and clear to Aisling. If there was something Garran desperately needed to know from Surratt, they could try and bring him back. But the odds would be worse than if he went into a coma, taking whatever information Garran needed with him.

"The coma," Garran said with a catch in his voice. "But he is to be under guard at all times, and only with people myself, Agent Larkin, or Detective Danaan approve of." He pointed to Reece and Aisling.

Aisling was surprised at her inclusion as well as Reece's. From the look that flew across his face, so was he.

"Agreed. He will have one of the private rooms upstairs." With a dismissive nod, the healer went back to her patient.

They were in the way, but Aisling was still feeling like someone had punched her in the head. Healing Maeve had been bad, but this was horrific. Regardless of what the male healer had said, she wasn't magically strong.

"Okay, let's walk out to the waiting area," Reece said as he helped her to her feet and he and Garran escorted her and her blanket out of the room. "I can give you a ride back, but where are you staying? My people have another safe house set up for you."

Garran nodded once they got her into the waiting area and went to talk to the police officers guarding the door as well as two more officers who had shown up. Aisling now realized they were detectives from other precincts but they were wearing beat cop uniforms. The high-end guns they had weren't standard beat cop issue though.

"Oh no, it's okay. My brother is waiting out there. I have a place to stay." She shook off some of her lethargy. "And I don't think you or your agencies need to know where I'm staying at the moment." She wasn't sure how long she could push him off, but she wasn't able to deal with him right now.

"We can protect you. After what's been happening, we need to keep you safe."

Aisling leaned back and folded her arms. "You do remember that I was kidnapped from one of your best safe houses, right?" She knew it was a stretch, but the fact was that the bad guys *had* found the house. Granted, they hadn't had time to act on it before Caradoc led them off. But the house had been compromised.

"We can find a new house. We can keep you safe." There were a few layers to his words that Aisling wasn't up to dealing with yet.

"Did your people find out who it was who almost blew my head off in the forest? Who in the hell was in that black chopper? Who took out that same chopper?" She got up and started pushing him in the chest. "There is too much shit going on and no one, not even the super spooks, know what the hell it is." She stared at him; for once his glorious eyes did nothing to her. She was scared and tired.

Reece took a hold of the finger that she'd been poking him with and gently lowered it. Then he wiped a tear she hadn't known she'd shed away.

"I'm sorry. He and I weren't friends, but losing Surratt is a brutal blow. He was a good man." Then he engulfed her in his arms. They were close in height, but standing like this she was aware of the few inches he had on her.

She thought about pushing away, but she was so damn tired. And it felt too damn good. "It's all of this. I need something to fight. No one knows what's going on, so I can't fight anything."

Garran came back to them. "If you two are done, we have a lead."

Reece dropped his arms and actually appeared embarrassed.

Aisling nodded. "On Surratt?"

"Yes. The cops that found him did a piss poor job the first round of checking for witnesses. My people found some." He nodded to Reece. "You staying on this?" It was a challenge; the lines between feds, cops, and whoever Garran's other people were had changed.

"Hell, yes." Reece started for the door. "I'll follow." The way he held the door, he left an open question if Aisling would ride with him.

Her reaction to being in his arms was too disturbing to deal with. Besides, Garran might actually give her some answers.

"I need to catch up with Garran. Make sure you keep up with us." She walked through the door.

Garran stayed behind until Reece passed them and silently went to the lot.

"Is there something you want to talk about?" Garran had his car up front in the police emergency spot, so it was a short walk. Which was good because his smirk was too annoying to be in public.

"I have no idea why everyone feels the need to get involved in my personal business." She slid into the passenger seat.

"If you're involved with a fed, I have the right to know. Besides, who else noticed?" He moved past the parking structure.

"Damn it, my brother." She held up her hand. "Not damn it that he noticed anything, like you, it's all speculation. But I need to call him; he gave me a ride here." She punched in his number.

He picked up before the first ring went through. "You're going out on a case," Caradoc said.

"Yup, just letting you know." Aisling paused, wondering how to ask him where in the hell she should have Garran drop her off. She trusted Garran more than Reece, but she wasn't wasting Caradoc's safe house, nor risking Maeve.

"I'll meet you at the Boolian Diner after. We still have those papers to go over. Call me when you're there." Caradoc clicked off.

Garran drummed his fingers on the steering wheel as they waited for Reece. "Didn't know you had a brother."

At least this might distract him from Reece. "I try to keep it a secret. My brother is Caradoc Larfin. He changed the family name years ago." It wasn't hard to channel some irritation into her voice.

"The business tycoon? The one who likes to take over entire bars for small parties?" Garran laughed. "One of you two fell far from the family tree. No wonder you don't talk about him."

"Yeah. He's a pain. But he's been taking care of me with the car and place to stay issues."

"Gotcha." He quickly got on the freeway once Reece's car pulled up behind them; obviously he'd gotten it out of impound at some point. "And no, I haven't forgotten about you and Larkin, but I'll let it slide for now."

She turned to him. "More importantly, where have you been and how long has all of this been going on? *What* is going on?"

"I was over in the UK for a few days to see if I could find anything about Maeve. The feds are sure she's here in the US and working against us. Surratt didn't believe it. Never found her though. As for the what and how long? Hard to say. We didn't notice anything unified until a few months ago. Too much noise and not enough."

That was one of his favorite sayings. Meant there was a lot of useless chatter in the underground world, but not enough meaning where there should be. Important pieces were remaining hidden.

"For what it's worth, I wanted to pull you in. But then Maeve took off and that flyer…" he shook his head.

"You suspected me? Or did Surratt?"

"Neither. We were concerned as to what attention you were already attracting. Thought you were out of it though, or else one of us would have been watching Heike." He went down a side street. They weren't that far from the station, but the rundown area felt worlds away.

"The witness was here, but I don't see anything…wait… that green car." He slowed and the hair on the back of Aisling's neck stood on end. A quick glance behind her showed that Reece was still behind them but no one else was.

No one was anywhere.

"Garran?" She watched all the houses; a few that hadn't had their shutters closed did as soon as they passed.

"I see it. Damn it, the source was good. One of my best CIs." He started slowing, but more like he was searching for someone.

Aisling knew they were being watched, probably since before they hit the street. Holding her cell phone to her ear would be too much of a tip off. She only glanced down briefly as she dialed Reece.

"It's a trap. They might not have noticed you're with us, so try to turn around and get out of here." She spoke loud enough that he should be able to hear her, but his response was almost too faint to hear.

"I think they spotted me. This is an area Leifen used to visit. They have lookouts up now."

Garran swore more as he approached the end of the road. "Larkin! Turn and run now! We don't have a choice." He pointed to a blockade of cars that completely obstructed the road, then swung his own car wide and flipped a huge U-turn.

Reece was turning right before him and racing back the way they came in. A hail of gunfire tore into his car and their own.

CHAPTER THIRTY

A ISLING SCREAMED, BUT NONE OF the bullets hitting their car came through. Even the ones hitting the windows melted as they struck.

"Sister of mine, you two might want to get the hell out of there before this gadget shorts out." Caradoc's voice came out of her phone, but she knew she hadn't called him. She still had the line open to Reece.

"You're in Reece's car? What are you doing?"

"You don't sound happy but that's okay, neither is he— didn't know I was in the back seat until now. I'm running a scrambler of my own invention on the gun fire. Not going to explain more. Follow us."

Reece's car took off down the street.

Garran shrugged. "He *is* your brother."

"He takes after our mother." She hung onto the dashboard as Garran tore to follow Reece and Caradoc.

"I heard that!" Caradoc yelled through the open phone line.

Having their bullets seemingly dissolve as they came near the speeding cars only increased the number of rounds fired.

Garran was swearing loudly now, and from her still open phone she heard Reece doing the same. Knowing Caradoc, Reece was probably swearing at him as much as the situation. It was a contest as to which one was a bigger pain in the ass.

They turned off the street and the gunfire stopped, but

three heavy motorbikes, the ones favored by the troll gangs, peeled out behind them.

"Seriously? Trolls?"

She looked back as two more bikes picked up the chase. Five troll bikers, in a town they hated, right outside of an ambush. She was going to run out of room on her murder board.

Reece was driving like a wild man, dodging down side streets with turns so fast that only an equally wild driver could follow. Garran had no trouble keeping up. Unfortunately, those biker trolls were the same level of speed obsessed. Or rather, four of them were. The final one couldn't handle the most recent turn and slammed into a tree.

The other four picked up the pace.

"You have to get closer to us," Caradoc yelled through the phone.

"If I get any closer, I'll be sucking your tailpipe!" Garran responded. But he did get closer. If Reece slowed, they were going to be in his back seat.

"Closer. Just a bit. You're almost within range." Caradoc's face was visible in the passenger seat as he turned.

Aisling wasn't surprised to see a large gizmo in his hand. "Do what he says. My brother is eccentric but he's good. He probably has something to make us fly or short out the bikes." She wedged herself as tightly into the seat as she could.

Garran crept up closer, but so did the bikers.

Aisling had no idea what Caradoc was up to. But a moment later he had climbed halfway out of the passenger side window and threw the gizmo.

It sailed right over Garran's car and slammed into the first bike. The heat from the resulting fireball could be felt through Garran's car. The other three bikes couldn't move away in time and they all went up as well.

Reece's car increased speed and this time Garran didn't need cajoling to keep up.

"What the hell? Did you throw a bomb at them?" Aisling was almost disappointed. If they got away, then it was effective, but seemed far too simplistic for her brother.

"As our mother says, old ways are sometimes the best. Now keep moving."

Reece's car whipped down two more side streets and went up an old access road to the freeway.

Aisling could still smell smoke and was sure that Garran's shiny new car had scorch marks on it.

"Is he always like that?" Even Garran sounded stunned.

Aisling shook her head. "Not sure. I don't hang around him much."

"I think we need pie. Or at least cake, and maybe some real food," Reece said through the still open speakerphone. He had been quiet, aside from the swearing, since the ambush. "Stay with us." He got off the freeway and headed toward a familiar diner.

"We were almost killed and he wants food? Is this a fed thing, Larkin?" Garran sounded testy, but he stayed close behind him as he went down the alley.

"Trust me on this," Reece said. He and Caradoc were getting out of his car when she and Garran pulled up.

"Do you trust him?" Garran hadn't turned off the engine yet.

"Caradoc or Reece?"

"Yes."

"I do. I think they're both totally mad, and had you asked me two weeks ago I would have given a different answer." She watched the two arguing about something. "But now? Yeah, I do."

Garran turned off the engine. "Good enough for me."

"You need to warn me the next time you're going to pull that kind of stunt." Reece was getting into Caradoc's face. Reece was about six-two but Caradoc was a few inches taller. That didn't stop Reece.

"Hey, if I hadn't hidden in your car, you'd all be dead. You, I don't care about so much, but I'm attached to my sister. And at least I had a plan, other than food."

"It's a valid plan," Reece said then shrugged as she and Garran approached. "I know it sounds odd, but this is the safest place I can think of." He clicked what looked like a car alarm and a shimmer danced over both cars, then disappeared. "The cloaking device is built into the walls." He pointed to an almost invisible series of tiny dots along the roof of the two closest buildings. "It will hide the cars for a few hours, longer if need be."

He led the way toward the mouth of the alley and the diner. It appeared to have recovered well from the attack of the smoke monster a week ago.

"This isn't just your favorite place to eat, is it?" Aisling shook her head at her own lack of observation. They'd parked in the same spot when he brought her here before.

"It is more than that," Reece said. "But it is also my favorite place to eat. Lucky happenstance, right?" He held open the door for Aisling and both men.

Stella was there. If she was surprised at Reece's company, she gave no sign. "Good to see you again, sugar." She gave Aisling a warm hug then her smile dropped and a line of worry creased between her brows as she studied them. "You want the room?"

"Thanks, Stella, full protocol."

"Damn it," she said, then motioned for them to follow. "The room took some smoke damage during the incident, a lot more than expected given how far from the door it is. We redid the filters."

Reece nodded but they all stayed silent as they walked past the diners. The room in question was toward the back and labelled storage. Aisling wasn't surprised when the storage room had another door inside that led to a good-sized conference room. Sneaky seemed to be Reece's middle name.

"Won't people out there wonder where we went?" There wasn't a crowd but Aisling still thought someone might have noticed them come in.

"Oh, they'll all believe that the four of you walked back out after disagreeing about the menu," Stella said. "In about two minutes." Her grin was wide.

"Thanks, Stella. I'm not sure how long we'll be here. Can we get some food and coffee?" Reece took off his duster and dropped it on the back of a chair. Aisling briefly wondered how many dusters he had—his last one was at the bottom of the ocean.

"He wants pie," Caradoc said as he came forward. "I'm Caradoc, by the way. Pleased, I am, to meet you." He took Stella's hand and bowed over it.

Stella winked. "I thought I recognized you from the papers. But I don't ask with Reece's folks." She leaned in closer. "And he always wants pie."

"I'm Gar, nice to meet you." Garran shook her hand. He was smiling but since he gave a shortened version of his name and no affiliation, Aisling knew he was still trying to figure out what Reece was up to.

"Nice to meet you as well. I'll be back with supplies." With a nod she was out the door.

The room looked like a standard conference room, a large table with about fifteen chairs around it. Nothing fancy, but functional. It wouldn't stand out at all aside from the fact that it was hidden in a semi-seedy diner.

"So, what is this? Did you find it? Build it?" Aisling walked around the room, but aside from a small door that led to a full bathroom and a wide screen of some sort on the far wall, there wasn't anything to see.

"Actually, my old partner had this in place long before I

joined the agency. It's not known by any of the agencies. It's a private 'when things go in the shitter' hidey-hole. She died fifteen years ago and left it to me. I keep it updated, but I've only had to use it twice since then."

"I think you were right that it's warranted this time," Garran said as he sat halfway down the table from Reece. He might agree with him, but caution was still his key word.

"We might not find this as safe as I'd hoped." Reece leaned back in his chair. "I'm worried that they had to clean the filters. This is a self-contained system. The smoke at the entrance of the diner shouldn't have gotten to it. Not unless that was the goal of that damn smoke monster." He gave Aisling a nod. "I did speak to our Seer, he agreed that it was a smoke monster."

Caradoc sat in the chair next to Reece. "Ah, you had the smoke monster event on your murder board. Couldn't figure out what one would be doing at a restaurant."

Aisling split the difference and sat in between all of them. Caradoc had apparently decided Reece was his new victim. He'd gotten too much of a reaction out of surprising him in his car and wanted more. As long as he got a reaction, he'd keep poking. "It came in, smoked the place, and would have done more but I think Stella stopped it somehow. Most people didn't know what it was."

"Including me." Reece shook his head. "We thought for some reason the target had been the diner. Considering that they got smoke in here, I'd say we can assume that was wrong. Whoever was controlling that smoke monster might have been happy to let the diner burn, but they were after this room."

Stella knocked and came in bearing an impossibly huge collection of covered plates. A hulking fey behind her brought in more and a carafe of coffee and huge bottle of water.

"No, I didn't forget the pie." She put a tray in front of Reece with sandwiches and assorted slices of pie. "I'm locking you down now, but if you need anything, ring." She and the huge fey left.

Aisling pulled a sandwich over to her. "While this is handy, and sneaky, I don't understand why trying to smoke out or even damage some fed's secret hiding hole would be a priority for any suitable villain."

Reece tapped the edge of the table twice and the right wall folded back to reveal a weapon storage panel. One with enough firepower to arm an entire police station. Possibly two. He tapped three times and the wall behind her opened. It was about five feet deep and filled with scientific equipment and gizmos. Aisling swore that Caradoc started drooling.

The fourth tap brought the screen she'd noticed on the far wall to life. Live views from all over the city appeared. Twenty separate boxes.

"What in the hell…" Garran got up, leaving his food untouched and went to the guns.

Caradoc went to the equipment side in reverent silence.

Aisling stayed in her seat, ate her sandwich, and took it all in. "This isn't any agency; this is all you?" There were too many layers to Reece and she wasn't sure she was ready to figure them out. This was all so state of the art, it was painful.

"It was all put in place years ago, but yeah, I've been adding to it with funds my former partner left me. The walls of this room are reinforced magically and physically. Even if that smoke monster had destroyed the diner, this would be standing." He frowned. "As long as they didn't break through the vents."

"So, you and this former partner of yours were preppers?" Garran managed to get a condescending snark in his tone. But he didn't pull away from the collection of guns.

"No. She felt there was something undercutting this world, some level of threat that we weren't seeing." He paused. "That the humans weren't seeing."

Garran turned around at that. Every few decades or so, small groups of humans would rise up and try to seize control of the world. Never mind that there were far fewer of them than the fey, and that without elven magic they wouldn't be able to reproduce enough to carry on past a hundred years. Conspiracy theories were usually a big part of it.

"You're part of the anti-fey contingent?"

"I'm half fey, Garran, so no. And neither was my late partner and she was a full fey. But the humans have some theories that, while extreme, are worrying. And on the fey side, the walls between this world and the old world have been growing thinner." Reece polished off his second sandwich before going for a slice of pie. "I doubt that's something the higher powered fey wouldn't notice."

Aisling shared a look with Caradoc as he resumed his seat. Walls between worlds getting thin could definitely go a long way toward explaining the appearance of vallenians. Not that she could tell Reece that. Their mother was one of the highest powered fey in the world, yet Aisling hadn't even heard a rumor. A worried look crossed Caradoc's face; that, and a single shake of his head, told her he hadn't either.

So whatever was going on, their mother either was being kept in the dark—an almost impossible task—or she knew and wasn't letting her two youngest know. A chill went through Aisling; maybe it had something to do with her recent insistence that Aisling get back into the family fold.

"I don't see the connections," Aisling said. "We have Gaelic mobsters invading each other's turf, yet also possibly working together, the Lazing spreading out and taking out said Gaelic mobsters, an iron drug poisoning fey, and it's all connected to a thinning of the wall between worlds? What in the hell?" She grabbed another sandwich and turned to Garran. "And who set us up just now? A troll biker gang within city limits? And you didn't know about it?" She had a hard time believing that. Things like biker gangs were like popcorn to Garran.

He shook his head. "That was news to me. They either just arrived or had been extremely well hidden. Which makes coming after us stupid. Broad daylight— even if they had caught us, they would have been on ten different city cams."

"I know I'm not a cop or a fed," Caradoc said, "but when I'm trying to figure out a tech problem, I start with the most recent issue and work my way back. The ambush and the trolls."

Aisling nodded and glanced around. "All of these things, and not a single white board?"

Reece smiled and tapped the table again. The wall of guns was partially obscured by a huge electronic screen that dropped into place, then solidified. The faint bluish glow told her it was a tech board. Not as good as an old school dry erase board in her mind, but three times as big. Sadly, she was afraid they were going to need it.

Aisling lifted an eyebrow as she approached the board. It lit up along the edges and greeted her, "Hello, Aisling." She spun back to Reece. A smart board was one thing, but she wasn't sure about something that knew who she was.

"It picks up who is in the room, even when it's down. Don't worry, it just knows your name," Reece said.

Aisling turned to the board and took the stylus. Even that simple tool was state of the art. "What was your CIs name?"

Garran settled into a chair. "Nuthlin. No last name, he was a dryad. Liked living in town rather than the forests and worked out well for keeping an eye on things. That was his green car in the trap, so we can assume he's dead."

"Could he have turned? The car could have been a trap," Caradoc said. He wasn't a cop, but he loved mysteries.

"Doubtful, very doubtful. And he hated trolls. There's no way that gang was so close to an ambush and not involved. He was either tortured or talked too much and they killed him."

Aisling wrote his name with a circle and slash through it. Then she added "Troll Bikers" and did the same. "Whose turf is that area?" Unless there was a homicide of a non-gang member, Aisling rarely worked with the gangs.

"The Scrubs, or it was." Garran rose and came next to her. Then he wrote "Scrubs" and a second later a circle and a slash. "They were a small gang, mostly imps and brownies. They wouldn't have worked with the trolls either. And whoever was firing at us had way more firepower than they ever had." He turned to Caradoc. "Thank you for the save by the way, care to share how you did it?"

Aisling knew something that could deflect bullets would be a huge item for the police. So did Caradoc.

"Sadly, that was the prototype. I didn't tell our fed friend here because I didn't want him more freaked out than he already was, but it was overheating badly after we made it out of the ambush." He shrugged. "That's what I threw at the bikers, so it had two purposes."

"We had a possible bomb in my car?" Reece glanced from Caradoc to Aisling.

Aisling put up her hands and shrugged. Normal people would be upset about both losing a prototype and almost dying. Caradoc wasn't normal by a long shot.

"And how did you get in my car anyway? I have sensors and alarms."

Caradoc smiled and faded out of view. Aisling could still see him but only as a vague outline and she knew that was probably because she knew he was there and she knew what to look for. Garran and Reece were squinting, but both kept shaking their heads.

He reappeared. "Eyes can be fooled and sensors can be overridden, my friend. Granted, yours were not easy and by the time I realized what was going on with you all, you were almost to your car. I got in and reset your alarm moments before you deactivated it and got in."

"Seriously?" Garran nodded to Caradoc then turned to Reece. "If he's that good, why in the hell haven't you feds snatched him up?"

"Because I don't want to be snatched up, and I fly below their radar." He winced. "Most of the time."

Aisling turned back to the board, walked to the far end of it and wrote "Agent Paselin."

"Who is that?" Reece asked.

Caradoc snorted. "She's not a real fed. Well, she is, but not one of the scary ones."

"You said yourself that you thought she was tracking you for people she didn't know were pulling her strings. How many patent agents hunt evil doers in the forests?"

"She's a patent agent? I'm seriously missing something." Reece looked between them both.

Caradoc stayed silent.

Aisling gave in. She wasn't going to sit through Caradoc being stubborn and Reece being equally so. "She was tracking him because he sold the government a research and investigation company and she feels he's keeping some of the inventions for himself. The company that Mott Flowers had worked at. Somehow she ended up in the car my kidnappers left me in."

"The inventions in question are legally mine. I left her in the forest where I found her and she was fine at the time," Caradoc said. "Maybe someone grabbed her because she saw Aisling's kidnappers."

There was no way they were letting Reece know what

had actually happened.

"Is she still alive?" Reece pointed to the board with all of the circles.

"As far as I know." Aisling added "Bilth" and "Hooded Man" to that side of the board. "I hid her when I heard Bilth and his people come up. The cops weren't far behind, so hopefully they found her."

Reece tapped the desk and a keyboard and monitor appeared in front of him. "According to the report, she was taken in for observation and released. She didn't recall much before waking in the back of the car she and Aisling were in. She mentioned a female detective had been with her, but ran away."

"I didn't run away—okay, I did, but I recognized Bilth's voice, so I figured it wasn't going to go well for anyone else around."

"Bilth? The elven gangbanger?" Garran had stayed silent, but now they were on his turf.

"We were undercover for narco when he showed up; pretty sure he was behind the Celts losing two of their leaders." Aisling spoke before she thought of who she'd been with. Reece was undercover as Dixon with the station; Leifen was Dixon's undercover persona, not Reece's. She turned to him with a nod, there were too many damn secrets going on, and one or more were going to have to give.

"You and Larkin? Why would a fed be on one of our narcotics cases undercover?" Garran narrowed his eyes.

Reece took a deep breath and shook his head. "This doesn't go out of this room. Garran, trust me, Surratt was on board with this and had been for the past year. I've been working in narco as a consultant named Dixon. We went undercover in Old Town as a small-time hood named Leifen and his woman. Bilth spotted us, blew up the Scot and Cymru leaders, and left us to die in the rubble."

"And now he happens to show up where Aisling and this patent agent were dumped?" Garran hadn't reacted as badly as Aisling thought he might about a fed hiding in plain sight in the station. Probably because narcotics wasn't his turf—or he already knew.

Aisling mentally scrambled for what could safely be said without compromising Caradoc or Maeve. "Someone tagged me with a tracker, but I've got no idea who or when. Apparently it got damaged by my kidnappers and was sending a signal. Wherever it came from, it had originally belonged to someone Bilth wanted to find." She pointed to her still bandaged shoulder. "According to my doctor, it was destroyed when I got shot by the coasties. They might have done something to it first though, it had gone dead, then started vibrating when we were brought on the ship." She added "Black Chopper" and "Coast Guard Captain" with a question mark to the board. Then she added a circle and slash to the "Black Chopper."

"That signal was what we picked up on to rescue you. I wasn't able to find out much about the chopper," Reece said. "It was flown out of LAX helipad, but not registered. I've got people working on it."

Garran scowled at the board for a moment. "Did the chopper have any symbols on it?"

Reece shook his head, but Aisling nodded. She hadn't thought of it at the time, but she'd been going through what happened in her head. "I noticed a small red triangle with marks in it right before we went down." One thing she'd received from her mother, a freakish memory for images. It wasn't as consistent as she'd like.

Garran went to the center of the board and made a large triangle, then added Japanese characters inside it. "Like this?"

Aisling couldn't have told any of them what was in the center of it before; until this discussion reminded her, she didn't recall seeing it. But once Garran drew it, she knew that was it.

"Yes, but my Japanese is rusty, what does it say?"

"Death to all before us." Caradoc's language skills had always been better than hers.

"That's sort of cryptic," Reece said. Even he seemed at a loss.

"Damn it." Garran pulled out his phone. "That's the Guardians of Death: the assassin arm of the Lazing, stationed in Japan. They never leave the East. *Never.*"

CHAPTER THIRTY-ONE

"WHY IN THE HELL WOULD they be here flying around in black helicopters? Marked ones?" Aisling wanted to second-guess what she'd seen, but now that she'd seen the image in her mind, she knew that was it.

"Few people would have a clue what that mark means, even most cops in Japan wouldn't recognize it. I have to call this in. Now don't freak out." He held up his hand as he turned to his phone. "Surratt? We have bigger shit going on. Yeah, I know you'll have to toss that burner now, but the Lazing are not only here, they've sent the Guardians of Death. That's who shot down Aisling."

Aisling was about to rip the phone from his hand. Reece looked ready to do the same. Garran kept one hand up toward them as he listened to the other end. Caradoc watched all of them like he was waiting for popcorn.

"We have to move you into higher security, now." More arguing from the other end. Then Garran pulled the phone away from his ear and gestured Aisling over.

"He wants to speak to you. Make it quick."

Aisling took Garran's phone. "Surratt? I felt your injuries and you were dying. What the hell is going on?"

"Aisling, good to hear you. Quickly, I was shot, but not badly. The healers blocked your healing so you wouldn't notice. We needed both you and Larkin to believe I was dying—you both have a lot of people tracking you whether you know it or not. But I want you to listen to Garran and Larkin like you would me. Stay alive. I've got to stay out of this for now, but listen to them." Without waiting for her to respond, he cut the line.

"The bastard is conscious? And going to live?" From the glare he was shooting to Garran's phone, Reece was used to pulling sneaky shit on others, but he didn't like it being reversed.

"Not after I find him," Aisling threw the phone back to Garran. "How did you two pull this off?"

"The attack on him was real. We disguised his injuries like he did for yours, making them seem worse. Part of it was to get whoever shot him and possibly murdered Heike to come out, but the rest was to see if another iron-infected fey would appear to try and take him out completely."

"You think that fey in the hospital was after me." It wasn't a question because she knew the answer. He had come right for her room.

"Pretty much confirmed it, but we still don't know who killed Heike, who she was working for, or who attacked Surratt and us. None of those activities seem like something the Lazing would do, but they've also never come here before."

An intercom that apparently had been imbedded into the table and only appeared when in use, squeaked to life. Stella gave a cough on the other end. "Reece, you might want to come out here. There's a woman asking for your lady friend. She's human, and bleeding badly. But she also has a fey rod aimed at my head." There was a shuffling noise as Stella turned away from the speaker, then came back. "Says her name is Maeve."

Caradoc and Aisling were at the door before the other two could respond. "How did she get out of the house? Open this damn thing, now!" Aisling couldn't imagine how or why Maeve was here, nor where she got one of the illegal fey rods, a device that could scramble the brain of any fey, in some cases permanently. But Aisling intended to find out.

"You knew Maeve was in town?" Reece's voice dropped and a line appeared between his brows.

"Not the time. Open the damn door." Aisling turned to Caradoc standing on her heels. "Can you blast it?" Her brother's magic was far more dangerous than her own. This door would take a lot out of him, and he didn't like to use his magic like this, but she didn't care.

"Here," Reece said, then released the door. Aisling and Caradoc were out before it had opened halfway. Reece and Garran silently followed them.

The diner was cleared out and only Stella and a hooded figure remained near the hostess counter. The figure was about Maeve's height and holding a rod. Aisling pulled out her gun; with the hood it could be anyone. She squinted at the fey rod. It had spell symbols written on it. Ones suspiciously familiar to Aisling. She'd done that as a mock-up for a training exercise with Maeve years ago.

"Drop your hood." Garran also had his gun out and it wasn't clear if he cared if it was Maeve or not.

With a shaking free hand, the hood dropped back. Maeve clutched her stomach and dropped the fake fey rod. "Sorry," she said to Stella before crumbling.

Aisling caught her before she hit the ground.

"Damn it, her wound is open again." Aisling turned to Stella. "Did everyone leave before she got here, or when she got here?" She needed to know if cops were coming. Maeve was a cop but was still wanted by too many people to let her be seen. Including Reece's agency. But that couldn't be helped right now.

"There weren't but a few, but they fled when she came in waving the wand." Stella picked up the wand and chuckled. "She kept it moving when she came in so I couldn't tell it was a fake. Smart girl. But we need to get her to a hospital."

Maeve was fading in and out of consciousness, but revived at that. "No!"

"We can't take her to one," Aisling said and looked toward the front door. There was no sign of anyone coming in, but eventually someone would tell the cops about the lady with the fey rod. Or someone might come into the diner to actually dine.

"Take her into the back room. We can sort something out there." By the scowl on his face Reece was pissed about Maeve but was willing to overlook it for now.

Maeve stirred when Aisling picked her up. "You need to know," she got out weakly and held out a box. Then she blacked out again.

Aisling's hands were full, so Reece grabbed the small box. The box was long and slim like an old-fashioned stylus box. Except it was made of wood from the enchanted forest. Even without touching it, the essence of what it was smacked her hard.

"Do not lose that box," Aisling growled at Reece as they rushed Maeve into the room. She didn't think he'd accidently lose it; she was warning him about deliberately doing so. Garran shut and locked the door behind them.

Aisling put Maeve on the table and Garran made a pillow of his jacket. At least there didn't appear to be any additional wounds, but the original one was seeping through the bandage badly. Damn it, Maeve must have lied about it not hurting.

Reece brought out a medical kit from one of the cabinets along the wall. "Your work?"

"Not the injury, but yes, I bandaged her." Aisling faced him and Garran. "Still not the time for this, but yes, we knew she was here. She showed up injured. Keeping her hidden from everyone, including both of you, was the best option. Now either help us or get the hell out of my way."

Garran smiled and came forward. "What do you need?"

If he was upset about not being kept in the loop about Maeve's arrival, he was happy that it annoyed Reece more.

Reece looked ready to say something snarky, then shook his head and handed her the med kit. "We all have secrets, too many, and you're right, now isn't the time for them."

Maeve was thrashing about as whatever was tearing her up inside got worse. Caradoc held her still and Aisling removed the bandages.

Garran started brushing the hair back from Maeve's face and murmuring soothing words. Aisling's surprise only lasted a moment—his children were long grown but Garran had at least twenty. His fondness for Maeve was clear; she was the human child he'd never had.

Reece held back, then stepped up to help hold Maeve still.

The wound was worse. It had been clean when they last re-bandaged her, but now it looked like an infection was taking hold. Aisling swore at those mystery elements that were still inside her that she hadn't been able to take care of before.

"Can you clean the wound? I need to focus." She nodded to Reece. He didn't hesitate but did what he could to clean it. Caradoc was holding Maeve down but judging by her thrashing she was in a lot of pain.

Aisling took a deep breath, forcing the past failure out of her head. Maeve was fighting for her life, and unless Aisling could save her, she was going to die.

"Think of Mother," Caradoc grunted out as one of Maeve's hands almost came free from his grasp.

"What?"

"Get angry. It will help focus your magic."

The moment he'd said Mother, she'd felt a flare. She'd never tried anger before, but she needed something. She shut her eyes and brought up every infuriating interaction she'd had with the woman who gave her life. There were plenty to choose from. Power as she'd never felt before flowed through her and pushed her healing to a higher level. She held her hands over Maeve's torso and focused healing magic. She almost pulled back as the unidentified invaders from before became clearer—minute bits of metal. But not iron. She focused on pulling them out and healing the paths they left. They were too small to have been bullets, even buckshot would be massively larger than them. But they were the source of what was killing Maeve now.

Her healing magic started to fade and she thought of her mother's tricks again—most recently the fact that she hadn't seen fit to warn her children that something was wrong with the veil. Healing magic, stronger than she'd been able to tap into before, rushed through her and finished healing Maeve.

It was almost a shock to return to the real world once she finished.

"Wow." She glanced at her hands. Not shaking. Unlike her normal healings, she was exhilarated, not exhausted. "That was a rush."

"Is she going to be okay?" Garran was still brushing Maeve's forehead, but looked up as Aisling pulled back.

"You keep that up, gnome boy, and I'll have to tell your wife." Maeve's voice was quiet, but there was no weakness behind it. "Where am I?"

Caradoc stopped trying to hold her down and helped her to sit up.

"Reece has been full of secrets, including a secret hidey-hole in a diner. Which, I might add, you somehow found." Aisling helped Maeve off the table.

Maeve peered at her bare stomach. There was no sign of the wound. "Am I dead, and you are all hanging out with my spirit?"

"Aisling healed you. Her brother pissed her off by telling

her to think of their mother—which is a dynamic I don't need to know about—and she glowed." Reece's face was inscrutable as he watched them both.

"I glowed?" Aisling turned to her brother and Garran.

"Yup, just like Mom when she's working something big and nasty," Caradoc said. The smugness on his face was annoying.

That couldn't be good. Aisling was glad she found a way to save Maeve, and stronger magic was usually a good thing—but her mother's magic was definitely not in the healing realm. With all the crap going on right now, the last thing she needed was to worry about becoming her mother. She shoved the concern aside.

"Sometimes glows happen. More importantly, why and how did you find us, and what were you doing with that box?" She held out her hand toward Reece. He hadn't lost it, but the way he'd been partially blocking it, he was hoping no one would ask for it until he got a look at it.

With a sigh he placed it in her hand.

It was lighter than it appeared, weighing about as much as a single page of paper. The carving that decorated it was thin and elaborate. And the wood sang to her soul with such force that she had to grab the table. To be safe, she slid into a chair.

The enchanted forest was a remnant of the old world, one brought to this one when the first fey came through the veil thousands of years ago. The trees were seedlings from the world they'd been forced to leave. There were relics made of some of the trees that had fallen over the centuries, but they were closely guarded by the ruling families. Aisling's family had one box, an elaborate forest scene with a deer on it. It was guarded better than all of the wealth they accumulated. No family would have allowed this box out of their control willingly.

CHAPTER THIRTY-TWO

CARADOC WAS HOVERING OVER HER and she knew it was only because there were other people around that he hadn't tried to grab the box out of her hands. Aisling ignored him and the others as she touched the wood. The carvings were intricate, and appeared to be words, but she couldn't read them. The language might be older than even her mother.

Finally she shook her head and turned to Maeve. "So? Talk. Breaking out of a locked house? Coming to the diner? Where did you get the box?" She couldn't help but continue petting the box; there was something incredibly soothing about it once the initial shock wore off.

"Sorry about breaking out, Caradoc, but I had to. There is too much going on and I couldn't put you two at risk anymore." She winced but it wasn't from her injury. "Although I might have made things a lot worse. Sorry." She nodded to Reece and Garran. "And now you two are pulled in. Anyway, I found this box stuck in the hedge. I don't feel it the way Aisling appears to, but I had an idea what it was. I'll be honest, I thought about taking it and running, or leaving it behind and running. But there was something about it that was disturbing. And I caught some creepy-looking guy watching me. Then I spotted the box and my gut went on fire. So I ran to find you. Thought maybe this was your family's."

Caradoc offered her a drink and a sandwich. "That's not from our family. What did the creepy guy look like?"

He could have been asking about anyone, but the hairs on the back of Aisling's neck rose. He thought it wasn't someone from this world. How she knew that was what he meant, or how he even guessed, she had no idea. It was instinct.

"Tall, skeletal, had a weird mask on, tall black hat and an old fashioned black cloak. Some sort of costuming I'd guess?"

Aisling's heart went into overdrive—another vallenian. And it let a human see it. It was taking all of her strength to not grab her loved ones and race for a dark cave somewhere in the hopes it couldn't find them.

"I'm not a super spook like Larkin here, but the look on your faces is impossible to ignore," Garran said. "You two know what she saw." It wasn't a question.

Aisling fought the terror and shared a look with Caradoc. Their best plan would be to hide and leave Garran and Reece alone so they could remain unexposed. Well, as long as Reece never regained the memory of seeing the first one anyway. She'd say Maeve too, but if the vallenian let her see him, whether she knew what he was or not, she was marked. "How secure is this room?"

Caradoc was already shaking his head.

Reece looked from one to the other with narrowed eyes. "Class one. I verified the smoke monster hadn't gotten through and upgraded the filtration system electronically while we ate."

"Magically, she means against magical beings." Caradoc was still shaking his head, but like Aisling, he realized there were few options.

"It's never been rated. But standard protocols are in place."

"Won't be enough," Caradoc said. He went to the wall with all of the equipment. After gathering a few of the machines and relocating them to the conference table, he started taking a few apart.

"What the hell are you doing? Tell us what you are both freaking out about." Reece walked over to him, but Caradoc held up a hand.

"Not until he finishes," Aisling said. If anyone could block this room from vallenians, her brother could. "I'm serious. If we can't block it, we can't tell you. Not if any of you want to live to see the outside of this diner again."

"Damn it, it's not working." Caradoc adjusted a few more things, then reached in his pocket and pulled out a small, round gizmo and added it to his conglomeration.

Aisling felt him fling a magical push at it, but the spell went right through it. She assumed from his swearing it was supposed to block it.

She jumped when her phone chirped from her back pocket. She was about to mute the call when she noticed the name—Harlie. Her brother had never called her in his life. She had kept his number identified in case that ever changed.

"Harlie?"

Caradoc looked up in surprise.

"Aisling, I can feel both you and Caradoc. And so can others. He needs to add a higher frequency or they will find you. The hunters are coming. I will see you soon." With that he disconnected the call.

Aisling pulled back the phone and glared at it. Although it was less cryptic than he usually was.

"Crap. He said you need to add a higher frequency and that others are searching for us."

"Who is Harlie?" Garran asked.

"Our brother—he's a mystic in Nepal," Caradoc answered but was focusing on his machine. He cast a spell on the equipment and adjusted two knobs. This time his test pulse flowed back at him. "Never doubt Harlie." He glanced around, then walked over to an electrical panel in the back of the room. "This for only our room or the entire diner?"

"The entire diner," Reece said but still looked extremely confused.

Garran and Maeve stayed silent, but a worry line was appearing down Garran's craggy face the more he listened and watched. Aisling was pretty sure he had a good idea what they were trying to protect against, but he was smart enough to not say anything until it was safe.

"Good." Caradoc quickly connected the parts to the panel and touched it with a spell.

Aisling felt it as it kicked on. A slight numbing of her natural perception of the world beyond this room. She shuddered. She also felt the pressure of a magic wielder vanish. One she hadn't noticed until it was blocked. "Damn it, they *were* searching for us. They planted that box."

"Okay, enough. Who was trying to find us and why are they now blocked?" Reece had been more patient than she would have expected, but he was at the end of it now.

Caradoc slid into the nearest chair. His hands were shaking. "If you even think about what we're going to tell you outside of here, you will die." He held up his hand as Reece took a defensive stance. "Not from me, nor Aisling. What Maeve saw was a vallenian."

Garran snorted, Reece looked worried, and Maeve looked confused. Aisling was glad that her head didn't explode by thinking of them. Whatever mix of magic and technology Caradoc had pulled off was damn powerful.

"They don't exist," Reece said, but he kept watching their faces.

Garran shook his head. "Aye, they do. But the High Council would know if they were making forays across the veil. And allowing a human to see them? Sorry, Aisling, I know you trust your brother, but I don't believe we wouldn't know. And only a few elven family lines would have the ability to do what he claims to have done."

Caradoc let a full magic flare show. It started like a soft light at first, then grew beyond the range of sight and into pure feeling. The hairs all over Aisling's body stood on end, and as his sister she wasn't being hit with it as hard as the others. The flare gave no doubt to his power. It also showed his lineage. Aisling sighed, and then did the same. The time for secrets ended a while ago.

Garran pulled back as if struck. "You're Lady Tirtha Otheralia's kids? Why didn't you say anything?"

"Because our mother is a powerful, psychotic bitch and I wanted a life not related to her," Aisling said. "She had to have known the veil was slipping and didn't tell us."

Reece slid into a chair as well. "So the vallenians exist, and they let Maeve see them." He nodded to both Caradoc and Aisling. "And I gather you two have seen them?"

Caradoc adjusted his clothing as if that flare had rustled him in some way. "Aisling has. I had to go into her mind to block them since they have an ability to follow memories."

Aisling watched them all. "There is another who saw one." Reece would probably hate her now, but he needed to know. "On our stake-out, when we were in that alley in your crappy car—we were followed by one."

Reece glanced around as if she was talking to someone else. "How? And why do I have no memory of that?"

Aisling hadn't told anyone what she'd done, and she avoided the eyes staring at her now. It was unethical as hell. "I mindwiped you. It's a side spell of healing. I had to, Reece. It was stalking us. And you seeing it? You don't want to know what they can do."

"My mother told me tales as a child. But how could you?" Anger warred with disbelief on his face and in his voice.

"She saved your life, boyo," Garran said. "One of the Old Ones would have gone right through you, cell by cell.

Makes the Iron Deaths almost look pleasant."

"Is there anything else that you blocked?" From the way he wouldn't face her directly, Reece was dealing with a lot of hurt and anger. But the fact he was pushing it aside meant he accepted Garran's words.

She thought about their fake make-out session. "Not a thing. You said you sensed something but couldn't see it. I turned and it was behind us. I didn't have a choice. One also appeared at the crash scene of Ryn Trebol. But no one else reacted like they'd seen it."

"Why did it let me see it?" Maeve had been silent, but was watching the enchanted forest box like it was a snake. "Damn it, it wanted me to find you."

"That would be my guess," Caradoc said. "But if you hadn't taken the box and found us, it would have taken you back through the veil in pieces."

CHAPTER THIRTY-THREE

M AEVE TURNED SO PALE IT looked as if her
wounds had opened again. "How can we defend
ourselves against these things? How can anyone?" There
was a fear in her voice that Aisling had never heard. "If
they are truly as the myths say, they can destroy everyone."

Caradoc leaned over and took her hand. "They are limited in what they can do on this side of the veil. All of the
Old Ones left on the other side are. But we can't ignore
that they are here, and that they are after Aisling for some
reason."

Aisling almost spit out the water she'd been drinking.
"What? That's a pretty damn big leap."

Garran shook his head. "I agree with Caradoc. You've
seen them with Larkin, at a crime scene, and now your
best friend, who has your psychic feel on her because of
the healings, has been targeted. They want *you*."

Reece finally turned to Aisling and it was worry, not
anger, that was on his face now. "She's safe in here though,
right? We all are?" At Caradoc's nod, Reece continued.
"Then she stays here. You said the protection would cover
the diner as well, Stella can get her food, clothing, and we
can set up a bed—"

"I'm not hiding while the people I care about go out and
try to figure out why the world is going to hell." Although
she'd been thinking of running away, she'd been thinking
of all of them going, not just her.

"What about your mother?" Garran said.

"I don't think even she could take out a vallenian," Caradoc said.

"No, but if Aisling went to her home, most likely she
or her cohorts might be able to track the vallenians. And
protect Aisling in the long term."

"Do I get a say? I'm not hiding here, and I sure as hell
am not going to her house. My skin is still crawling from
last week."

Reece opened his mouth to argue, then shook his head
as another thought hit him. "Was that the last time you
were around her?"

"Yes, the evening before the first iron death victim. She
was staying at their LA house for a few weeks."

"And less than two days before you first saw the vallenian—the one that I sensed." At least there wasn't any
hostility in his voice as he spoke. Aisling was sure he'd
bring up her mind wiping him many times down the
line…providing they all survived.

"Could they have been watching your mother? Caradoc? Were you there?" Garran asked.

"I wasn't there. Actually, Mother didn't tell me about that
family conference until I was already tied up with that
damn patent agent Paselin. She didn't want me there."

Maeve had gotten her color back, but hadn't pulled
her hand back from Caradoc's. "You think they are after
Aisling because of your mum? The woman's a nasty piece
of work, but isn't that a bit much?"

"Think about it, if they were searching for a way in
to take out our mother, Aisling would be the way." He
shrugged at Aisling's scowl. "You're the most removed
from her and the rest of the family, and no harm meant,
but you're not the strongest magic user." There was no
cruelty there, just the facts.

Aisling shook him off. "Fine, I might be a way in. But I
don't get why they think showing themselves to me and

those near me will help them destroy our mother. Nor what they have against her. We have plenty against her, but we're family. Pretty sure she hasn't been beyond the veil. Even she isn't old enough to have been in the first crossing." The Leave Taking, when the first fey fled their plane and came to Earth, was over five thousand years ago. Few fey were alive today who'd come through then.

"I still say you should stay here until we figure something out, regardless of why they are after you. Garran? You agree, right?" Reece wasn't backing off.

Reece's phone rang before Garran could respond. "Larkin." His face paled as he listened to the other end. "Damn it. We're on our way." He disconnected the call and took a moment before turning to the others. "There was another feral fey. In the station. Fachie complained about his skin feeling itchy about half an hour ago. Then he went feral and started attacking people. He's dead and four other fey cops he grabbed won't survive but are being taken into isolation rooms at a human-only hospital. The station is under quarantine."

Although Caradoc had never met Fachie, or most likely any of the four who were now dying painful deaths, the look of horror and shock was the same on his face as the others. There was no way to know what had happened to any of the fey who had died of iron poisoning and not be emotional. But it was worse when it hit a friend, and possibly more.

"Who...who were the other four?" Aisling's voice shook but it was justified.

Reece shook his head. "That's all I got. Garran will probably have to find out details for us."

Garran's phone rang. From the sorrow on his face, it was the same information. He said a few terse words then cut the line. "Same information as you. The station is on lockdown. We need to go in. I'm now the acting chief."

Aisling got to her feet, but Reece shook his head. "You sure as hell can't go now. You're connected to both this vallenian and the iron fey deaths. The first had someone leave a message for you. The third was running for your room in a corridor of hospital rooms."

"The second had nothing to do with me." She took a step into Reece's space and folded her arms.

"He was connected to Maeve, your best friend and police partner." He held up a hand. "And you also saw a vallenian there. The more coincidences, the higher the level of bullshit that is going on."

"Maybe I need to be out there to draw them out."

"Or maybe you'd risk everyone," Maeve said softly as she came next to her and Reece. "The fed has a good point. I originally took off to save others, but I think you need to hide, at least for now."

Caradoc nodded. "I can work on blockers, something that will mask you from searches, once I figure out how they are tracking you. But for now, you need to stay here." Even her brother was on Reece's side.

Aisling studied the faces around her. Even after admitting that she'd destroyed some of his memories, the main expression in Reece's eyes was concern for her. "Fine. But Maeve's staying here too."

"Obviously." Maeve flopped into one of the chairs then pointed at the wall of monitors. "Do any of those screens get television stations? I'm behind on some of my telly. Oh, and we'll be needing a lot more food before you leave."

If Reece was surprised at her demands, he didn't show it. Wordlessly, he pulled out a remote, clicked it, and the screens all went off except four in the center that formed a single screen. He handed Maeve the remote with a bow, nodded to Aisling, then unlocked the room and left.

Garran followed but he was already on the phone barking orders.

Caradoc nodded to the others. "I'll keep an eye on them and find out what I can. And keep your phone on scramble mode."

"My phone doesn't have that...what is that?" Aisling jumped as her phone gave a chirping buzz as an update hit it.

"It does now, lower screen for the apps—small purple box. Click it. Calls might go through slower, but they will be almost impossible to trace." With a nod, he followed the other two and shut the door.

Aisling was about to launch into a nice pissed-off tirade when a knock came at the door.

Stella was there with a pair of pitchers of beer and a cart of unhealthy snacks. "Not sure exactly what's going on, but I shut the diner. Reece said you two might need some comfort food. Mind if I join?"

Aisling laughed and stepped out of the way. "You come bearing great gifts, please be welcome." She had no idea what all Stella could or couldn't be made aware of—she'd bet a lot considering she'd been hiding this room for a few decades. But either way, her joining them would be a nice respite. Besides, Aisling liked the taste of beer, even if it didn't do anything for her.

"We haven't been formally introduced," Maeve said as she rose to her feet. "I'm Maeve, no hard feelings about the fake fey rod? The situation was pretty desperate on my end."

"You're British! How charming, I couldn't tell from your blood-loss mutterings." Stella started laying out food. "And no worries at all. Actually, I could have taken you out before you actually used it, had it been real. But I could tell you were in distress and honest." She smiled.

Once all three got settled in with mugs of beer and snacks, Stella turned to the blank screen. "What's your plan? So you're aware, I have a class four level clearance."

She held out a small wallet with an agency logo—FBI.

"Very impressive," Maeve said. "Is the diner a long-time cover?"

Stella took a long sip of her beer and sighed. "Other way around actually. Reece's predecessor, Leticha, got me the clearance when she created the room we're in. I'm a changeling, but also a pretty heavy magic user. I built this place over two hundred years ago in the middle of three ley lines." She grinned. "Lots of good mojo here. And, while I just met you two, I am an exceptional judge of character. I know damn well you two aren't going to sit here and watch television."

Aisling laughed. "The sitting here is true, at least for now." A level four FBI clearance was actually a level higher than Aisling and Maeve. Anything they knew, Stella could as well. She gave her a brief rundown on the current situation. As brief as she could anyway—there was a lot going on.

"I knew it was bad, but I had no idea this bad. Feral fey I had heard of. Reece read me in after the poor flyer girl, but the rest is new. I do agree with you staying hidden for the moment however." She grinned. "Which doesn't mean we do nothing."

"Quite." Maeve flicked the remote and the original surveillance cameras replaced the TV screen. "Don't suppose he has one in the station?"

"No, never could risk setting a camera up there. But he does have one outside of it," Stella said. Maeve handed her the remote and she flicked through a few more screens. There were twenty screens, but Reece had far more cameras up.

"This is wild. He has more eyes than five agencies combined." Aisling couldn't decide whether to be terrified about that or not.

Stella stopped flicking and a view of the police station

appeared, then she expanded it so it took over most of the other screens.

Aisling laughed once she'd sorted out where he had the camera. There was only one possible location based on the angle. "He put the camera in the palm tree? Isn't that cliché? I would have loved to have seen him shimmy up there."

"He's a very stubborn man," Stella said. She shot a quick glance to Aisling and nodded. "He doesn't give up once he's set his mind to something. Leticha had about a dozen cameras set up before she passed. Reece has added at least thirty more."

They watched as a security screen around the station flared into being as someone approached it. They didn't have sound, but Aisling knew a loudspeaker would be telling people of the emergency and the location of the Fary Street police station.

Reece's car tore to the front a moment later, followed by Garran's car. Caradoc was riding with Reece, which Aisling was sure wasn't making the fed happy.

"What did they do, drag race there?" Maeve shook her head and helped herself to some chocolate.

"Most likely, and both have lights on their cars. I'm impressed that Reece beat Garran though." Aisling knew how both men drove, and she still would have bet on Garran over Reece based on their cars. Of course, she had no idea what Reece actually had under the hood.

The three walked to the security screen with both Reece and Garran holding up their arms to display their wrist tattoos. Caradoc did a moment later.

"What in the hell? My brother does *not* have a badge tat. He's not law enforcement." Aisling watched to see if the other two would respond, but they both walked into the station with him. "Damn it, whatever Caradoc is pulling, he told them about it. I'm seriously getting tired of being the last to know."

"He's doing something," Maeve said with a laugh. "I do like him, never afraid to jump into whatever is about. You need to hang out with him more."

Aisling shook her head. Caradoc bent the rules, all rules, so far they were little more than over-cooked noodles. Aisling preferred her rules intact—at least most of the time. "Can we split the screen with the hospital Surratt is at and wherever they took the dying fey?"

Maeve clicked through a few more screens and the monitors split into three. Both hospitals also had security screens up. Hover bots were dangling over a few people as they tried to get any information.

Maeve held up her hand before Aisling could speak. "Already pulling up the big networks. At least we can hear them as opposed to Reece's cameras."

"A chemical attack at the local police station has left one dead and more critically injured. No further information has been forth-coming. A news conference has been announced for one hour from now."

"Why aren't there reporters at the station?" Stella asked.

"They can't, not if a news conference has been announced. If they go to the station before the conference they will be kicked out. Good move of Garran's, or whoever thought of it." Aisling texted her brother. They'd been inside the station long enough—she needed to know who the other four soon-to-be-dead were.

It took longer than normal for the text to show as received—most likely that scrambler he had on it slowed that too. Whatever worked and kept her hidden. Vallenians might not need technology to find her, but she was damn sure whoever was behind the Iron Death killings was from this side of the veil.

His text came back a few moments later. "The ones we're losing are Smythe, Radicison, Theila, and Berris, and of course Fachie." Out of those, only Fachie was someone she worked with regularly. But it didn't change that five good cops were dying horribly.

Maeve dropped the volume and shrunk the TV portion to a small corner. "We need to figure out what the connections are. Visual might give us an idea." She tapped in the hospital where Surratt was. "Now, where did you go after you left him?"

Aisling filled her in on the location of the ambush and the troll biker gang. There weren't cameras near where the gang met its demise, and a quick check of the news feeds showed the collision was attributed to a rival gang—no one had gotten a shot of Caradoc lobbing his gizmo at them.

"That's Scrubs territory. Surratt thought they had something to do with Heike's death? Or her betrayal of all of us on the force, and then her death?" Maeve narrowed in the camera as much as she could but there wasn't much information.

"The Scrubs were taken out two weeks ago," Stella said. She shrugged. "A lot of different types come into my diner. The gangs claim it's neutral territory."

"Do you know who by?"

"No, but it was an offshoot of one of the bigger gangs. Everyone else was worried. That's what brought the troll gang into town. But I think they might have been working for the new gang, or at least ended up that way. How many followed you?"

"Five." Aisling watched the camera that focused on the place Surratt was attacked. But there wasn't much that had changed. The cars that had blocked the road at the far end were gone, and people were going about their business, but aside from that, it looked the same.

"They started with twenty. And none of them left town according to my customers."

"Shite," Maeve said. "This new gang chewed up fifteen troll bikers?"

Trolls were pack creatures most of the time, even the ones not in a biker gang. If twenty came in, twenty would be going out—together. Had there been more still alive, Aisling and the others would have found all of them on their tail.

"I don't suppose you know where they were from?" Maybe if they knew what gang had sent the bikers, they'd get a better idea of what was going on. Trolls didn't come into the city without a reason and something drove them to come into the new gang's territory—and cost them their lives.

"No, unfortunately. But they'd only been here a week. The people coming into the diner were trying to avoid them. There were rumors one of the gang world's big hitters brought them out of the mountains, but I never heard much beyond rumors."

"I think that—" Aisling cut herself off as two people walked up to the station. There was something familiar about the woman. "Maeve, can you close in on those two?"

The screen enlarged and narrowed in. Whatever effort Reece had gone through to get the camera up that palm tree, at least he used a high quality one.

"Mott Flowers and Agent Paselin. What the hell are they doing there? Reece said Mott was locked up somewhere, and still unconscious. That lying bastard." She narrowed her eyes. Mott wasn't moving like a man who was still recovering from the beating he'd taken when she rescued him.

Both walked to the security screen and started talking to whoever was monitoring it. Aisling furiously texted Caradoc—both of them were his issue.

"They make a nice couple," Maeve said. She zeroed in on both. "Those aren't them."

Aisling was still waiting for her brother's response but looked up sharply. "Yes, they are. I saved his ass a few days ago." The hair on the back of her neck started going up the more she watched. They looked like them, but there was something a bit off in the way they moved. "Changelings?"

Stella rocked forward. "That is speciest you know. Every time there is something that is appearing to be something else, everyone blames us…I'll be damned. They aren't changelings." She pulled an old cell out of her pocket and started punching numbers. "Reece? Damn it, whatever you do, keep people away from the two malgi at the station shield. They look like someone named Flowers and an agent—but they are malgi." She paused as he responded. "Don't sass me, boy. I know what they are. Get everyone away from the security screen, lock the station, and get as far back from the street as you can."

Aisling looked down as the delayed text came back. "Will go get them now." She grabbed the phone out of Stella's hand. "Reece, stop my brother—he's going out there. Tackle him if you have to. Stop him."

Reece's response was lost as the camera they were watching flared when a massive explosion engulfed the security screen and flowed over the station. Reece's phone went dead.

CHAPTER THIRTY-FOUR

A ISLING DIDN'T CARE ABOUT BEING traced. She dialed Caradoc's number. A knot of pain hit her gut. He couldn't have...no. *Damn it, answer the phone.* The line rang through a few times then went dead. The knot in her gut grew worse. "What in the hell were those two?"

Stella shook her head as she tried to get any of a number of phones to dial through to Reece. Finally, she shook her head. "Malgi. Magic nasties. Bastardizations of changelings created by a sick mage hundreds of years ago. The mage was tossed back through the veil, but some of her automatons are still around. For sale to the highest bidder. Someone paid thousands of dollars for those two for a chance to destroy the station and everyone in it. They were triggered to blow too early though. Whoever sent them wasn't counting on the delay at the security screen. They can take any likeness and will destroy themselves on command. Their biggest danger is that they can talk and respond just like the originals."

How had she never heard of these things? Aisling swore; she was sure her mother knew exactly what they were. Just a little more of the censored upbringing she'd had. She turned to Stella. "How powerful are you?" She didn't want to run out of the diner and risk being spotted until they figured more things out, but one way or another, she was getting to that station.

Stella looked at her phone for a moment, then turned it off and dropped it back into her pocket. "Very. I am over two thousand years old. You do not get to this age by being weak." The diner matron was gone now and an age she'd hidden through her changeling ability showed in her eyes. Now that she'd released her spell masking, Aisling felt the power emanating from her.

"Can you disguise me?" A tricky thing, but some of the higher-powered changelings could extend their abilities over others for a short time.

"Aye, but you're not going without me. Reece might not be my brother or son, but he's my responsibility." Her fingers flexed and arcs of magic snapped between them.

"Not without me either," Maeve said, then held up her hand to hold off any argument. "No. I've stayed hidden too long. I went along with it before because I knew I was injured. I'm not anymore and those are my friends dying out there too."

Aisling gave her a nod then turned back to Stella. "Can you disguise all three of us?"

"Damn straight." Stella closed her eyes and arcs of magic snapped around the room. "Close your eyes, it's going to get bright in here."

Aisling did, as an intense light slammed into her. Her entire body tingled with magic as Stella's spell went through her.

She waited until the light pressing against her eyelids vanished before opening her eyes. Judging by the two total strangers standing in front of her, the spell worked. "Maeve! You look awesome as a redhead." Her friend was now a tall and slender red-haired woman. Stella was now a short black man. Aisling held out her arms. Heavier than before, human not elven. "What do I look like?"

"I've got a mirror in the diner. You should be aware that this spell will only hold a few hours at the most. Might go out before that."

The three walked out to the diner. Aisling stopped in

front of the mirror around the corner and took in the dark hair and brown eyes. She also had some impressive tats up and down both arms. "You made me a biker chick? I like it!" They locked up the secret room and double-checked all the locks on the diner; the amount of locks alone should have announced that this wasn't a normal restaurant.

"One problem, they took their cars." Aisling checked her phone, but no texts or messages. The closest camera to the station, besides the one that blew out, only showed a giant ball of smoke. The news stations were scrambling but they had no information either.

"I've got us covered," Stella said then led them around to a wall on the side of the diner. With a grin she clicked a small remote and a garage door appeared. Another click and it opened to reveal a cherry red fifty-year-old Mustang.

"Does Reece know you have this? He's a car junkie," Aisling said and shoved the concern of whether he and the others were still alive deep in her gut. They had to be.

"He does," Stella said. She clicked again and all four doors unlocked. "He says it's a gilded tart and not a real muscle car. Ignoring that I beat him on the 5 one night at two a.m." She slid into the driver's seat with a smile; Aisling beat Maeve for the passenger seat by a second.

"On the way back that's mine," Maeve said as she climbed in the back. Once the car was out of the stealth garage, the door slid back into place and vanished from view.

"Is the sneaky garage you, Reece, or his predecessor?" Having recently been driving with both Reece and Garran, Aisling had her seat belt on and hands on the dash before Stella floored it.

"Me. I built it when I bought this beauty. The room you were in was initially my speakeasy when nectar and booze were outlawed a hundred years ago. Didn't need it for that anymore, so when Reece's predecessor showed up, I set her up there."

They could still see the smoke rising from the station but it seemed to be thinning out. It must have been more from the initial explosion than any resulting fire. Even if there had been a fire, the station had more than enough fire suppression spells placed around it to knock it out.

The entire block to the station was cordoned off with a police barricade. Aisling automatically raised her wrist to flash her badge, and then dropped it. Even if she wasn't under a changeling glamour, her badge tat was gone. Maeve's would still be there, but it would be hidden by the glamour as well. Damn it. There was no way they were going to be able to talk their way inside.

Stella lowered her window and held out a badge wallet. "Agent Ricken. Two of my agents were in the station. Call it in, I have clearance. These two are with me."

Whatever was on the badge must have been impressive. The beat cop nodded, saluted, and motioned them through.

"Just what does your badge say?"

"FBI special op. Reece got it for me for special occasions." She slowly drove forward. The fire was out, but so was the security screen. The explosion from those two automatons had taken out the screen, the sidewalk, and the entire walkway leading to the front of the station. The actual doors were damaged, but wide-open and medics were wheeling people out.

Aisling didn't want to wait for Stella to park the car, but without flashing badges of their own, which they didn't have and wouldn't match if they did, she knew they couldn't go without Stella.

Stella parked on a blocked side road and all three quickly walked through the staging areas. Then she marched in the front of the station, flashing her badge as needed. Aisling and Maeve stayed on her heels.

Aisling watched every stretcher that came out. Judging by the people she recognized, and the condition of the lower floor, the small crimes unit was hit hard. She didn't see her brother, Reece, or Garran.

Stella stopped a medic who was guiding things. "Is everyone out?"

"Except the injured and the dead. Those with light injuries are in the tent across the street, along with most of the uninjured. They are still searching, but the building hasn't checked out as clear, so we need everyone out." He wasn't chasing them away, but the encouragement was there.

Aisling didn't want to cause a fuss, so with a last glance upstairs, she followed Stella and Maeve out.

"If they were still up there, they wouldn't have been killed. Probably over at the tent." Maeve's pep talks were usually a lot more believable, but she was carrying a lot of concern as well. There was a good chance that cops they both knew were dead or dying.

Aisling's phone rang as they were crossing the street; it was an unknown number, so she was about to let it go to voice mail, then a text appeared. "It's me. Caradork." The deliberate misspelling of his name made Aisling tear up. She used to call him that when she was a kid. She answered the call but kept her voice low. "It's me."

"Thank goddess; I was hoping you'd pick up. Whatever you do, don't leave the diner. We're okay, but along with going for destruction, Reece thinks this was to draw someone out—most likely you."

"Too late."

"Crap. Wait. Dark hair and tats? Or the red-head? How are you doing that?"

"Dark hair is me. Maeve is the red-head. Our diner owner has skills."

"Okay, good and bad. Reece is swearing like a banshee on speed now that he knows that's you. He wants you three out of here now. And Garran is arguing with him."

Aisling rolled her eyes and stopped Maeve and Stella. They had crossed the street but the recon tent was up a hill. "What do you want us to do? We're almost there."

The phone fumbled as Caradoc had it taken from him. "A—okay, you. You all need to leave. At least you. But the others should go as well." Reece stumbled as he almost said her name, but recovered.

"I can't not have them involved, Larkin. And two of them are my people now." Garran had that perfect pitch. He came through clear on the phone even though Reece probably still had it, but Aisling knew no one around them would think he was speaking louder than a normal conversation.

"This is a fed case," Reece wasn't backing down either.

The phone jumbled again. Caradoc appeared out of a smaller tent, but still the size of a good-sized office, off to the side from the injured staging area. He held up the phone. "Come up here, Garran is bigger and meaner; let's stay on his good side."

"Agreed," Aisling said, then disconnected the call. "The boys are having a pissing match up there. Caradoc wants us to bet on the winner. Let's go up."

Stella and Maeve must have heard enough of the odd conversation and agreed. They all started up the hill.

Caradoc greeted them. "They're fighting again. I knew you'd want a list of the dead and seriously wounded." He held up a mag-pad.

There was only one good friend listed, Goldkowsky. He was listed on the hospital-bound injured list. But the note indicated he was expected to pull through. Six other officers had died and five more were probably going to join them. She handed the pad to Maeve.

"Damn it, who attacks a police station?" As she asked, she looked around the tent. It was larger than it appeared from the street and set up like a base of operations. Reece, Garran, and Caradoc had taken over a far corner, but the place was filled with high-ranking police. "Where's Losien? I didn't see her on the injured list." Not a good sign considering what they suspected of her.

Garran broke off his fight with Reece. "She called out sick the past two days. Wouldn't answer her phone today. Had a black and white drive by her house—it's cleaned out."

Just as Heike's had been.

"Why didn't you tell me?" Now Reece had a new topic to be pissed about.

"We were busy not dying and keeping others from not dying. Let me guess, your agency was after her too?"

Stella walked between them. "This fighting is what's going to get more people killed. The agency, the police force, whatever it is Caradoc actually does, there is too much at risk right now. No case jurisdiction. Work together."

A tough mom speech coming from a short, balding black man was a little odd, but it hit all three of them.

"I can't speak for my entire agency," Reece said. "I'll do what I can, but you took a huge risk coming here."

"We watched the malgi explode and then your phones were dead. What the hell were we supposed to do?" Aisling didn't like being exposed and, even with her disguise, she felt like she was. Being without her badge wasn't helping that feeling.

Reece leaned forward. "Maybe stay in a safe place?" His voice had dropped and the troublemaking smartass was coming back. "Not that you'd ever do anything smart."

Aisling laughed. "You were one of the ones I came to rescue, so yeah, I'm not very smart." She shook her head. What the hell? People were dying, she was being stalked, and she was flirting.

Reece must have had the same thought; he took a step back. "Anyway, I make it a goal to never be at odds with Stella, so let's get all of our information out on the table."

"Chief? We want to show you the footage the sky cam got." Ellis from homicide came over to get Garran, but took the chance to study Aisling, Maeve, and Stella. Ellis wasn't the most curious elf, but even she wanted to know who they were.

Garran nodded to the rest of them. "You all sort this out and I'll expect to be updated when I get back." Garran had always been a lone fey, but not now. He never wanted to be captain, but if they wanted to keep Surratt out of things, and right now they apparently needed to, he had to step in. He did it so easily that Aisling wondered if there was more to his past.

The five of them stared at each other in silence for a moment. Well, four of them did. Maeve kept watching the other cops in the tent. She hadn't seen any of them for a few weeks and it was visibly difficult for her not to respond as herself as familiar faces walked by.

"I'm not sure why you think I was the target, they disguised the malgi to mimic two people who Caradoc is dealing with," Aisling said. "Actually, you've been dealing with Mott Flowers, so that could have been aimed at you as well." She folded her arms and gave Reece her best glare.

"True, but I know Mott is still in a secure hospital. Granted, whoever set that up might not have known that I check in on him regularly. Per Jones, he's still unconscious, by the way. As for them targeting you, what better way to bring you out of hiding than threaten your brother?"

"Most people don't know we're related."

"But anyone who has seen you in the past few days might have guessed," Stella said. "There's a similarity in your faces."

"I haven't been that hard to find, other than the past few

hours. I was at the hospital, in the car, I'm visible."

"But you went to ground after you were shot. Once you left the hospital, you were gone. No one could find you until we picked you up in the forest." The tone of Reece's voice was more that *he* couldn't and if he couldn't, then no one could.

"Or, they knew Caradoc was inside, knew of his connections to Mott and the agent. And used that to try and gain entrance and take out the police station," Maeve said. She'd turned back to them. "Never make things more complicated than they have to be, although I guess complicated and sneaky is second nature for a fed."

"Which brings us back to how bold does someone have to be to take out an entire police station in broad daylight?" Aisling didn't doubt that, for one reason or another, she was involved in this; there were too many things pointing to that. But this was beyond her.

"I think it's probably whoever is behind the iron drug," Reece said, but kept his voice low. "Had Fachie not fought the infection like he did, isolating himself before he went feral, he would have infected a lot more people. He could have decimated the station." He turned to Aisling and Maeve. "We learned a few things before the explosion. Fachie locked himself up the moment he realized something was wrong. It was only when his friends tried to help him that people got exposed. The scientists in my agency believe the Iron Death reaction is mutating, with or without help. In the first cases it wasn't contagious. But in the man at the hospital who went after Aisling and in Fachie it was. Touch will spread it while the first victim is alive."

The noise from the command center around them became louder as all of them went silent.

Aisling swore. "There is something big coming in and they want us out of the area. Yes, cops from other stations will cover the beats but it's going to be thin. Feds will come in too, but not enough, at least for a while. They are planning something soon. The malgi were their backup in case Fachie didn't take everyone out."

CHAPTER THIRTY-FIVE

REECE WASN'T HAPPY. "WHAT'S THE point of removing the cops from an area just so they can move drugs in? There must be something else going on beyond Iron Death being brought in. Yes, they might be able to get through undetected, but the station will be back, and the agency will send more people to fill in any gaps. What good will it do them? They also wasted their two high-placed plants—Heike was shot execution style and Losien is either dead or on the run. And how the hell is Mott Flowers tied into this?"

Maeve turned to Caradoc. "What did you say that Mott did for your company?"

"He was our mathematician and one of the key inventors. We were in the early stages of work on a predictive algorithm for events when he started to become secretive. Without warning, he took off with all of his files and some weapon prototypes, which was why I was trying to find him."

"The same reason we were," Reece said. "He was involved in a brain trust a few years ago that had been recently shown to have been accurate at predicting certain events—scarily so."

"You said you'd been checking on him since I found him, how is he?" Aisling almost felt upset about not asking earlier, but it had been a long and twisted few days.

Reece shrugged. "He's still in a coma, but stable. Who-ever left him meant for him to die, but I don't get why they didn't just kill him. We arrested the leader of those thugs and the troll. Neither were in condition to escape before the uniforms slapped cuffs on them." Reece shot Aisling an approving grin. "The troll was clueless, but the leader finally handed over what they'd taken off of Mott, but it was only an empty wallet and a beat-up watch."

Caradoc perked up at that. "Do you still have the watch?" There was too much interest in his eyes. That focus was rarely good.

"What is it really?" Aisling narrowed her eyes at her brother. She knew him. He'd find a way to get the watch and replace it before Reece knew. Sneaky super-secret fed versus her brother—she'd bet on Caradoc every time. Normally she wouldn't care, but the time for secrets from each other was over—good or bad they had to work together to stop whatever was going on.

Caradoc flashed the grin that usually only made an appearance on magazine covers or interviews. "Sentimental reasons."

"You're not even trying, mate," Maeve pulled back and gave Caradoc a serious look over. "Even I didn't believe that."

"Not to mention that grin was a dead giveaway." Reece shook his head at Caradoc's look of surprise and annoyance.

"I can't believe you've brainwashed your friends against me." But his fight wasn't there—for the first time since they were kids, Caradoc looked tired. And concerned.

"Considering that only Maeve knew you existed before today, that was all you, brother mine."

Caradoc studied at the buildings around them. "We need to get somewhere more secure. A half-assed parabolic could hear us from a mile away. But let's say it is of interest."

His comment brought nods from everyone, including

Garran, who'd come back after organizing the cops in the tent. "I can't leave, but I want you all to go. Caradoc gave me one of his secret phones." He held up a small phone that appeared to be the twin of Aisling's. "You need to get clear. If your other brother was correct, there are still some unhealthy searchers."

Stella had been quiet, but nodded now. "I think they need to go back to my place, in the room, at least for tonight. There are folding cots and supplies in the closet. The diner and the room locks are now coded to all of you. I'm staying here. The glamours on Aisling and Maeve will drop once you're at least a mile from me." She flashed her badge to Garran. "I think this will stop questions about my right to be here, and I have a feeling I can help. Whoever we're up against is using some old school ways. I haven't seen a malgi in decades, but I *have* seen them, unlike many of these younglings."

Garran nodded. "Agreed, we could use the help. You all go do what he/she said and check in with that mystic brother of yours to see what he's sensing. I'll contact you when we have more information."

"Good idea. They should go until it's safer." Reece was already studying the station. It appeared that the medics had cleared out the injured, they could start assessing the damage soon.

"You too, Larkin," Garran said. "Sorry, this is my crime scene. I know you will get pulled in officially at some point, but something already found you—all of you—even if Caradoc didn't notice. I need that element removed from here right now."

Aisling glanced at the cops around her. "As much as I'd like to disagree, and none of us are good at waiting, I have to say he's right. This is too volatile right now, we shouldn't compound it." Up until the subtle reminder of the vallenians, Aisling had been willing to fight Garran. That shut her up. The last thing they needed around here were Old Ones.

Maeve shrugged. "I can't talk to anyone I know, being here is making things worse, and if that thing I saw is what you've said, I want to be somewhere protected. For a bit, anyway."

Reece wasn't a cop; he could do whatever he wanted as long as he left the station. Garran wasn't going to allow Dixon to show up for a long time, if ever. "I think we need to stick together, and my agency wants me to stick to Aisling. No, I haven't told them about Maeve or Caradoc." He almost seemed embarrassed about that, as if he was admitting to caring about something other than his work and that was weak. "Guess it's a good thing my car holds four." He nodded to Garran and headed down the hill. Caradoc followed.

"You'll keep us updated, right?" Aisling said to Garran and Stella. She knew there might be things that Garran wouldn't pass along, but Stella might.

"Aye," Garran said. The smile he flashed was classic Garran, the mischievous fey she'd always known. "And you keep yourselves safe. I know you're damn good cops, and you're with a sneaky fed bastard who can definitely handle his own—same could be said for Caradoc from what I can tell. But watch your backs—there is a lot of bad coming down the pike."

"Deal," Aisling said. "And I promise not to tell Reece you said something nice about him." Garran turned back to the cops as Aisling and Maeve went down the hill.

Reece's car was a bit further than Stella's was but he and Caradoc waited at the corner.

"We're making a detour; someone wants his car back." Satisfied that everyone was together, Reece continued walking to his car.

"It's sitting in a hospital parking lot not five miles from

here; I think we can afford the detour. And I'd hate to have it towed." Caradoc shot Aisling a grin.

She wanted to smack him but while Reece being a step ahead of them meant he didn't see the grin, he would hear her hitting her brother.

"I've heard getting a car out of a tow yard can be a real bitch," Maeve said from behind all of them.

Aisling turned and shot her a glare. Seriously, they needed Reece to stay on their side. Letting him know who left his car to be towed was extremely low on her list of things she wanted to do this year.

Reece was either too focused on whatever he was thinking about or choosing to ignore them. He didn't say anything until they got to his car.

"What did you say, Caradoc?" He'd been listening to something on his phone.

Caradoc sighed. Games were only fun if there was some-one to play with. "I'd like to get my car before we go into exile."

Reece unlocked the car. "Fine, but after I drop you off, I'm going to check something out. There's been some unusual increased activity reported in some gang areas." He held up his hand to stop all the comments. "No, you can't go with me. Yes, I will be back at the diner right after, and you heard Stella, the locks and alarms will work by touch for any of you—including the back room. I'll return as soon as I can. If we *are* facing some sort of Old One invasion on top of the rest of this, I don't want to be target number one."

Either he'd decided he did need more folks on his side, or whatever he'd heard on his phone was massively dis-turbing. He wasn't concerned about them going into his super-secret lair without him or Stella being there.

"I'm going with you." Aisling settled in the front seat and folded her arms. Whatever was going on, she was in the middle of it. Time to take a stand.

"No," Reece said.

Followed by Caradoc. "No way."

"Not without me." Maeve finished it off.

Aisling shook her head. "This isn't negotiable. I need to get a better handle on what I'm up against before we go to ground. I know you guys want to as well, but we need people who know what we're doing to be safe." She left the 'in case we don't come back' part dangle in silence. "I'm a damn good cop and can take care of myself. Worst case, healing can be used as a weapon." She glared around to all three.

Her mother had made sure she was trained extensively in it when she was young. It wasn't a great defensive ability, but it was something. Her mother had been disappointed that Aisling wasn't magically strong, so she'd wanted to make sure Aisling could defend herself. Once Aisling started training for physical defense, she didn't need it anymore. She'd only had to use it once—on a boyfriend who got way out of line.

"I'd listen to her," Caradoc said. "I was one of her training victims when she was a kid—it's not fun. But you two need to come back immediately. Harlie wasn't kidding that something is tracking us. I should be able to figure out mobile blockers, but it will take time."

"I need to do this alone. Leifen needs to go to Old Town. And check on some contacts."

"Unless you want to have Leifen's woman chasing him through the worst sections in town, you'd better back off and let me join you." Aisling wasn't in the mood for whatever issues he was working through. She was going.

Reece stared her down—or tried to. He finally gave in and shook his head. "Fine. Come on."

"I still can't believe Surratt is fine, or mostly fine," Aisling muttered to herself as Reece pulled into the parking lot.

Hopefully Surratt would get a migraine from how hard she was thinking bad thoughts in his direction.

"I know he had a good reason—our animosity was for show—but damn it, that move pissed me off." Reece pulled into the parking structure, but since he'd never seen Caradoc's car, he had no idea where to go.

"Surratt is a sneaky bastard, that's for certain." Maeve didn't sound any happier about his lying than the rest, but she looked like herself now. Aisling looked in the visor mirror and she did as well. Stella's spell had worn off.

"Go up one level to the left, black SUV," Caradoc said. He didn't know Surratt, so had no vested interest in his living or dying.

Reece pulled up behind Caradoc's car.

"Don't stay out there too long," Maeve said. She handed Aisling a pair of small knives and paired wrist braces for them. "You might need these more than I do right now." She leaned into the window on Aisling's side. "Take care of yourself, and don't let the fed do anything stupid. And Larkin? My girl better come back in the same condition we're leaving her in. Or you won't have to worry about Old Ones finding you." With a pat on the side of the car, Maeve and Caradoc went to his.

"I don't get why no one trusts me," Reece said then drove out of the parking structure.

Aisling laughed. "Because you've spent quite a lot of time and effort to make that happen? Don't forget that I watched you and the cops on the dock. They liked you. I'd say they trusted you. You're a fed, yet they treated you as one of their own. Even if they had known I was one of them—they wouldn't have been as friendly to me as they were to you."

Reece was silent for a few moments. "I guess what you and Stella said has merit; for good or evil, we're thrown together and we can't afford secrets. There have been some rumblings going on for a while now, over a year. Garran was off about the timing, but he wasn't pulled in initially. The situation with Surratt has been longer. He used to do black ops work, and his bosses and my bosses wanted us to be able to work together—but indirectly. Dixon was born and, with a good enough backstory from high up people, was given access to most all of narcotics. Losien had been a good cop at one point. But she had no idea who Dixon really was. Then, a few months ago, Maeve's name popped up as a person of interest, so I worked harder to spend more time with your cases, but I kept the annoyance factor up to keep everyone at bay." He started swearing. "I just realized my top agency bosses might have been messing with me about where she was. They tried to make me believe she was traveling north when they had to have known she was here."

Aisling hung onto the dash as he tore up the on-ramp to the freeway. "In all fairness, they probably didn't know. Caradoc made it appear that she went through the Gloven forest, and she was hidden pretty well."

Reece shook his head. "How in the hell did he fool the FBI and Area 42? Yeah, that's my real agency, and no, not discussing it now."

Aisling gave a low whistle. Area 42 was so secret most people doubted it existed. That was one item she would definitely be asking about later.

CHAPTER THIRTY-SIX

"YOU JUST MET HIM, BUT my brother is as crafty and sneaky as all those articles about him imply. Not to mention, he managed to sneak inside a car owned by an Area 42 agent and not be caught."

He sighed and ran one hand through his hair. "True. But how did you hide Maeve for any length of time?"

"Caradoc has a safe house, one that is far more comfortable than a diner back room." She frowned. "One he either feels is compromised, or not as secure as your hideout." She hadn't thought of that. Caradoc liked controlling things. It would have made more sense for him to take them all over to his safe house.

"He's concerned that the Old Ones found it. They found Maeve outside of it, but the house itself could be compromised." The hushed tone in his voice told her that, while Reece didn't recall seeing the vallenian, part of his soul did.

"That would be my guess. Do you recall anything about them?"

"No, and I should be furious for what you did, but I'd rather be illegally mind wiped than dragged through the veil. We should change. We look too much like a cop and a fed." He pulled into an alley, a nicer one this time. Most likely these houses were originally built with back alleys, before front facing garages became popular.

"I don't have anything to change into." She could try and tramp out her clothes, but it was a pretty basic outfit.

She'd end up looking like a schoolteacher trying to go wild.

"Maeve left you something besides the knives, she left a satchel in the back seat." Reece got out of the car and went to rummage in the trunk.

That was weird; what was Maeve doing with a satchel of clothes? Aisling started laughing as she pulled out the skimpy clothing. Maeve had left Caradoc's house on the run, but she didn't have much of her own clothing, so she borrowed some of Aisling's old club wear. She'd been planning not only on running, but going undercover as well. Aisling took out her ponytail and put on a loose but low-cut top. It was long enough to tie up in the front but leave the back down for her gun in the waistband of her pants. She kept her pants and low shoes on. They weren't going to Old Town to party, and if things got ugly, she'd need to run and fight.

Reece was still behind his car with the trunk up and was grumbling to himself.

She went back to check on him. He stood there bare-chested and holding two shirts in the air. "Neither of these work."

"You could go like that; it would certainly distract people." Aisling wasn't going to try not to admire him. He always wore his duster and a dress shirt, so previously it was impossible to tell if he was in shape or not. But he was and he worked out—a lot. He wasn't bulky, but there was more than enough definition to give most fitness models a run for their money. And his abs were way beyond a six-pack.

"Funny." He lifted both shirts again. "These are all I have, and neither are something Leifen would wear."

Aisling didn't do much undercover, and she didn't know anyone else who did it as much as Reece. Telling him it didn't matter wouldn't work—it could matter, and it might for her as well if he didn't play his part.

"Can you rip the sleeves?" She pointed to the plaid shirt on the right. It was less like Reece than the other one. "Maybe a t-shirt with that over it and the sleeves ripped off?"

Reece went into a gym bag and pulled out a black t-shirt. He pulled it on, modified the other shirt, and added it. Then he added the glam box spell and his coloring faded to Leifen's paler skin and eye color.

He looked up as if noticing her for the first time. "That works. A bit high end for Leifen, but, ya know, he's been moving up in life." He slammed the door, then they walked around to the front.

"Isn't this going to be a problem?" This was his Reece car, his Dixon/Leifen one could change how it appeared, but others wouldn't know that.

"I would prefer to change cars, but we need to get there quickly. We can park further out and go in on foot." He scowled. "I know elves are fast. I can't go as fast on land as in water, but I can move faster than I should be able to."

He was trusting her with another secret. More and more he was displaying talents that no half breed should have. It was more than a little dangerous if the wrong people on the fey council found out. That he was still telling her this after finding out who her mother was said a lot. The fact she clearly despised her mother probably helped resolve any fears that she'd tell her about him.

"So we jog in, probably better. Did *they* say what was going on?" She was afraid to say Area 42 out loud.

He got them back on the freeway. "No, they're being more cautious, even over our secure lines. I know they lost three agents last night and they were certain it was the Lazing, but they still haven't been able to pin down how many of them are over here. The agents who died last night did get information that tonight something big was going on. It appears to be some intel as to who is smuggling in that iron drug. Unfortunately, that information didn't get found until an hour ago when they found the bodies and the messages they were able to encode before they died."

That was reassuring. Three fully trained Area 42 agents killed doing what she and Reece were about to do. "What *are* we doing?" She really didn't want to die, but she also wanted to help stop Iron Death from killing more people. Julilynn's face from the photos before she died haunted her.

"Just recon. Not getting involved. You and I are out on the town and visiting one of Leifen's buddies, Clark Smythe."

She glanced over to see if he was joking as he parked the car. "The drug runner? Narco brought him in a week ago, and he died the first night. You know that." Reece spying in there for over a year meant there was probably nothing in that department he didn't know.

"Reece knows that, Dixon would know that, Leifen wouldn't know that. He's not a regular in this part of town. He's there enough so people should recognize him when we go in, but not beyond being Smythe's buddy." He got out of the car and waited until she did the same. "I will be suitably crushed when I find out he's gone. We can see what is noticeable, and then high-tail it out of there. My people have a few other teams hitting the area, but we can't risk anything—this is information gathering only."

"I'm on-board with that." Aisling ran her fingers through her hair to make it a bit wild. "You lead."

Reece nodded, he was almost thug-like and far more muscular in the tight t-shirt, and started off at a jog. His movements were deceptive, he looked like he was moving at a quick jog, but he was at a speed closer to a flat run for a human. He led them through mostly empty streets, slowing when a stray car got too close. Running was too suspicious in this part of town. Aisling kept up but was impressed at his speed and his sneakiness.

The part of town where the Celtic gang bosses had been killed was bad—and not someplace anyone would casually visit. The part of Old Town they were in was so bad no one visited unless they had a gun to their heads. Or they desperately needed information.

The center of Old Town was more like what might be found in an old village in Europe. A large square with dilapidated businesses, some still open, but owned by gangs, with rows of tiny houses circling it. Small groups of people, men and women, fey and human, gathered in small groups talking to each other.

And watching Aisling and Reece.

They'd slowed to a walk well before any of the Old Town guards should have been aware of them, but Aisling had a feeling they were waiting for them.

A tall, skeletal fey stepped toward them. "Hey, there's Leifen. What ya doing here, *Leif-en*?" The emphasis placed on the name caused a shiver to run through Aisling's gut.

"Looking for Clark, he owes me money." Reece had been a foot ahead of Aisling, but he stepped back to her side now. "Taking the woman out."

"Nice piece of ass. Too bad Clark got bumped off in prison last week. Word has it he was a narc, with a fed friend."

Aisling let her hand drift toward her back, but Reece's hand beat hers. He kept it there, appearing as if it was around her waist under her shirt, but she felt his fingers on the butt of her gun. She did the same to him. If things were going like they seemed to be, two guns wouldn't save them, but at least they could take some of the assholes with them.

"No shit? Damn it, he owed me money." Reece was keeping his voice balanced between Leifen being a bit stupid and also showing a respect for the gangs. Leifen wasn't in a gang, but he drifted around and helped them with things.

Judging by the scowls around them, they no longer needed his help.

"What say we think you did know? Rumor is you set him up to turn. That you're a narc too."

Aisling tightened her hold on Reece's gun. It would be quick now.

Gunfire and the explosions of spell balls erupted behind the row of houses toward the right side of the circle.

All of the gang members ran toward the gun fire, but the one who had approached them grabbed two others as they went by. "Lock them up. I want to find out what they know before we end them." He pulled out his gun and ran toward the sounds.

The two he'd grabbed were both thugs and while Aisling thought she and Reece could take them, she waited to see his move. A cop would handle things far different than an undercover fed. She hoped his way kept them alive.

Hopefully, whichever gang these two belonged to, they weren't valued as great brains. Common sense would say to frisk anyone you're going to lock up and torture. Neither man did so, each grabbed one of them and started pulling them deeper into Old Town. Both were watching the area with the gun battle, and it was obvious by their glares they were pissed about not being there.

Reece waited until they went down a small street between houses, and more importantly, were out of sight from the center courtyard, and jerked his arm free of the thug. He pulled out Aisling's gun and shot the one holding her in the forehead. He turned to shoot the one who had been holding him, but Aisling shot him first, with Reece's gun.

"We can't go back out there. Whatever is going on is big. And coming this way." Aisling held out his gun and they swapped.

Reece jogged forward a few houses, then ran for a door and kicked it in. It appeared to have been abandoned for a long time, and hopefully once they propped the door closed, it would still appear that no one was inside. They went as far to the back as they could and hunkered down in the kitchen.

Aisling studied the dilapidated room. There was a door in the back, but it was heavily boarded up. And the bit of window she could see through indicated there was nowhere to run in that direction anyway. "This wasn't what Leifen was planning, I'm thinking." There was a good chance they'd only delayed the inevitable. Even if they called for help, they'd probably be found before a large enough force could get to them. "Any idea who was attacking them?"

"If I had to guess, I'd say a rival gang—one that shouldn't be in this country." He checked his clip then put the gun back. "Based on the timing, someone gave them the same information we got."

"Lazing. So what do we do now?" Aisling duplicated his moves with her own gun, but kept it out next to her.

Reece jumped, then grabbed his back pocket. He had the phone's volume off, but it was vibrating. He started to shut it off, then swore and answered it. "Larkin." His face grew grim as the person on the other side spoke. "We're trapped. You're right about a leak. They knew Leifen was a cover. I think the Lazing are hitting them right now." Another pause on his end. "Understood. Larkin out." He turned off the phone but stared at it for a moment.

"Well?"

"That was the agency. The other operatives were all exposed. They're dead and we're on our own."

"What options do we have?" Aisling prided herself on being able to think her way out of things—but there didn't appear to be many choices. Once the two thugs they'd shot were found, there would be a massive search.

"Wait until we see who survives?" The tone in his voice said even he didn't believe that. The Lazing finding them would be worse than the local gang.

The sound of gunfire was definitely moving closer.

"Calling the cops won't work. They have too much happening on their own right now, and this is a full gang battle. We'd be dead before they got in here."

They sat in silence. In their jobs there was always a chance you'd go out on a call that you weren't coming back from. Still, you always hoped it wouldn't be this one.

"If this is it, then I am going to do something possibly extremely stupid," Reece said. He leaned forward and kissed her. It was tentative at first, then became far more involved as Aisling joined in. The shock of him kissing her wore off, and she found herself pulling him closer.

Finally, they broke apart. "You're still a pain in the ass, Larkin," Aisling said. The kiss left her more rattled than the gunfire around them did. Her reaction to him was startling to say the least—and not something to mentally address in gang territory.

"Likewise, Danaan." He smiled and gently pulled her forward for one more kiss, a short and passionate one, then rocked back again. "I have a way to get you out. I run to the center with this, detonate it, and you run like hell the other way. You still might not make it, but at least you've got a chance, and I can take some of these assholes with me." He was holding a small bomb. Extremely small; it sat easily in the palm of his hand.

"Is that an Icarus bomb?" Tiny little balls of massive explosive power—hypothetically speaking. They supposedly didn't exist yet.

"Yeah, a prototype." He started for the front door, but Aisling grabbed his arm.

"You seriously think you get to go out in a blaze of

glory? You seem to forget, fed boy, that while you are some sort of weird, mutant breed, with abilities you shouldn't have, that I am still a full-blooded elf. I'm faster and stronger than you." She grabbed the bomb, planted a quick kiss on his lips, and then shoved him at the back wall. She was gone before he hit it.

The alley was empty except for the two bodies, but the sound of gunfire was just past the entrance to the main courtyard. She'd run as fast as she could, but there were fey out there with guns as well; they'd be able to hit a running elf. As long as she could take them out as well, it was a hell of a lot better than waiting to be tortured to death.

She picked up speed and hit the center of the wide courtyard at a full run, waiting to feel bullets tearing through her. She skidded to a stop when silence surrounded her. Not only silence, frozen people. The gun battle hung around her like a piece of virtual reality put on pause. No one moved.

CHAPTER THIRTY-SEVEN

MEN AND WOMEN WERE FROZEN all around her in whatever they had been doing. Shooting. Dying. Just frozen in the air.

A cold pressure built directly in front of her and three vallenians appeared. A thin, foot-long wooden box landed at her feet.

Aisling contemplated the bomb in her hand again. Maybe she could take them out too.

"Time." The word came from the one in the front, but it was only in her head. He pointed to the frozen tableau around them.

"Life." The second one pointed to the box.

"Lady." The third didn't move at all, but Aisling knew it was that one who spoke.

Then they vanished.

Reece must have taken off after her immediately, because he skidded to a stop behind her as the vallenians disappeared. "What in the hell happened to the gangs? And were those…?"

"No idea, and yes." Aisling was fighting a number of terrors right now.

"Are you going to pick that up?"

"I don't want to."

"But?"

"Damn it." She bent and grabbed the box. That it was made of enchanted wood wasn't a surprise. "How long of a delay does your toy have?" She wasn't sure, but she thought she spotted a tiny bit of arm movement in a gunwoman in front of them. Whatever the vallenians had done to freeze time, it was wearing off.

"A minute, hit the blue button. The eggheads are still working on making it longer."

"Then hang on." Aisling pressed the delay on the bomb, threw it behind her, grabbed Reece, and ran like hell.

The explosion felt like it took much longer than a minute, and they'd gotten a good distance away, or so she thought. They were still slammed to the ground when everything exploded.

She'd been half-pulling Reece along since, while he was fast, she was still faster. But he'd pulled himself out of her grip right at the end. When the explosion lifted them up and dropped them, he dove to cover her.

"Damn it." Aisling slid out from under him and looked behind them. Old Town was a giant fireball, one that collapsed in on itself as she watched. No more flame, just a lot of smoke. "Is your toy supposed to extinguish the explosion it made?" Reece hadn't moved.

"Reece?" She pulled his arm, then stopped when he groaned.

"Yeah, I'm here. And yes, it is supposed to wipe itself out after destruction. I'll tell the eggheads that part worked." His groan turned into a yelp as he rolled over. His entire left side was riddled with holes and seeping with blood. His shirt and t-shirt had been punctured by shrapnel.

"Can you move?"

He let out a big breath. "Yes, just surface wounds. Might need help getting up."

There were sirens in the distance, but they sounded far away. At this point Aisling wasn't sure who could be trusted, so getting to the diner as quickly as possible would be the best thing.

She tucked the enchanted wood box under her arm, got

to her feet, and pulled him up with one hand under his good arm. From the amount of blood he was now losing, they were more than surface wounds.

Normally an explosion would have brought some people running. But people in the areas that surrounded Old Town weren't the type to go out and investigate. The few people she did see were going into their homes and closing their blinds.

Reece was walking, mostly, but he was listing to one side as they went.

"Damn it, your leg took a hit too." His entire lower left leg was bloody. That would cause listing, but so would blood loss.

"I'll be fine." There was no conviction behind that.

Aisling moved as fast as she felt was safe and got them to Reece's car. She propped him up against the vehicle and started patting his pockets.

"Is this really the place for that?" His voice was weak, but the snark was still there.

"I'm trying to find your car keys, you perv." She finally found them.

"You aren't driving my car. You'd never handle her." He'd been fading since he got injured, but mention his car and he perked right up.

"No, I can handle your car, but you might not be handling staying conscious for much longer. Something inside you is bleeding and I sure as hell am not going to try and heal you here. We need to get to the diner." She opened the passenger side and gently put him inside. That he didn't fight back was scary.

She'd buckled him in and gotten into the driver's seat when her phone vibrated. The caller ID flashed Caradork. She clicked to answer. "What? Things went south, Reece is hurt badly, and we're on our way there."

"We saw the report of a major explosion in Old Town,

thought it might be you, but don't come here—it's compromised. We're safe inside, but there are people on the roofs watching—I think they are waiting for you and fed boy. Go to my place. Call when you get there but keep it short." Caradoc cut the call.

"Okay, change of plans, you get to see my brother's secret home."

She headed for the freeway and kept up mundane chatter about life in the police station, anything that might keep Reece focused. The trip was uneventful, but Reece was unconscious by the time she drove through the hedge.

"Sorry about this," she said as she picked him up and carried him into the house. Not easy since he was taller than her and dead weight, but she did it.

She placed him on the sofa on his good side and cut away both bloody shirts. A quick examination of his leg showed it appeared to be a bullet wound, or possibly small shrapnel, but it went completely through his calf. Whatever got his side hadn't gone through. His bare torso resembled raw meat, which wasn't attractive, but something must have gone deeper. She dropped to the floor next to the sofa and held her hands over him.

Something had cut through a lot of tissue. When she narrowed her search, she found it was a piece of shrapnel and a bullet. She focused on trying to pull them both out and heal the damage they'd already done, then recalled Caradoc's suggestion and started thinking about her mother. Whether it was something about her mother specifically, or anger in general—it worked. The pieces of metal were pushed to the surface and the tissue was repaired as it exited. Then she healed the smaller injuries and the wound on his calf.

She felt tired, but not as completely drained as she normally would have been. Maybe the anger principle was helping with that as well.

"Am I still pretty?" Reece muttered without opening his eyes. But he also scratched the healed side which was a good sign.

"You've never been pretty—I can only work with what is there," Aisling said and batted away his hand from his side. "I just need to make sure you'll live." A quick pass confirmed he was healed, not a mark on torso nor leg to show he'd been injured. "You're going to live though, and you're welcome for that." She rolled to her feet and took over a chair.

He opened his eyes and patted his side. "You do good work. The agency's healers only do enough to keep us from losing too much blood."

He looked far more innocent than normal, not that someone who knew dozens of ways to kill a person could be innocent. But there was a vulnerability she'd never seen before. She let herself meet his eyes. Mistake. She wasn't certain how he did a lot of things he did, but there was seriously something up with his eyes. Combined with the kisses they'd shared when they both thought they were going to die, his gaze brought heat to her cheeks.

She forced herself to turn away. "I couldn't save your shirts, sorry, but I can get you something from Caradoc's room." She glanced at his bloody and torn pant leg. "Pants too." She was on her feet and passing the sofa when he reached out.

"Are we going to talk about it? Ignoring this isn't a great idea."

She sighed. Ignoring it had been her plan. Falling for Reece was not on her list of things to do this week. "Neither is talking about it." She held up her hand to cut him off when he opened his mouth. "Not with everything that's going on. I don't know how I feel about you, I really don't. It's as if you're brand new to me. The jackass I thought I knew wasn't real. And while that was one hell of a kiss, I don't think pushing it further at this point is a good idea."

Reece finally nodded then gave a crooked grin. "One hell of a kiss, eh?"

"Don't be a smart ass—you felt it too."

"I did, and I agree, this isn't the time. But I have no intention of letting anything drop once we get through this." His eyes had gone serious. "You might not have seen the real me until the last few days, but I've known you for a while."

They watched each other for a few moments, then Aisling shook her head. "Let me get you some clothes. And bedding. For out here. The diner is being watched, so we need to stay here tonight." She went to Caradoc's room to get clothes and called to check in with her brother and Maeve.

"You made it? Will fed boy live?"

"We did, and he will. Won't talk long, but we ran into three Old Ones."

"Damn. Okay, the watchers are still in place, but if they're not gone by morning, I'll take care of them. Stay put, and don't do anything I wouldn't do." Again he clicked off without letting her respond.

Aisling put the phone in her back pocket and pulled out a t-shirt and sweatpants for Reece. Tomorrow he could riffle through Caradoc's closet and pick out something better—right now she needed Reece clothed and falling asleep—alone—in the living room.

"Here you go. There's a bathroom in Caradoc's room, and feel free to rummage through the kitchen. This is Caradoc's safe house so not sure how much food he normally keeps here."

Reece put the clothes next to him on the sofa. "Does he have alcohol? It's been a long shitty week and I could use something." He got to his feet and followed her into the kitchen.

She opened the fridge. "Beer?"

The warmth of him standing directly behind her told her they needed to keep their thoughts on the case. At least she did.

"Anything stronger?"

She turned and was an inch away from him. "Pretty sure," she said softly but in trying to avoid looking into his eyes she focused on his mouth—not a great option. Ignoring the part of her mind that was reminding her who said they needed to dial things back, she leaned forward. "Damn it, why did it have to be you?" She glanced into his eyes, pulled him close, and kissed him.

Reece had started it the other time, when they were pretty sure they were going to die. This time that wasn't a driving force. Something far more confusing and basic was behind this.

She ran her hands up his back. He really did waste this body under the dress shirts and duster. He gave a soft murmur and moved them toward the counter. His hands started sliding up her shirt in the back. Then he stopped and backed away with his arms out at his sides.

He was rattled. "You started it, after logically saying that this shouldn't happen—you started it again." There was more than just lust there, but it was hard to separate all of the emotions.

"I know. I'm sorry. I shouldn't have—"

"And I shouldn't have responded," he said and smiled as he dropped his arms to his sides. "I'm a grown boy, you didn't attack me. I do agree we need to hold back though. Unless we're sure we're going to die again. Then all bets are off."

She laughed. "Deal. End of the world, we'll bang like bunnies. Now, the hard booze would be here, if he has any." She went to a small cabinet. This might not be Cara-doc's real house, but most people were creatures of habit in where they put things.

No nectar, thank goddess, but two bottles of whiskey.

"Bang like bunnies?"

"I was trying to lighten the mood."

He laughed and found a pair of glasses. "Thought you might want some too."

She poured them both a small dab; there was no way to know how long it would be before something hit the fan, and being drunk wouldn't be a good thing for him. He looked like crap, sexy as hell, but still crap. How he'd manage to go from annoyingly-cute-but-a-pain-in-the-ass to damn sexy in a week was something she might have to talk to a therapist about. Later.

They took their drinks out to the living room. He set down his glass, pulled on the borrowed shirt, picked up the sweatpants and went to the bathroom.

Aisling shook herself from watching him walk. Damn it, her libido was like a sixteen-year-old's. It was such an odd reaction, but thinking back she realized that on some level she'd been interested in him even when he was a prick. But he'd been such an ass, on purpose, that the interest never went beyond acknowledging he was attractive and trying to stay away from his eyes.

He came back out wearing Caradoc's sweats and looking sleepy. He sat and took a long sip of the whiskey. "What were you thinking about? You have an odd expression on your face."

"You. Just trying to figure you out." She finished her whiskey and stood. "I'll get you a pillow and blanket. Will you be okay out here?"

He finished his whiskey, watching her carefully. Then put down the glass and flopped back on the sofa. "Nothing for me thanks, I've slept in worse places. Thanks for the whiskey. It helps sometimes." He said the last bit softly, but not to her, so she let it go. She knew nothing about his life, but right now wasn't the time to find out.

"Night."

"Sleep well."

She went to her room. Alcohol didn't affect elves like it did humans, but she was exhausted. She slipped out of her clothes and into her sleep shirt and shorts, and tumbled into bed.

CHAPTER THIRTY-EIGHT

A SOFT KNOCKING ON HER DOOR brought her out of a deep sleep, but like before, the sun was shining through the window, so it couldn't be that early. Aisling squinted at the clock. Seven forty-five. Seriously? They went to bed at two.

She rolled out of bed, adjusted her sleep clothes to make sure she was decent, and opened the door.

Reece appeared as groggy as she felt and had obviously slept without the shirt. The sweats hung low on his hips. She forced her eyes back up to his forehead. Damn it, she was going to order him to only wear loose dress shirts, baggy slacks, and that duster whenever he was around her.

"What?" It came out mad, which she was, but most of it was directed at herself.

"That box you brought in is glowing." As he spoke, her phone started hopping around on the desk where she'd tossed it.

"Hold on." She grabbed the bouncing phone. It was her brother again. "What? You don't want anyone to sleep? I was up all night saving our fed boy." Yes, Reece technically woke her up before Caradoc called, but he was compounding things.

"Is that what the kids are calling it these days? Kinky. But that's not why I called. The snipers—as they left, I spotted their weapons, and they *were* snipers—left about fifteen minutes ago. And whatever you two did to Old Town, it was serious. Most of the worst area is completely gone.

The channels can't pick up what caused the destruction."

"Reece had a prototype device that I'm not going to talk about until we're in person. Did you call just to tell us that?" She rolled her eyes for Reece's benefit.

"Not really, although you might come over here, or we could go there. It seems the Old Ones are gone."

"How do you know? Wait, Harlie called again?"

"Harlie is *here*. Showed up with a backpack and a motorcycle about half an hour ago. Glared at all the snipers until they left, even the ones I hadn't spotted, then came in, and told us the Old Ones are back on their side of the veil."

That news was good, the snipers might come back, but her freaky older brother had sent them packing somehow. And she was extremely glad the Old Ones were out of the picture for now. But Harlie being in LA was almost more disturbing than everything else combined. Even when she was a child, he never left Nepal. She'd only seen him in person twice. Once, when her parents took her to him to introduce them, and the second time when she was ten, for something her mother refused to tell her about.

"Did he have any other information?" As she spoke, Aisling pushed past Reece and went to the living room. The box the vallenians had given her was glowing along the seal. There was no way that was good, even if they were now out of this plane.

"Nope, wait." Harlie's voice was saying something in the background, but the phone wasn't picking the words up clearly. "Okay, he said you might want to put that box in a safe."

"This thing is glowing!" Maeve yelled from the background.

"Crap, the box she found is glowing and Harlie is getting agitated. Where'd you get a box anyway? Is it glowing too?"

"Our friends from the other side gave it to me in Old

Town. They also did some other scary stuff that I don't want to talk about on the phone. Yep, it started glowing before you called. Does Harlie know why?"

Caradoc pulled away from the phone and spoke to their brother then came back on the line. "Yeah, no. He's running blind here, just like we are." There was muttering in the background but, again, Harlie wasn't speaking loud enough for her to hear his words. Aisling could guess though. Caradoc called it and Harlie was refusing to admit he didn't know something.

"But we should get it in a safe? Yours too?"

"Yup. Can you put Reece on? We'll need the combo. My safe is in my room in the floor under the rug. Zero-eight-two-five-five. And yes, I will change it afterwards."

Aisling handed her phone to Reece. "You heard the man, give over your code."

He looked ready to argue, then shook his head. "Five-five-three-two-four. I take it that you already found it?"

"Thanks. Harlie did. He now isn't sure that we should stay here. He thinks it's secure, don't worry. But he wants us all together."

"Your place is larger than the diner." Aisling took back her phone and Reece grabbed the box and went into Caradoc's room. "But there aren't going to be enough beds over here."

"There could be," Caradoc's smirk came through even though she couldn't see his face.

"Not going to respond."

"You used to have a sense of humor. Fine. There is another floor in that house. End of the hall, small indentation, then pull the panel at the end. Full glamour on it, there are three more rooms."

"There hasn't been a lot to laugh about as of late. Thanks."

Reece came out of Caradoc's room without the box and went into the kitchen. Then stuck his head, still with a shirtless upper torso, out of the doorway. "Tell him to bring food and coffee."

Aisling started to relay it, but Caradoc spoke first. "I heard him. Demanding fed boy, isn't he? Per Harlie, we're going to leave the box in the safe here. He won't say much about them, or why they are glowing, but he doesn't think they should be together."

Aisling knew there wouldn't be much more from him until he got there, so she ended the call. Then went to the living room, grabbed the t-shirt she'd lent to Reece, and marched into the kitchen and tossed it at him.

"What, my manly self too much for the elf princess?" He said it with a laugh but slipped the shirt on over his head.

"Yes." She turned and walked back to the living room.

He followed. "I was joking, but if we're going to play fair, you should be wearing more than that." He nodded toward her sleepwear, then handed her a cup of tea and sat as far from her as he could and still be in the living room.

She thought about staying dressed as she was; after all, he'd thought nothing of parading around half-naked. But it was probably best for both of them for her to change, not to mention Caradoc and Maeve would give her crap if they found her with him and dressed like this. She did take a long sip of her tea, watching him over the rim before she got up though.

She threw on the least sexy clothes she could find; baggy jeans she wore to paint her apartment and an oversized t-shirt. Reece was reading a text on his phone when she came back.

"Surratt has been moved, and Garran has him under heavy guards hand-picked by him. There's more evidence that he was a primary target. Stella is staying with Garran for a while longer. The police infected by Fachie have all died, and part of your station is cleared to move back in. You, however, are still out of the official line up and Garran says if he sees your face before he brings you back, he'll lock you up. That means that officially, unofficially, you're assigned on loan to Area 42."

Aisling had slid back into her chair and resumed drinking her tea, but almost choked on his last statement. "What? A cop can't just lend me out like that. And wouldn't Area 42 screen me first?"

"You have been screened and vetted. By me and Jones." He had a sober expression on his face as he leaned forward. "Being in Area 42 isn't pretty. It's hard as hell and one of the reasons I sometimes have a drink to go to sleep. But we need you with us. This case is the test. If you pass and we all survive, there will be a formal offer."

"I…have no idea what to say to that. I simply don't. I do wish I had been told all of this was going on, but keeping me in the dark as of late seems to be popular with a number of agencies, including my own." Part of her was interested, very interested. The kinds of things an agent with Area 42 could investigate would make being a homicide detective in the LA police department seem like being a school crossing guard.

"Life of a super-secret spook, sorry. We often are left in the dark by higher ups. No glamour attached to it, I'm afraid."

"Where is Jones? Does he just appear out of thin air when you need him?" She'd seen what Reece could do on other shared cases; he was dangerous. But he wasn't as disturbing as his friend Jones.

"Almost. He was black ops over in Asia for fifteen years during the Huong uprising. He saw too much and quit. Then he got bored three years ago and showed up on Area 42's doorstep—without an invitation." He laughed and shook his head.

"I'm thinking that went over well."

"For five days, they'd send someone to either take him

out or at least subdue him enough to bring in under their control. He'd leave the agents tied up and unconscious but alive on their doorstep the next morning. On the sixth day they gave in and opened the door. I was his partner at first, then I got put on the case at your precinct and he got reassigned." He glanced over to the far wall where her murder board had been shoved. "Old school?"

Aisling got up and rolled it over. "Yup."

"Who put you in the middle?"

"That's what I'd like to find out."

He tapped the board. "No, here. Who wrote this, you?"

"Yes. Too many things appear to be connected to me, and I don't know what or why." She took one of the pens and added Paselin and Fachie.

"No black chopper?"

She pointed to the "Lazing" on the board. "Since they've been identified, I'm not including them. They weren't a separate problem but part of whatever in the hell the Lazing are doing. I'd like to know who killed them though, but it would be to send a thank you, not to add to my murder board."

Reece started to say something, then his phone rang. He glanced at the number. "What?" Whoever it was, it wasn't one of his superiors. "Seriously? Why?" He looked over at Aisling and scowled. "Him too? Why not an entire party? Are you sure the healers are okay with this?" More silence from him, but whoever was on the other end was talking a lot. "We're waiting for him now and we'll be there in a bit." He hung up.

"And? That is a lot of annoyed fed for one little call."

"Speak of the devil, it was Jones. Mott Flowers is conscious but is refusing to speak to anyone except you. And your brother. I don't know how he knows you're siblings, but he does."

"Caradoc will probably be pleased. No clue as to why he

wants us?" She should be concerned that he knew about her and Caradoc, but nothing surprised her anymore. Now, if he knew about the rest of their family, she'd be pissed—and worried.

Reece ran his fingers through his hair. "Not a one. Jones can't use his usual forms of persuasion since Mott isn't a suspect at this time. He can make people talk by other methods as well—but he can't get anything. You planning on going to see him dressed like a house painter?"

Aisling looked at her clothing. "No. I'll be right back." She quickly showered and changed into one of her court suits. They were extremely stodgy and perfect for testifying in court. But the dark blue pants, jacket, and white shirt were all made of a special fabric that allowed a lot of movement. Low dress shoes that were equally misleading completed the outfit. She glanced in the mirror; her hair had been down since they went to Old Town, but if Mott wanted her, he was getting professional her. She pulled her hair into a high ponytail and stalked out into the living room.

"Now that is the Aisling we all know and are annoyed by." Reece smiled as he took in her outfit.

"Is this a new game? The frat boy and the lawyer? Don't let us interrupt," Caradoc said as he swung open the front door. Aisling hadn't heard them come up the walk. Knowing her brother, he'd been waiting outside until he could catch her with Reece, even though he was juggling three bags of groceries. Admittedly, Reece did kind of look like a frat boy right now.

"You might want to change too—I can fill them in on Mott." Aisling waved Reece off and turned to the others when Reece went to Caradoc's room. Maeve was right behind Caradoc, and Harlie was behind her. He was taller than even their father and gaunt almost to the point of appearing ill.

344   MARIE ANDREAS

Aisling hadn't seen him in person since she was a girl, so she wasn't sure how to react. Harlie stepping forward and engulfing her in a massive hug was possibly the last thing she expected though. He actually lifted her up in the air about a foot.

"It is good to see you, little sister. I am glad you are still alive." He put her back on her feet and patted her head. There was a level of oddness in his dark brown eyes, but love too. His rich, almost-black hair extended past his waist in a braid.

"It's good to see you too, Harlie, and I am also glad you are alive. So the Old Ones are gone?"

Harlie nodded and then sat on the recliner. "For now, but I can't see the pattern of their actions, and it is disturbing."

That was something they hadn't had a chance to check into—precogs and the like losing their abilities. Reece hadn't said anything more about it lately, but she was pretty sure his abilities hadn't come back—although he'd insisted they weren't precog. The issue at Old Town for one; no one would walk into a death-trap like that if they knew about it.

Maeve came up and hugged Aisling as well. "Thank you for not exploding. That would have been bad form, you know."

The door to Caradoc's room popped open and a damp Reece, wearing nothing but a towel wrapped around his hips, stood there. "Any clothes I shouldn't borrow? I can get my own after this, but we'll want to get on the road quickly."

Caradoc and Maeve both looked at him, then at Aisling, then back at him. Harlie watched everyone with a small grin.

"Naw, anything in there is fair game." Caradoc's voice said he was trying to process a few things and his response wasn't what it could be.

Reece nodded and shut the door.

"Holy shit, girl," Maeve said and hit Aisling in the arm. "Where did that body come from?"

"A hell of a lot of time at the gym, I'm thinking," Caradoc said. "So why are you geared up and why is he... damp?"

Aisling shook her head at Caradoc—she wasn't going to take the bait. "Reece's buddy called a few minutes ago. Mott Flowers is conscious, but he won't talk to anyone but you and me. It's stressing the feds out."

"I'm still focusing on what just came out that door." Maeve was seriously drooling; she also shot Aisling a knowing grin.

Which Aisling wasn't about to respond to in a room with two of her brothers. "Mott also knows that you and I are siblings. Since he's been unconscious since we started publicly being seen together as such, it implies he has a lot more details on us than we might want."

Caradoc's grin dropped. "That's not good. We should go once your pet fed is dressed, but Harlie and Maeve need to stay here."

Harlie nodded, then took some of the groceries and went into the kitchen.

"Oh, come on, with everything that's going on, you still want me to hide?" Maeve threw herself onto the sofa.

"Not sure about hiding, but walking into a secret federal location when a lot of my bosses want to talk to you wouldn't be the smartest move. Unless you feel like being interrogated for a few weeks." Reece came out of Caradoc's room wearing a black turtleneck and jeans. An extremely fitted black turtleneck. He flashed her a grin and Aisling knew he did it to taunt her. Bastard.

"Damn it, sexy and smart. Fine. I'll stay here," Maeve said. She got off the sofa, grabbed the final grocery bag from Caradoc, and went to join Harlie. Aisling was a bit intimidated by her eccentric oldest brother, but Maeve had him laughing the minute she walked into the kitchen.

Aisling gave Reece a long once over, shook her head, and went out the door. Caradoc was right behind her. "Anything you want to talk about?"

She looked over her shoulder at him and scowled. "No, and why would you think I would share anything with you?" There were plenty of things she would share with her brother—her love life wasn't one.

She stood between the two vehicles while Caradoc and Reece caught up to her.

"We could take his, and maybe this time I can climb halfway out of the window with some exploding box." Reece went to his car. "But, since I don't think you know where we're going, we'll go with mine again."

"Shotgun," Aisling said. "The seat, not an actual gun. Caradoc can be pushy about front seats sometimes."

They got in the car and after a few minutes where Reece tried to figure out how to get through the hedge, they were back out on the street.

"I was unconscious by the time we got here. How was I supposed to know it was an illusion?" Because of that, it also took him a few false turns to get out of the neighborhood, since he wasn't completely sure where he was. Aisling finally got him pointed the right way.

Caradoc gave up taunting Reece and leaned forward between their seats. "So, no idea at all what information Mott has? He and I didn't work in direct contact that often. We'd trade ideas, but often weren't in the same building. I'm not completely sure why he wants me there."

"My guess would be that whatever he's gotten into is tied to that company you had," Aisling said. She gripped the dash as Reece made some sharp turns. He was being far more cautious of followers than normal. She knew enough evasive driving to know when she got tossed around by it. "Which could be a bad thing if you sold a dangerous company to the government."

Caradoc's scowl told her he was already thinking the same thing.

"Hopefully, whatever he tells you two will help resolve that issue as well. That business deal was examined in the smallest detail when you made it—nothing was found." Reece got off the freeway near a business park. "Of course, even our best might not have known what to check for, so who knows." He drove through a few empty blocks of office structures.

Aisling shook her head as one bland building followed another as they passed through. "Your super-secret agency is hiding its super-secret lair in the middle of a business park? Is that allowed in the world of spies?"

"You should know by now that many things aren't what they seem." The smirk on Reece's face was far too familiar. He flicked a switch on the dash, and the wall in front of them swung up, and the parking spots below them started tipping at an angle. The car rolled down and Aisling noticed Reece's hands weren't on the steering wheel. "Don't worry, anyone following us wouldn't be able to get in." A track was pulling the car in without any guidance from Reece.

The path was lit by rows of thin lights, but aside from that it was dark—even for elven eyes. "You guys blocked out the fey spectrum," Caradoc said. One of his companies had spent years trying to isolate fey abilities, including better eyesight, in an attempt to increase them for everyone. The search eventually came to a dead end.

"Yup, we have many fey working here and they all have the same reaction. Taking away the ability to drive, or see, from someone, does help control them."

"Isn't Mott in a hospital?" Aisling had been expecting the one they'd taken her to after her apartment blew up.

"We have a small hospital wing here, and no, it's not where you were taken," Reece said, in answer to her unspoken question. "That place is secure, but this is impenetrable."

They kept going down and Aisling realized they were quite a bit under the building they'd approached. A wide blue and green band scanned the car.

"Light stream scanners? I didn't think those had been proven viable yet?" Caradoc was practically drooling on the window as they passed. Aisling wasn't sure, but she thought she heard him try to open the door to get out.

"We've had them for two years. They were officially proven to be unreliable outside the agency, and we're going to keep it that way. They can detect any substance down to the smallest detail. Too many ways they could be misused. And yeah, you can't get out while we're in the tunnel."

Aisling wasn't the only one who heard her brother try to make a break for it.

They continued past the scanners and into what almost looked like an ordinary underground parking lot, if not for its location, and the two heavily armed guards standing near a bright doorway. They were so suited up in full body armor, it was impossible to tell what they were. Aside from not being small.

Whatever track had pulled them inside also took them to a parking spot. The car doors unlocked as Reece turned off the engine.

"Anything we should know before we go inside?" Aisling wasn't sure about any of this; the level of security was making the hairs on the back of her neck stand up.

Reece turned to face her and Caradoc. "Watch what you say or do. My superiors will be analyzing everything. Don't mention anything, or *anyone*, you don't want them to know about." He gave them both a pointed look about the 'anyone' portion. That was something she'd have to bring up to him later. They all knew his bosses wanted to talk to Maeve, yet at no time did he suggest giving her up.

With a nod, they got out of the car. The guards didn't acknowledge them. But as they passed, Aisling was even more impressed, or terrified, by their gear. The suits were so armored they were like tiny tanks, and the guns they carried were longer than her legs.

The almost blinding light of the doorway was made so in part because of the extreme darkness in the tunnel and parking area. Plus, it was extremely bright. Another way to disorient any would-be attackers.

A whoosh of air passed over them as they entered what looked more like a long, sterile hospital corridor than the entrance to a secret federal agency. Completely bright white and no doors except for one at the far end. Even though there was nothing visible, Aisling knew they were being watched, scanned, and recorded. Most likely if something didn't look right, they could be knocked out or killed at the push of a button.

Reece led, keeping two feet ahead of them. Aisling and Caradoc stayed next to each other. Aisling had thought about grabbing her gun when they left Caradoc's, but had talked herself out of it—now she found herself reaching for it.

Walking behind Reece as they were, Aisling was able to watch him change as they walked down the hall. No magic, that she could tell, was involved, but he appeared taller, his shoulders broader, and his stride longer the further they got down the hall. It was difficult to tell who the real Reece was. She wondered if he even knew.

At the end of the hall, the doorway they'd seen grew more defined, but it didn't open.

"Reece Larkin and requested guests." Even his voice seemed lower than before.

There was a whirling sound, then the door slid open. Yet another hallway. But this one at least had a curve to it, and she could hear people somewhere beyond the bend. She wanted to ask, but this new and serious Reece took some getting used to. If he was this way, there was a reason. Reece was exceptional at playing a part, but now she knew that she could use his behavior to gauge situations.

She stood straighter and lifted her chin. She caught Caradoc doing the same thing. They were their mother's children after all; they could play the game.

They went around the corner and it changed from kind of creepy secret lab to regular office building. One that happened to be underground in a business park and full of super-secret spies and weapons. Aisling noticed that Reece's physical demeanor didn't change though. He might be wearing a borrowed black turtleneck and jeans but he looked extremely professional as he led the way down the hall.

He stopped outside of an open door. Jones stood at parade rest right inside of it. "Anything change?"

Jones gave a small smirk at Reece's clothing. "Nice civilian wear, going for a cover model shoot after this? But yeah, nothing's changed. Second room on the left."

Reece sighed and stalked down the hall. Jones grinned at Aisling. "Not sure what's going on, but he's been fun to poke at lately. If you're part of it, thanks." He nodded to Caradoc as they passed.

The second door to the left had two stoic-looking guards in front of it. Like Jones, they exuded capable killing abilities even though they weren't doing anything.

Mott Flowers lay propped up on a standard hospital bed. He still had tubes attached, but he looked alert and aware.

"You made it." His voice was raspy but that could have been due to the tubes from when he had been in a coma. He turned to Caradoc. "Hey, boss, I got caught."

Aisling watched her brother. He'd said that Mott took off with some inventions. She thought he'd be angry. But he looked sad and a bit embarrassed. Hopefully he'd keep that to himself until they got out of there. There was more going on, but even with all of his secret inventions and gadgets, Aisling doubted Caradoc could win against Area 42.

"I said you were heading into trouble." Caradoc approached the bed and patted Mott's hand. "If it weren't for Aisling, you'd probably be dead now."

Mott's grin showed he was still getting some good drugs pumping through him. "I know, isn't she wonderful?" That dreamy look had better be part of the drugged state he was in. He must have been sober enough to catch it, or he caught the look on her face. "Sorry, thank you. I heard you saved me from thugs." His voice was coming back.

"After someone else had already beaten and dumped you. You don't happen to recall who?" Reece had been standing off to the side.

"I like you, Larkin, and this new look works. But I wasn't kidding when I said I only want to speak to them." Mott pointedly looked around the room. Two nurses and three agents. "In fact, I won't talk until the rest of you leave."

The others all turned to Reece. He waited a moment, then gave a sharp nod. He was the last to clear out and shut the door behind him.

"Thank goddess. I assume you're packing?" Mott sat up straighter in bed and nodded to Caradoc. He sounded far better than he had before the others left. He still didn't look good, but Aisling had seen photos of him before he got beat up—he hadn't looked good then either.

"You're taking a damn big risk, but yes." Caradoc took out one of his little gizmos, tapped it once, and sat it on the edge of Mott's bed. He turned to Aisling. "You'll want to come in closer, with the tech Area 42 has, this will have a limited range and it won't be able to last long."

Aisling scowled and stepped forward until she was a foot

away from Caradoc. They were up to something, and she was sure it wasn't good. "You're scrambling their sensors." She folded her arms. She had no idea what Area 42 would do to someone who brought a de-bugger into their own headquarters.

"I kind of thought it might be a good idea."

When he didn't appear inclined to elaborate further, Aisling turned to Mott. "So, what do you recall? Those punks that were rolling you found you at the edge of the park near the station. Any idea how you got there? And on a personal note, how in the hell did you know I'm related to Caradoc?"

Mott's grin was less drugged perv, but still irritating. "I got jumped. I thought I was doing pretty good at hiding. Larkin and his people were a step or two behind me, but it wasn't until that last place that they almost caught me. No idea who finally caught me though—I know it wasn't the cops or the feds, but that's about it." He held up a hand as a thought hit him. "Actually, I do know I was grabbed by some trolls. They picked me up for someone else who wanted to trade me to some gang." He scowled but it seemed to be at himself. "But something went wrong and the chick they were trading me for escaped…can't recall her name. They weren't worried about me hearing things, so whoever they were trading me to was never letting me free." He sounded cavalier about it. "As for you and Caradoc, I research my employers, and I also remember one day he walked you to primary when your nanny was out."

"You have a freakish memory." Aisling would take his word about Caradoc walking her to school one day; she sure as hell didn't remember it.

"I should warn you," Caradoc said. "He's also wicked smart. And incredibly stupid. I was protecting you, no one could have taken you, or your inventions had you stayed." He glanced at his watch. They didn't have much time.

"I know, but there were things going wrong. That girl died because of me." Now Mott looked ready to cry. Aisling returned to her original premise of a lot of drugs in his system.

"You knew Julilynn Marcos?"

Mott nodded sadly. "I knew of her. She was a runner for the lower gangs, but she sang so sweetly when I'd see her in the park. I knew she was into something bad, so I tried to watch out for her. Someone noticed my attention and killed her."

Aisling shared a look with Caradoc, then turned back to Mott. "Isn't that a pretty big leap? She was a gang runner, and one of her handlers didn't like that some obscure math and invention wiz liked listening to her in the park, so they killed her?"

"No, there was more than that." He looked at his bed. "I invented the chemical that killed her. I made Iron Death."

CHAPTER THIRTY-NINE

"WHAT?!" NEITHER SHOUTED IT BUT Aisling and Caradoc got the same word out at the same exact moment.

"You're fey, how in the hell could you invent that monstrosity? *Why* would you?" Aisling didn't know Mott. She literally hadn't seen him since primary school. But it was horrifying to think someone she once knew, no matter how far back, was capable of such a thing.

"It wasn't supposed to turn out as it did; it wasn't my fault. I thought I was working in a think tank. It was hypothetical, nothing more. They said it would be something to help move into space exploration."

"A way of getting iron into a fey's blood and killing them would help move forward space exploration?" Caradoc's face was a conglomeration of horror and total confusion. "How could you think those two went together? You have got to be the stupidest smart person I've ever met."

"No, it made sense at the time, it really did," Mott said as he rubbed his head. "I don't know why it doesn't now." The more he was thinking about it, the more upset he got.

Aisling shook her head. "What if someone was doping him or using magic? Not enough to make him not be able to think, but enough to make him not be able to remember. He recalls you walking me to school one day, two hundred years ago, but not something like this?"

Caradoc ran his fingers through his hair. "Agreed, something magical or chemical was used. This isn't good. And to be honest, I'm not sure that keeping this from Area 42 is a good idea."

"You promised," Mott said. He was back to being ready to cry.

"I know, damn it." Caradoc turned to Aisling. "Mott doesn't trust officials. Or feds or cops, present company excluded I assume. Actually, not many people in the government. That's why our set-up worked. I was the one who dealt with them. But this might be larger than that fear, Mott."

Aisling sat on the edge of Mott's bed and gave him her best speaking to a scared puppy smile. "Think hard. This wasn't your fault. If they used drugs or magic on you, you weren't aware of what was happening. Try to recall anything about the place where you invented this chemical. Walking in, the people, anything." Part of her was screaming that they needed to get out there and find a way to stop this, but the other part knew they would need to take it slow with Mott.

He pulled on the hair at the sides of his head, leaving him looking more gnome-like and less elf-like. "No. But maybe?" He glanced around frantically and Aisling was afraid he was going to try and run. "Pen? Paper? Pad?" His hands made little grabbing motions.

Caradoc caught on faster than she did and stepped over to a desk and found two pens and a pad of paper. He didn't speak until he was closer to the bed and back within the protection of his electronic toy. "Why?" He handed them to Mott.

"Drugs or magic might not have latched onto all aspects of my memory. Written memory might not be…aha. Still blocked, but something is there." He started scribbling furiously and soon had two pages written.

Aisling was peering at them upside down, but she didn't know if she'd be able to decipher it even if it were right side up. "I hope you can read his writing."

Caradoc leaned over as well. "Not sure. Can you write slower?"

Mott looked slightly deranged as he shook his head, shrugged, and kept writing at the same speed. Two pages turned into fifteen by the time Caradoc's little tech blocking gizmo started smoking.

"Damn it. It's going into destruct mode—we're out of time. Do you have a bathroom?"

Mott kept writing, faster now, but pointed to a door with his non-writing hand.

Caradoc took the smoking gizmo into the bathroom and a flush was heard. Mott stopped writing, folded the pages in half, hid them under the edge of his sheet, and lay back on his bed.

"Thank you for letting me use your restroom, Mott. I'm sorry that you didn't recall much more of what happened. But we'll tell Larkin and the others about the gang who grabbed you and the trade they were trying to pull. It might mean something to the feds." Caradoc came alongside Mott's bed. He turned to Aisling. "Might want to tell your new captain as well. He's got gang connections. Who this gang was and why they were trading Mott for someone else could shed some light."

Aisling caught on; they were going to let that part of the story out, and not the other. How Caradoc figured Area 42 would deal with not hearing or seeing anything for almost ten minutes was beyond her. Honestly, she was surprised that they hadn't come busting in within the first minute.

"I'll make sure to bring it up with Garran. It's warm in here." She was still sitting on the edge of Mott's bed, but couldn't figure a way to get the pages he'd scribbled without being noticed on camera. She took off her jacket and placed it over the sheet where the pages were.

"Thank you for coming to see me. I'll be in contact,

probably through my keepers." Mott might not like feds, or government officials, but the tone in his voice wasn't one of a prisoner. If Aisling had to guess, she'd say he figured out that he was safer here than outside.

"They'll find us if you need us, and if you recall anything else about the gang who took you, let someone know." Caradoc shook Mott's hand then headed for the door.

"Thank you for saving me," Mott said to Aisling with a smile.

"Only fair. Rumor has it that a certain lactic junkie might have been trying to kill me when someone saved my life." She picked up her jacket and the collection of papers from Mott's bed.

He blushed. "I figured you had him, but there was something off about him, something more than just a junkie. Glad I could help."

Aisling thought of the iron shavings that Reece said they'd found in the backseat of the car with the junkie's stuff. "Thank you again. What happened to the gun, by the way?"

"I destroyed it. That invention shouldn't be used by anyone. Knowing what something does in theory is different than seeing it."

"Can we come back in now? Caradoc is in the hall harassing Jones," Reece said as he poked his head in. More nurses, doctors, and agents seemed to be behind him now.

Mott sighed. "More tests, I'm sure. Come in." He nodded to Aisling and she left.

The rest of the incoming group went into Mott's room, but Reece turned and followed Aisling out.

"So? What was so big that he could only tell you two?"

"Nothing huge, he really doesn't like feds." She gave him the information about him being kidnapped, the proposed trade, and a few other innocent bits as if she didn't know he'd already heard them all. "How's your agency doing?

How many did they lose in Old Town?"

"Ten total. They'd had a few agents near there that had been murdered before the explosion. Found their bodies but didn't previously know they'd been in that area. My immediate report agreed that if I had another place to stay for a bit while we work on this case, it might be a good idea. It appears there is a leak, and they're afraid personal information is out as well. Agents are being relocated from their homes." He said the last part as they came upon Jones and Caradoc bonding over items of destruction.

Caradoc nodded to Reece. "My safe house is your safe house. Maybe Jones wants to move in too, if the agency is trying to get everyone working on this case out of their homes, it might not be a bad idea. Did you know that he was the first to use my micro tent and survival kit? Got stuck up on Everest tracking a case and it saved him." One of Caradoc's most useful inventions for general use, fit in a pocket but could expand to fit two people and keep them at survival temperatures for up to a week.

"Your brother saved my life, no joke. Funny that no one knew you two were brother and sister until Mott mentioned it." Jones kept his voice neutral, but there was a prying look in his eyes.

"I don't want to be connected to his wild lifestyle. Hard to be a detective when your brother's photo keeps popping up in the mags." She shuffled the jacket between her arms to keep the folded papers hidden. "Is there a restroom that's not in someone's hospital room?"

Reece nodded and pointed down the main hall. "Second door to the right."

"Thanks."

Once she got in the stall, it took some doing to fold up the papers small enough and fit them in her pockets without leaving a bulge. Luckily, along with being stodgy and comfy, the jacket was a bit too big. She stayed inside the stall until she was sure nothing was noticeable. The restroom itself was most likely under surveillance, but she hoped even Area 42 wouldn't scan inside the stalls. A quick flush, washing of hands, and checking herself in the mirror later and she was back in the hall with the guys.

"What next? You did drive us, so we're kind of stuck for now." Aisling hoped they weren't going to have to stay there. The white on white on white sterility of the place would bug the crap out of her; no wonder Reece was always at her station—he didn't want to be here. She still wasn't sure how she felt about Reece's comment that she was on loan to Area 42, or that they might recruit her.

"Detective Danaan?" A woman's voice came from behind her. She was petite with softly curling gray hair and sharply pointed ears even longer than Garran's. Many of the fey had pointed ears of some sort, not all, but most did. The woman before her was a Gridgen, feys that preferred places deep underground who used to be miners in ancient times. She shook Aisling's hand. "I'm Captain Driyflin. Agents Larkin and Jones have said some good things about you. I'm looking forward to meeting you again once this is over." With a smile that encompassed the group, and nods to her two agents, Captain Driyflin went down the hall to another doorway. The sounds coming through as it opened briefly sounded far more like an active police bull pen than the sterile area out here.

"You aren't all automatons, that's good to know." Aisling gestured toward the doorway the captain had gone into. "I can't say I like what you've done with this part of the place, but it's good to know there's some life here somewhere."

Jones laughed and hit Reece in the shoulder. "I like her, she mostly has good taste. I hate this section as well. And since I'm off my watch-the-guests-as-they-come-in duties, I think I'll take you up on hanging out with you folks for a bit."

"If I'm staying at Caradoc's place, I need to get clothes and supplies from my house." Reece pulled on the edge of the turtleneck. It was obvious that he'd chosen it to bother Aisling, he didn't look comfortable in it. It did look disturbingly good on him though.

"Good idea, I can't have you going through all my clothes," Caradoc said. "I guess we all go to Reece's."

"I can give you two a ride if you don't want the detour." Jones reached back inside the doorway he'd been standing by and grabbed a black satchel. "I was on a quick trip and just got back when they told me about Mott. I'm packed for a few days."

"That would be great. I have some ideas for improvements on my survival line. I'd love to hear your take on them," Caradoc said.

Reece shook his head. "How am I going to get back if you two are with Jones? Yes, I came out of that area, but I have a feeling that without assistance, or guidance, getting back won't be so easy?"

"Nope, it wouldn't." Caradoc started patting himself and Aisling was sure he was looking for another directional gizmo like he gave her the first time she drove to his place. He started swearing.

She held up her hand. "Ya know? I can find our way back. I'll stick with Reece. Seeing the cave he lives in might prove insightful."

Caradoc narrowed his eyes, then laughed. "She doesn't want to listen to us talking shop. That's the real reason she tried to pretend she didn't know me all these years, too much shop talk."

"Got it in one," Aisling said and started walking back the way they came in. "I assume we can get out this way?"

Reece said a few words to Caradoc and Jones, then jogged after her. "You don't like hearing about his inventions? Your brother is brilliant. A pain in the ass in many ways, but brilliant."

"I like it as much as I like talking cars—he likes those, too." She waited when the door they came in didn't open as she approached.

Reece shook his head at that then turned to the wall. "Reece Larkin and guest." The door slid open long enough to let them out, then snapped shut behind them.

"You don't want people getting out unless they're allowed. Nice paranoid secret agency." Although if Mott changed his mind about feeling safer inside than outside she had a feeling that he'd find a way around it to get out. Caradoc admired Mott, and that was rare. It meant Mott was smarter than him, and Caradoc was the smartest person she knew aside from their brother Harlie.

"It has its charms." Reece grinned as she slowed at the next exit. "Larkin and guest." Again, the quick door open and close.

He opened the car door on her side then went to his. Once both doors shut, he turned to her. "So, what did he really say? Good move on whatever Caradoc used, by the way. Pretty much only heard some coughs and sounds of people sitting on the bed until right before we came in. The image was grainy but had enough movement to match the sounds."

"He was writing things for a bit, but that was about all." She buckled her seat belt quickly. She didn't think he'd have a chance to speed until they got out of the parking area, but better to get in the habit with him. "That's what I don't get. You're in Area 42 and a bunch of other agencies. There were nods as you walked in, they respect you, and most likely you're a high-ranking whatever. Yet you're helping us hide Maeve from them, you have a secret hideout they don't know about, and you feel that something went on that Area 42 missed, but didn't bring it up to them? Just who and what are you?"

Reece was silent as the same system that brought the car in, took them back out.

Finally, he sighed. "There are layers within all of the agencies. And a long time ago a small group of super-secret leaders, as you'd call them, decided that they needed to have some agents with a more autonomous nature. I've been an agent for almost twenty years, and when Leticha brought me on-board with her hideout in the diner fifteen years ago, I was granted that autonomous status. To tell you how good Jones is, they granted him that status after a year." He drove through the business park slower than she would have expected. "They trust us to work outside the chain of command, but still get things taken care of. I've seen Maeve—talked to her, but I don't think that right now any agency needs to talk to her. She didn't do what they thought she did, but until I can prove that to them, I'll help keep her hidden."

Aisling watched him for a few moments. Trusting him with Mott's secret was huge, but he'd kept Maeve hidden without even being asked. She needed to talk to Caradoc before she spilled the rest of what Mott said. The notes were going to stay with them until they were figured out.

Her phone chirped as a backlog of calls suddenly came through. "You guys block cells all the way to the street? What do the people renting those business buildings do?"

"There's no one actually in them. Cars come, folks come, but it's all for show. Who is calling you so much? We weren't inside that long."

Aisling clicked on the screen. A dozen calls from Harlie. There was no way that was good. She checked messages—nothing. "I need to call my brother."

Harlie answered before the first ring went through. "We've got a problem."

"I sort of expected that with the number of calls. Why no messages?"

"If they can block the calls, they might get the messages—don't trust them. Hello, Reece."

Reece nodded and got on the freeway.

Aisling put the phone on speaker; if Harlie didn't want Reece to hear this, he wouldn't have said hello to him. "What's the problem?"

"Maeve escaped and I didn't stop her. She got a call on a cell she had sewn inside her jacket. She looked quite disturbed. The man said he knew what she did and where her belongings were. He said she could have it, all of it, and the emphasis was on the word all, but she had to go meet him. He mentioned having information on that iron drug. Then he signed off by saying he's sorry it wasn't her in the forest, but he had you being watched just in case. If she came to him, he would leave you alone."

CHAPTER FORTY

———◆———

REECE SWORE AS HE HEARD.
"You knew all of that, and you didn't try to stop her?" Her oldest brother was eccentric to an extreme, there was no doubt on that score, but he wasn't stupid.

"I thought it might help you solve some issues. I believe your 'man with the hood' in the forest was her caller."

Aisling figured that as well with that not very veiled comment. "But there's no way for us to find her. Getting answers is good, but not if Maeve loses her life and can't tell them to us."

"Littlest sister, have you no faith? I have a spell tracker on her. It can't be picked up by any scanner, magic or technical, unless I allow it."

Aisling screamed and dropped her phone as a shock zapped through it and into her hand. Luckily, Reece was a good driver and the car only wobbled a bit in the lane.

With her other hand she gingerly picked up the phone. "What in the hell, Harlie?! My fingers are numb."

"They'll be better in a bit, but you and your phone are now synched to Maeve's tracker." The phone clicked and a rough map of LA appeared. A small, moving red dot also appeared.

"That dot is her? How in the hell did you do this? Never mind, you can tell me later. Can Caradoc do this too?"

"No, I can only clear one follower at a time, and it takes a while to create something unique to them. I will explain it to him when he gets back here." How he knew she and

Caradoc were traveling separately, Aisling had no idea. But the spell tech Harlie was using was far beyond anything she'd heard of, so knowing who was in the car wouldn't be difficult for him. "I'd better get the house ready for the new guest." Without a goodbye, Harlie cut the call. If that was becoming a thing with her brothers, she was going to have to nip it in the bud.

"We'll need to turn around, the dot's going the opposite direction of us. I don't know how far she'll go and that jackass who almost killed me in the forest isn't playing. I don't know what in the hell she's thinking, going right to him. Nothing could be that valuable in her belongings—she would have taken it with her. Or locked it in a vault."

"There's you," Reece said as he pulled off the freeway in a slightly seedy neighborhood. It was better than a lot of areas of town, but still not a place anyone would want to stay in for long. Aisling figured he was just changing directions, but he parked the car near a dirt lot and faced her. "There was more to that threat of keeping an eye on you. That guy might not have known who you were when he almost killed you before, but he found out. You shouldn't go find her."

She poked him in the chest. "There's no way that I'm not going after her. Besides, you heard Harlie, right now I'm the only one who can track her." Yes, he could possibly un-do whatever he did, then transfer it to someone else, but they might not have time. Not to mention, if anyone got to save Maeve from doing something heroically stupid, it was going to be her.

Reece studied her face for a moment then shook his head and laughed. "Wasn't really going to suggest it. I wanted to state the obvious. I would never expect you to follow logic or self-preservation in a case like this." His smile vanished and his eyes dropped to her mouth. "You need to be careful. I'm not letting you out of my sight. For a number of reasons." He leaned forward and kissed her gently.

She responded in the same vein. This was more intimate than the other times. Lust was one thing; this was something else.

"I was counting on you being with me on this, thank you," she said when he pulled back after their kiss. "Let's get this show on the road." She pulled up her phone. "Looks like we're going back into the woods."

Maeve's light was moving faster than before; either she'd hired a driver or stolen a car—depended on how hard it was to get a driver. To be fair, whenever she did "borrow" a car, she always left money behind to pay for gas and incidentals.

"Same area? That's not a coincidence." Reece got the car back on the freeway but going north this time.

"It does seem to be a common dumping ground. That car I was in wasn't what I arrived in, and it had been torched a few times." She still had to dance around what had happened during and after that night in the safe house. Telling him what she and Caradoc did to him and Jones wasn't going to go over well.

"I ran a check and there are no known hideouts of any major gangs in that area, but there could be a few solo criminals. If they know the forest well they could have escape routes all the way to the deep mountains."

"I wish I knew who in the hell it was," Aisling said. "He tossed me that patch, which I noticed you never gave back to me, and implied he'd killed Tyr. That puts him with the Iron Death group. But he is acting like a solo rather than gang participant, and he knows Maeve from way back or he couldn't have pushed her buttons like that." She tilted her head, trying to recall anything he'd said that might give her a clue. "He was British, but trying to hide it, or another part of the UK and trying to hide that even more. I didn't catch it at the time, but adrenaline can mess up attention. There was a slight catch in some of his words."

"So, probably from her MI6 days. Which Tyr was also a part of. And the gangs who appear to have been bringing the Iron Death in were the Scotties and the Cymru. He's gotta be a freelancer for one of the Celtic gangs."

"That's not as helpful as you'd think though." Aisling sighed. Without a computer to cross reference lone wolves with the Celtics they couldn't narrow it down. Knowing who they were up against could help them on a plan of attack.

"What if we can narrow down the options of who he might be?" Reece flashed one of his smart ass, insufferable grins and tapped a slight indentation in the ceiling of his car. "Processing on. Galaxia, run the following on known lone operatives of the Celtic gangs." He rattled off the information they had.

"Three candidates fit your description. None are currently known to be in the US." The computer voice seemed to come from all around them. "Nix Stealian, Roman Carloff, and Steve Jarlia. All three are known associates of the Celtic gang families."

"You have a computer in your car? Not just a computer, but a link to Interpol databases?" Aisling pointed up at the ceiling. "I know where that voice came from."

"If you know all of my surprises, what will keep you coming back for more?" He gave her a wink. "Yes, I do have a linked connection to some of the databases. It's limited, and I can't use it often. I figured this would be a good time for it though. Galaxia, any connection between them and Maeve Halithi or Tyr Trebol?"

The roof was quiet momentarily, then came back. "Nix Stealian and Roman Carloff. Nix Stealian was picked up by the MI6 officers twelve years ago, for narcotics. And Roman Carloff worked as Agent Trebol's CI on a case with Agent Halithi."

"Doesn't it mean former agents? Neither are still MI6."

"Negative. MI6 rosters show Agent Halithi as temporarily inactive and Agent Trebol as deceased."

Reece shot her a quick glance that said he hadn't known that. He was looking to see if she did.

"What in the hell? How could she still be MI6 and a LA cop? What am I talking about, you're in a dozen agencies. But she lied to me." Aisling couldn't count all the times that Maeve had mentioned being happy she was out of MI6 and all the intrigue. However, Aisling didn't realize she just meant temporarily.

"There are a lot of layers within the agencies. Maeve could be working for them in a reduced capacity. Or she might not be aware she's still in the database."

"Seriously? She told MI6 she quit, and what, they didn't believe her?"

He shrugged. "There's a chance of that. Whatever the reason, let's work on getting her back and bringing down this asshole. Then you two can have your throw down." He pressed a small button on the side of the steering column. "Can you call Caradoc? Tell him he and Jones might want to get weapons and follow us."

"What's that button?"

"Tracking device. Had it installed after my car went missing. It's connected to my phone, my office back at headquarters, the diner, and Jones' phone."

Aisling shook her head but called Caradoc. "Hey, I'm sure Harlie told you about Maeve, we're tracking her now—back into the Glovin forest. Reece sent a signal so you guys can follow us with Jones' phone. Reece says grab a bunch of weapons and join us as soon as you can. I think some gizmos would be a good idea too." She was thinking specifically of the one that wiped out Reece's and Jones' weapons. Right before they got skunked and forgot the entire thing. They could be impressed anew.

"I had a long conversation with Harlie about not letting people out of locked places even if he believes it needs to happen. Or at least asking us first. Jones is not happy and is already armed. What do you have? Your gun is still here."

Aisling looked to Reece. He smiled, nodded, and pointed to the trunk. "I think Reece has me covered. Just follow us when you can. Oh, and not sure if you or Jones have any intel on them, but we think the guy she's meeting, the guy with the hood who tried to kill me, is either Nix Stealian or Roman Carloff. They are independents with ties to the Celtic gangs. Neither are officially reported to be in this country, but we know how that goes."

There was some noise in the background. "Yeah, Jones is inventing new swear words. He knows Nix, says Reece does too. Also goes by the name 'The Murtair'."

"Shit. How come I've never heard the name Nix?" Reece sped up and weaved in and out of traffic like a race car driver in the final lap. A second later he hit a switch on the dash and cop-style bar lights and a siren appeared. He increased his speed.

"The connection was made recently. He almost got caught and got sloppy with his DNA so they were able to tie the names together." Jones had taken over Caradoc's phone. "Officially he is somewhere in Northern Ireland right now."

"The guy is literally calling himself 'The Assassin'? Isn't that a bit pretentious?" Aisling hadn't studied Gaelic languages since middle school, but she'd liked them so much that she recalled quite a bit. 'The Murtair' was 'The Assassin' in Scottish Gaelic.

"It is, and he is good. He's an elf, an old one from what intel we have. Never has played well with others. Twenty-eight years ago, he was the head of the Caldian gang in Anglesey," Jones said.

"They were all killed in a raid." Aisling might not be an international spook, but that had been big news at the time.

"Nope. He killed them all. He took control of the gang quickly and violently and some older members took exception. He killed most of them and Interpol killed the rest in a raid. He's been solo ever since."

"And that's who's after Maeve." It wasn't a question but a statement of terror.

Caradoc came back on the phone. "Jones says he's sure that it's him. No doubt. Harlie is trying to find the connection between everything. He says it's out there somewhere. He'll keep us updated. We're on our way now." Caradoc paused. "Stay safe. This guy might be alone, might not, but he's a serious bastard. Bye, Aisling."

"Bye, Caradoc." The twist in her gut as they said goodbye hit Aisling hard. This was a time that a quick hang-up with no goodbye would have been welcome.

She looked at her phone for a moment before putting it away. "Okay, how screwed are we and is there an army we can call in for support?"

With the lights and sirens on Reece's car, other vehicles were moving out of their way quickly. Reece was still focusing on the freeway though. Finally, he shook his head. "Sorry, trying to pull things together in my head. We're extremely screwed and I don't think having a lot of people would help. If it were only to shut down Nix, I'd say call in the hordes and blow him off the planet, but we do want to get Maeve out alive. A few of us will have a better chance than a large group." He looked bothered more than worried.

"Still no super spook precog?"

"I'm not a precog," he said automatically. "Hells, maybe I am. Or was. And yeah, absolutely nothing about this case, or anything else."

"It's not only you. Harlie *is* a precog, spotty interpretations of what he sees, but he's a strong one. He's been shut down recently as well."

"I shouldn't be one, breeds can't have extra abilities." Reece's voice was quiet, more to himself than her.

"They can't. You also shouldn't have been able to turn into super fishy boy swimmer, either. But you saved Jones and me in the ocean with ease. There's a lot of little shit going on that needs to be figured out, but not until we stop this bigger shit from destroying things."

Reece laughed. "Profound. I knew I liked you for your verbal skills."

A familiar red sports car pulled up alongside Aisling's door. Stella had on old fashioned driving goggles and was waving. "Stella's joining us?"

Reece glanced over and shook his head, but Stella smiled, gave a thumbs up, and dropped back behind them. "Damn it, what is she doing?"

"She doesn't normally hide as a cop and then join dangerous missions?"

"No. She's always been satisfied with hearing the stories after." He looked back in his rearview mirror. "Damn it, does she have someone with her?"

Aisling looked back as well. "Yeah, someone tall but I can't see who."

"Damn it, she brought Grundog. Troll-minotaur buddy of hers. She lives in these forests most of the time. She might have been in the city for supplies."

Trolls were often not the brightest of the fey, and minotaur blood could make them extremely unpredictable. "Well, maybe having someone who lives there might be a good idea? Why else would Stella bring her?" Reece's concern was reasonable. Having someone who knew the forest would be good—two unpredictable civilians out on a joyride wouldn't be.

Aisling jumped as her phone buzzed. "Hey Stella, what are you doing? Reece is getting a little more stressed than he already was."

"Is his left pinky twitching?"

Aisling glanced over. "Yup, it is. We're kind of in the middle of things."

"That, my child, is the understatement of the millennia. Grundog and I are here to help. Tell Reece to take a deep breath, I know what I'm doing. And I know what's happened. We will get her back." She paused. "Oh, bother. I wanted to tell you that we're aware and will follow Reece's command. But can you call your brother and tell him to get Jones off our ass?" She hung up.

Aisling looked past Stella's car and sure enough Jones and Caradoc were right behind her. The three cars probably made a great sight. Reece running with full lights and siren being chased by a sports car and a death mobile. She punched in her brother's number. "Caradoc, why is Jones trying to crawl into Stella's back seat?"

"He's trying to get her to back off Reece. I told him I knew who that car belonged to and he said Stella never leaves the diner."

"She will and she does, right now I think having you two follow this close is a bad idea. Back off."

She heard muttering in the background. Then Jones backed his car off, followed by Stella backing off. They still had three cars speeding off a freeway, but at least now they weren't on top of each other.

"He's not happy and wants to know who is with Stella."

"A troll-minotaur breed friend of hers named Grundog."

Reece might have been pissed about the addition, but Jones found it hysterical and raised his voice so Aisling and Reece could hear him through Caradoc's phone. "Well, this might be a good thing. Stella is far more dangerous than she appears, and we are heading into Grundog's turf.

Sorry about that, Reece." They cut off the phone as all three cars took the off-ramp.

"Why did he say sorry? And your pinky is seriously twitching." She'd never noticed it before but now that she did, she'd know what to look for.

"Stella told you." He shook his hand to make it stop. "There's been some issues with Grundog in the past, but we'll be fine."

Aisling's phone buzzed with a text from Caradoc. She laughed and read it out loud. "Jones says Grundog has the hots for Reece."

"She decided she wanted to be my mate a few years ago. I convinced her otherwise, but trolls have a hard time with 'no'."

Aisling's laughter stopped. "Is this going to be a problem? We can't have a lovesick troll in the middle of our fight."

"She'll be fine. After the fight, if we live, we might have a bit of uncomfortableness."

Aisling watched him, but his pinky had stopped twitching. She looked at the map that was tracking Maeve. She had gone off the main access road and was taking one of the smaller side roads that went deep into the forest. Luckily, not in the exact same area Aisling had been left at. They followed in silence for another mile. Then Maeve's light slowed and stopped. Reece slowed and stopped with the others stopping behind them.

"We're about a mile behind her still, should we move closer?"

Reece watched the empty road, and finally shook his head. "No, I don't think so. I think we need to—" He groaned and clutched his head.

Aisling grabbed him and pulled his hands away to look for an injury. Nothing. "What happened?"

Reece's breath was coming in heavy pants and he wouldn't open his eyes. "Stay here. Walk in. Ambush."

The words came out through clenched teeth. Then his eyes opened and he wiped away tears. "Okay, that sucked. Something hit me hard. Full sensory overload. If all full precogs get hit like that, I never want to be one. We have to leave the cars here and hike in. They—it's not just Nix— are waiting for cars to come through. Not us specifically, but they are expecting someone. I know exactly where they are."

"Where?"

He tapped his head. "It's up here. I can't see any of it now, but I know. Can you tell the others?"

She quickly told Stella, but had a harder time reaching Caradoc. It took him five rings to answer.

"Sorry, I was on the phone with Harlie. He said a cognition flare almost took off his head. Precogs and sensitives across the globe are reporting it online."

"Damn it. Reece got hit, too. He knows where Maeve and Nix are, there are more people out there, and they are prepared for car traffic, but not foot. We hike in."

"We'll come to your car. I have some toys for everyone." He ended the call.

"How's your head feel? It was worldwide and if anyone can find out what caused it, it will be Harlie. Like it or not, you are officially some level of precog." She held up her hand. "And no, aside from our merry band of misfits, I'm not telling anyone."

Reece leaned back and rubbed his temples with his thumbs. "Thanks. That was horrific. I can only imagine what it was like for full precogs. We should check if other talents spiked."

"Right in the middle of a case?"

He leaned forward. "Sorry, talking to myself, making notes for later. Since this event was global, I'm pretty sure it isn't related directly to us. In fact, hopefully Nix has some precog and has his brain leaking out his ears right now as well."

Stella appeared at Aisling's window and a large shadow moved over to Reece's side. Aisling shrugged and got out of the car.

Stella engulfed her immediately. "Oh, my, you two have had lots of adventures." She tilted her head and a small knowing smile appeared. "Of many types. Good on ya's both. Not the almost exploding, but I am glad you could save him. He's like the son I never had."

The car rocked a bit. Reece had started to come out of the car, but Grundog grabbed him in a hug and lifted him a good foot in the air. Reece wasn't small, nor particularly light, as Aisling could attest, but he looked like a rag doll in the troll's arms.

"Grundog, put him down. He's fine." Stella shook her head. "She's been worried since Old Town fell. I left Garran late this morning and she was waiting for me at the diner. She somehow knew something was wrong with Reece. She also might have accidentally snapped a few sneaky snipers in half. Not sure where the bodies went."

Caradoc and Jones joined them but stayed on Stella and Aisling's side of the car.

Stella introduced Caradoc and Aisling to Grundog as if they were sitting around having pie at the diner.

Grundog was interesting. Like most trolls, she had some tusks, but they were smaller than usual. She was also practically willowy for a seven and a half foot tall troll maiden. But one look at the size of her arms and hands reminded everyone what she was—and what she could do. Those snipers found out the hard way.

"You good," Grundog said to Aisling. Then she turned to Caradoc. "You *very* good." Most trolls spoke Pidgeon, including the highly educated ones; it was more cultural than anything else.

"I always said I was better than you, Aisling." Caradoc

beamed up at Grundog as she gave him the very good.

"Yes." Grundog picked Caradoc up similarly to her embracing Reece. Then she set him back on his feet.

"According to the magazines, you are single, right?" Stella asked Caradoc with a serious look on her face. One she couldn't hold long. "Pish, non-troll males are always thinking troll women are after them. She's just friendly."

Caradoc gave an odd smile, then shook it off and reached into a pouch he carried. He handed out familiar looking small, flat gizmos to everyone. "Okay, these are my own invention. No, you can't take them and have someone reverse-engineer them. They will self-destruct before they get out of my control." He looked around the group but focused on Reece and Jones far more than anyone else. "These little babies will short-out the magic component in any weapon. They aren't perfected yet and we each have one because their range isn't wide. Plus, they will only work a few times. But once they short out a weapon, it stays out for at least twelve hours."

"Won't it short out our weapons as well?" Jones was holding the small device like it was a scorpion he found in his shoe. Considering he would have never seen one of these before, except when Caradoc used one against him and Reece, and those memories were wiped, Aisling wondered if somewhere his body recalled the pain from being zapped.

"Only if you aim it toward yourself. It's a cone projection of two and a half feet around. If you aim it at one of us, then yeah, you'll short out our weapons too. And whoever is holding the weapon will get a nasty sting. More than a sting if you take out something bigger than a handgun."

Aisling didn't like the way Reece's forehead was crinkling up—as if searching for a memory. She nodded to Caradoc and his scowl said he was concerned as well. Skunked memories stayed skunked for a long while, so why were they remembering?

Everyone else was armed, so Reece motioned Aisling to the trunk of the car. She hadn't seen weapons in there before but this time he pulled loose a wide flap that was sealed to the trunk top. Lots of weapons. He took two guns near the left, then nodded to the rest. "Help yourself. Extra clips are in the second gym bag."

She pulled two out and some extra clips. She preferred smaller guns than what he used—she'd seen Jones with larger guns as well. It was either a guy thing or a fed thing. Probably both.

Reece looked at her suit. "Are you going to be able to hike and fight in that?"

"Not much of a choice. I don't think whatever they are planning to do to Maeve will wait until I go home to change." The suit was comfortable for most things, she wasn't sure hiking through the woods was one of them.

Caradoc had been having a discussion with Grundog, but he overheard her. "Dang, almost forgot. Hold on." He jogged back to his car and grabbed a bag out of the trunk. "Realized whatever we were doing, a suit probably wasn't appropriate. Brought you your normal cop clothes."

Aisling took the bag. "How do you know what my normal cop clothes are?"

"Anything that doesn't look fun."

She shrugged and stepped to the other side of Reece's car. Stella made the boys turn around while Aisling quickly changed into jeans and a dark shirt. They weren't cop clothes, but they'd be much better than her suit. Of course, now she and Reece looked like they were trying to dress alike. Knowing Caradoc, that wasn't by accident. She secured the guns and the extra clips.

"Thanks, Caradoc." She sat in the car to change shoes into hiking boots—actually high-top running shoes that she pretended were hiking boots.

"So, we walk in off the main trail, that way." She pointed a bit off the road. "But you don't know more than that?" The red dot that was Maeve hadn't moved since the cars stopped, but there was no way to know what was going on. Aisling forced the thought of her being dead out of her mind.

"Probably in this barn compound." Caradoc had another one of his toys. It looked like a phone, but it could project a 3-D image in the space above it. In this case it was a large barn shape and outlying buildings surrounded by trees. The barn looked odd until Aisling expanded the image. It and the other buildings had camouflage screens over them. Although it was a large clearing, none of the buildings would be seen from the air.

"That's it," Reece said and tapped the image. "We should approach from this side, go around the entire compound. And probably move our cars off the road and hide them before we go." The last part was sudden.

"Another precog flash?" Aisling didn't think he looked in pain this time.

He shook his head. "No, sorry. My scrambled brains are catching up. Only one road in or out and my flash indicated they were expecting someone. Three cars sitting out here might be a bit suspicious."

Caradoc took his image device and swiped through a few pages. "We should all be able to get through this fire access road back here. Drop back half a mile, make a left and go a bit until you see the dirt fire road, then keep going once you're on it until you can't see this road."

Reece looked ready to argue, then shook his head, and patted the roof of his car. "Sorry, honey, off-roading for you."

It wasn't long before all three cars were down the fire road. None of the cars fared well during the off-roading but Aisling thought the owners were overreacting.

Caradoc pulled up his electronic map and oriented it to their new location. "That way. There's no way to know who might be out here. This is an interactive map, not real time."

Reece and Jones pulled out guns, and Aisling followed. Caradoc looked at them and shook his head. "I'll trust the law enforcement folks to get first jump, I'll work on navigation."

"And Grundog and I will bring up the rear." Stella checked the ammo in her gun and nodded to Grundog. The troll wasn't carrying weapons, but she probably never needed them.

Jones stepped back to let Reece and Aisling follow after Caradoc. "Might as well keep some of the firepower spread out."

The woods were silent and, surprisingly, so was their group. Aisling didn't think any of them, aside from Grundog, were forest people, but the path was clear enough to keep quiet.

They froze behind a clump of trees and tall shrubs as four slowly moving cars came from the main road. Caradoc nodded for them to keep moving after the vehicles passed the area.

Aisling looked at her phone a few times, but Maeve's dot still hadn't moved. She put it in her back pocket when the first outbuilding came into view. Caradoc shut his map and dropped behind her and Reece. Aisling knew he had gun training and wasn't squeamish, but he was also a strong believer in having experts on hand to do what they were good at. Even better than an LA cop like herself, were two super-secret fed boys.

Jones and Reece moved as if they were in communication with each other—but no words were said. A few rapid hand signals and even Aisling could figure out that there were no guards, and Jones was going to the left. Caradoc followed him.

Aisling looked to Reece, he nodded, then motioned for her, Stella, and Grundog to follow him around the right side, which was his original plan. He hadn't seemed upset about Jones and her brother going the other way. He and Jones must have seen something on the way up that changed their plans.

Aisling had no idea why in the hell anyone, especially someone who had destroyed an entire gang, wouldn't leave guards on his perimeter. Then she looked closer at the ground around the closest outbuilding as they passed. The ground was oddly scuffed up. The second building looked the same. However, while a layer of pine needles covered most of the roof, one section was clear to the edge. As if someone had been up there and was removed. Maybe Nix *had* had people out here—those four cars that came in might not have been his associates at all. The cars were conspicuously absent.

They came around to the side of the barn and they were out of options. Maeve was inside and they needed to get to her one way or another—even if it meant doing something stupid. Aisling looked for Jones or Caradoc but couldn't see them. She was half-way facing Reece when Stella tapped his shoulder and pointed behind the barn, then motioned to her and Grundog. They were going to cover the back. Reece nodded. After they left, he turned to Aisling and smiled. "Let's get her back." He said it softly, but Aisling heard him. "And no need for bunnies this trip."

Aisling had to stifle her laugh. The door they were at was small, not the main entrance to the barn. Two locks, old and rusty but still solid looking, held the door shut. Reece pulled out a small lock-pick kit from his back pocket and got the locks open in moments. They cracked the door open and snuck inside.

CHAPTER FORTY-ONE

THE INSIDE OF THE BARN was dark and, judging by the level of dust as they brushed past things, not used much. Old farm equipment was piled up on the sides, leaving a narrow path to walk through. Aisling was close enough to Reece that she felt him tense as they moved forward. The center of the barn came into view, and any images of an elaborate and fancy seat of crime were dashed. It looked more used than the section she and Reece were hiding in, but was mostly just an empty and abandoned barn.

Reece held up a closed fist which Aisling didn't need since there was no way she'd go out there until they knew what was going on and where all the players were. She and Reece settled across from each other in the shadows of the corridor of junk they'd come through.

There were five heavily armed men and women in the middle of the barn, and ten more in the rafters that she could see, probably a few more that they couldn't see. Like the lack of guards outside, the fact that the way she and Reece came in was unguarded spoke to someone else planning on joining Nix; someone who had taken out a number of his people and was waiting to see what Aisling and the others were going to do. No criminal worth international status would have trusted those old locks. Nix would have had guards outside this door and around the compound.

The center of the barn was set like an arena, with a group

of six people gagged and tied to chairs, facing a single person—not gagged, but tied to a chair. That person had her back to Aisling and Reece, but Aisling knew immediately who it was.

"One more time," Nix said as he strode into view around one of his people. There was no disguising that voice, even if it now had a full Irish accent. He wasn't wearing a hood this time, and his short red hair accented his elven ears and sharp features. Some elves showed their age in their features—Nix was one. Not as old as Harlie, but probably only a few hundred years younger. "Maeve, darling, let's go through this again. What did you have in your possession that the Scottish and Cymru gangs were coming to get? Don't act innocent. They were coming to negotiate for it. Someone was blackmailing them and everything points to you."

Aisling frowned. He had Maeve's possessions and knew that what he was looking for wasn't there, yet he didn't know what exactly he was looking for? She could see Maeve trying to trick gang leaders into something, but blackmail wasn't her style. Then again, she'd been keeping a lot of secrets from Aisling.

"I have no idea, Nix. Why the hell would I have come out here if I was holding out?"

"Because you thought I'd found something. And you knew I was tracking your elf cop buddy and could kill her. Even traitors can still have some loyalties."

"I don't have anything the gangs want. I was kidnapped and brought to the States to be traded for someone else. The deal fell through and they dumped me. I'm still on your side."

Aisling pulled back at that and Reece looked at her questioningly. She shrugged. There was a trust between her and Maeve that went beyond many years of saving each other's asses. It would take more than Maeve bargaining for her life before Aisling would think she'd been betrayed.

One of the tied-up group squirmed. Nix nodded and one of his people took the woman's gag off. It was Losien, looking a lot worse for wear. "She's lying. She's not with you. I worked with her and she's still MI6."

Aisling was glad that little revelation had come to her before now. Better to be shocked and disturbed before facing a barn of armed gang members.

Nix's smile had no warmth and he used his gun to lift up Maeve's chin to force her to look him in the eyes. "Is that true? You never could lie to me. Is it true?"

Maeve took a deep breath and gave a short nod. "Inactive. But yes. It allowed me to get info I couldn't get by being a detective. But Losien is working for the Lazing. Didn't know who she was with until I got back here, but she's with them."

"Thank you for confirming that, but I was already aware. They actually gave her up to me after I let rumors slide that she was the one who blew up their chopper."

"What?" Losien now looked wild and tried pulling on her ties. "I didn't do that! They can't believe I would."

"They quickly told me where you were hiding," Nix said. "Or rather told my representative, they didn't know it was me. I told them you did it to get back at them for what they did after you blew up that detective's apartment. They wanted her alive for some reason, but you probably realized your mistake."

"If they wanted her alive, why the hell did they send a chopper after her? I saw the intel." Losien was cocky for someone who was tied up and surrounded by guns.

"Not sure, and I don't care. With the recent losses, I'll be taking over the Celtic gangs entirely. I planted a bomb in the Lazing chopper when I found it in a hanger simply because I don't need competition from them as I move into my new role—they shouldn't be here." Nix shook his head. "I'm done with this conversation." He nodded to another one of his people, a troll woman, and she lumbered forward and broke the ties on Maeve's wrists and pulled her to her feet. Then he handed Maeve his gun. "You said you were still one of us earlier, that the lawful side was a ruse. Here, prove it. Kill Losien."

"No, you can't. I still have intel on the Lazing!" Losien was pulling away in her chair, but being tied up meant she wasn't going anywhere.

Maeve raised the pistol, and then without turning her body, twisted the gun and shot Nix.

Or would have. It was unloaded.

"Maeve, Maeve, Maeve," Nix said as he ripped the gun out of her hand. "I should kill you where you stand, but I still need that item, whatever it is. Besides, I have fond memories of us." He had gloves on now and carefully loaded the gun. Then he used it to smack her hard enough to send her to the ground. "But, in case you had any idea of escaping and going to the cops, the feds, or any of your friends…" He barely looked but quickly shot all of the tied-up people in the head, starting with Losien. Aisling noticed that one hostage was the Coast Guard captain. "We'll doctor the footage and send it along with the gun with your prints on it to MI6."

Maeve stayed on the ground but wiped the blood from her mouth. "Losien I get, but the others were working for you."

He let out a long sigh and dropped the pistol into a bag and sealed it. "Yes, and they collectively failed. This little exercise keeps you in line until I get what I need, and serves as a warning to everyone else to not fuck shit up."

Aisling had startled when Nix smacked Maeve, then twitched with each shooting. Reece reached over, took her arm, and shook his head. Then he tapped under his left ear and pointed to the other side of the barn…and the back area. She'd have to presume he and Jones had subliminal communicators. Stella must have one too. That would have been a nice thing to let her know about. They couldn't communicate words per se, but preset simple codes would go through. They were timing their attack.

Maeve was getting to her feet when all hell broke loose.

Jones and Caradoc came through the side of the barn a moment before Stella and Grundog. They aimed the gizmos Caradoc made to strike Nix's people without overlapping each other. Reece nodded to her and they did the same.

Nix had pulled out a second pistol when Jones appeared, but threw it, swearing, when the gizmo shorted out his gun and shocked him in the process. His hench-people did the same. Except a couple that were up high in the rafters above them. Aisling tried to reach them but aiming the gizmo directly did nothing, they were outside the reach of it. She still had her gun, so she shot them. Reece fired at the same time. "Mine," they both said as the gunmen tumbled to the barn floor.

Nix made a feint to grab Maeve but instead threw one of his now unarmed men at her. Jones shot him. The rest of Nix's people were too stupid to quit and had to be shot as well. Or they knew that failing Nix wasn't an option.

Aisling spun on Nix, but he'd vanished out the main door. Reece started to run after him, Aisling heard a burst of gunfire followed by the whine of a land mine before it exploded. A moment later, Reece heard the mines as well and skidded to a stop right inside the door. There was no missing the series of small explosions outside.

Maeve and the others came to the door and cautiously went out the way Reece and Aisling had come in. They hadn't seen the four cars that had passed them on the way to the barn, but she'd guess the smoking remains on the outskirts of the clearing were them. There were many bodies. Or parts of them at least. Nix suddenly burst out of the furthest outbuilding on a motorcycle. The bastard fired a crossbow at the barn, then vanished into the woods.

Caradoc started pushing them all away from the barn. "Move! It's going to blow!"

CHAPTER FORTY-TWO

C ARADOC PUSHED TO GET THEM to run faster, but they didn't get very far before the arrow hit the barn roof. The roof caught fire and exploded.

The smell of smoke was overwhelming, and it felt like half of the barn fell on her. Then part of it moved and she realized that Reece had again covered her with his own body and was still lying on her bottom half. "If you got punctured again, I'm not healing you this time." The pieces of the barn were removed, Reece rolled off, and Aisling was helped to her feet by Garran.

It looked like everyone was okay, only bumps and minor cuts for the most part.

"How did you know where we were? And get here so fast?" There was no way Garran and his crew, including five fey who were heavy magic users and were suppressing the fire, could have gotten here this quickly from the station.

"You're welcome for saving your asses. Although whoever was on that bike is long gone." Garran nodded at Stella. "She told me as an FYI before she went after you. So I tracked her phone." He looked around. "Damn, you killed all these Lazing?"

"Nix had explosives around his compound; if the Lazing hadn't triggered them, we probably would be in pieces." Reece walked over to the nearest body. Then went to a few more. "Grunts, from what I can tell, no high-ranking members from any of the tats that I can see, but they have a lot more people in this country than we thought. Or they did."

Garran shook his head. "Nix? As in the Irish thug?"

"As in The Murtair, one and the same," Aisling said. "He was the one on the bike."

"Damn it. We had the bastard right here," Garran said as he stomped around to look at the dying barn fire. "And anything he didn't take with him is gone too. No one knew he was in the States."

Maeve looked the worst of the bunch, with plenty of bruises to show, but Nix was to thank for that. "He had been here for a while, he was bragging before my rescuers arrived." She gave a half smile to Aisling. "I was trying to save you from him, but I misjudged what he was after. Anyway, he's after a scroll I had, one I'm damn sure is still in my house here. He pulled out the rest of my belongings when I went back to London." She turned to Garran. "Can you get people to my house to guard the place until we get there?"

"Actually, I have your scroll. It's secure." Aisling continued to dust what felt like half of the barn out of her hair.

Maeve stepped in close and kept her voice low. "Where did you find it?" There was an odd combination of worry and hope in her light colored eyes.

"In the far back of your upper kitchen cabinet. Nice spells. Whoever you got them from, you got your money's worth." Aisling also kept her voice low. She was pretty sure the rest of their people would find out about it, but Garran's extra cops didn't need to know.

"Thank goddess." Maeve took a deep breath, then winced and rubbed the growing bruise on her jaw. "He always knows exactly where to hit. The bastard."

Aisling still hadn't figured out what exactly the scroll was, but the spells on it alone were enough reason to keep it safe. Right now, it was lurking in the same opal spell chamber that her clan jewelry was.

Garran watched them with a slight scowl. "I think we need to have a talk. What was Nix doing here? I refuse to use that stupid moniker of his."

"He was definitely involved with the Iron Death infiltration, but I don't know that he was the start of it. He was focusing on taking over the Celtic gangs and viewed that as a way to speed things up." Maeve stood still as Caradoc took a med kit and started working on the cuts on her face. "Can I please be cleared to return to duty? I know Reece's people want to find me, and I'll tell them whatever they need to know at this point. I need to stop hiding."

"I can talk to Captain Driyflin," Reece said from where he was still examining the remains of the Lazing. "I think there are more of Nix's dead thugs back behind that building as well. Looks like the Lazing took them out, we came up, and they sat back to see who was going to win. Then Nix triggered the land mines and blew them all to hell. You need to make sure it goes through the channels that it was an Irish mobster who took out those Lazing. They will take revenge."

Garran nodded and sent two of his people over to gather the other dead mobsters. "Oh, I will get it out to every source I can—and also make sure people know who The Murtair really is. The Scots in particular will be glad to have a real name for that bastard. Maeve, as for getting you back on the force? You never left. But I will officially declare you off vacation."

Aisling held up her naked wrist. "Can I get my badge tat back? How many people did Heike remove them from anyway?" She'd been painfully conscious of it being missing these last few days.

He nodded. "Aye, the station isn't fully functional yet, but important parts are working. We can get you re-badged. As for Heike, she only fully removed yours. And she did undercover glams for a number of big cases. Something about you made her bosses anxious. Still not certain, but it looks like she was working for the Lazing."

"I have no idea what caused them to focus on me. I'm just another detective. But I will feel better once it's back."

Garran nodded. "After you get cleaned up, you and Maeve report in, we'll get you back up and working." A large van pulled up and the other cops started loading the bodies. Another pair of cops had mine excavators and were searching the perimeter for any mines that hadn't gone off. Doubtful, judging by the thoroughness of the mess left behind, but this would be an active investigation for a bit—so it was better to be certain. Garran went over to direct them. He might not want to be chief, even temporarily, but he was doing a damn good job.

Grundog and Stella had stayed off to the side, but Grundog was looking more and more agitated. Aisling walked over to them. Grundog kept looking deeper into the woods.

"What's wrong?"

Grundog scowled and shook her head.

"She's concerned that Nix went deeper into the forest. She's afraid he might have a hideout in one of the troll enclaves."

"Damn it. Why can't he go back home?" Maeve came up and held out her hand to Grundog. "I'm Maeve, thank you for rescuing me." Then she nodded and gave a few words in native troll.

Grundog stopped staring toward the mountains and shook Maeve's hand with a massive grin. Then she picked her up and hugged her. "You good, too." She sat Maeve back on her feet then turned toward Stella. "Things not good. I need go."

Stella nodded. "I'll go with you, my car will be fine where it is, it can protect itself. Garran, thanks for coming." Grundog gave a distracted nod to everyone, but had already started into the forest.

Aisling stopped Stella as she went to follow. "If you two need anything, call me."

Stella smiled. "Thank you. I've got a vacation sign on the diner, but Reece knows the back way in. Plenty of food stocked up for the lot of you." Her smile faded as she watched Grundog head out. "I have a feeling this is only the start—keep each other alive for me." She quickly caught up to Grundog and the two were soon out of sight.

"I can get our rescued detective back to Caradoc's place. If you don't mind swinging by my house, I'd still like to pick up some things. None of Nix's failed flunkies that he slaughtered were connected to the agency in any way—so whatever leak exists in the agency is still there." Reece had been briefly on his phone before he walked over. Most likely, once he dropped them off, he'd be having a long conversation with his bosses.

"That would be great if you could take them back, I want to run by the office and show some prototypes to Jones. Things not related to survival equipment." Caradoc had been studying the dead Lazing and was making notes. Considering that it looked like standard land mines had killed them, Aisling wasn't sure what he saw that others didn't.

They made their way back to their cars. Reece, Aisling, and Maeve were all lost in their own thoughts, Jones and Caradoc were discussing something very animatedly. Most likely world domination.

Maeve finally broke the silence. "So, we're all going to live together like one happy family? Jones too? How long?"

Aisling looked to Reece, but he was still working something out in his head. "At least for now. I don't have a home at the moment, who knows how much insurance will cover for a townhome blown up by a pissed-off and now dead chief of narcotics. You have a home, no belongings until we figure out where Nix hid them, but the gangs are probably looking for you, so you should stay at Caradoc's until things die down. Reece's bosses are trying to get a free safe house for their super spooks, so he and Jones will probably stay."

That got Reece's attention. "What? Oh, Caradoc's place. We won't be there long, but there has been increased activity in the neighborhoods where some of the Area 42 people live. Places no one should know about. The captain isn't panicking, but she does want us to change up our living quarters. Jones and I can move to the diner if you prefer." He was looking at Maeve, but Aisling knew the question was aimed at her.

Maeve raised her hands with a grin. "I've no problem with a cozy house. Caradoc welcomes all." She shot a look over to Aisling.

"I don't care either. But having tasted my brother's cooking, we might want to sneak into the diner from time to time. Stella has it locked up but left food for us." Aisling narrowed her eyes and shook her head at Maeve. Seriously? Like anything was going to happen between her and Reece with all this shit going on and four other people in the house?

Maeve just grinned.

Caradoc looked over when he heard his name, then shrugged and continued his conversation with Jones. He was a genius at many things, and he knew it. Cooking wasn't one, and he knew that too. Aisling couldn't throw too many stones at him though; she didn't cook much either.

Reece unlocked his car and held up the gizmo Caradoc had given him. "I'm thinking you'd like these back?"

"They're dead or nearly dead at this point anyway, but I can always recycle them," Caradoc said. "And thank you for being a good super spook and not trying to take them back to your leaders."

Reece shrugged and gave a nod in Maeve's direction. "They don't need to know about everything, at least not immediately. We'll see you back at the house."

Aisling got in the car. She knew that Reece and Jones were free agents within Area 42, but Caradoc hadn't been in the car for that conversation. Jones could fill him in on it if he wanted.

Maeve got in the back seat. "That was stupid, especially since one of the reasons I went to him was to save you. But thank you for bringing the rescue posse. Nix has gotten worse."

Reece turned the car around and started heading toward the main road and the freeway. "You knew him well?" His tone was that structured level that meant he had a hell of a lot more to ask.

Aisling wondered if they taught them that inflection at super spook school. She'd heard Jones do it a few times as well. It was similar to the tone a cop used when interviewing a cagey witness.

"Normally I wouldn't tell you, but you did just save my arse, kept me secret from your agency, and Aisling seems to like you—so I guess you can be trusted. I joined Nix's gang, his original one, fifteen years ago, before he started destroying the competition if they wouldn't play his way. I went undercover for MI6 and almost didn't make it out. He was a right bastard back then, but now he's an unbalanced right bastard. Power hungry and stability issues aren't a good combination."

"Did you find out anything about Iron Death?" Aisling asked.

"Not much. Mostly when I was brought in it was him prancing around showing me the people who had all been working for him but failed. He is behind it though, at least the testing and distribution part. The first three deaths we found were him testing it and working through some anger issues. The girl pissed him off. Tyr betrayed him, and Konel, the one who went after you in the hospital, was his highest lieutenant. Nix feared he was coming for his job, so he set him up in the hospital. It sounds like there was a drug called Iron Death, which didn't have iron in it, nor cause death. Surfaced in the underground a few years ago in Bulgaria. Made its way to the good ol' UK where it got modified."

"I still don't get the point," Aisling said. "A drug that's fatal to fey, and contagious. Unless that's the point." That was a sobering thought. The fey had been in charge since the humans almost all died in the plague. But humans and fey had been on almost equal grounds since the 1820s. What would happen to the human population if all the elves died? A small percentage of humans could still breed without assistance but, after almost a thousand years, they hadn't been able to improve on that. Without elven healers, the human race wouldn't survive long either.

"Maybe they are still fine-tuning it. America is a much larger testing ground than the UK." The tone in Maeve's voice said she was thinking the same thing as Aisling.

"But Nix is fey. He's evil as hell, but do you think he'd be helping propagate a drug that could kill him?" Reece had been in his own thoughts, but was still listening.

Aisling looked out the window as they went through the forest. "Maybe he's immune to it. We need to get Caradoc, Mott, and anyone else of their scientific mojo ability together to see if there is a cure and if there is an immunity among fey. He's shown no loyalty to anyone, and if he were to destroy most of the fey, who would be able to stand against him?"

All three went silent at that, most likely thinking of more than a few grim scenarios. Reece had them out of the woods and on the freeway in minutes. Jones and Caradoc were behind them but took the third exit off. Who knew which company or secret lab Caradoc was leading Jones to. Aisling had to admit it had been nice having Caradoc around the last few days. Not the circumstances behind it, particularly with this new revelation, but it was good to have him in her life again. Keeping him out had been her choice—tied to keeping her family connection out of her police life.

She was finding that, with everything that had been going on, she wasn't worried about it anymore. She'd still fight tooth and nail to deny she was her mother's daughter. But it was time to let Caradoc and Harlie back into her life.

The neighborhood that Reece drove to was disturbing in its normalcy. If each house had a picket fence Aisling wouldn't have been surprised. She was more surprised when he pulled into the driveway of a nice, neat, two-car garage, hit the garage door opener, and drove in.

"Is this a secret entrance?" She didn't get it. There was no other car inside, but enough car junk to look like it belonged to Reece.

"Nope." He closed the garage door and turned off an alarm on the house.

Maeve looked to Aisling, but she just shrugged as they followed him inside. Secret super fed lived in the middle of suburbia?

"It's not much, but it's home." He dropped his keys in a dish near the door. "Have a seat. I need to go get some essentials." He waved to a small and neat living room then went down the hall.

"Are you as weirded out by this as I am? Please tell me you are?" Maeve sat on a normal-looking sofa.

"Oh, I'm weirded. This doesn't look like any secret lair I've ever heard of or seen." Aisling wasn't sure how this worked with what she thought she knew of Reece. She'd known him for a while but their closeness this past week, both forced and not, had made her think she was getting to know the real Reece. Until this.

He came out of the back room slowly, with three good-sized bags and a serious look on his face. "Keep your voices low, and when I say go, I need the two of you to make your way to the car—quickly, but not running. Grab the keys and get the hell out of here."

"What?" Aisling got to her feet but kept her voice low. Maeve rose next to her.

"Whoever is hunting Area 42 agents found my house. I triggered a reaction of some sort in my room, the place looks bugged as well, but cheap pieces only. I can't let go of these bags and I can't move fast; the explosion will go off before I can get to the door. You two can make it before the entire place explodes." He stared at Aisling until she met his eyes. "Please."

Damn those eyes were definitely fey-powered. Aisling found herself taking three steps toward the kitchen without thinking. She stopped moving. "Maeve, can you go in front? Get the keys and start the car." She kept her voice low but smiled as if nothing was wrong. If they had bugs they probably had cameras. Maeve nodded and walked to the door and picked up the keys.

"Now." Reece didn't shout but put enough emphasis on the word to send a shiver down Aisling's spine.

She took another step away from him as if going for the garage, then spun around at full elven speed, grabbed him, luggage and all, and sped toward the door into the garage. Maeve figured it out even though Aisling knew at the speed she was going no one but another fey could have seen her. Maeve had the garage door up and the car running with the back door open. Aisling ignored Reece's complaints and threw him, the luggage, and herself in the back of the car then pulled the door closed.

"Go!" Aisling yelled as explosions started coming from the house; small, more like gunshots, but she knew they'd get louder.

Maeve had the car in reverse and down the street before Reece managed to dig himself out from the luggage.

"What in the hell? You both could have been killed."

"How many times is this going to happen? Why do you think it's okay for you to take risks but no one else? Maybe you have a white knight syndrome, but get over it." Aisling didn't know if she wanted to kiss him or punch him. She dropped her voice. "And don't think we're not talking about that trick with your eyes. Never do that to me again."

He pulled back at her last comment, but there wasn't enough room to get far from her, they were still in a pile with his luggage, but his confusion seemed real.

They'd reached the end of the street when a fire-ball went up. Exactly where Reece's house had been.

"Maybe hiding in suburbia wasn't the best idea." Maeve tore through three side streets, then pulled into an alley and stopped the car. "Keep down, we might have had a tail." She slid low in her seat and Reece folded over Aisling.

Aisling had a good place to hear his heart—it was still racing. She'd seen him in worse situations, many in the past few days. But this freaked him out. Not that she could blame him; her heart had probably been racing when her townhome got blown up.

Maeve finally sat up. "Okay, it's clear, you two stop snogging. We're getting the hell out of here." She whipped the car out of the alley and down the street. In minutes they were on the freeway.

"What the hell was that?" Maeve glared from the rear view mirror. "And I agree with Aisling, you don't get to decide to throw your life away unless we say so."

"I couldn't have made it, look." He lifted up one foot. It was chained to the other in a gooey pile of weird dark vines. "It's organic, so my home sensors wouldn't have picked it up. Whoever planted it made it so I couldn't get out. But you two could since they didn't know I'd have guests."

Maeve laughed. "They weren't counting on a stubborn-as-hell elf princess."

"I am not a princess. And yeah, I don't let people die on my watch if I have any say about it. That goes for both of you. Stop trying to protect me and putting yourselves in danger. I'm faster and stronger than either of you. And have the heritage of a real bitch to draw on. So knock it off." She was also far more bendable than Reece and maneuvered her way around so they weren't piled on each other.

Neither Reece nor Maeve tried to defend their actions. Good thing too. She was so angry right now she might really channel her mother if they had.

Finally, Maeve broke the silence. "How about why your secret lair was in suburbia? If all of your agents live like that it's no wonder you're being found out."

"You two were with me, so you didn't feel the glam worked on it. As soon as we got within three blocks, my car, myself, and anyone with me is under a glamour." He looked to Aisling. "Yes, it's unbreakable. Anyway, people see an aging family man and his wife and kids. A really powerful fey, maybe someone on the level of your brother Harlie, could break it—but it would take a long time. Mine makes the third house they've found and destroyed. And no, not all of them are in the suburbs."

"One of your agents is a mole," Aisling said. He'd mentioned that there was a leak, but obviously didn't think it was an actual fellow agent.

"In Area 42? There can't be. The level of screening for a

full agent is intense, and long. Years."

"What about someone like Jones? You said yourself they took him in quickly. I'm not saying it's him, but what if there are others who also went through expedited routes?" She turned to him, he was trying to free his feet, not easy in the back of a car. "How else are they finding you? You guys are so secret most people don't believe you exist. The reason you all hide behind other agencies is because they are helping you to not appear to exist."

"I have no answer," Reece said. He finally surrendered to the goo locking his legs together and stopped pulling on it. "But if someone has managed to get an agent mole in Area 42 we are all screwed."

Silence fell again. Within a few minutes, Maeve had run through the hedge and they were back at Caradoc's place.

"Ya know, you don't have to bust through it," Aisling said as she helped Reece out of the car and toward the door. "It's an illusion spell."

"I know, but it felt good." Maeve pocketed the keys and beat them to the house.

Harlie opened the door as they walked up. "Good to see you're all alive." He looked at Reece's feet. "A vine leash? I haven't seen one of those in decades. Centuries actually. Who is still using those?"

Aisling got Reece to the sofa and he flopped down. "You've seen this? It's fey?"

"Oh yes, very fey, and extremely old school. As shown by you not recognizing it. I doubt Caradoc would either unless he's done research." He was far more animated than he'd been before; like Caradoc, give him something obscure to focus on and he was in for it. He dropped to Reece's feet. "Do you mind?"

"Could you get it off? I agree finding out who and how someone got this on me is important, but I'd like my legs back. It seems to be tightening."

When he'd first come out of his room at his house, he could move, but only small steps. His legs were almost completely stuck together at this point and he didn't look comfortable.

Harlie had been staring at the goopy black vines and shook himself out of it. "What? Oh, yes, sorry. It will be easier to look at it once it's off of you." He grabbed it and muttered some spells words. The vines glowed briefly, then went back to black.

"Tighter now." The pain was clear on Reece's face as both of his legs appeared to be trying to occupy the same space.

"Whoever was behind this was far stronger than I thought—I am sorry. They are not better than me though." Harlie grabbed the vines again, and this time the spell words were heavier and dark. They vanished in the air before Aisling could process them, but they sent a shiver through her.

The vines glowed again, then tried to go back; another word from Harlie, and the vines turned white and fell off of Reece's legs.

"Thank gods!" Reece started rubbing his legs. "Thank you, Harlie. Those were going to kill me."

Harlie had gathered the limp vines and was looking at them like a child with his new favorite toy. He started walking toward Caradoc's room, he had equipment there, but stopped. "Oh yes, they would have. A painful way to go, I assure you. Good thing you didn't die." With a nod he went into the room and shut the door.

"Great bedside manner he has, but as long as he got that thing off me, I don't care." Reece rubbed his legs fiercely. His pant leg came up and angry welts went from his ankle up his calf.

"Those don't look good, might need to go to one of your spook doctors." Maeve had gone into the kitchen when they first got there and now came back with three beers. And scissors, which she set on the table with a shrug. "I was going to help cut if off if need be." She handed Reece and Aisling each a beer.

Aisling went to her murder board and added "Nix" and "Reece's House" to the diagram. She also drew a slash through the Coast Guard captain and Losien. "Damn it, we get rid of some players and get an entirely bunch."

"Nix will go to ground," Maeve said as she came over to the board. "He might have another base of some kind deeper in the mountains. I think Grundog's fear was justified. If he sticks to his MO, he'll be alone, not rallying more troops—at least for the moment. He goes through people like toilet paper, but he always attracts more."

"Whoever is going after Area 42 agents' homes is a major concern too." Reece stayed on the sofa. "And if you folks will excuse me, I need to call that in. Caradoc said something about extra rooms?"

"Yup, I checked them out when I was waiting here with Harlie. I can take you up." She turned to Aisling. "Did you know your brother can sit there for hours and not respond to a single thing another person says?" She shook her head and led Reece to the end of the hall.

Aisling trailed behind to see how it opened.

Maeve placed her hand on an odd indentation in the side wall, a stairway appeared out of seemingly thin air then dropped down. "The rooms are decent, and all have en suites. Weird affectation your brother had when he had this built, but I for one am all for it."

"Thanks." Reece took his bags and went up the stairs.

When Maeve walked away, the stairs stayed.

Aisling followed her back to the living room. "I have an odd feeling he was planning this as a bunker of some sort. It looks like a house, but secret rooms? You never know with him."

They went back to the board. "So, nothing else about Nix while he had you? Just checking in case there is still some mistrust on your end of our fed." Aisling smiled. She also was now wondering how much Maeve was telling her.

"Nothing. He was looking for the scroll, but had no idea what he was looking for, only that he didn't find it. Which makes me wonder how in the hell did he know he hadn't found it?"

"I was thinking the same. He was looking for a specific magic signature I'd think, something that's on the scroll. What is that thing anyway?"

"Be easier to explain if I get it. Although, wherever you're keeping it might need to be its home for a bit. He'd said that he sensed it when they emptied my place, but hadn't sensed it for a few days—most likely when you secured it."

"Yeah. Clan jewelry needs to be in a special protected charging box. The boxes are completely spell-proof as well." Aisling went into her room and pulled out the box from her dresser and brought it to the living room. "Here ya go." She got a shock as she handed the scroll over to Maeve. "That thing bites."

Maeve laughed. "It does. Has a lot of old spells piled on top of each other. And it's really old, which makes it cocky." She gave Aisling a sideways look.

"I'm not cocky, I'm good. And if you're referring to my earlier comments in the car, I was stating facts. You're good, but you're human. Reece is appearing to be some sort of fey breed with powers, but he's still a breed."

"Yeah, how can that happen?"

"No idea. And we can't mention it to anyone. My mother's council would probably take him for study and he'd never see the light of day again. A breed showing fey powers is one of the signs of the apocalypse for them." She nodded to the scroll. "So? What is it?"

"It's the secret for turning iron into gold." She shrugged.

"Or something like that. I got it from a dying MI6 agent about twenty years ago. She said to guard it with my life, and I have. But I honestly don't know what it is. I can't translate it." She handed it back to Aisling. "It makes me nervous having it out. Maybe your two brainiac brothers can figure it out later. Right now, we need it to stay hidden."

The shock was less this time. Aisling put the scroll back into the spelled box. More like it was saying hello. "Okay, that was freaky." After the box was locked and put back in its hiding space, she turned to Maeve, "I swear it was trying to talk to me."

"How did you know where to find it in my house?" They walked to the living room.

"I cast a spell for anything that had your imprint." Aisling dropped her voice. Reece was still upstairs, but that could change. "I didn't tell Reece or Jones."

"Probably a good idea." Maeve settled in with a beer. "I need a vacation."

Aisling sat as well. "You had one. You blew it going undercover and trying to get killed."

"Yeah, I was never a quick study."

Reece came pounding down the stairs. He was dressed in his normal loose work clothes and duster which Aisling was grateful for. Hard enough to deal with the crap that was flying around them, she didn't need him distracting her.

"I've got to leave. There's something going on across town, but I need to talk to my boss in person first. Don't get comfortable, things are getting worse." He ran for the door, stopped, and held out his hand to Maeve. "My keys?"

Maeve grinned and tossed them to him. "Thought you'd figure it out."

He nodded to them and took off.

"You could have held them until he told us more. I've

started to realize he only gets in a rushed mode when things are almost catastrophic."

"You think he'd talk?" Maeve laughed. "Although, speaking of him...so?"

Aisling thought about brushing it off, but it wasn't worth the effort. "Yeah, him. Don't ask me to explain it, but he's not the asshole he's been playing the past year."

"I noticed," Maeve said. "I think it's good you've found someone. I question the wisdom of getting involved with a super-secret spook, because I know what that life is like. But lust wants what lust wants. And he's hiding a seriously nice bod under that duster."

"It's not just lust. I'm not sure what it is. Seeing the real him is...interesting."

"It is interesting. You took the words from my mouth." Harlie came out from Caradoc's room waving a clear box that contained the vine strands. "They're safe now. It's a spell blocking box and they can't sense them."

Aisling looked at her beer. Nope, hadn't changed into nectar. Harlie's statement wasn't confusing because she was drunk—he was just being Harlie.

He sat his box on the dining room table.

"Do you want to clarify that for those of us who aren't in your head?" Maeve asked before Aisling could.

"Ah. Sorry. The vines are neutralized. And they are protected against being sensed by the powers behind them." He scowled at the vines. "Which is good."

"Wait, you know who created them and tried to kill Reece?" Aisling wished he would start with the important parts.

"Yes. It's not good. No one else can know." He stared at them until they nodded. "The High Council. The signatures vanished once they realized I'd traced them, although the council can't tell that I was the one who tracked them.

Tricky spell to do that. I sensed our mother in the mess before it vanished."

CHAPTER FORTY-THREE

"THE HIGH COUNCIL IS TRYING to destroy Area 42 agents?" Aisling wasn't sure what she'd been expecting, but that was totally not it. "Why in the hell would they do that? Why would *she* do that?"

Harlie shrugged. "I have no idea, but I know what I felt. The genetic link between us was probably why I could identify her before someone on their end realized they were being tracked and the connection vanished."

"You two have a seriously messed-up family." Maeve finished her beer and went for another.

"You don't know the half of it," Harlie spoke softly, more to himself than to them. And there was an old sorrow on his face. "So, we know the council is doing something to interfere with Area 42. Probably other investigative branches of law enforcement, as well. Something they are foresworn from doing." His eyes lost focus as he drifted somewhere else, then he shook himself out of it. "Earlier, I was searching Caradoc's recorded data on the dead flyer case, the same magic signature that was behind those vines was also behind the magic signature next to the pixie fey."

"What? Someone on the council did that? Our *mother* might have done that? That's beyond sick. That's...wait how did Caradoc get that information?"

Harlie shrugged. "Most likely by hacking the police files. He is very good at that sort of thing."

Thinking about why the council put a spelled message next to Julilynn Marcos would have to be added to the pile of questions invading Aisling's life. But it wasn't something she could sort out now. "Crap. What are we going to do?"

"Right now, we keep this information hidden. We need to know what they're doing. Don't trust anyone in the family besides us and Caradoc, we have to assume the rest of our siblings are involved." He got to his feet. "I'm going to be working in Caradoc's room, there's some food I brought from the diner in the kitchen. Good night." With a small nod he left.

Maeve got to her feet first. "I'm going to try and do some research myself after dinner. But let's eat. You can dish about Reece."

There wasn't much dishing involved as they were caught up in their own thoughts, and Aisling wasn't sure she felt like describing her feelings toward Reece. She wasn't sure she could. When Maeve went off to do her research, she decided to see what she could find out about the people Nix had killed.

———◆———

The next morning, Aisling heard voices in the front room a good twenty minutes before she decided to move, let alone open her eyes. Yesterday had been a long, hellish day and she was feeling it. She slipped a robe on over her night clothes, checked the mirror to make sure she didn't look too out of it, and went out. There was no saying who might be there.

Harlie and Maeve were playing a card game, no one else was around.

"Morning, where is everyone?" Normally she'd not worry about three adult males who could easily take care of themselves. But there had been too many weird and dangerous things going on. Had none of them come back last night?

"Judging by the kitchen, all three were here at some

point," Harlie said. "I saw Reece leave about an hour ago. Caradoc and Jones had were gone when I got up. Caradoc's mess in the kitchen is distinctive."

"Did they leave a note?" Aisling got some tea then went back into the dining room.

"No," Maeve said as she picked up and put down a pair of cards. "Troxie. I win."

"Since when do you play Troxie?" It was an elven language learning game that Aisling had played as a kid.

"Since this morning." Maeve took the cards, shuffled them, and handed them back to Harlie. "Oh, I snuck into your room and took your spell box while you were asleep. Harlie opened it and we were trying to figure out the scroll. I snuck back in to put it back when we couldn't figure it out."

Aisling wasn't happy Maeve had gone into her room, but she'd been exhausted and that was better than waking her up.

Harlie nodded. "I think there might be a reason the scroll came into Maeve's possession. I can't translate it, and I know the ancient elvish language. She might be able to translate it, as it responds to her, but she doesn't know the language." He shrugged. "This game will work. It will take time, but it will work."

The chirping of Aisling's phone from her bedroom broke into the card shuffling. She went in and grabbed it, then looked at the caller ID twice before answering. "Yes?"

"Aisling, thank gods I reached you. Reece is going into a trap."

"Surratt? What are you talking about?" She came back into the dining room and nodded to Harlie and Maeve. It sounded a bit like him, but this was his old cell number.

"He's going into a trap and I can't get to him. You need to go to Area 42 headquarters and get him."

Aisling paused. "How's your trip to Sweden?" Surratt

hated Sweden.

"It's fine. I'll be back soon. You have to go—"

Aisling cut the line and set Caradoc's shock system on the number. Whoever it was would get a nasty surprise if they called back.

"I take it from your face that wasn't Surratt? Where do we need to go?" Maeve went into her room and came back with a few guns. That she was still in her pajamas was a little disturbing—weapons before clothing.

"No, it wasn't. They were using an old phone number of his, but he and Garran are using burners. Changing them almost every time they use them. He wants me to go to Area 42 and save Reece."

"Damn sloppy, don't you think? Someone is watching you and would follow if you took the bait." Maeve added a garrote and a few other toys to her collection, then finally noticed her pajamas and darted back into her room.

"Very," Aisling said as she punched up Reece's phone. Or tried to. It just bounced back with his voice mail. A quick call to Caradoc's did the same thing. She didn't have Jones' number or she would have tried him too. "Voice mails on both Reece and Caradoc—what are the odds of that?"

"Unlikely as hell," Maeve called out. "Trap or not, we have to get a warning to the feds—someone is definitely after Area 42."

Harlie started to get a faraway look in his eyes—he was probably trying to calculate the odds.

"It's okay, Harlie. It wasn't a real question. We need to let Reece and his people know that there is a serious risk to Area 42. Without leading anyone right to it." The council was forbidden to get involved in law enforcement because of their combined magical strengths and powers. If they were ignoring that to go after Area 42, there was a *very* serious threat.

"Agreed. There are too many layers of spells on this place

for them to see where you are," Harlie said. "But if they know the general area you're in, they can find you when you come out. I might be able to mask it somewhat, but you'd still have to be quick and extremely careful."

"There were tails on us when we fled Reece's house yesterday. But I lost them," Maeve yelled from her room.

"And they would have been tracking Reece's car, so somehow he lost them already if they are calling me." Aisling went to change into jeans and a t-shirt, checked the ammo in her borrowed guns from Reece, then added her cop firearm. "Caradoc's car is still here, right?"

Harlie nodded. "He's still riding with Jones. The extra set of keys are hidden under the second potted plant in the window." He shook his head, at whatever thoughts he was working through. "Someone else could track you though, even if I mask the car. Without a tracking device. Or rather, through a genetic spell." His look became pointed at that.

Aisling almost dropped the potted plant she was holding as the conversation of the night before came back. "Our mother?" She sort of hated the woman a lot of the time, and had most of her life, but thinking she was greedy and power hungry was far different than thinking she was trying to use her to kill people. "She could have tracked us yesterday, when Caradoc and I went there."

"Not if she didn't think of it. Or realize where you'd gone. Or with whom. If she saw you with Reece at some point she knows she can use you now. Or maybe someone else on the Council is convincing her to use your connection with Reece."

"So, I stay here, hidden? While she and her cronies try to infiltrate Area 42?"

"No. I can spell you genetically well enough to hide you from her, you'll physically look the same but different on a magical level. I'm going to have to hide Caradoc and myself too." He shook his head almost as if he was carrying on his own conversation—with himself. "Again, I remind you to stay clear of the rest of the family. Too bad about father though, he's always been decent." He'd already mentally written off most of their family; but he didn't seem upset about it as he set the spell on Aisling.

Maeve had finished changing and arming herself and shrugged. "I don't want to know about your family dynamics. But if that wasn't Surratt, and Reece and the secret spook agents might be in real trouble, shouldn't we get going?" She held out her hand for the car keys.

"Why do you get to drive?" Aisling kept them behind her back. "It's my brother's car we're taking."

"I could drive." Harlie perked up at that.

"No!" Maeve and Aisling yelled at the same time.

"Sorry, Harlie, you told me you've been living in a cave in Nepal for a few hundred years—not a lot of driving experience." Maeve turned to Aisling. "And you keep having accidents. I'm not saying they are all your fault, but it might be better if I drive."

Aisling handed over the keys. "You'd better stay here, Harlie. We're not sure what's going on, and while you're insanely powerful, you're not a fighter."

He shrugged. "Aye, you might be right on that. I can help from here, though. I'm making improvements to Caradoc's lab. Speaking of which…" He nodded to her phone a moment before it chirped.

Caradoc's name flashed.

"What?" She was pretty sure the council couldn't hack his phone; her mother was ruthless, but she wasn't tech strong. But better to be sure.

"Nice greeting. Wanted to warn you that someone is impersonating Surratt. Badly. They're trying to get people to lead them to Area 42."

"Yup, already got the call and added the number to the shock list. I just tried calling you and Reece and your numbers went to voicemail."

"The phones have been having problems, use the security system to reach me. Slower, but it'll keep away hackers."

Aisling looked over to Harlie and tilted her head.

Harlie narrowed his eyes, focusing on something only he could see, and then he gave a quick nod.

"There's more. About the people hunting Area 42 and their agents." She paused; Caradoc didn't like their mother any more than she did, but it was still hard to say. "It's our mother, possibly the entire council, but definitely our family. Don't trust anyone except Harlie or me. And Harlie needs to put a block on you against her."

"Damn it. I knew she was up to something, but why the hell go after Area 42? I'll have Jones drop me off at the house. Put the car keys back." He clicked off.

"I can give them to him when he gets here." Maeve sat on the sofa. Nothing worse than being ready to go kick ass and suddenly having nowhere to go.

Aisling's phone rang again. "Seriously?" She shook her head and answered. "Hey, Garran."

"Aisling, good, who's with you?" Garran sounded as close to seriously worried as she'd ever heard him.

"Just Maeve. Caradoc, Reece, and Jones took off at some horrid hour." He didn't need to know about Harlie and she seriously doubted that was who he was looking for.

"We've got a problem in Old Town."

Aisling pulled the phone away from her ear to check the number. Yup, Garran. "We kind of blew up Old Town."

"Not all of it. The east end survived. The tunnels are the problem."

Crap. The tunnels were closed off eighty years ago. A rebel tribe of gnomes had tried to build a kingdom under LA. Stupid and dangerous. They were eventually stopped, sent to live in the Antarctic, and the tunnels were blocked. It would take a hell of a lot of magic to get through those barriers.

"Someone is attacking the tunnels?" Even though it was referred to as the tunnels, it was really just a single massive one. There had been off shoots, but they'd collapsed during the extraction of the gnomes.

"Nix and some new associates went down there last night—with a ton of equipment and supplies of some sort. There was a large flat of some substance, but the cameras we picked it up from were too far away for details. He destroyed the closer ones."

That incident at the barn must not have slowed him down at all. "Oh crap."

"Exactly. I'm calling in everyone I can, but we can't pull from the other districts much right now. That psychic wave yesterday has put everyone on edge."

Aisling hadn't felt it, but Reece and Harlie had and it almost took them down. "Maeve and I were waiting for Caradoc and Jones, but we'll meet you now. Reece is with his people."

"Reece just pulled up with five cars full of agents. This isn't looking good. Get here as soon as you can." He hung up.

"We need to get to the tunnels, there's something big going on."

Maeve was on her feet and at the door before Aisling finished talking.

Aisling followed her, then turned back to Harlie. "Tell Caradoc to use one of his other cars." He hadn't shown them all to her, but she knew he had at least a few. Car junkies always did.

Maeve was already in the driver's seat and had the engine running when Aisling got to the car. She'd just buckled her seat belt when her phone rang again. More calls in the last ten minutes than in the past month. "Hey Caradoc, we're taking your car."

"Good. There's something big going on at the tunnels. The agency is swarming all over the area. Another dozen fed cars just showed up to join a mass of LA cops."

"We're already on our way." Aisling cut off this time. Mostly so she could hang onto the dash with both hands as Maeve tore out of the drive, through the hologram hedge, and down the street at a speed Reece would have loved. "You and Reece seriously need to go drag race somewhere and get this out of your system."

"People get out of your way faster when you drive like this." Maeve bobbed and weaved until they hit the freeway. Then she went faster.

"You know there's no siren or lights on this thing, right? We get pulled over and there may be issues." Aisling shook her head as Maeve slowed a bit, but not much. "Area 42 is out in force on this one, everyone's heading for the tunnels."

"For Nix? Doesn't that seem extreme?" She slowed a bit more, now only about ten miles over the limit.

"It does, but there must be more to it. Something drew them out." A nasty thought popped into her brain and she punched Reece's number.

"Aisling?"

"How many agents are left in your headquarters?"

"What? How do I know?"

"I can't explain, but someone is trying to go after the agency. They were trying to get inside, and they would have seen all of you coming out."

"We're not that sloppy—"

"Garran said you had at least five full cars of people with you and Caradoc said another dozen just rolled in. How many times have that many agents gone on a call at once? Things would have been rushed. There's going to be an attack."

"I'll call you back." He cut the line.

"You really think they'd try to take out Area 42? There are more branches of them worldwide."

"But this is their largest research arm. Damn it, can you go faster?"

CHAPTER FORTY-FOUR

"WHICH? THE TUNNELS OR AREA 42?" Maeve had slowed more but only because she was going to have to choose between two freeways.

"Damn it," Aisling said as she weighed the two. Area 42 was a trap, but the tunnels probably were too. "The tunnels." There wasn't a logical reason, it was all emotional. Nothing against the people at Area 42, but there were people she cared about at the tunnels.

Maeve picked up speed as they got on the second freeway, and Aisling didn't ask her to slow down this time. This close to the tunnels probably any cops on the road would be heading there as well.

The side streets leading to the tunnel entrance were empty, but the police barricade stopped them a few blocks from the entrance.

A large minotaur cop flagged them down. "These roads are closed right now. You'll need to turn around." Aisling didn't recognize the cop, but this area bordered a number of precincts.

Maeve held out her wrist with her tat. "We're with the 626. Call Garran, tell him Maeve and Aisling are here."

He looked into the car, but Aisling didn't have a badge to show him. He narrowed his eyes and reached for his phone. "You'll need to stay here."

He stepped back and talked animatedly for a few seconds. Then he shut up and turned red. Yup—the sign of a pissed-off Garran chewing someone's ass.

He stepped back to the car. "Go ahead." He nodded to the other two cops standing near the barriers to let them pass.

Aisling watched the cops as they drove by. "He should have been okay with your tat alone, what the hell was that about?"

Maeve shook her head as she drove down the road. Cars were all along the sides. There were a hell of a lot of black and whites, and most likely the rest were detectives. Aisling was a little pissed that Garran hadn't called them in sooner.

"Ready?" Maeve finally found a place to park, and then double-checked her weapons.

Aisling checked her own as well. "As ever."

The street, while full of cars, was eerily empty of people. The wide area at the entrance to the tunnel was another thing entirely.

The front was being guarded by a split group of cops and feds. Neither group looked happy, but they were working together.

Garran was standing at the front barking orders into his phone. He clicked off the call and turned to them. "We've confirmed that Nix and his people are down there, with enough Iron Death to wipe out half of the fey in Los Angeles. We've sent some people down, but we can't reach them by phone or walkie. I'm holding off letting more go down until we know what's going on."

"Every law enforcement agency is looking for him. How in the hell did he get here without being seen?" Aisling looked around. "Where is Caradoc?"

"Your brother went in with the first wave, claimed he could block weapons. Surratt called, the real one, and told me to let him do whatever he needed to do. Anything else you'll have to ask your fed friends about," he said and glared over to the black, tan, and beige crowd. "Stella got a hold of us a few hours ago. Nix did have a mountain enclave, one far too close to a major troll outpost for their liking," Garran said. "They didn't find any drugs, but it appeared to have been a processing plant of some kind. The trolls and Stella destroyed it with extreme prejudice. The feds were tracking him but somehow lost him, his people, and the drugs late last night."

"Why would Nix use a chemical that could kill him horribly? That rat bastard doesn't do anything without a monetary motive," Maeve said.

"We think we know."The voice came from behind them and was so uncharacteristic that Aisling almost didn't recognize Mott. "He's built an immunity to it." Mott didn't look great, but he was standing and wrapped in a large cloak. "I realized that I didn't participate in the creation of the Iron Death—I was helping build an immunity treatment. They did a damn good job blocking my memories."

Garran nodded. "Yup. That's our best theory. This is a massive power play. Take out Los Angeles as both a show of power and as ground zero for a fey takeover. A single fey, that is. Cameras show he brought in a lot of equipment and explosives. If he decides to blow the Iron Death up and get it out over the city, the resulting cloud could kill tens of thousands of fey and will affect millions. He would be left as one of the most powerful fey alive, with a kingdom of humans."

"Then who's after Area 42? Where's Reece?" Aside from their captain, she didn't recognize any of the feds. There could be ones from other agencies, but she'd guess most were from Area 42. Something changed his mind about taking her warning seriously.

"No idea who's after them, they don't share information. He and Jones went back to Area 42 to get people out."

A disturbance in the air crackled through the entrance. Everyone was slammed to the ground as a blast of air exploded out of the tunnels.Yelling followed but the winds were still too strong to get up.

"What the hell was that?" Aisling used her healer senses to tell if there was anything in the air, like Iron Death, but it just felt strong, not deadly.

"No idea," Garran yelled back as he fought to lift his phone to his mouth. "What happened down there?"

The winds were dying down and Aisling pushed herself to her feet. She didn't wait to hear what the person on the other side of the phone said, and she ran into the tunnel.

"Aisling! Wait! Damn it, Maeve. Stop!" Garran's voice told her whose feet were right behind her. Well, drifting back behind her. She wasn't happy about Maeve joining her, but she wasn't slowing down. Caradoc was there somewhere and something big had pushed a deadly amount of air out.

There were dead gangsters and cops laying along the tunnel as she got lower. She was pretty sure it wasn't from the explosion; they looked like bullet wounds from what she could tell at this speed.

She slowed when she reached people who had collapsed and didn't have visible wounds. Some were torn apart, but there were no other signs of an explosion—just serious winds. A few people were stirring. She punched three gangsters and took their guns as they tried to roll to their feet. A few feds and cops were getting up too. "Here." She gave them the extra guns and took off running again.

"Caradoc!" Her brother was directly before her as she reached a wider section of tunnel, no wounds that she could see but he wasn't moving. She skidded to a stop, the bodies around him were mostly gangsters, but there were a few cops. None of them were moving. Still no sign of an explosion, but they had to be near where it happened.

She grabbed her brother and rolled him over. Tiny wounds and scratches marked all of his exposed skin, and his eyes were closed, but he was breathing.

Maeve stumbled to a stop next to them and dropped her hands to her knees. "Damn it. Forgot. How. Fast."

"You shouldn't have come down here."

"He's my friend too." She nodded her chin toward Caradoc.

"He's breathing. I can't tell what's wrong." Actually, having Maeve and her variety of weapons with her was a good thing. Aisling would be exposed when she went into a healing trance. Maeve would cover her. She placed her hand on Caradoc's chest and started to close her eyes.

He grabbed it. "You try having all the air ripped from your lungs and see how you hold up." His voice was weak, but he opened his eyes and smiled at her.

"Shit, what did you do?" Maeve came forward, then turned back to the closest bodies as someone moved. They were human gangsters, but they could have still survived. "Two are dead, and this one is the winner of a nice pair of cuffs." She slapped her cuffs on the moving gangster, then went to check the cops.

"I am honored that you think I have that much skill, but this wasn't me." He let Aisling help him to his feet. "It came through the tunnel. I threw the strongest magic I could to shield against it, but it still mowed us down. Doesn't help that this damn tunnel messes with magic—I'm more drained than I should be."

Maeve turned back to them. So far only a few feds and one cop were on their feet. "If you didn't put up a shield, I'd guess that none of you would have survived."

"Where's Nix and the drug? Garran thinks he's planning on blowing it out over the city, but there wasn't anything in that wind." Aisling's immediate goal had been to find Caradoc; now that she had, they needed to find the madman behind this.

"As far as we could tell before he tried to blow us all up, he's at the bottom of the tunnel with a fair amount of his goons—the ones in the forest weren't his only lackeys. Not sure what that burst of air was though." The look on Caradoc's face wasn't good. He looked ready to run down there on his own for the sole reason that he had no idea how Nix created the huge force behind the deadly wind.

"We're going down together. With back up." Aisling nodded to the recovered cops and feds as more got up and joined them.

"I wasn't planning on…fine. Maybe I was." Caradoc reached behind him and pulled out a small gun. "Look, I even have firepower."

Maeve nodded and dropped her voice. "What about your gizmos?"

"This tunnel is too small, we'd end up wiping out our weapons as well."

"Detective Danaan? We'll follow your lead." A younger looking cop came forward. She looked like she'd just gotten out of the academy, but Aisling spotted the tiny lines of a changeling on her face. It said a lot about their dedication that there was a high percentage of fey down here. They were willing to die horrible deaths to stop this nightmare.

Aisling studied the people around her. About twenty-five had survived. And there were at least that many who weren't ever getting up again. "We go in. No matter what, Nix has to be stopped and the drug taken confiscated. Don't anyone touch it—even if you're human." She pulled out her gun and started jogging down the tunnel.

They couldn't be silent any more than Nix or his people could get past them. More bodies, some with bullet holes, some not, attested to the fight that had happened before the winds. The tunnel grew wider and lamps flickered the further they went. Aisling was impressed that the lights had held up under the wind.

The tunnel turned in a wide curve, blocking them from seeing more than a hundred feet or so in front of them. A whirling sound, at first nothing more than a high-pitched whine, came from the bend.

"Everyone get against the sides!" Caradoc pushed Maeve and Aisling up against the wall and the others followed suit. "Get as low as you can!"

The wind that tore past them didn't seem to be nearly as fierce as the previous one, but it was more focused. It tugged on her hair and clothing as it went past, then shot up into the roof of the tunnel. And vanished.

Caradoc was the first to pull himself away from the sides. He ran to the center of the tunnel, trying to get a look at where the wind had gone. "There's a tunnel in the ceiling." He stepped back as parts of the tunnel rained down.

"He's using a weaponized wind to punch new tunnels?" Maeve looked up but didn't join Caradoc in the center. "That doesn't sound like the Nix I know and hate."

"He has to know we're here," Aisling said. "Why isn't he aiming at us?"

Caradoc finished his study of the new tunnel, or the attempted new tunnel, and came back. "There's something else he wants more and thinks he can do it before we stop him."

"Now that sounds like Nix. Literally and figuratively." Maeve gestured down the tunnel. Someone was coming. A number of someones.

"Take defensive positions the best you can." There were outcroppings in the tunnel but not many. At this point the curve of the tunnel was the only thing blocking them. "Stay here—everyone." Aisling fixed her brother and Maeve with a glare, then ran to the bend. Several dozen heavily armed Celtic gang members were walking their way. They all appeared human. They were going slow because some of the original fed-cop contingent had made it down this far earlier and the gang members were checking to make sure everyone they passed was dead.

Aisling ran back to Caradoc. "You have to use your gizmos. There are too many to fight." A fire-fight down here would be horrific, especially for the side with fewer guns.

"In this tunnel, we'll lose our weapons as well. The gizmos I have left are larger than the ones we used before."

"We don't have a choice. There are too many of them and they have too many guns. Hand to hand is our best shot right now." She nodded to the cops and feds around them. "We need to quietly warn our people." Aisling, Maeve, and Caradoc got everyone to lay down their guns—they quickly complied when Aisling told them what would happen once Caradoc's device went off.

Caradoc crouched as well as he could and crept to the bend in the tunnel. With a nod, he got to the ground, rolled out into the center of the tunnel, and fired. Judging by the screams, there had been some very heavily armed people.

The Celtics dropped their weapons and charged forward. The fey feds and cops ran to meet them, with the humans bringing up the rear. The fight didn't last long. The Celtics had been injured by their exploding weapons, and even though there were more of them, the fey were stronger and faster.

After the gang members were killed or captured, Aisling had most of the cops and feds follow her; leaving several behind to handle the dozen surviving prisoners. The tunnel expanded into a wide, rounded hall-like cave with an impressive amount of equipment in it. Nix stood before it, looking like he was the one with the upper hand.

"How nice, you found your friends." He stepped near an odd machine, one that looked like a massive wind generator used by movie studios. Only this one was the size of a house.

"Just give up, Nix. There are more cops coming. There's no way out." Maeve stepped forward.

"You never were the brightest, were you?" Nix held up his hand and a blast of focused wind slammed into Maeve and the five cops nearest her.

Aisling pulled the rest back a bit. Maeve and the others were breathing, she could see their sides still moving. But they were unconscious.

"He's got a remote on that damn thing. Highly focused pressure—" Caradoc's words were swallowed as a blast sent him and ten others against the wall.

There were three people left standing besides Aisling and they all ran forward as far apart as they could. Nix grabbed the first one by the throat and flung him against the wall. The remote was still in his other hand, but he appeared to enjoy fighting this way.

Aisling ran straight to the equipment. Right behind the massive wind machine was a sealed pallet almost as tall as she was. She recognized the sealant—a neutralizing compound used by narcotics to handle shipments of dangerous and contraband drugs. He might have killed Losien, and she might have been working he and the Lazing against each other—but she had helped him with this. There had to be enough Iron Death wrapped in there to bring down an entire city.

Nix came running after her and she moved as far into the wide area as she could. Her plan was to distract him long enough for the others to recover. He pocketed his remote and charged her with both hands outstretched. She flipped him over her, but he twisted and pulled her backwards with him. She kicked herself free and scrambled to her feet. When he came at her this time, she responded with a hard kick to his gut that sent him back a dozen feet on his ass. He rolled back up and charged again.

His punch connected with her jaw as he grabbed her right arm and spun her toward him. "I want Maeve to wake up and watch me kill you."

Her phone rang at that moment and she kicked back into his shin. He released her arm, but ripped the phone out of her pocket. She moved further away from him but was limited by the tunnel wall.

"A fed calling? Not as good as Maeve, but she might already be dead. This will work." He answered her phone. "Hi fed. Want to see your friend die?" He held up the phone in one hand, and his remote in the other. "Say goodbye."

Aisling ran toward him, determined to get to him before the wind pushed her back. The blast wasn't as harsh as before and was aimed above her rather than at her. She dropped to the ground and curled as tight as she could as the ceiling collapsed on her.

Aisling must have been knocked out. The sounds she heard when she came to were more deliberate than a ceiling falling.

"Aisling, damn you, say something." Maeve's voice sounded far away, but annoyed, and worried enough that it supported Aisling's theory that she'd been out for a bit.

"I'm here." She tried to yell but didn't feel like she made much sound. The rocks pressed around her, but she curled in tighter against a large one. Judging by the shape, it had managed to keep the falling rocks from crushing her. She slowed her breathing, both to reduce her air consumption and to keep her panic from growing.

It seemed like forever before light and fresh air came in through a tiny hole near her head.

"She's here! Move over here, but be careful. The rocks aren't stable." Maeve's voice was louder now, and she could see Caradoc.

Slowly the rocks were removed and Aisling was pulled out of the rubble.

Caradoc patted her down, checking for broken bones, then hugged her gently. She threw her arms around him and hugged him tighter. She was bruised, but nothing was broken.

Maeve joined in a group hug, then pulled back and handed Aisling her phone. "I found this. It looks like Reece called."

Aisling thought of the last images Nix would have sent and tried calling Reece back. Nothing.

"Might have to wait until we get back up top." Caradoc started leading them out.

"What happened to Nix?" The equipment was still there, and the still sealed Iron Death. But no insane gangster.

Caradoc pointed to another tunnel in the ceiling, right at the edge of the large wide open area. "I came to just as he fled. He made that, then got pulled through it."

"Wait, he used the wind machine to push himself through the tunnel?" Aisling looked up as they walked by it. It was about as wide as she was tall, but it didn't look like it would be fun to be shoved through.

"No. That's what was weird. He shut the machine down and ran toward the new tunnel, like he'd been expecting it. Then it pulled him up like there was suction."

"His yell when it sucked him up would have been far more satisfactory had it ended in a blood curdling scream." Maeve looked up into the tunnel like she was going to follow Nix even if she had to climb through the tunnel on her hands and knees.

Caradoc put a hand on Maeve's shoulder. It looked relaxed, but his fingers were holding her still. Aisling wasn't the only one who thought she looked like a flight risk.

"He might not have survived whatever sucked him up. We're alive and we have the Iron Death." Aisling raised her hand before Maeve could say anything. "Yes, he might be able to make more. Or he might not. Between us seizing this equipment and what the trolls did to his mountain enclave, his operation has been seriously curtailed. The scientists should have enough of it now to find a way to permanently neutralize the drug."

A troop of humans in hazmat suits moved into the tunnel. Aisling, Caradoc, and Maeve followed the line of injured making their way up. The human researchers, along with fey long-distance ones, would be analyzing the drug for quite a while.

"I still don't like it." Maeve gave one parting glare at the tunnel Nix had vanished into. She turned to Caradoc and pointedly looked at his hand still on her shoulder. "You don't have to worry; I won't run after him. For now."

He laughed. "Aisling's told me how sneaky you can be. I might need to keep a closer eye on you for a while."

Maeve smiled and patted his hand. "That might not be so bad."

They got up top where the crowds of cops, scientists, and EMT's were staging more groups to head down. Aisling pulled out her phone to call Reece.

"Aisling!" Reece's voice was heard before he was seen as he came from behind a group of seven-foot tall Syliarn fey EMT's. Jones was a bit behind him, moving faster than usual, but still not rushed. The broad smile on his face was unusual though.

Reece grabbed Aisling's arms at first, then shook his head and hugged her. "I was afraid you were gone. The phone…Nix…and then the phone cut out."

"So was I. Nix managed to bury me, but Maeve and Caradoc got me out." She and Reece pulled apart a bit. "But we're here and you guys survived. How's Area 42?" She didn't want to let go of him, but surrounded by pretty much every law enforcement agent in an eighty mile radius wasn't the place.

Reece's smile dropped and Jones joined them. "We

couldn't get there in time—it's gone."

"It exploded? Damn it. I'm sorry." Aisling knew her mother and the council were the prime suspects in her mind for who was going after Area 42, but she'd thought it was to break in, not destroy it.

Jones shook his head. "Not exploded. The early camera footage appears to indicate that it vanished." He handed a wrapped package to Reece. "You left this in the car."

"Vanished?" Caradoc looked from one to the other.

"How does a building vanish if it doesn't explode?" Maeve asked.

Aisling nodded. "What both of them said."

Reece shrugged. "They'll be tearing apart the footage for a while, but it was there one moment, as we were pulling up to it, then it just wasn't there. There's a huge crater where it was. A perfectly carved out crater."

"I've seen enough exploded buildings in my time, this didn't match anything like that," Jones said then tipped his head toward the package. "You going to hang onto that all day?"

Reece scowled. "No." He handed the package to Aisling. "We wrapped it up, but it's unscathed from what I can tell. It was just sitting in the middle of the hole that used to be Area 42."

Aisling looked at them for hints, but Reece and Jones had their stoic fed faces on. She unwrapped it, but as the wrapping came off a rock grew in her stomach. The shape was familiar.

"Another family box?" The enchanted wood's essence came through the final layer along with a familiar pull. "*Our* family box?" Yup, there it was. She'd only seen it once, as a child, but she knew it was the highly guarded box of her family.

Caradoc took it out of her hands. "This isn't a fake." He looked up. "Who, or what, has the power to steal a massive compound and leave a highly guarded family heirloom in its place?"

"That's a damn good question. But whoever it is, they've got my attention," Reece said.

Aisling nodded and looked at the bodies being brought out of the tunnel. "We won this battle, but I think war has been declared. And not just by Nix."

THE END

DEAR READER,

Thank you for joining in on the flagship adventure for the Broken Veil series! I hope you enjoyed it as much as I enjoyed writing it.

The second book, AN UNCOMMON TRUTH OF DYING will take off early 2021. The war against the fey, and even the humans, is just starting!

If you're also interested in a little bit of space opera, please check out the first book in The Asarlaí Wars trilogy- WARRIOR WENCH.

Magic, mayhem, and drunken faeries run loose in THE GLASS GARGOYLE, the first book in The Lost Ancients fantasy series.

I really appreciate each and every one of you so please keep in touch. You can find me at *www.marieandreas.com*.

And please feel free to email me directly at *Marie@marie-andreas.com* as well, I love to hear from readers!

If you enjoyed this book (or any book for that matter ;)) please spread the word! Positive reviews on Amazon, Goodreads, and blogs are like emotional gold to any writer and mean more than you know.

ABOUT THE AUTHOR

MARIE IS AN AWARD WINNING fantasy and science fiction reader with a reading addiction. If she wasn't writing about all of the people in her head, she'd be lurking about coffee shops annoying innocent passer-by with her stories. So really, writing is a way of saving the masses. She lives in Southern California and is currently owned by two very faery-minded cats. And yes, sometimes they race.

When not saving the general populace from coffee shop shenanigans, Marie likes to visit the UK and keeps hoping someone will give her a nice summer home in the Forest of Dean or northern Wales.

More information can be found on her website *www.marieandreas.com*